Judgment Day

Judgment Day

Rasha al Ameer

Translated by
Jonathan Wright

The American University in Cairo Press
Cairo   New York

First published in 2011 by
The American University in Cairo Press
113 Sharia Kasr el Aini, Cairo, Egypt
www.aucpress.com

Dar el Kutub No. 24413/11
ISBN 978 977 416 481 1

Dar el Kutub Cataloging-in-Publication Data

al Ameer, Rasha
    Judgment Day/ Rasha al Ameer. —Cairo: The American University in Cairo Press, 2011
    p.   cm.
    ISBN 978 977 416 481 1
    1. Judgment Day (Islam)   (S.H)
    I. Title
    297.23

1 2 3 4 5 6 7 8   14 13 12 11

Designed by Sebastian Schönenstein
Printed in Egypt

A missing signature and inadequate thanks. I wanted this book to bear at least two names: my name and that of my brother and friend, and incidentally my publisher, Lokman Slim. The day I completed the draft of this book I entrusted it to him to tell me what he thought of it. After reading it, he asked me to give him some time, then asked for yet more time. I agreed, and he spent many hours laboring over it. When he gave the draft back to me, he had added his comments to the margins. I found myself approving many of them, and felt he deserved the status of co-author. I asked him to add his signature to mine but he declined. But if this book does not bear his name alongside mine, it does bear his fingerprints.

This book also owes a debt to Mahmoud Assaf, a scholar and teacher of Arabic who promotes the love of the language, as most of the books published at Dar al-Jadid are indebted to his other talents. I doubt that words can do justice to the ample thanks I owe him, and so, reluctantly, I recognize that the only recompense I can offer him is to acknowledge my debt.

Rasha al Ameer
Beirut, September 2001

And how can you know what is the Day of Judgment? Indeed, how can you know what is the Day of Judgment?

(Quran 82:16–17)

Introduction

This is your book, so how can I dedicate it to you? Trust my good judgment, even if we both know there's an element of doubt about whether I have completely recovered.

Some days ago, for the first time since I moved to this faraway country "for worldly benefits" and for a woman I love,* you packed your bags and set out on a journey—a short one, though it seems long to me. Surely that means you are confident I have sufficiently recovered and you need not worry I might have a relapse. Or perhaps, as it occurred to me when you told me you were leaving for that conference, it means you would like to do an experiment, to put my recuperation to the test.

In a few days you will come back and discover I have not followed your instructions to look after the antique wall clock, which requires one to flex one's steely muscles every day so that the hands keep spinning.

---

* The caliph Omar ibn al-Khattab narrated: "The Prophet said, 'The rewards (for deeds) are according to the intention, and everybody will get the reward for what he has intended. So whoever emigrated for God's and His Prophet's sake, his emigration was for God and His Prophet; and whoever emigrated for worldly benefits, or to marry a woman, then his emigration was for the thing for which he emigrated.'"

1

Then you will have suspicions about me, firstly that I weakened the moment you abandoned me and surrendered to the devils of a past that refuses to fade away, preferring to throw myself into the depths of that past and wait for you to come back and pull me out. I will have fun teasing you with 'the truth'—the truth that, knowing how dear that clock is to you, I wanted to protect it from my rough hands, which are untutored in spite of the books they have handled. Then you will shake your head and frown in disapproval and reproach.

Rest assured, and believe me rather than the clock. In any case, as soon as I finish writing these lines, the matter will be over and it will be written in the record of your life that, unlike mothers, you did not give birth to me just once but several times, giving me each time a new life.

❧

Rumor has it that what lay behind our relationship and behind 'the scandal' which is synonymous with my name and about which people in our two countries have such fun telling anecdotes (most of them figments of their imagination) was the fact that I, the venerable sheikh, fell so in love with you that I 'sacrificed' everything for your sake. While some believe that love is enough to account for my 'disgraceful' behavior, others insist that the story has other dimensions and that in fact I deserve pity as 'the foolish victim of a major ongoing conspiracy,' which targeted what I represent and not my humble person. They say you were the instrument of this conspiracy, sent to seduce me, and that you succeeded in the mission assigned to you. Whether I fell in love with you, and love you now, and took pleasure in loving you and still do, is not in doubt. If I am 'the victim' of my love for you, then what a wonderful way to be a victim . . . if that were the case, except that it is not.

Those few still interested in our story can stay up late and argue about it, while I breathe a deep sigh of relief that I have almost paid off a debt to you. So, this early morning, spontaneously and not out of boldness or daring, I decided to record without the slightest hesitation, not in my private diary but in the form of publication to all and sundry, that I have loved you and that I fell in love surreptitiously when I was in charge of that house of God, and that today, when we live under the same roof in a country where we are both strangers, and where I am merely a teacher of the language of God's book, His eternal home, I love and adore you openly and publicly. In doing so—and my pen runs merrily as I write these simple words—I do not believe that anyone but you and I fully appreciate how many deaths I have suffered, or how many lives I have lived through, in order to speak out. They do not appreciate what it means for a man who has been full of talk about religion and the world on every occasion, giving advice to people of all kinds and all ages—what it means for such a man to bare his soul to himself and to others.

Firmly but lovingly, you have pressed me to reclaim my life from the versions of others by publishing my own story roughly as you would have inspired me to write it. Perhaps if I called this task the latest of my births under your auspices, it would help anyone interested in reading these pages to share my appreciation of what it means to me to publish them. That way the reader can also help me bear the burden of thanking you for all the favors you have bestowed on me, whether you bestowed them in full awareness of what you were doing, or unintentionally, without affectation or ulterior purpose.

✑

The morning light, which slowly floods the world, and the wall clock itself—although its hands have been immobile for some days at some random hour—show me that the time has come to prepare for a new day's work. But fortunately it is Wednesday and my first class is at eleven o'clock, so there is no need for haste, except that I am in a hurry to finish this introduction, which on the day you left I promised myself I would complete before your return, to be my gift to you.

Without conviction I describe these pages as the introduction. They are the introduction to this book but the conclusion to this story. That's why I am reluctant to embark on it and why I have put off completing both it and my book, our book, time after time over the last few weeks.

You convinced me I should publish the diaries and jottings I was inspired to write down in that refuge where I spent fifteen months 'to save my life' (it was under threat at the time in the name of God, His Prophet, and His Book on charges which may or may not have had divine authority). But after going over them with a view to publication, I have been uncertain, as a newcomer to writing in the first person, about what I should call this thing I am supposed to write by way of an introduction, as though my aim should be to let the appellation guide me as I felt my way toward what I wanted to say or, more precisely, as though my aim was to procrastinate in fulfilling my promise, postponing a book which I was destined to write.

Now, without any appellation to take me by the hand, the matter is decided: it is your book, and my only merit is that I followed my inclination and wrote it. Take it. I do not dedicate it to you, because who dedicates something to the person who lent it in the first place?

This book, written in the form of notes and jottings and then rewritten in the form presented here to the reader, consists of twenty-four chapters and a conclusion. They were not written in this order according to some predetermined plan but rather (and especially the parts that have become the first chapters) in installments and sporadically. Besides, converting them into a book required that I merge some parts with others so that they form a sequence with a beginning and an end. In order to structure them in this way, in many places I found myself compelled to omit some parts, rather than to make additions.

I have omitted absolutely none of the facts, even those that I am surprised today I was able to put in writing. In fact, I have confined the omissions to pages of repetitive lamentation that overwhelmed me with boredom when I read them. If I have fallen short and have not cut out everything that should have been cut out, then may the reader forgive me and generously ignore those passages. He should rather follow his intuition and move on to passages that do not embitter him toward me or make him judge me to be tedious. Since I have not been afraid to make omissions, many a reader may wonder in other passages of this book what my motive was for sparing long descriptive passages that may in their turn also appear tedious. In those cases I did not subject them to omission because what I described, sometimes to excess, reflected what for me was a discovery or a first experience. In their discoveries and experiences, people have lives that cannot be measured in years.

Then, when I broke up these diaries and notes and pieced them together and offered them to you for your comments, you suggested that, out of respect for prospective readers, I should clarify the references and terms in the text, and those I came across or picked up, sometimes deliberately and sometimes inadvertently, from domains of knowledge that we have explored and still explore together, and that might be obscure to some readers. I hesitated to take up your suggestion, for fear that I might not be able to distinguish clearly between the references that needed footnotes and those that did not. At your insistence, I suggested that we work together and that you identify for me the points you felt required clarification, while I would undertake the rest. So it has been, and for that, too, this book is indebted to you, and for that you are answerable!

1

I t is seven o'clock, your hour. It comes to me and I am on my guard. I take a deep breath, like someone preparing for something that has to be faced, even if anticipated.

For months past, months when you were absent, seven o'clock has crept up on me uninvited, taking advantage of my torpor. It throws down its walking stick, drops its bags in my small courtyard, outstays its welcome, and takes charge.

Impotent, or maybe intent on death, I have tried to keep it at bay each time I rise from the dead, desperately defending, as they say, what little control I retain over my life. I have tried, but it has overwhelmed me. Intentionally, not just out of impotence or because of the sense of death that resides in me, hangs over me, and clings to me, I have tried to summon all my resolve to ignore it, but in vain.

Your hour . . . but if for you it has reverted to its proper place in time, an hour that is neither prized nor despised, that brings neither joy nor sadness, nor makes your heart flutter, how can I explain that for me it is still the hour, the hour that has no rival and no equal?

For as many months as one's hands have fingers, seven o'clock or thereabouts was our rendezvous almost every day. We agreed on that and persevered, not because we saw a good omen in the magic of the number, but in deference to my duties and formalities, and throughout the months, throughout all my worries and concerns, throughout the unrest and on many occasions violence, and the disturbances in my mosque, I would await seven o'clock to stand at your door, knock gently, and it would open. Now, throughout the day, I only have to wait for seven o'clock to come, and although I have nothing to do but wait, it's almost as if I am more worried than I was then.

The hundredth seven o'clock struck a while ago. As usual, it arrived neither stealthily nor unexpectedly. Everything is as it is, and it frightens me how life has stabilized so quickly here, as though I have been in this place for three years, not three months and a bit. With the bleak manliness on which I was brought up, I suppress my emotions, even here where there is no one to report on them if they come to the surface in the obvious form of tears or sighs of sadness and pain. I suppress my emotions, but not my fantasies: they have free rein. I do not try to contain them and they do not desist of their own accord. My fantasies . . . when I say those words, I tell myself I should put them between quotation marks—'my fantasies'— emulating the caution you insisted on whenever you used a phrase or expression on impulse and then worried it might seem exaggerated, or feared that on first hearing it might be understood in its most obvious sense. But I am not putting the words between quotes, because I fear that to do so would deal the fatal blow, and when I say the fatal blow I do not mean it metaphorically: I mean the blow that really paralyzes and silences me. If I so much as shied away from openly attributing these fantasies to myself, if I denied they were my fantasies, then my tongue would be tied and my right hand shackled. Sometimes I think there must be something more than the two extremes between which I waver—at times imagining myself basking in the relationship we had, rather than other parts of my life, and at other times feeling imprisoned by it. But at many other times, I admit that there really is nothing more and that I awake and fall asleep to fantasies, and that the only thing left that can bring me to my senses and calm me down, psychologically and physically, is that little part of me that is worth mentioning, most of which happens to be what we shared for no longer than a few months, rather than the rest of my life.

I often disagreed when you chanced to attribute my hesitation and confusion to humility, or when you thought I was deliberately belittling myself. Similarly, tonight I would have to disagree if you disputed my claim that, of my whole life, however full of incidents, people, and situations it might have been, the only part worth mentioning is what we shared.

It should not surprise you that I date my life by you—by meeting you and by what followed, not by the public events that transformed me within months from being the imam of a humble mosque, frequented by the poor and by immigrants on the outskirts of this city (your city by birth and mine by migration), into a 'star,' as you liked to describe me after I began to appear regularly in public and in the media, and then into an outcast who sought refuge with the government against justice administered by those who were once my brothers in God and in Islam. It should not surprise you, because, were it not for you, what happened would not have happened and today I would not be who I am. Perhaps other things would have happened, and I would be another man somewhere else, above or below the surface of the earth.* But definitely I would not be where I am now, my thoughts would not be as incoherent as they are now, or perhaps I would not be plagued by any thoughts at all. I say 'thoughts,' but obviously I do not mean what I say, but rather my fantasies, that mixture of memories and delusions. The hand that turns the pages of my life story (I was about to describe it as invisible and I wish it were so) insists on slowing to a standstill on the pages filled with those fantasies, so I see myself only as I never saw myself before I knew you: I see myself in your company, poring over the dictionary and tracking down some elusive word, or each of us poring over the other like a couple reluctant to save for the next day any of the pleasure of their communion today.

In those days I had two lives, or rather my life was divided between two worlds—from early morning till seven o'clock they called me by the title 'mawlana,' and from seven o'clock until a little before the dawn prayer I was just a man and you were my woman. It was not easy for me to hold water and fire in the same hand,† and as I can see now, it preyed on my mind somewhat and occasionally distracted me from you and my visions of you. That was until, guarded by an escort fit for a VIP, I was

---

* "If you gave me friendship, then wealth is insignificant and everything that is above the soil is dross." (Al-Mutanabbi)

† "Combining water and fire in my hand was as difficult as combining good luck and understanding." (Al-Mutanabbi, from his elegy for his grandmother)

9

brought to this remote and mountainous resort, which the government has chosen as the strongroom where it stores people like me—people called moderates by some and "government clerics and agents of the regime" by others, people the government sees as ammunition is still live and they might decide at some stage to thrust back into the thick of battles that are sometimes secret and sometimes open. Since I came here, all I can do with those two lives of mine is live them in reverse, and my daily sustenance is whatever was lucky enough to stick in my memory, my heart and my body.

Perhaps, despite your instinctive distrust of the whims and heroes of the common people, you would have preferred for me a fate that was more valorous and more in tune with the poetry that brought us together. But this was my only possible fate, other than being handed over to have my throat slit by one of those whom, in my professional capacity, I had undertaken to guide to the True Path. Yes, I do sometimes regret I did not let myself be killed and that I saved my skin by coming to this room, knowing how safe it is and how I am staying here for my own protection. I know I am on death row, as prison people call it, but worse than all this is the folly and nonsense I sometimes indulge in, such as telling myself reproachfully: "What harm would it do if you let yourself be killed? Wouldn't being killed be your last chance to see the course of your life changed?"

You must wonder what it is that makes me write, especially as writing in the first person has never been my style, nor the style we used together. Because you think well of me, you might imagine that in this safe refuge of mine I have been overwhelmed by an impulse to meditate on what happened, what brought me here, why others have ended up in dungeons or worse, and why a third group has been promoted to positions of power. But that is not the case, and it is no compensation to know that I am pampered and cosseted compared to some of my brothers, whether or not I want to be brothers with them, brothers who this very night are being forced to recount the events of the last months and years of their lives, incident by incident—events in which they were unwitting participants, as well as acts they engaged in deliberately and knowingly.

I feel for these brothers of mine as much as I pity myself, but I am not so virtuous as to claim that I do not sometimes envy them their ordeals. I envy those of them that are steadfast and calculating, who sculpt their silence into words in which they see the truth take form, just as I envy those who cannot hold their tongues when their will is broken and who withdraw defeated, balanced between despair and hope for the mercy of God.

How could I not envy them, when my inability to express myself is such an obstacle that the only way around it is to have you mediate between me and my thoughts? Yes, my lady, I appoint you mediator, but for hour upon hour, all I ask of this trick of mine is that it bring me close to you and make me indifferent to myself, leaving me alone to flounder in my thoughts at will.

To be close to you, my lady: I ask to be close to you in soul and in body. And although it was you who taught me that the soul is just one part of a human and no better than any other part, for the moment I will keep it simple, ignore the soul, and draw close to you little by little, until I find myself embracing you, indivisible from you, and then perhaps I will not fear that my soul might ask for its share of our union.

*

For some forty years I have taken responsibility for this body of mine, for better or for worse, until we have grown used to each other. My body no longer complained when I failed to fulfill my obligations toward it, and I no longer rebuked it for demanding that I fulfill those obligations until . . . yes, my lady, until you came between me and my body and gained irresistible power over it. How can I not resent it when you helped me overcome my inhibitions and taught me to explore and delight in my own body as much as I have with yours? How can you expect me to tame my body when you have driven it wild?

As I review the panorama of my life, I do not forget to give credit to all those who have thought well of me—my family, my teachers, the sheikh who mentored me—and then I come to you, and I find nothing to say except that no one else, man or woman, has done to me what you have done—and no wonder, for those others treated me well, each by virtue of his relationship with me, bartering favors, whereas you . . . why did you take it upon yourself to extricate me from the way I had lived all my life before you? Was it to gratify yourself or your vanity that you took the trouble to do so, or was it for some other reason that escapes me?

A solitary man is prey to fantasies from every quarter, and here is one of them, so forgive me if you can, and if you cannot, then rest content

11

anyway: is there any argument more eloquent for what you have done with me than the fact that I am now revealing to you so impetuously all of my inner self, without leaving out those aspects that may offend you?

⁂

Many times you lost patience with my persistent silence and urged me to open my heart to you. You have been kind enough to seek ruse after ruse to make me more candid. I shall never forget the sound of your voice, half making fun of me and half giving me advice, the day you told me: "You're in enough trouble already. When you speak, your breathing is precise and the articulation of your consonants is perfect, but beneath all that there is a noticeable hesitation. What's the matter, man? Words are home remedies for the likes of us. Even if they don't work, they will do no harm. Try them, and perhaps . . . "

I may or may not have been wrong not to try out your advice when you were with me, and now the only therapy available is that home remedy of yours.

2

I t was not by inheritance or by any deliberate act of volition that I acquired the title by which you know me—imam of the Mosque of the Expatriates. All that happened was that my parents were so poor that they had no choice but to enroll me in our village school, which was more like a Quran school than a modern institution, and for various reasons, including the fact that I was the youngest of my brothers and that I showed a natural inclination toward academic study, I advanced stage by stage in Islamic learning ('the science of the poor') and ended up, like dozens if not hundreds of others like me, as a graduate of the seminary. I did not choose this college in preference to others, but the students at this college, unlike those in other colleges, were remunerated for the learning they endeavored to seek and benefited, especially when they proved they were capable and earnest, from grants that made them dependent on the college and those who ran it. When I suddenly became a sheikh, since my graduation coincided with the complete nationalization of religion in my country, I found myself a civil servant in a newly created ministry, which was responsible for all the mosques and religious endowments that had passed into state hands; a ministry that had a mandate to ensure control over the faith of the people, who were suddenly labeled 'citizens,' although citizenship in this fledgling republic, established on rubble rather than firm foundations, was a concept that fluctuated with the vagaries of its politics.

I have neither good nor bad memories of that period, because my student years brought no change in my introverted nature and my indifference toward mixing with my peers. My only legacy from those years was the 'friendship' that arose between me and a few of my teachers, a friendship based on admiration rather than affection. Believe it or not, I can date the time when I left the confines of the seminary and embarked on a 'working life' as a civil servant in that ministry, living alone in a small rented apartment, by the fact that I then stopped performing the dawn prayer, because in my college days communal prayers in the morning were 'a timed prescription'* and anyone who missed the prayers once would think twice about doing so again, thanks to a giant tattered register that every student, before leaving the mosque, had to sign alongside his name and the date.

Does it make sense that a boy who, unlike his brothers, insisted on accompanying his father to pray in the village mosque at dawn every day, who learned how to wash for prayers in water so cold that he shivered, who learned how to pray before he could decipher the alphabet and who lived with people who advocated strict adherence to Islam, its rituals, and its laws, does it make sense that such a person should date a stage in his life by the moment he ceased to pray? I fear you might misunderstand me or misinterpret my conduct, or attribute to me an attitude toward Islam that I do not maintain. Don't jump to conclusions: I stopped praying, except on special occasions, but that made no difference to my faith. How so? I myself cannot describe it well in words that are clear and easy to understand, in spite of my pressing need to explain it to myself rather than to others. Give me a little time and for the moment accept what I say, despite its inadequacy . . . I do not have anything better or more convincing than that.

Although I stopped performing dawn prayers in the mosque close to my home, I did not abandon my habit of waking up early, and so my days began at dawn and ended around midnight, opening and closing with hours of study (because as soon as I graduated from the seminary I enrolled in the Arabic language department at the Faculty of Humanities), with work hours and a siesta filling the gap. That is how it was and that is

---

* *Surely the prayer is a timed prescription for the believers.* Quran, 4:103

how I lived for years, without changing the rhythm of my life even when I moved house or advanced up the civil service hierarchy.

Given all that, and all the knowledge and academic qualifications I acquired, how is it that the day I met you it was as if I had never done anything, as if my life before you was insignificant?

My academic zeal and my devotion to carrying out my professional duties as fully as possible distinguished me from my colleagues, especially in the eyes of some of my superiors, but that did not turn me into an 'enthusiastic worker' in the conventional sense, because enthusiasm in our ministry, as in other ministries of course, was a virtue for employees only in a metaphorical sense that was a substitute for reality. The enthusiastic workers were not necessarily those who carried out their duties fully and properly, but rather those who excelled at pleasing their superiors and winning their favor: those who were good at shifting from one loyalty to another, or at dealing adroitly with the guardians of the republic, even at the expense of relatives and friends. As for the likes of me—and they were a minority—in all modesty, we did not count for much and if those in charge could have dispensed with our services they would not have hesitated to do so, but it so happened that such people were almost indispensable, so it was not possible.

I do not pretend that I was born with a strong, instinctive moral sense, or that this was what deterred me from emulating my colleagues and imitating the deceit and hypocrisy they indulged in. All I can claim is that, by virtue of a strict rural upbringing, the principles of which have stayed with me till today, and despite my 'religious culture,' I have never treated 'good morals' as an ambiguous text that could be read in seven different ways, but rather as a form of chivalry. Thus, I can almost say that behind my disdain for emulating my esteemed colleagues lay the remnants of an ancient chivalry, which came naturally to me, and not the 'morals' prescribed in books or the things that the laws of heaven and earth unanimously condemn, because the world, my lady, this world which our common language likes to call 'wide' rather than long, whenever we want to emphasize its size, did not in my case extend beyond the confines of that mountain village where I was destined to be born and to grow up until my early youth. As for the sky, from there, from that village nestled in the hills, I did not see it as a vast and lofty firmament, as I later learned to do. For me and my peers, the sky was a meadow that differed from the open meadows surrounding the village only in its shades of blue and in whatever made it dark or bright, and this sky, with all the heavenly bodies and atmospheric phenomena, was closer to us than the nearest town. That is the way it was, and I do not exaggerate.

There, at about two thousand meters above sea level and a grueling two-hour journey from the provincial capital, I was born among people whose thrifty way of life and demands on the world were as modest as their meager harvests, but not to the extent of misery and poverty. That's how I explain to myself the "simplicity of their ethics," some of which I have inherited, and the fact that ethics did not feature prominently among their concerns. The most they expected in life from their religion and from the world was to tell right from wrong. Endowed, I would claim, with this minimal set of binding rules of conduct, I do not recall ever harboring any feeling of envy toward the material gains and promotions that my colleagues succeeded in procuring for themselves, and I never had any sense of resentment. On the contrary, all this only made me more attached to my silent aloofness.

Was it because of my alienation from people and from my colleagues that I decided to resume my university studies in the Arabic department of the Faculty of Humanities, or was it in fulfillment of a plan ordained by some omniscient power, some decider of fates who decreed that I should acquire the knowledge that would make it both possible and plausible that we should meet?

Accept my claim that I do not favor one explanation over the other, and do not argue with me when I say that I did not foresee the possibility of meeting you when I obtained that degree in the literature and history of the Arabic language. Try to forget that at the time it did not occur to me that this degree would lead to anything more than a place in the teaching profession, which I saw as an escape from a life sentence to a career that I had not chosen, but which was imposed on me like a punishment. And even today I can scarcely believe that by expanding my horizons in this way, which at first seemed no more than a change in vocational nomenclature, I have come to the threshold of forty, and that, were it not for that degree, I would not have met you, my life would not be in danger, and fate would not have brought me to where I am now.

Time and again you have asked me about my 'past' life, and sometimes you have pressed the question. Rarely have my brief and evasive answers satisfied your curiosity, and rarely have you accepted the truth of my account, the substance of which is that for years I lived 'in the shadows,' like thousands of my compatriots who were indistinguishable from me, either by their jobs, their titles, or anything else. Often you cast doubt on my account and invited me to concoct a version that was less modest and more plausible, and often your invitation aroused in me anxieties which I did not dare divulge; or rather, even after reflection, I could not see how they *could* be divulged. The more you insisted, the less I was able to express myself. Perhaps that is why I began to imagine my 'past' life—that is, what happened to me before I met you—as something like a tightly closed seashell, and I greatly feared that, if I prised it open, I would find absolutely nothing inside it.

For various reasons, the least compelling of which is that impulse to take stock which everyone experiences at moments of adversity, especially when that adversity includes the risk of death, I am now less attached to the idea that the shell of my 'past' life is empty, yet more convinced that the people and events it contained (I don't know whether to call them part of a 'first life' or a 'last life') are gone and never can return.

That life ended, or more precisely began to end, in the aftermath of upheavals that "put our republic on the right track," as was said at the time. One day I was summoned by a sheikh with whom I had a long history of mutual affection, despite the difference in our ages and his distinguished reputation. Since this mentor of mine had been a professional politician from his early youth and had lived the vicissitudes of politics, sometimes going to jail and sometimes holding high-level positions, and since he supported the 'reform movement' that had seized the reins of power in our tormented republic from the gang of military men who had wrested power from the previous owners, I had no doubt that he had summoned me for some reason connected with these 'developments.' My guess was not mistaken, but he exceeded my expectations in a way I had not anticipated. After a brief greeting, without any sham courtesies, the sheikh brought up the reason why he had summoned me, in his usual style—resolute and at the same time effusively cheerful: "Unless I was sure you would not let me down, I would not have called you. For once, I can say with confidence that we are now in charge. Your place is not behind a desk on the second floor of a government office building. I want you to prepare to travel urgently. I have recommended you for the position of imam, preacher, and teacher at our mosque in . . . "

17

The sheikh had hardly finished speaking when there was a knock on the door and an officer came in. I could not easily decipher the stars and pips shining on his lapels, but fortunately the sheikh quickly introduced us by our titles and, in a courteous allusion to his familiarity with me, he deliberately called me "my son, Sheikh So-and-so." Without any preliminaries other than a broad smile and a gesture that meant 'over to you,' the sheikh consigned me to the officer.

The sheikh had not taken the trouble to warn me that the officer was about to join us or to explain his intrusion, and the officer, like someone conveying a message rather than someone engaged in a dialogue, took me by surprise with a lengthy lecture, the gist of which was that the reputation of our republic abroad was no less important than other political and economic matters and that, in view of my spotless personal conduct and my academic qualifications, on the basis of the sheikh's recommendation and after consultation, it had been decided to appoint me imam, preacher, and teacher at the mosque that served our citizens in the neighboring country.

I was not unaware that I was being pushed into something that had nothing to do with me, and that if I accepted this position I would be succeeding a colleague of the same nationality and profession, who had either damaged the reputation of our republic in some way or whose only fault was that he had fallen out of favor. Nevertheless, I received the news of my appointment submissively and compliantly. The officer might have found my reaction difficult to interpret, but he praised my attitude, especially what he described as my "equanimity," as if he knew in advance what was awaiting me.

However precise the reports submitted on my humble person might have been, and regardless of the extent to which they covered the aspects required (that is, just about everything), I doubt they succeeded in showing how lonely and dejected, if not melancholic, I was, or even paid any attention to that. Or perhaps I am fooling myself, and in fact they saw my defects as exactly what was needed!

I move on to this phase of my life as cautiously as someone entering a ruined building, not as someone discovering virgin territory, even though, trust me, this is the first time I have done so, and is possibly the last.

Another impossible thing to explain today is how easily and carelessly I agreed to take on the job as imam of this mosque, when I knew of its unique status. If I were to attribute it to 'personal reasons,' I would not be credible, and if I suggested 'non-personal reasons' for my selection, such as the fact that during my student days I had favored certain political positions rather than others, I would appear to be exaggerating.

Although all mosques in all four corners of the world are dedicated to God alone, perhaps before any other consideration they are also defined by the imam and his congregation, and the Mosque of the Expatriates was no exception to this rule. Originally and officially, it was called the Mosque of the Two Omars, but since it had been built with contributions from compatriots of mine who over the decades had taken refuge in your country and since it stood in the neighborhood where they had settled, the name Mosque of the Expatriates prevailed. Because of this, and because most of the congregation lived in the neighborhood (with the passage of time, the neighborhood had expanded into a whole suburb, and in turn the services provided by the mosque had also expanded), it become customary for the imam and preacher to be named by consensus between the authorities in the two countries.

Naturally, it was not unknown for this consensus to break down from time to time through 'tensions in relations between the two countries,' leading to divisions in the committee charged with managing the endowment and its activities, and to all the other problems that arise in such circumstances.

My agreement to carry out this 'responsibility' was the context without which my life would not have come together in the form of a drama. I leave that aside for the moment. My priority is to make clear that at the time it did not occur to me that, when explaining why I accepted, I would ever have to defend myself against suspicions that I was collaborating with the new rulers.

The desire to please my superiors was the explanation current among my colleagues who, because of my reputation for keeping aloof from them both in work and in pleasure, were surprised that I was chosen. But even this explanation they were quicker than me to assume, for the simplest of reasons—the fact that I myself had no fear of any consequences if I turned down the new job.

Who would believe that I was deeply dispirited at the time, and that what is closest to the truth is that, in agreeing to take on this responsibility, I was acting out of a mixture of apathy and curiosity—apathy in the sense that I was confident deep inside that I did not owe anyone an explanation or a favor, and curiosity in the sense that from making the move I looked forward to broadening my horizons and to some relief from the monotony of a life that was not only hardly a life but from which I thought there was nothing more to be gained? Besides, I was quite sure I would not be alone in running the mosque and looking after the congregation. Would it make sense, I said to myself on that day, for the government to leave me posted alone at such a vulnerable front-line position? On top of all that, and perhaps most importantly, I had no sense of guilt or of compromising myself; no sense that I was abandoning one conviction and falsely and hypocritically embracing another one.

3

I am impatient to write about you, like a man impatient for an appointment on which he has long pinned hope. Writing about you means many things, all the things that we have shared together, things that teem in my mind and in my body. Can what we have shared be counted? Or does my lack of confidence in myself and in whether I deserved to meet a woman like you lead me, time after time, to doubt whether what happened between us really happened? The only way I know to dispel that doubt is to try to tell myself our story, again and again, in tedious detail from start to finish.

I was wanted as imam of this mosque, and I was willing to play the part, so I began to minister to my very small community with my little learning and my considerable tenacity. I soon realized that this was all that was needed to carry out the duties of the job, because most of those who frequented my mosque, that house of God, came in to unburden themselves of the worldly concerns that troubled them, rather than to magnify His name as they were supposed to do. I do not think I am exaggerating, and if you ever had a chance to hear their complaints you would know what rubbish I had to listen to and what worries I had to imbibe. You would also understand my excitement and my confusion when you came to me and, with a spontaneity that, I realized only later, came so naturally to you, and in language of a simplicity, clarity, and firmness unfamiliar to me, invited me to other concerns closer to my own and more stimulating than the concerns of the mosque, which threatened to sweep me away like a flood.

After a while, I again have doubts that what happened between us was real. As soon as I slay the dragon of that doubt, another one springs up at me, this time in the guise of the idea that what happened stemmed from pure chance, from mere coincidence, and might not have happened at all, and that for this reason, and however much I might embellish it, it is liable to contestation. The only way I can counter this possible original defect in our relationship is to say that had we not become friends I would have remained hostage to my two prisons: my mosque and that neighborhood of the city, a neighborhood that bore the imprint—the language, the smells, and the noise—of the people who had moved there, and that had gradually become a cocooned casbah. All it needed was a tall minaret and all those entering the area would know they had to take off their shoes before crossing the threshold.

Even now, when what happened between us is an established fact, part of a story which cannot be amended or expurgated, it troubles me that I am still seeking evidence that it had to happen for some good reason and did not come about just by chance.

Now that you do not know where I am, do you understand why I sometimes disappointed you when you encouraged me to stare at your naked body and have my fill of it, and, when I was inside you and running my fingers through your hair, do you realize how much effort it took me to raise my head and look you straight in the eye at the moment of orgasm? Do you understand why my excitement left me speechless and why I would close my eyes and leave it to my hands to caress your body from one end to the other? How could I dare to open my eyes and let a word pass my lips, when for years upon years I had known nothing of life or had turned my back on it? And how could you have known?

After our first brief telephone conversation I did not think there could be any common ground between you and the likes of me. That impression was reinforced by the misplaced respect that your tone of voice betrayed and by the grandiloquent titles by which you addressed me, titles which I am not accustomed to see or hear before my name except at public ceremonies, printed on invitations I receive or in certain circulars relevant to the affairs of the community. It was also corroborated when you came to visit me for the appointment we had made by telephone, especially by the inexpert way in which you tied a scarf to cover your hair for me and by what I imagined was your disappointment with my 'modern' dress and with my behavior, which you later described as 'easygoing,' one day when we were reminiscing together about the events of that first meeting.

That was the first time, as you told me later, that you had ever entered a mosque, or "a place of that type" as you quickly rephrased it. What we agreed to call my mosque was in fact a walled enclosure containing three independent buildings: one rectangular and two square, linked by pathways that were haphazardly paved to save pedestrians from sinking into the mud in winter. The rectangular building, rather like a large shed despite its gilt door, was the mosque itself; and one of the square buildings, hidden behind the mosque from the eyes of those entering the compound from the main gate, was small, low even for a two-story structure (but it had to be that way so as not to be higher than the minaret). The janitor occupied the two ground-floor rooms, while I had the two upper-floor rooms. Unlike this building, the other square building was exposed, facing the mosque, and did not aspire to be tall. It was designed to provide the mosque with a hall suitable for 'cultural and social activities.'

The building work had been a struggle, and not enough money was available to finish off and furnish the inside, so it remained as it was until I arrived. I then appropriated a section near the entrance and turned it into my office, and put some chairs in one corner to elevate its status to that of a 'meeting hall,' while the rest of the space became a storeroom for neighbors and local shopkeepers lucky enough to obtain the consent of the janitor.

Anxious not to waste my time, you took control of the tone and pace of our first meeting. After thanking me for agreeing to meet you, in spite of the many duties you assumed I had, and after speaking highly of those who had recommended me to you, you briefly laid out your reason for visiting me. Then you took out of your handbag a neat dossier that you said contained a detailed explanation of what you were proposing. When the call to prayer reached us in my office, where we were meeting, drawn out somewhat because the tape in the machine had stretched from frequent use, you quickly took your leave and asked if you could phone me in a few days to hear my views on 'the project.'

Stumbling over my words, I tried to tell you that there was no reason why we should not continue our conversation, despite the call to prayer, but I did not succeed; perhaps you thought my suggestion was merely a deferential courtesy. Anyway, after you took your leave, I took advantage of the minutes we stood standing to express my great interest in 'the project' and to say I was willing to put my modest learning at its disposal. My remarks at the time were no more than platitudes that might have applied to anyone and to any 'project,' but I deliberately took my time in order to emphasize that I was serious about inviting you to continue our conversation. As though the tenor of my message had reached you, you gently interrupted my explanation to ask me when I thought it would be convenient for you to call me back and whether it would be possible for us to meet outside the confines of the mosque, that is, at your place, as you hesitantly put it. At that point, after I left it to you to decide the time and venue, all that remained before we met again as soon as possible was for you to leave. That is how it was.

I had trouble getting through the rest of that day, which as usual I allocated to receiving women seeking advice and counsel, in fact mostly asking me to intervene personally with their husbands, with what they supposed was my moral authority, to deter the men from hurting them or from wasting what little they earned on their vices. Fortunately I had only three visitors that day: one of them came to thank me for an intervention which had succeeded, and I delegated the official in charge of what we call social affairs to look into the matters that had induced the other two to knock on the mosque door. My visitors did not tire me and it was not an exhausting day, but I did not breathe a sigh of relief until I withdrew to my room, after bluntly asking the janitor only to disturb me for something momentous.

That night was very much like my nights here: stretched out on my bed, resting my head on my interlocked hands, with my eyes closed and pleasantly drowsy, I began to go over the events of my fleeting meeting with you, just as I do here when I go over the events of our relationship, and what surprises me most is that, now that I am the only person I can narrate them to, the months we had together seem as fleeting as that first meeting of ours.

As I lay there that night, I could hear you talking. In a tone quite different from the confused tone of our formal first telephone conversation, you were explaining that al-Mutanabbi may not be the only Arab poet for whom it is worth dispatching a scientific campaign to explore his world, so that the results can be deposited in an encyclopedic book, but he is certainly the one with the most compelling poetry and career. To the timbre of your voice, I closed my eyes that night without thought for the morrow, or for anything.

4

I f what came over me that night was sleep, then I can only conclude that I had never known sleep before. If it was not sleep, then I must have spent large portions of my life asleep. After dawn prayers, which I would have missed had the janitor not knocked persistently on my door, I spent hours as a prisoner of this thought and similar thoughts less subtle and more truly substantial. To stop him intruding on me again as eight o'clock approached, I quickly notified him that I had been feeling unwell for the last few hours and had to stay in my room. I also asked him not to disturb me except in emergencies, and not to transfer any phone calls to me except . . . I remember clearly that I did not complete this sentence, but checked myself and retraced my footsteps to my room, assuming that the janitor would attribute my mumbling and absentmindedness to my alleged indisposition. But was this indisposition a mere invention? Throughout the days between our meeting and your subsequent phone call I remained uncertain whether or not I was ill. I met all the criteria for sickness, but the trouble with my illness was, and still is, that it did not have a name. There in my room, the question nagged me: "Except . . . ? Except . . . ?" like a chronic cough. I tried all the answers that came to mind and of course none of them were convincing or served the purpose.

I wanted to make an exception only for you, but how? How could I make an exception for a casual encounter with a woman who had nothing in common with the women who usually visited me, and on what basis could I do that?

Where are you now, my lady? And how are you? Are you in the company of al-Mutanabbi, who brought you to me? I never heard you mention him other than by his first name, Ahmad, and I was secretly surprised to find a young woman on familiar terms with such a vast amount of poetry, history, and Arabic language lore—a woman of such mystery.

Later, when al-Mutanabbi brought us together in our passions, my surprise changed into something akin to jealousy, and how can I say just jealousy, when I am jealous of a dead man who is in fact more alive than anyone I know?

                       ⟋⟍

You clearly did not know what a sore spot you had touched when you came suggesting I take part in your project, because one of the symptoms of my premature senescence, which I needed no doctor to diagnose, was that, as my modest ambitions foundered on the rocks of routine, I had lost my appetite for the books which had once kept me up late into the night, including the poetry of your friend Ahmad, "who thought himself a prophet."* It is no credit to me that I had spent long hours in his company; rather, the credit is his. Lest you might think I am exaggerating or trying to flatter you, I have hesitated to tell you anything else about my relationship with al-Mutanabbi: that his collected works was one of those books that I not only read but also forced myself to copy out by hand, in my eagerness to pay him homage. And more: in my spontaneous resistance to the premature senescence that I felt creeping up on me, al-Mutanabbi's was one of the few books that I rebought here, when I first took on my new job, and I depended on it to provide me with an escape from the comfortable misery in which I found myself wallowing, unwittingly and in spite of my occasional attacks of anxiety.

---

* The name al-Mutanabbi is usually interpreted as meaning someone who pretends to or aspires to be a prophet (nabi). The sheikh and his friend discuss possible theories about the nature of al-Mutanabbi's 'prophethood' in detail in Chapter 22. (Translator's note)

27

If I go on talking about trifling matters—when I first saw you, when we first met, the coincidences that sometimes meant more than anything planned—I might end up reducing al-Mutanabbi to the role of the matchmaker who brought us together, and nothing more.

I will not do that but, within myself (I would normally have said "between me and you"), the only way I can now get close to you is through him.

When I had the idea of conjuring you through al-Mutanabbi, I did not intend to perform a divination, but inadvertently I found myself doing it.

I picked up the two volumes of his collected works, which had been lying flat since I bought them because the bookshelves in my office were too small to take them standing upright, and I opened the first volume at random, like someone engaged in bibliomancy, not to read it.

If it was a book I had read repeatedly, the spine would have been broken in such a way that it opened automatically on certain pages, like a book in which one often reads certain passages, giving one away if it falls in the hands of someone else. If that was the case, you would accuse me of cheating, but it was not like that.

I say I did not intend to perform a divination, but what can one do in a situation such as mine, obsessed by your specter, when al-Mutanabbi, so boastful, such a braggart, so bombastic, takes one by surprise with verses which appear to speak so clearly on one's behalf?

> *Close to you I feel at ease*
> *Even if that closeness is marred by some distance.*
> *What use is it to me that barriers between us have been lifted*
> *If a single barrier stands in the way of my desire for you?*
> *I am sparing with my greetings, not wishing to annoy you,*
> *And I hold my tongue, so you need not answer.*
> *There is much I would like to say, but you are so discerning*
> *That my silence speaks for itself, and sends a message.**

Applying the verses to my own situation, and ignoring the fact that they were addressed to a male, I interpreted the verses as though I were interpreting any other verses I came across.

---

* From al-Mutanabbi's eulogy of Kafour, after which he did not meet him again.

28

Whenever I read a line, it felt as though the line dissolved and your features took its place, as in my mind's eye I liked to imagine them, and when I read new lines, you appeared to me in yet another guise, and so on and so on, all day long, undisturbed until, after the evening prayer, I heard the echoes of an argument taking place in the courtyard of the mosque.

Although I was preoccupied with reading and with the thought of you, I could make out the voices and could sometimes anticipate the opinions and arguments that each voice would come out with, regardless of the subject that lay behind the heated discussion. I was often surprised by their enthusiasm for disputation, and by the way they took pleasure in repeating the same arguments and using the same analogies. Often my lack of interest puzzled them, but they saw it as wisdom and composure.

Wary that the small community of worshipers might start wanting to visit their sick imam if I stayed away too long, I pulled myself together and closed the book, with my eyes on the last image of you I had conjured, determined to show my face the following day to my inquisitive charges, who no doubt would speculate readily about my absence if I hid from them another day.

The next morning I did not wait for the dawn call to prayers from the loudspeakers before I left my room. I reached the mosque even earlier, deliberately arriving before everyone else, or rather ensuring that the congregation would arrive just as I was busy performing the two customary prostrations. I took my time on these prostrations, then stood up to take part in communal prayers with the few people zealous enough to perform this ritual in the mosque, knowing that if I did not lead them in prayer, then my own prayer would not count. When it comes to prayer, besides the question of intent,* there is another question that has haunted me from that day on, whenever I found myself compelled to perform my prayers:

---

* Intent means resolve to perform an act of worship in order to bring oneself closer to God Almighty, and without intent prayer is not valid.

since a man who needs to urinate* cannot pray, how then can a man pray when his mind is full of thoughts and fantasies much more repulsive than the impurities in his bowels? Besides, the body has well-known channels for eliminating these impurities and if they were obstructed the body would malfunction. But what can a man do when he has such thoughts and fantasies, and how can he rid himself of them?

All I remember is that after I had finished praying and all the others had gone on their way, I stayed where I was until I had run over in my mind all the images of you I had imagined the day before.

God alone knows if I was reckless enough that day to say to myself that one man's misfortunes are another man's blessings. In fact, I thanked God for my indisposition, which had distracted me from you and from waiting for you.

By eight o'clock, I had already spent hours struggling to prepare the sermon for the coming Friday, which on the anniversary of the first reform had to be about patriotism. Suddenly, I heard a commotion from beyond the mosque wall, followed by the relentless pounding of fists on the thick metal door. I was as confused by the banging as the janitor, and it seemed to be gaining in tempo. I rushed out of my office toward the door, but the janitor, who was in his sixties, had beaten me to it to find out what was happening. Before I reached the door, I saw the janitor's hand trembling, hesitant to slide the bolt to keep them out. The banging was more like a threat than a sign that someone wanted to come in. For a couple of seconds the janitor stood his ground and resisted the threat, but suddenly the door swung open, or rather burst open, and I found myself facing a seething throng with raised fists, shouting incomprehensibly at the top of their voices. My timid attempts to retreat did not succeed: the crowd was too fast and too unruly. It swept me away like a wave, and like a wave it pushed

---

* Specialists in Islamic law are unanimous in their disapproval of praying when one wants to urinate or defecate, based on a saying of the Prophet, narrated by his wife Aisha: "No prayer can be (rightly said) when food is present or when the worshiper is resisting the call of nature" (*The Sahih of al-Bukhari*, Book 4, hadith no. 1139) Scholars of the Shafii and Hanbali schools of law include in the same category those who are hungry or thirsty. They say that someone in such a situation should first urinate, defecate, or break wind, and then satisfy his hunger or thirst, even if it means missing communal prayers, based on a saying cited by al-Bukhari: "If anyone of you is having his meals, he should not hurry up till he is satisfied, even if the prayer has been started."

me back across a pathway toward the small circular open area facing the mosque door.

The crowd stared at me and in what seemed like a single step it pushed me into the circle. Then it began to break up and regroup behind me in human chains arranged in concentric semi-circles matching the curve of the circular area. The throng, made up mostly of juveniles and youngsters, with some older men, was shouting insults, pushing and shoving with shoulders and fists, and it seemed to me it was divided into two equal halves: one half lined up to my right like a solid wall, the other likewise on my left. There was no enemy in front of me, just an empty space, and there was no sea behind me, just onlookers. But to my right and my left stood hostile forces.

Once the scene was established in this way, the intensity of the uproar diminished spontaneously and turned into a murmur, which soon subsided in its turn. At that point, a local man known for his prestige, dignity, and integrity appeared from I know not where and stepped toward me until he was right in front of me. In a voice audible to the two disputing sides, he began to recount the reasons for the disturbance: early in the morning, one man's family had received news that the man had been detained on arrival at the airport, and the family suspected that his detention was the result of a denunciation and that the informer was the son of so-and-so. Before he raised his hand to point out the suspected informer, who led one of the two groups, I interrupted him for fear his gesture might reignite the brawl, and in a tone of rebuke I urged the family leaders to have their followers disperse and to accompany me into the mosque, along with some of the local notables, to discuss the matter.

Reluctantly, the two sides did as I asked and, when I was somewhat confident that the brawl would not resume, we went into the courtyard of the mosque and from there walked to the corner that we insisted on calling the 'meeting hall.' With the help of some peacemakers, I arranged to seat the two sides in a way that brought them close together but did not upset either of them, while preserving the middle ground for myself and the neutrals. To make sure that neither side spoke first, I opened the dialogue, after a bismillah and a blessing for the prophet Muhammad, by reproaching them for allowing themselves to be carried away by impetuous youngsters on both sides, and when I felt that my reproach had tempered their fury and that making a distinction between them and the youngsters might help reconcile them, I went on to praise the virtues they shared and finished by reminding the family of the detainee that *if an ungodly man comes to you with news, use your judgment, lest you hurt people unwittingly and then regret what you have done* (Quran 49:6). I told the family of the suspected informer that *if you do good openly or in secret or pardon an evil, surely God is all-pardoning, all-powerful* (Quran 4:149). Addressing the two of them, I cited two readily comprehensible sayings of the Prophet, the first to the effect that "insulting a Muslim is sinful and fighting a Muslim is heresy," and the second to the effect that "one becomes many through one's brothers." I then prayed to God Almighty to free all innocent detainees, without neglecting to mention that we were guests in this country, dependent on its bounty and generosity for our livelihoods, and that it was in no one's interests, either as individuals or collectively, that our deeds should tarnish our reputation as a community or the reputation of the country from which we came. I said no more than that because I felt that the group had listened to me long enough and it was time to let them speak, after I had steered the discussion in the right direction, and on top of that, so that I did not go too far and say something that one side might interpret as an argument against the other side. The head of the suspect's family was the first to take advantage of my silence. After a prayer wishing me long life, he quickly swore the most solemn oath that his son was innocent of the allegations against him in this case in particular and of the charge of "collaborating with the security agencies" in general.

In case swearing by God and His prophet might be seen as empty rhetoric, he coupled his oath with thorough abuse of the government and its security agencies, as though these insults were more eloquent proof of his truthfulness than the oaths themselves!

My lecture, followed by the speaker's barrage of insults against the government and its security agencies, chastened the family of the detainee. The head of the family set about cursing the devil and the times, and, with everyone seeking an honorable way out, the conversation took a more general turn. This whetted the appetite of those present and they began to share the latest local news they had heard, from the brutality of the security agencies to the high prices of goods and the shortage of medicines, competing with each other to exchange the latest rumors and speculation.

With an impassioned appeal from me to deal with matters amicably, to avoid any repetition of what had happened in the morning ("because all of you are community leaders and responsible men"), and a promise that I would give the matter my personal attention to establish the details, the session broke up after about two hours and everyone left the mosque except two of the peacemakers, who thought the conversation should continue and preferred to stay on.

That was their right, my lady, because the mosque is the house of God, and home to everyone at a time when they might feel uneasy or anxious in their own homes; except for me, maybe because I have no other home in which to take refuge!

Politely and with difficulty, I declined to continue the conversation with the peacemakers and withdrew to my room, leaving them to discuss the affairs of the community in general and what had happened that morning in particular and putting myself at their disposal if they were to call me.

⚶

As I expected when I agreed to guard this vulnerable frontline position on the borders of our republic, it was no more than a few days after my arrival that I realized I was not the only guard, and that some members of the endowment committee and of the congregation itself shared this task with me on behalf of people I could not precisely identify. Fortunately this fact, which did not surprise me, was well known to the people of the neighborhood, and although it inspired some wise guys to tell me that the imam here reigns but does not rule, it also set me up in the eyes of some ordinary congregants as an intermediary between them and those who had the power to make or mar.

Such a situation may not appeal to someone who seeks authority and is anxious not to share his prerogatives with anyone else; but overall it suited me, even if I did not always like it. I was reluctant to confront those who encroached on my authority, and I left them alone, without concern that their encroachments overshadowed my status. Perhaps this supercilious attitude of mine, from the moment I arrived, was what conferred on me, and on my position with respect to both them and the congregation in general, a prestige of mysterious origin, which they were the first to begrudge me.

Without a summons, my war council would convene at times of crisis and on the eve of major occasions, and that is how it was on the day of

33

the confrontation. A little before the sunset prayer, unusually, and as though in response to an invitation that could not be refused, a number of elders began to descend on the mosque. We performed the prayers and, when some of them stayed around waiting for the next prayers, I asked them to leave and invited those I knew should be invited to join me in the meeting hall. I did not need to open the session with any kind of question or introduction because we were all well aware of the reason for our unexpected meeting. But I did find myself opening the meeting with some useful remarks, "You know better than I that there's an old feud between family X and family Y, and that they brought the feud with them in their baggage when they came to this country," I said. "They revived it here, and it died down only after great effort and after a laborious reconciliation, which some of you helped to mediate and to which some of you acted as witnesses. After what happened this morning and in light of the new allegiance of many members of family X, both young and old, an allegiance evident in their long beards and short gowns,* I'm very worried that this feud might resume, if not flare up, and not only in the name of family pride, so I would be grateful for any guidance you can give me."

I did not really expect any of them to give me advice, because I knew that every one of my secret partners in protecting the community had come to listen to what I had to say and report it back to his master or his patron and, besides, I knew much less about the incident and its background than each of them knew. My suspicion was correct, and the consensus was that what happened was a portent of something worse and that it was not clear what precautions should be taken.

The expected call to prayer brought our meeting to an end and we arose with heavy hearts to join the people in the mosque. Confused, and with wavering zeal, I led the small group in prayer and, as soon as the prayer was done, I hurriedly took my leave and went back to my room.

❧

The least that can be said is that I urgently needed to be alone, if only to take stock and sort out my thoughts and the events in my small community.

---

* These forms of dress are conventional among modern salafist Muslims. (Translator's note)

I do not recall that I managed to achieve that purpose. Probably I fell asleep as soon as I took off my shoes and undid my belt—a sleep punctuated by both dreams and nightmares. If I had merely had nightmares, I would have dismissed the night as a passing phase, and if I had merely had dreams I would have wished never to wake up. But to have the two together—such that one moment I happily started to go over our meeting in general and in detail, and the next moment I imagined that people were hammering on the mosque door—was more than I could bear, or so I fancied on that night.

5

I do not think I am any different from the rest of humanity when I divide memories into three categories: pleasant ones, which we hope to keep alive forever; memories of unpleasant events, which we wish had never happened; and embarrassing ones, the most difficult ones to deal with because of what they share with the other two: with pleasant memories the impulse to mull them over and with unpleasant memories the fact that we want them completely forgotten.

The telephone conversation we had after our first meeting was of this latter kind. I am wary of remembering it, but I have no choice. Without the slightest effort or any desire whatsoever on my part, it is deeply engraved in my memory, along with all the words I spluttered out in the course of it. Do not ask me how or why. Throughout those days I was obsessed with waiting impatiently for you to reemerge, if only by telephone; that was all I was interested in. In such a state, how could I not get flustered and stammer when you asked me, "frankly," as you put it, if I would agree to meet you at exactly seven o'clock the next evening at an address you dictated to me, and that you described merely as "my place?" It was as if you were asking me, "Would it distress you, you sheikh of over forty, to leave your house of God and visit a woman in her home, in spite of the contrast, if not the inexorable conflict, between the two places?"

I was at a loss to respond or even attempt to respond, but fortunately an expression such as "God willing"—even if your poet described it on the eve of his murder as "a phrase which can neither avert the inevitable nor help bring about a particular outcome"*—is on such occasions a response that cannot be contested.

---

* "We wrote to Abu Nasr Muhammad ibn al-Mubarak al-Jabbuli, asking him for an explanation (of how al-Mutanabbi was killed). Abu Nasr was an elder of the Tunnaa', a Persian community in that region, and a courteous and respected man. In reply he sent us a long letter, reading: 'As for your question about the murder of Abul Tayyib al-Mutanabbi, may God have mercy on him, let me explain it as follows: 'He left Wasit on a Saturday, thirteen nights before the end of Ramadan in the year AH 354 and was killed at Bizaa, an estate close to Deir Aqoul on Wednesday, two nights before the end of the month. The man who organized his murder and the murder of his son and his servant was from the Banu Asad and was called Fatik ibn Abi al-Jahl ibn Faris ibn Badad. It is said that when he killed him, he said, 'Shame on this beard, you slanderer.' This was because he was related to the mother of Dabba ibn Yazid al-Aini, whom al-Mutanabbi had mocked in a poem, saying his mother had long flabby breasts. Some people say that Fatik was Dabba's maternal uncle and he was enraged when he heard her described as ugly in the poem. It is in fact the silliest and the worst written of al-Mutanabbi's poems, but nonetheless it led to his murder, the murder of his son and the loss of his possessions. Fatik was a friend of mine and he lived up to his name (translator's note: Fatik means 'killer or destroyer') for the blood he spilled and for his fearless spirit. When he heard the poem making fun of Dabba, he was offended and the offense began to rankle. He even reprimanded Dabba, saying: 'You shouldn't have let a poet find a way to attack you.' He did not reveal his true feelings, and he tracked al-Mutanabbi's movements when he left Persia for Iraq and passed through Jabbul and Deir Aqoul. Along with a group of cousins who shared his views on al-Mutanabbi, he was never off his horse, seeking him out and asking everyone he met for information. Fatik was terrified that al-Mutanabbi might elude him, and he would often come and stay with me. One day he was at my place, asking travelers about al-Mutanabbi, and I told him: 'You've made such a big deal about this man, so what do you intend to do if you meet him?' He replied: 'I have only the best of intentions—to rebuke him for his slanderous poem.' 'I wouldn't expect anything less of you,' I joked. He laughed and said: 'By God, Abu Nasr, if I cast eyes on him, if he and I are together in the same place, I will massacre him, crush his life, unless something stops me.' 'Refrain from such talk, God forgive you,' I said, 'and go back to God. Clear your heart of such thoughts because the man is famous and of great repute, and killing him because of a poem would be wrong. Poets lampooned kings in the pre-Islamic era and caliphs in the Islamic era, but we've never heard of a poet being killed for his satires. The poet said: "I have lampooned Zuhayr and then praised him / The high and mighty are still lampooned and praised," and yet his offense did not carry the death penalty.' 'God does what he wants,' he said

On the way from the mosque to 'your place' I did my best not to anticipate how it would be, but instead concentrated on preparing myself to appear before a woman who would decide whether or not I had the qualifications required for her project.

I tried to interpret the furniture of the room where you received me, to see what kind of place this 'your place' was, and although I had thought it was probably a place of work and only by extension a place of residence, what I found strongly suggested the opposite. I wavered between these two

---

and went off. Only three days later I came across al-Mutanabbi with mules loaded with gold and silver, clothes, perfumes, jewels, and other things, because when al-Mutanabbi traveled he never left at home a single dirham or dinar, nor clothes nor anything worth more than a dirham. He was especially solicitous of his notebooks because he had selected his best verse and written out corrected versions. He said, 'I received him and invited him into my house and asked what news he brought, who he had met and how his journey had gone. I was gladdened by what he told me: he began describing Ibn al-Amid, his kindness, his politeness, his learning and his generosity, as well as the tolerance of King Fanna Khusraw, his interest in literature and his affection for his people. When night fell, I asked him what they were agreed to do, and he said, 'I'll ride by night, I find it more comfortable.' 'That's the right thing to do,' I said, hoping that the night would conceal him from his enemies and that he could travel far by daybreak. 'You'd better take along some of the men from the town, men who know the way and all the frightening places along it. They could lead you all the way to Baghdad,' I added. But he frowned and said, 'Why do you say that?' I replied, 'They'll keep you company!' 'When I have a sword on my neck, I don't need any other company,' said al-Mutanabbi. 'That is indeed the case and you'd do well to take my advice.' 'This allusion of yours sounds like a hint, and a hint often heralds candor, so why don't you spell it out clearly?' 'That ignoramus Fatik al-Asadi was at my place three days ago,' I said, 'and he has a grudge against you because you lampooned his sister's son, and he said things that make it vital to be cautious and on the alert. He's with about twenty cousins of his on horseback and they are all of one opinion.' His servant, who was smart and sensible and had heard our conversation, said, 'Abu Nasr is right. Take twenty men with you to go ahead of us all the way to Baghdad.' But al-Mutanabbi was furious and viciously insulted the servant boy. 'Don't you ever say of me that I traveled under any protection but that of my sword' he said. I said, 'Come on, I'll arrange for an escort to go with you and protect you.' 'Are you trying to frighten me with auguries, are you worried on my behalf about the Banu Asad? By God, if this scepter of mine lay on the bank of the Euphrates and the Banu Asad hadn't had a drink for five days and they were looking at the water like the bellies of snakes, not a single foot would venture to reach the water. And if anyone thought of doing so, God forbid, I'd deal with them in the blink of an eye.' 'Say "God willing, "' I said. 'A phrase that can neither avert the inevitable nor help bring about a particular outcome,' al-Mutanabbi replied. Then he rode off and it was the last I knew of him."

Mahmoud Muhammad Shakir, *al-Mutanabbi* (Cairo: Madani Press, 1977)

theories, uninterested in anything else, throughout the minutes you were away making tea, not out of curiosity or to keep myself busy but because I had little familiarity with private spaces, especially those such as 'your place,' a room that within a few square yards brought together furniture, electronic gadgets, books in various languages, and decorative items, to create a microcosm of a motley world, tended day after day by an elegant and ingenious manager.

You could see clearly that I was flustered and, when you tried to make me feel at ease, you too were almost overcome by embarrassment, but then you took the initiative, assumed the role of a pupil addressing a teacher, and invited me to take one of the three chairs, comfortable despite their unfamiliar shape, which surrounded a round table supported by a single square leg, rounded at the edges. The table was made of a strong, dense wood of a kind that suggested an exotic origin and gave the impression it was cut from a single block.

On a lower table nearby, you put the tea set you had brought on a copper tray, which you carefully set aside out of sight, I don't know where. Ill at ease in my seat and counting every breath, I followed all your doings, careful not to look at you in a way you might interpret as intrusive. In pouring the tea, you had to bend down a little and turn your head to the right. You were wearing a token headscarf, which held together the locks of your jet-black hair but did not cover them completely. When you bent down, our eyes might have met if you had turned toward me, by accident or on purpose. At that point I looked away from you sharply and lowered my head to the right, pretending to examine the titles of the books stacked regularly on top of each other to my right, and holding this position until you offered me my cup of tea. Perhaps your "please" and my "thank you" were the first words we exchanged after the initial greetings, when I had deliberately said the usual "Good evening," instead of using the religious salutation "Peace be upon you."

You sat to my right, as I had expected, because I had noticed a book there, with small pieces of paper slipped between the pages and covered with notes in small, neat handwriting, along with an elegantly bound notebook of medium size and a collection of pens. You swiftly brought an end to the silence by pressing me to drink my cup of tea before it went cold, and then repeated your invitation, encouraging me, as much as you could, to break my silence and relax. You explained that you had neglected to offer me a choice between tea and coffee because you assumed I preferred the former, based on what you observed when you visited me in the mosque. I confirmed your observation. Since we felt the need for a subject to break the ice and to overcome our shyness about listening to and looking at each other, we embarked for some minutes on a comparison of the two drinks, and when we had had our fill of this unavoidable routine, you turned to the conversation we had at our first meeting, asking whether my busy schedule had left me enough time to read the plan for 'the project.'

You did not wait for my answer, but picked up the notebook and opened it at a double page on which you had drawn lines of boxes with great geometrical precision. Some of the boxes were still empty, while others were filled with careful writing in the same tidy hand. At the head of each group of boxes there was a title in the same hand, but slightly wider, and between the boxes small arrows had been drawn, running in various directions.

When the two pages were laid out in front of me, I could not help commenting by citing the line of al-Mutanabbi, written on the eve of his flight from Kafour's Egypt: "Alas this plan!"* You did not respond, even out of courtesy, to what I imagined to be a joke, but instead you turned immediately to the subject at hand, with a seriousness that was somewhat exaggerated. "As I told you in brief at our first meeting, and as I hope you were able to discover from the folder I gave you, the *Guide to al-Mutanabbi* is meant to be the first issue in a series of encyclopedic books exploring the world of the founding fathers of Arab culture. What I'm doing now, on behalf of the regional organization that is sponsoring the project, along with colleagues in other countries, is making contact with those whose participation in the project we consider vital to its success, in order to seek their views on the project as a whole and find out to what extent they might be willing to take part in it."

As far as possible, I avoided looking at you directly as you spoke, and I contrived to do that by continually nodding in agreement, deliberately closing my eyes whenever I leaned forward. I recall with embarrassment that some seconds elapsed between the time you stopped speaking and the time I stopped nodding my head. Instead of pulling myself together to

---

* The full line reads: "Alas this plan! Alas for one accepting it—for the likes of it were created the long-necked Mahri camels."

make up for my absentmindedness, I felt weak and a little faint. I think my cheeks flushed and I do not rule out other signs of embarrassment showing on my face. You suggested more tea and, before I could answer, you rose from your chair and attended to my cup slowly, as though urging me to recover my strength and pull myself together. I do not know to what extent on that day and other days I went too far in interpreting your doings as responses to my own states of mind, but I certainly did interpret them in that way, and all I can do now is admit it, in the hope that my admission will give me some relief.

You resumed the conversation by asking me what I thought of the project and whether I would be willing to take part in it. Did you really expect me to give a satisfactory answer, or even to answer at all? I fell back on the eloquence that my profession had instilled in me and lavished praise on the project in general terms consistent with your question or any other question. I ended by saying I was quite prepared to do whatever you thought I was qualified to do.

I felt that, either out of kindness toward me or out of disappointment in my answer, you were taking the same timid approach as at our first meeting, colored this time with a little apathy and arrogance. "I'm sorry, I hope I haven't taken up too much of your time," you said. I took that as a signal that I had gone too far, and interpreted it as meaning, "Up you get and leave, you. You're not for me or for what I'm about."

6

I took my leave and you said goodbye. The lights of the cold city welcomed me, but I took no notice of them nor of the false life they were trying to create. I quickened my step to reach the bus stop as fast as possible, and thence to my humble bedroom, my only refuge and the place where I could safely hide from everyone and from myself. I would be lying, not just exaggerating, if I were to say that on my way from your place to my place, whether walking or riding the bus, I was thinking. Yes, thoughts were turning and teeming in my head, assailing me, mocking me, and doing whatever else thoughts can do to destroy a man. But was I thinking these thoughts? No, definitely not.

The most I can claim is that I was angry with myself, with you, and with the whole world without exception. I was also in a daze, or else it would not have escaped me that it was only minutes after nine o'clock and I would have realized that the door to the mosque compound was closed but not locked and I would not have tried to put the key in the lock. When I failed and the part of the door with the lock swung open anyway, it only made me angrier. The voices I heard from inside the mosque did not detain me. I just gave the people there a casual greeting and slipped like a thief in the night to my room, where I undressed and lay down as quickly as a man who has spent the day in constant toil. Needless to say, that night did not pass peacefully, because of all the specters of you that began to assail me, nor did I obtain the rest I wanted after such an exhausting day. I woke up early, perhaps for fear that the call to the dawn prayer would catch me wrapped in thoughts of you rather than in the solemn guise of a sheikh, and, as on the previous day, out of an overzealous desire to cover my tracks. I opened the mosque doors before the janitor arrived and sat with my back against the pulpit, pretending to read, impatient for the few dawn visitors to come so that I could lead them in prayer and then go back to my room and to my bed, where I would wrestle with my thoughts.

This infantile behavior of mine should not surprise you, even in a man of almost forty whose profession it is to urge people to follow the right path in life. In fact what other behavior would you expect from a man who at this stage in life discovers, without warning and despite himself, that he has never been in love, in spite of his great learning; a man who, until he met you, had not known what love was; a man who was, in the words of an imam of a kind no longer produced by Islam, "indistinguishable from a wild ass in the desert"?*

❧

Ever since I came here to your country I had never had any regrets about my hasty agreement to come, but that evening I did, or rather for the first time it struck me that there is a price to be paid for living in your country— an emotional rather than financial price. That's not because of me or you, but because of what our countries have in common and what divides them.

The fact that our countries share the same religion and language and are in the same region has not prevented their paths from diverging in recent decades, and some common features have disappeared to the extent that someone traveling from one country to the other might have the impression he is crossing from one continent to another. Judging by what those in power say, each country seems content and committed to its path, but that has not really been the case, neither in the practice of the leaders

---

* "If you have not loved, and do not know what love is, you are just like a wild ass in the desert." (Amir al-Shaabi, a collector of hadith who lived in the first century of Islam)

in your country, who have long been suspicious of the policies of their successive counterparts in my country, nor in the eyes of the great majority of the people in my country, who look with jealousy or rather envy at your country, which is rich, stable, liberal, and the source of their livelihood. I share with the people of my country their frustration, their hungry looks, and their amazement, for example, that a woman might run her own life and live alone, even if my mission here requires me to distance myself from my little community, from you and from everyone else I meet, and act as an experienced and impartial observer who, with his learning, his equanimity and patience, can handle the diversity of what he experiences.

My natural reluctance to mix with people, and my preference for keeping to myself as much as possible, ensured that those who came to the mosque daily—the janitor and colleagues responsible for financial, social, and administrative matters, as well as some of those who prayed regularly—could see in me none of the changes that might have betrayed the passions raging in my mind, my heart, and my body. Besides, the curiosity of these people did not go beyond checking I had recovered from the indisposition I had feigned to justify my absence the day after you visited me in the mosque, and my only response to them was a brusque and dismissive "Thank God."

From the start of our acquaintance you were always in control. I do not pretend that this was as clear to me then as it is today, but my instinctive sense that everything was up to you and that you held me by a tether,* such that you could pull me close or let me wander at your pleasure, imposed on me a kind of submission that was irresistible. You could have me neglect the duties entrusted to me and spend my days in the company of al-Mutanabbi's works, waiting for you to think of summoning me, which may not happen at all, in which case it would be said that "the sheikh has gone mad."

I did not let anyone, even you, suggest that I was going mad. I mean this, and do not merely say so out of pride. Sometimes I look at my case and can see that madness was only an arm's length away or less, and I had only to reach out and pick it like a ripe fruit. At other times I pretend that I struggled with myself and with my weakness to fend it off, and that it is

---

* "By your life, death never misses its man, like a loose tether it holds by one end." (Tarafa ibn al-Abd, a poet of the sixth century)

thanks to me that I did not go mad. Today I admit that madness was a possibility that loomed from somewhere I did not expect, and as usual I shied away from seizing it, out of cowardice.

Just because I was too cowardly to go mad because of you, it does not mean I was deterred from taking up a longstanding invitation to make a speech on the anniversary of the foundation of an association that looks after the affairs of our community in a province a day's journey from the capital. I made amends for my failure to answer the invitation by sending the organizers a telegram in which I deployed every possible expression of apology and of congratulations on the occasion, confirming that I would attend and saying I was willing to spend several days before the anniversary visiting the community, learning about their conditions and needs, and answering their questions on points of Islamic law.

Do not ask your bashful sheikh how this idea flashed to his mind—this idea, which, in spite of its naivety, seemed to him a trick of the most exquisite cunning to escape the mosque, that is to avoid waiting for you to appear there through the telephone lines, which at that point brought calls between us only one way: from you to the mosque. (You did well not to entrust your telephone number to me because by doing so you relieved me of a great burden: I cannot imagine even today how I could have borne it, because I have no doubt that my courage would have failed me whenever I wanted to call you, and I know how angry I would have been with myself and with God because of the injustice fate had inflicted on me for reasons that would have felt obscure to me.)

My trick, or what I deemed to be a trick, worked, and I received a welcoming answer. I notified my colleagues at the mosque of my unexpected journey and packed my belongings, which I noticed that day were no more or less than on the day I arrived, though they had become more shabby, and I headed to the station with a view to boarding any bus that would take me closer to my destination, even if it did not take me there immediately.

After a night of travel, I felt as though I had not left my mosque or my neighborhood, the only difference being that the neighborhood in that town was a back road in every sense of the word, parallel to the tourist

45

avenue that overlooked the sea, and the mosque was on the first floor of a building that was decrepit despite its recent construction, like all the other buildings in the street. But the people were much the same, with idiotic faces, their ears pricked up despite their deafness, their throats waiting in ambush for the shortest pause by the preacher to comfort themselves with prayers and cries of "Allahu akbar!" The questions, including those on aspects of Islamic law, were also much the same here and there. They generally began obscurely, sometimes pedantically, until someone came forward and prefaced his question with remarks such as, "Sir, there are no taboo subjects in religion," and I would know immediately that he was going to ask about some aspect of sex, marriage, or ritual purity. I would do my best to fend off the embarrassment I felt at their questions, especially the sexual ones, which, it seemed to me, probably had their origins not in the marriage bed but in television programs they watched or in their dreams by day or by night, when they sailed away to the islands of the houris.

Yes, although I had answered most of them many times, and although the answers had been passed down from sheikh to sheikh from the classical works of Islam, I never succeeded in handling them in the same way I handled questions about aspects of ritual or social life. That day, the questions troubled me more than ever, and I found myself having to make much, much more effort than in the past not to stammer or falter when I gave them the ready answers I had memorized to satisfy their curiosity. With every question they dreamed up, I repeated to myself: "He who digs a hole for his brother falls into it," and cursed the hour when I tried to outwit the need to wait for you. I wanted the time for evening prayer to come quickly, so that I could break off the session on the grounds that we should wash for prayers; then I would lead them in prayers and go on my way.

The questions and requests for fatwas from those 'men' that evening exposed me, and showed me clearly what a wretched state I was in and how fragile was the title I hid behind, that conferred on me respect and status I had done nothing to deserve. How did I differ from these 'men,' apart from the fact that I was more timid than them?

Anxious to be hospitable and respectful, my hosts saw fit to lodge me in one of the hotels on the tourist avenue. It was not the most luxurious or the best-located hotel on the avenue, but nonetheless, as the three stars glittering under its name at the entrance confirmed, it was at least worthy of the name 'hotel,' and I felt obliged to recognize my host's generosity.

Accompanied by the members of the association, I was escorted slowly on foot to my modest hotel. My obligation to be polite and courteous, which required me to take part from time to time in their noisy conversation about the details of the celebration (which sometimes drew the attention of passersby), did not wholly distract me from my worries or from examining the place and its environs. It was clear that the avenue was the respectable facade of a tourist district that included all varieties of amusement, 'innocent' and not so innocent. It was also clear that whatever was not fit for the avenue itself found ample space in the lanes and alleys branching off it. As we were passing one of these alleys, I caught sight of an illuminated sign in the shape of woman, showing visitors to a nightclub or some similar place, and before we crossed the street I caught sight of the silhouettes of women loitering deliberately in the dark corners, some leaning against the wall, others against signposts or against cars, and it seemed to me—and I do not think I was imagining it—that the people in my group suddenly started to chat more loudly and more rapidly, almost by consensus, whenever we came close to the mouth of one of these side streets, as if talking about the association and the anniversary celebration would make us look away and prevent us noticing what was going on around us.

I felt no curiosity to explore my room, where my bag had arrived in advance, and it did not occur to me to unpack my ragged old clothes, which had been arranged carelessly in that small bag, or, for the sake of the next day's ceremony, to remove some of the additional creases that long packing would have produced.

Fate determines the habits a man adopts. From my fate and from my lack of a companion, I was in the habit also of taking refuge in bed whenever I felt ill at ease for any reason, and much more so when I had a thousand reasons for feeling ill at ease. After a struggle, long or short, I would end up drifting off into something like sleep, and that night I was gambling that my struggle would come to an end in such a way, and that sooner or later I would find myself in a new day of my life and of the

47

calendar. I told myself that with a few strokes of my hand I could satisfy the sexual desire aroused in me and in my limbs by the sight of so many women displaying their charms to passersby. So I did, or rather almost did, because, as soon as my eyes closed and I fantasized about a woman, I was uncertain which face to attach to her. As soon as my hands touched my erect penis, and before I reached orgasm in my imagination, a thick liquid spurted out, sticking between my fingers, while other drops scattered over my lower stomach between my navel and my pubic region. Yes, my lady, that's how much I despised myself, my body, and my humanity; that's how simply I satisfied my impulses. As on every occasion, I thought I had won the round, or in fact I did not think anything at all, but rather succumbed to the numbness into which I habitually sank whenever I relieved my lust with my hand. Adding to the hypocrisy, and lest my reason rather than my conscience rebuke me, I set my mind to work thinking about the lecture I would have to give the next afternoon on the occasion of the association's anniversary. My mind was willing and did not wander off in undesirable directions. In this capacity, I imagined myself as a preacher and some sentences and tolerable quotations quickly came to mind. "Don't waste this chance, man. Get up, find yourself a pen and paper, and write down your inspirations before it's too late," I said to myself. For that I had to get out of bed, clean up the lower part of my body and rinse off the semen that was stuck to my fingers. I did all that at high speed, took a pen and paper out of my bag even faster, and wrote down the fragmented sentences and the key quotes that were still in my head. It was no surprise that I had already forgotten most of them but it was even more surprising that my desire for women began to revive with ever greater force. Do you understand how desire for women can take hold of a man, especially a vulnerable man like me? Ignore the nonsense I talk, call me a liar and fraud, but doesn't it ring true to you when you read what Mujahid, Ibn Abbas, and others say in their exegeses of the Quran? Open *The Revival of the Religious Sciences* at the chapter on sex and read what the great imam Abu Hamid al-Ghazali writes: "Qatada said the Quranic verse, *Do not lay upon us what we have no power to bear* (Quran 2:286) was about lust. And Akrama and Mujahid say that the verse *For man was created a weakling* (Quran 4:28) referred to man's inability to resist women. Fayad bin Najih says that when a man has an erection he loses two-thirds of his common sense, and some people say that he loses a third of his faith. In one of his exegetical remarks, Ibn Abbas says that the verse *I seek refuge from the evil of darkness when it gathers* (Quran 113:3) refers to a man's erection, which he describes as an overpowering affliction which neither reason nor faith can resist, even if it is useful because it gives rise to the life of this world and to the afterlife . . . and it is the devil's most powerful instrument against mankind. He referred to this when he said: 'I have seen nothing more damaging than you women to the reason and faith of sensible men,' because of the desire they arouse. The Prophet Muhammad himself said in his prayer: 'I take refuge with You from the evil of what I hear, what I see and what I feel, and the evil of my semen.' He also said: 'I ask You to purge my heart and preserve my genitals.' And if the Prophet has asked God to preserve his genitals, how could it be permissible for others to be careless with theirs?'"* Do you now understand better why that night I was not only unable to control my desire but also found myself shamelessly giving free rein to it? I told myself: "As long as your needs can be met quickly, and given that the fates have thrown you here, where no one knows you, and if anyone thinks he recognizes you then he might well observe in amazement that God has created forty or more men in your likeness, then why should you not resort to the services of one of those women, whose profession it is to meet the needs of men like you for a fee?"

Do not ask which devil trained his powers on me, changing my instinctive hesitation into firm resolve and my lethargy into dynamism. That devil took me by the hand, from my room to the receptionist, where I deposited my key, then to the door of the hotel, which was somewhat set back from the avenue, then to the avenue itself and then to the dark side streets and the entrance of that building where she was standing, leaning against it like the women in pictures—on one leg, with the other leg bent backward at the knee, a woman in the prime of life. I slowed my pace as I passed in front of her, and she invited me softly to come to what she had to offer, to her. I turned toward her, initiating a negotiating process, which quickly ended. She just whispered a figure and I nodded, and she opened the entrance into a long corridor. I followed until we reached a door that I thought was locked, but it opened when she gave it a gentle push. She led me into a poorly lit room, and the door quickly closed behind us.

---

* Ghazali, Abu Hamid Mohammad ibn Mohammad. *Revival of the Religious Sciences,* vol. 2 (Beirut: Dar al-Maarifa, 1980), 28.

I was worried about entrusting our seclusion to a door without a bolt or a key, but there was nothing to be done.

Unlike me, she had few clothes to take off, and undressing in the presence of a strange man meant little to her. She stripped gracefully and methodically, took her place on the narrow bed, and smoked a cigarette to pass the time while I fumbled to take off my own clothes. Could she detect what kind of man I was? I could almost swear she could, and that she interpreted my fumbling as inexperience, because she vulgarly hurried me to join her. I obeyed and approached the bed, bearing my nakedness like a heavy burden, confident that she could manage the subsequent stages of our secret encounter. I was not mistaken. With experience, if not skill, she took my penis in her hands, which were smeared with some viscous substance. When she was sure it was erect, she inserted it in a condom she had prepared. With an acrobatic twist, she lay on her back and pulled me toward her until I was mounting her in the usual manner.

What happened between me and that woman, whose body and womanhood I hired for some minutes, was nothing memorable. I had sex with her like someone having sex alone, in fact with even less pleasure. But what I felt inside me, I leave to your imagination.

7

I went back to my nearby hotel exhausted, by day from the association headquarters, by night from the red light district. I washed myself more thoroughly than prescribed in any chapter on ritual purity in any book of Islamic law. I then applied myself to penning a speech to suit the occasion for which I was invited, but resolved that on the next morning I would tell the organizers that unexpected news necessitated my immediate return home—this would spare me joining my hosts in their celebration. With difficulty, I managed this. In the hours I spent on the bus I did not pretend to be reading a book or browsing through a newspaper to dissuade any of my neighbors from opening a conversation to alleviate the hardship and length of the journey. For once, I felt within myself a strange ability to deter anyone from approaching me, either by looking at me or speaking, or even by smiling. I was anxious to understand how I could control myself in spite of all the images, fantasies, and feelings that festered inside me. When I was immersed in worry, what I feared most was that I might overestimate my resilience, and today I am compelled to admit that this fear of mine was justified.

My evidently lugubrious mood, which most of my colleagues at the mosque interpreted as travel fatigue (and which a pedant among them took as an opportunity to show off sayings of the Prophet on travel that he had memorized), prevented them from insisting I join them at the modest dinner table where they were gathered. But I hardly cared how they interpreted it, because that night, as on every night, my need to be alone in my room, and nowhere else, was a pressing and urgent physical need that had to be met immediately, more than just an emotional need which could be ignored or remedied by some psychological exercise.

<hr/>

I enjoyed my pain that night, or rather, that was the first time in my life that I felt my body was a boiling kettle from which pleasure rose like steam, hot and moist, clouding my vision but also clearing my mind. It was pain, but it did not matter to me that it coincided with what I was experiencing. That wasn't the only reason, but also because my pain was not a particular pain that affects a particular organ or a particular limb, but a pain distributed evenly throughout my whole body, from the top of my head to the soles of my feet.

Faced with a pervasive and evenly distributed pain such as this, no part of one's body can play the role of sympathetic spectator to the rest, as can happen when pain grips a particular organ or limb. Faced with a pain such as this, the soul admits to the body that it is part of it, embedded within it, sharing every affliction, and the body thinks it is in union with the soul, not just bonded and closely related. Even more so if the body has spent its whole life looking down on itself, on its pleasures and its pains, never daring to be alone with itself, even when it resorts to its hand for some passing pleasure, and even more so for a soul that treats the body as a wretch that crosses its path from time to time, inspiring feelings of pity and grief.

My head was spinning like a drunk's, all the more so because for many years it had not spun at all. In spite of all the faces the world had revealed to me from time to time, I had spent my life wandering aimlessly, my own face veiled with a thousand veils—a thousand veils, none of which it had ever occurred to me to touch, let alone lift or even try to lift. Call it an epiphany, call it what you will, but all there is to it is that by that night I date the first true ritual ablution I ever performed. Although the days would prove that it was to be my lesser ablution, at the time I deemed it the ablution to end all ablutions.

✍

I do not know if the symptoms I have described have a recognized generic name. If they, and the accidental properties that go with them, do have a name, then so be it. If they do not have a name, I am not at all proud to know with certainty that I am not made of the same stuff as those who have revelations and visions and who overnight are transformed into holy men and saints. I said dawn prayers with my colleagues and went back to bed, where without any significant resistance I fell into a deep sleep, or what is so named, from which I awoke late.

It surprised me somewhat that I did not feel guilty about sleeping late, as I was wont to do since I went to university, where I acquired a weakness for expanding my knowledge and began to set myself a monthly reading quota that I could meet only by staying up so late into the night that it was hard to wake up early. There was at least one reason why I should feel guilty—the fact that, although I had gradually abandoned the reading schedule that I had once set myself, I had not rid myself of my anxiety about waking up early, even if nothing urgent made it necessary.

And so, starting the day by allowing myself some extra moments of sleep, without feeling ill at ease or angry with myself, was the first of that day's surprises chronologically, if not the most significant of them.

✍

My mail at that time consisted of a money transfer sent to my eldest brother on the same day every month, as well as the circulars, invitations, and bureaucratic correspondence that came to the mosque. So when I was opening the mail from the previous days, with the indifference of someone who does not receive news by mail every day, my curiosity was aroused by a small rectangular envelope that bore my name, written with childish care in a tidy hand. Who might this be from? I wondered. All the other envelopes, because I knew in advance what they contained, I would open roughly, even tear them open if they offered the least resistance, but this

53

small envelope clearly called for gentler treatment. I cut the top of it open with one slice of a letter opener in my right hand, and carefully took out a thick card of dazzling whiteness. It had your name written on the top right in a cursive Persian-style script, and after the greeting the following words: "I tried to call you by telephone but was told you were away. I wish you a safe return and hope to hear from you in the near future." Your telephone number followed between brackets, and below that your initials. It was joy that I felt, but a calm inner joy that did not express itself in visible emotion. I wanted, trust me, to rejoice more, very much in fact, as befitted the place I had set aside for you in my heart and in my mind, but how could I do so after the previous night?

I did not proceed to phone you immediately or allow myself to indulge in possibly demoralizing interpretations of aspects of your brief message, such as the phrase "in the near future," or disturbing questions such as whether you were waiting for my phone call literally or metaphorically. Instead, I turned to my worldly business, inquiring about the latest news of the two family factions and whether those detained had been released. My colleagues told me the latest about the neighborhood and the town, and I led them in communal prayers. When I was done with all that and had fulfilled my obligations toward God and my small community, I went into my room and locked the door behind me with two turns of the key, although I knew there was no security reason for doing so.

Millions of humans turn millions of keys twice in millions of locks all the time, but I was not one of them, or so I had always imagined, until locking a door in this manner became one of my habits and I forced myself to ignore how, and in response to what concern, I acquired this habit. What reminds me of this, or rather what brings it to light, is the list of security instructions hung on the door, which I see facing me now, as if for the first time, when I look around this cell on death row.

When I was first brought here, to this so-called tourist village, a stronghold despite the comforts it contains, I was not assigned a private wing. In the name of security, I was placed in the central building, which over the previous months had already taken in a number of journalists and other writers and opinion-makers who were under threat for articles they had written or positions they had expressed in public. There was nothing in my dress or general appearance that would have given away my profession, not even my beard. When I left college—where growing a beard was a way to please the stricter sheikhs—and became a civil servant, I soon began to keep my beard trimmed to a minimum, and I have continued that way, not letting it grow longer or cutting it shorter, and that has become part of my image. Even so, my reputation had arrived ahead of me and I found myself unable to prevent people looking at me as 'a man of religion' and addressing me as such. Worse yet, I found myself trapped into a way of speaking and acting that in my whole life I had never adopted as much as I was forced to in the first weeks of my stay here; that is, until my minder, my patron, my guardian angel (call him what you will) contrived to meet my urgent request that I be assigned one of the wings built around the central building and obtained the necessary approvals for that.

Among the security measures prescribed in the list on the door is an instruction to lock the door from the inside with all three bolts and not to try to open it for anyone or for any reason, except on the advice of the security officer on duty. With the wooden door of my old room I needed only to turn the key twice in the lock to be sure that I was alone and that I, my body, and my emotions were safely insulated from a world that was only a few steps away. But this door of uncertain solidity, despite what I am told is anti-tank plating, despite three inner bolts and various guards and mechanical devices that would prevent anyone reaching it in the first place, does not inspire me with confidence or give me any sense of safety or privacy. Is it because it is a door over which I have no control and no key, and because on this side of it lies only an endless wait? Probably. And because one thing reminds one of another, let me confide in you, if belatedly, that I never enjoyed those readings that you set for us one time, the ones about doors leading to doors and so on . . . and my digression on comparing this door and my old door has nothing at all to do with those doors in those readings. Besides, I was speaking about the two doors literally, not metaphorically!

⟨⟩

Your telephone number is imprinted in my memory. That's what I discovered when I began preparing to call you and was about to take the envelope out of my jacket pocket and then take your card out of its envelope. "No use procrastinating, then," I said to myself. "All you have to do is lift the receiver, dial the number, and wait a few seconds." But another voice, this time inside me, was making me flustered, whispering things such as: "How will you greet her? How will you introduce yourself if she doesn't recognize your voice immediately? How will you stop yourself getting confused and how will you prevent your voice shaking?" Because of all that, when I pulled myself together, picked up the receiver, and dialed the number, I was hoping to wait on the line as your phone rang in vain. Then I could have escaped by saying there was no reply, and put off the ordeal till the morrow, reassured that I had at least made the attempt.

It was a relief when you quickly recognized my voice, and your spontaneity and easygoing tone gave me no chance to hesitate or stumble. It was not a dialogue that we had. How could it be? For you to speak to a man who is 'a stranger,' in the sense that specialists in Islamic law use the expression and in the sense it usually carries, is something you are familiar with, but when it came to me addressing a 'strange' woman, and on top of that a woman who was the object of my hopes and desires, then it was a matter with a 'before and an after,' implying certain apprehensions. Even so, because you were the first to ask how I was, what I had been doing, and how my trip was, it was your questions that set the rhythm for what we said in those two minutes, and after our conversation I did not think I had stuttered or that my voice had trembled, as I had feared, although I was aware that I had managed to evade your inquiries by answering them only with conventional expressions suitable for any context or occasion.

※

Congenially and willingly I set about the rest of my day. I smiled at my visitors and spoke at length and at ease with my colleagues on community matters that I had put off discussing for weeks. I even led the prayers and performed them with a cheerfulness and liveliness that took me by surprise; in fact, I would go further and say "with good intent," even if good intent and sincerity of intent are things for which it is difficult to provide proof.

I doubt the appointment we agreed for the following day affected your character and your behavior as much as it affected mine. And here we come to the crux of the matter, or, if you wish, its sanctuary. You are who you are in secret and in public, whereas in my case no peace is to be expected between my secret and my public self.

The next day's appointment confirmed to me that you had not lost hope in me or expelled me from your kingdom irretrievably, as I had dreaded. My pure, unadulterated joy did not make me forget that I was a man with an appointment with a woman and that for such an appointment he had a duty to prepare himself mentally and physically. Mentally, I did not think I had fallen short since the start of our acquaintance: I visited al-Mutanabbi's works several times a day, and I had enriched my little library with two other books about your Ahmad, one of which I had almost finished reading. As for physically, I conceded without argument that it was a thorny question. I asked myself: "What can I do to improve the way I look and the way I dress? What if I misjudge and am so well-groomed that I look unnatural rather than stylish and smart?" In the end, I decided that all I would do was pass by the barber's.

One of the characteristics of someone like me or someone in my position is that he imagines that his doings are an open book, that others, near and far, can read what is going in his head and what he is planning. On the short trip to the nearby barber's, this notion had such a hold on me that I almost retraced my steps. "How might people interpret my desire to have my hair trimmed twice within one month, when my usual practice is to visit the barber only once a month?" I wondered. "Apart from the barber's tendency to gossip, assume the worst: what if one of my colleagues notices my erratic moods and behavior in recent times, based on my melancholy in the days before my sudden trip, my hasty return, the fact that in the last few hours I was acting so eccentric that I was having my hair done, as well as the fact that on Thursday evening I was going to tell my colleagues and my charges that I could not attend their weekly club meeting? What if someone put all this together and concluded that something unprecedented had taken possession of their sheikh?"

My apprehensions and thoughts were interrupted by greetings from some of the local people and I quickened my pace in case my hesitation betrayed me. At the barber's, the rituals proceeded without change: after the usual pleasantries, he invited me to take my seat in his adjustable chair, cloaked me with a shabby and faded cape, and raised the chair so that my head was within reach of him and his instruments. After all that, either on my behalf or by reading my thoughts, he spontaneously volunteered an explanation for why I was visiting him twice in the same month. "These little hairs at the back of your neck are too much in the heat," he said. His theory emboldened me to add, somewhat cautiously: "If you could trim my hair all over, that would also reduce the impact of the heat." He received my remark with approval and with an obsequious "So be it" that scarcely concealed his delight that I had given him clearance to lay into my hair as he wished.

Confident that I would stay some time in his shop, the barber seemed to have no reservations about discussing the minor affairs of the neighborhood while he dealt with my hair, as though it were not yet the right time to delve into matters of destiny. But in the end, the moment came. The barber put his left hand on my crown, I leaned my head forward until my chin touched my collarbone and my mouth was firmly shut, and from somewhere he produced a razor with an ivory handle. Then he cleared his throat like someone preparing to say something weighty.

I do not recall which of the two made me shudder, or rather which made me shudder first—was it the twinge I felt from the cold, sharp blade on living flesh, which was in fact no more than the barber resting the tip of the blade for an instant on the part of my neck where he saw fit to start shaving, or was it the way he started speaking, in a tone more of rebuke than of gentle remonstrance? "Mawlana," he said, "I'm not one of them and it's not them who led me to the mosque and taught me to be pious, to pray and fast . . . I'm not one of them, but it's indefensible what the government and the security people are doing in the name of imposing law and order, and we here have started to suffer the effects . . ." I thought he had not finished his sentence yet, and I was right. After a short silence while he sharpened the blade of his razor, he launched into another sentence, more forceful than the first. "Frankly," he said, "I don't agree with what you said in your speech last Friday." Too modest to attribute this opinion solely to himself, he continued: "And I'm not alone in that, because many of the local people and my friends were surprised that in your speech you only spoke about the two groups. You listed the faults of our side in minute detail, but you completely overlooked the government and its outrages, which come to light day after day, as well as the misdeeds of its agencies, which people only dare hint at, such as the way they intervene in every little incident."

Unconsciously, or perhaps because he wanted to keep talking, the barber kept his hand pressed on my crown, bending my head forward and holding my mouth closed, so I responded with just a murmur, meant only to indicate I had been listening to what he was saying. But he understood it to mean I objected, or perhaps he did not hear it, so he went on to talk about the argument that had taken place between the two families that morning. He took the opportunity to praise what he called my wisdom, which "prevented the argument getting out of hand," and he did not mince words in expressing his fears that what had happened might recur.

Then he perhaps had second thoughts and wondered if he had gone too far in silencing me and upbraiding me for the sake of those little hairs. Or perhaps his left hand grew tired of pressing, firmly but gently, on the crown of my head. When he suddenly turned to asking me how was so-and-so, someone who was my neighbor as much as his neighbor, if not more so, I felt that this torture session was about to end and that he did not want it to end as it had begun. I felt him slowly lift his left hand, which he had been using to bend my neck, and I felt a brush on my neck and on the area down to the first vertebra, brushing away the little hairs that had stuck to my skin and that he had failed to blow off with his occasional puffs as he plied his razor.

It was rude not to comment, even in general terms, on everything he had said so effusively, especially about last Friday's speech, which had so upset him, but I did not want to miss these short moments of tickling from his brush, which I very much hoped would last, so I pretended to look pensive.

Unlike me, he seemed to be in a hurry to hear my response, and he indicated he had finished by tapping me on the shoulder twice, urging me not to come to him again until I had found a wife, and then awaiting my response.

When I stole a glance in the mirror, I did not notice any significant difference between before and after I entrusted the barber with the task of grooming my hair. But I did not give up hope that his fingertips, his combs, and his sharp instruments had in fact improved my appearance, and I thought that perhaps I would notice the difference if I took a closer look.

As usual, he tried to resist when I stuck my hand into his shirt pocket to slip him his fee, but I put an end to his resistance by resuming the conversation about his grievance. I said I was sorry my speech had been so misunderstood that I appeared to have taken sides with one party against another. Lest he see this as an evasion, I quickly explained that I did not exonerate either side, but that I agreed with the words of the Prophet Muhammad when he said: "If your Muslim ruler does something you disapprove of, you should be patient, for whoever becomes separate from the Muslim group, even by an inch, and then dies, he will die as those who died in the pre-Islamic period of ignorance." I also said I agreed with the view that it does not serve people to have a proliferation of rulers, and they should submit to one authority, whether righteous or unrighteous, and that in any case tomorrow comes soon to those who wait.

8

Tomorrow comes soon to those who wait. But for those to have to wait through what I had to wait through, nothing is more distant than the morrow; in fact, they almost dismiss it from consideration, even if it happens to be a Friday.

As the time for our third meeting approached, my good cheer began to diminish, to be replaced by a strange mixture of excitement and anxiety. I was not surprised at how my mood had changed, but my constant apprehension that people were watching me behind my back gave me reason to be cautious and keep to my room, although I had intended to perform the sunset prayers in the mosque with my colleagues and then slip away to your place. It was no use resisting the waiting. Then that mixture of excitement and anxiety gradually began to grow as time progressed, and I found my small room and the wait oppressive. In low and high spirits, I left the mosque an hour and a half before our appointment, holding under my arm a small bag that I had dusted off for the occasion and that hardly had room for the two volumes of al-Mutanabbi's works, and I decided to walk the long distance to your place, or at least some of the way. It was a good choice, because the more streets I crossed, the more certain I was that no one was reading my thoughts and emotions or was interested in exploring my inner self or my motive for heading into your neighborhood. Were it not for this growing confidence that neither I nor my worries would attract anyone's attention, I would definitely have been too timid to buy you a modest bunch of flowers, and were it not for that despondent cheerfulness with which I had emerged from the hell of the last few days, I would have thrown the bouquet into the first rubbish bin I encountered, for fear that I might not present it to you properly, because, as you can guess, that was the first bunch of flowers I had ever bought to give to a woman.

I could not wait the last ten minutes before seven o'clock and I knocked on your door with apologies for coming too early. As usual, even if it was not yet usual at that stage, I was saved by your hospitality and your spontaneous questions, which I tried my best to answer properly and in full sentences, not with the ready expressions I could produce on demand.

A moment of doubt almost overwhelmed me: that moment when you were in the kitchen making tea and, as I later discovered, arranging the flowers in two containers. It occurred to me to speculate on what you were thinking, and I imagined you were making fun of me and my flowers and wondering: "Now what to do with him? How do you deal with a sheikh who falls in love at first sight?" I fancied you trying to allay your fears with thoughts along the lines of: "It's true it's the first time a sheikh has fallen in love with me, but fending off an infatuated sheikh is not necessarily any harder than fending off an admirer whose profession is teaching or commerce or anything else!"

You saved me again by coming back with my flowers, stamped with your imprint, because you had arranged them in two slender containers, which I thought were not originally designed to be vases, instead of just putting them as I brought them in one ordinary container. I waited for you to come in and then stood up, ignoring your request that I stay seated. In fact, I stayed standing, waiting for you to come back again with the tea things. In case it might seem artificial to be standing, I approached one of the bookcases that covered most of the walls of the room, and started to browse distractedly through the titles in various languages, with just enough concentration to work out that the library probably owed its richness and variety to at least two generations of readers, and not just to you. When you came back with the tea things, you confirmed my guess, as though you could read my thoughts. You explained, in such detail that I almost thought you were apologizing for owning so many books, that they were family heirlooms you were merely preserving, though from time to time you did slip into the shelves some recent publications.

You asked me about the mosque library and its contents, and I replied that we were working on organizing it, because I was too embarrassed to tell you the truth about it—that it consisted of several large Qurans of mosque format, sumptuously bound and gilt to the point of vulgarity, which visitors to the mosque treated like icons, and a collection of books on hadith, the sayings and doings of the Prophet, which I doubt ever aroused anyone's curiosity. You did not ask for more details, but instead asked if you could inquire about my trip. I took the occasion to test the informality with which you had infected me. What exactly I told you does not come to mind. Of course I did not tell you the story of my trip as it really was, why I took it and why I cut it short, nor what happened in the course of it, but rather for the occasion I patched together a trip with pieces from here and there, embellishing it with imaginary touches where possible. The reason for that was not just shame at the reality but because the truth in that situation, then, in your presence, was my last concern and your last concern, too: it was unnecessary, futile, and there was nothing to be gained from it at all. Because the truth is not 'the truth,' or else I would no longer have a pretext to accept your invitation to continue our conversation. I'm not fooling myself so don't try to fool me. We had nothing to say to each other, but what brought me to your place that day was the fact that you wanted it for some reason you alone knew. All that mattered to me was to untie my tongue and address you as an equal. That was my sole concern and intention, and I do not think I am exaggerating if I claim success.

Chatting with you casually and spontaneously made me somewhat uneasy, as much as it excited me, and I did not know if I should leave it to you to go back to the subject of al-Mutanabbi and the book project, or whether I should take the initiative. Beneath this unease there was another unease and a question that was more difficult to answer: was this small talk, on the margins of the 'official' purpose of my visit, just a stopgap while we finished our tea, or was it the harbinger of a familiarity tentatively seeking a basis on which to flourish?

I did not want to miss the opportunity of casual conversation, so I asked you in my own style—inserting a superfluous "God willing," that is—if you had any news about 'the project,' although my intention was not to confine my inquiry to that.

You replied that there was nothing new, other than the issues that any project ran into in this country, starting with the shortage of workers who combined competence with humility, and then the competition for the title of 'editor-in-chief' and other titles, even before the project produced anything to be supervised, and then the smell of corruption that had started to spread when it came to travel tickets and hotel bills.

I do not know from where you dredged up the eloquent examples with which you illustrated what you had spoken about briefly, or how you were able to take such a cold and pessimistic view of things, while at the same time keeping your enthusiasm alive.

I was listening to you with my eyes as well, and when I felt that seeing you talk, with your body language as well as your voice, was about to overwhelm me, I could not help but interrupt your outburst with a timid and pompous question. "And what is to be done, my lady?" I asked.

I had to look at your lips, your eyes, your hands and breasts—that is, every part of you that moved—to remind myself that you were not just a figment of my adolescent imagination, but a woman with a spirit and a body of which you were in full control.

My question provoked you as if you detected some sarcasm in it, and you replied with something to the effect of: "There's nothing to be done, nothing at all, 'let's aspire to a kingdom . . .'"* but before you finished the sentence or indicated that it ended there, your voice took me by surprise with an unaccustomed tone. "Anyway, that's not what our meeting is about today and I don't know whether, in what I'm about to suggest, I am addressing the right person. It's a long story, but I will try to be brief. Toward the end of my university studies I was pained to discover that I had lost touch with Arabic and Arabic literature, and that's why, besides working as adviser to the organization sponsoring the project, I went back to university, not to get another qualification, but to satisfy myself and possibly my pride.

"In short . . . I have long wanted to read some Arabic books with someone trained in the language. Are you willing and do you have the time

---

* "Let's aspire to a kingdom, or find in death an excuse." (the pre-Islamic poet Imru' al-Qays)

64

to help me? Or at least we could try, and since we are indebted to al-Mutanabbi for introducing us to each other, how about taking on his complete works and reading them together from start to finish?"

Something in your voice revealed that you had had your 'eureka' moment, that you had found the door that, once one crosses the threshold, leads to places unknown. I did not hear in your voice on that day what I hear in it now, and it did not seem to me that it was one of those doors that were so dear to you. All I cared was that I saw in your suggestion an invitation to pursue our meetings, regardless of what happened to 'the project.'

⁂

In brief, that's how our story started. I have gone over the whole story from start to finish and backward, but it does not convince me. I tell myself I have forgotten or overlooked something, on the grounds that this beginning was not worthy of our relationship, besides the fact, of course, that no one would believe that a man and a woman, with nothing to make their meeting inevitable, would in fact meet one day over Ahmad who called himself a prophet, and that they should behave in the way ordained by nature for a man and a woman, and I would go further perhaps, and note that absolutely no trace of their meeting survives, not even a report—half-rumor, half-fact—to the effect that so-and-so fell in love with so-and-so.

It seems, my lady, that in our relationship I was a loan we were lent and when the time came it was repaid.

And so Ahmad al-Mutanabbi become our password, and seven o'clock, neither earlier or later, became the time. As for the people at the mosque, those close to me, I worried that one or two of them might speculate that the sheikh had gone mad, but little by little they grew accustomed to my absences and to the way my character had suddenly turned mild and gentle—a change I doubt they failed to notice. It was no great effort to explain my absences. It is true that I was not proverbial for the level of my enthusiasm for taking part in public occasions or even for performing my social duties. But was it unreasonable that someone like me, in such circumstances, acting as mother and father to a community, however small, should have appointments outside the mosque? As a precaution I started to accept more invitations to public events. For the same reason, I sometimes

65

expatiated in the hearing of mosque visitors on "the al-Mutanabbi project," and gave it as an example of how, "in spite of everything," our country did not lack "civilized initiatives." Of course I would talk about 'the project' as if it were advancing toward inevitable success. And when my absences began to lengthen and I started to stay out later and later, I added meetings outside the city to my imaginary schedule.

With time, my colleagues became less and less receptive to the cover stories I deployed to deter their curiosity. In reality, this was not because they challenged the truth of the stories but, as I gradually realized, because they had little interest in what I did as long as my doings did not change their lives in any way. In fact, I was greatly surprised to find out that by leaving the mosque at certain times in the week, with my bag under my arm, I had aroused the curiosity of the neighboring shopkeepers, who made inquiries with the mosque janitor, rather than that of my retinue, the ones I was worried about.

Seven o'clock after seven o'clock, you grew accustomed to me and I to you. Neither of us became familiar with the other easily or quickly, and we did not have the dimmest idea of where the bond that had started to form between us might finally lead. Sometimes it occurred to me, after day dreams or dreams at night, to broach the subject with you. I prepared my question and rehearsed it while awaiting a suitable opportunity to spring it on you. "And then, my lady?" I would say, and I imagined you acting naive and answering me with a "Then what?" I imagined our conversation continuing by allusions until it ran out when you picked up Ahmad's works, which you had put aside in the meantime, and it fell open at the last lines of his eulogy for Sayfaddawla, the one beginning: "My tears answered . . . ," and you suggested I help you memorize those two absurdly impossible lines, which consist of just a string of forty imperatives, many of them derived from the obscurest of verbs. I imagined you saying, "Let's go back to where we were, each of us back to his basic principles."

But I never dared to do that, to tell you that my imagination inspired me to fantasize about us together, going as far as a man and a woman can go together, but what deterred me was that whenever I likened you to other women (though I have little experience of them), something in you took me by surprise, and helped bring me back to my senses, and reminded me that you were not the kind of woman whose ultimate expectation with a man was to say, "Take me," and have him listen and obey.

Feel sorry for me, even here today, hostage to this cell on death row, where I can expect neither a lucky break nor the mercy of earth or of heaven, where I need fear no scandal-mongering neighbor, where I eke out in morbid rumination all that remains of what we shared. All I can do now is offer a metaphor to describe the ultimate togetherness between a man and a woman. If you were to ask me today what was behind this expression and my metaphor for it, you would find me, as for several months past, unable to reply on two counts, for quite different reasons. Previously, I had been unable to speak because I was afraid that my place with you might be usurped, whereas now it is because I sometimes despair that you will still have space for me. But in fact my metaphor from the start was self-sufficient and did not in fact refer to anything at all, rather like those jellyfish that, as soon as they are out of their element, dry up, shrivel, and expire, never to revive: they seem to be an aspect of the element in which they swim and feed and which provides their needs, not creatures that stand upright and have a grip on themselves, an independent existence. That was my metaphor: the element was my musings, my fantasies, and a medley of my delusions, and whenever I tried to put them clearly into words, they vanished, inevitably or of my own free will, leaving nothing to tell of.

I never imagined I would have such trouble with something I was writing. I have spent the last three days struggling to put pen to paper, or rather in exhausting contestation with myself—a contest with no set time, no referee, and no rules to which the two parties are committed. The fact that today I am resuming my tedious narrative does not prove that one side has won the contest or that the contest will not resume.

The three-day ordeal began with me remembering you. Does that make sense? Does it make sense that I should remember you when you are present, incessantly and unannounced, and like a throng, not as an individual. It does make sense, my lady, when you recognize that remembering is not necessarily the accurate retrieval of things that happened but sometimes, and often, a replay of them despite the difference of occasion, place, and time. When I said "ultimate togetherness," I wanted to divert my thoughts from all those beautiful and enjoyable hours we spent talking to each other or loving one another, or talking *and* loving one another. I wanted to use that expression as a means to escape from my childish craving and ravenous lust for you, but I took the wrong boat or went the wrong way, or both. Would it not have been better if I had admitted that psychologically and sensually I lusted for you? Did I have to go through all those detours and evasions and go to such lengths and depths, only to realize that I was like a man trying to dive in shallow water and that whenever I bumped into the bottom I blamed myself for being a poor diver, instead of admitting that the water was shallow?

Lying on my narrow bed like a corpse that has been washed and shrouded, staring at the ceiling of my room, that phrase took shape before my eyes—"the ultimate togetherness between a man and a woman." Sometimes I would read it slowly, sometimes in a flash. Then I would shut my eyes and it would vanish, but as soon as I opened them again it would reappear, over and over. In the meantime, between one blink and the next, I would fly into a suppressed rage at my failure to extract the slightest meaning from the phrase, and at how I was throwing myself into perdition.

In those hours, the most honest description of which would be 'critical,' I was pure desire for you but also for other hours that are still fresh in my mind, hours I spent recording my thoughts in this notebook and winning back my life from the versions of others, even if winning it back this way does not make the slightest difference now and does not change anything of what I have written and am writing.

I thought that if I gave up seeking the meaning of 'togetherness,' I could go back to winning back my life as though nothing had happened, by narrating it in the way I was starting to narrate it. So I gave up the search and escaped from the valley of the shadow of death where, inadvertently and unaware of the consequences, I had strayed. At that point, I discovered that going back to my story, to my version of the story, was not such a simple task.

Again a form of paralysis befell me and stopped me continuing my story, and along with the paralysis came its twin brother, fear—fear that for some reason I would run out of time to complete it. I wanted my story to be the only testimony to my life, if I am destined to live, or the only gravestone on my grave, when my time comes. In the meantime here I am, in this stronghold of a death row cell, a place that is like all the other places I have ever stayed in since I left the village for the capital and then moved to your country: it is not a home where I can take refuge nor a resting place where I can feel at peace. This room, here and now, is superior to the other rooms in some ways, for in it, for the very first time, I can live at the pace and in the manner that suit me, far from overseers or monitors. I can live what I have lived through these past forty days, churn the forty days like a miserly woman and extract the cream.*

As in the case of other questions that I cannot resolve, I do not know whether the metaphor for 'togetherness,' which I choked on, as your poet says,† was really the heart of the matter or just an occasion to set me against myself again, and I no longer care to know. After emerging alive from this ordeal, I was absolutely certain that this expression tormented me because I insisted on trying to fathom the essential meaning of it, which presupposed that it did have an essence, sealed in a bottle in a stormy sea. But what if the whole episode stemmed from my fear that pinning the expression down in the real world might detract from the magic of it? Please agree with me, my lady: agree that it was so and that a fear of this kind makes it worthwhile to die for three or four days and then to be troubled by one's conscience when one comes back to life, because one was not dead longer!

---

* "Even if God churned the years like a miserly woman, it would produce the cream of the ages." (Abu Tamam)
† "I choked on my tears until they were about to choke on me." (al-Mutanabbi)

9

U nder the wings of darkness and of al-Mutanabbi, my clandestine
excursions from the mosque to 'your place' became frequent:
weekly at first, but then they rapidly lost any regular pattern and
started to take place whenever I could make it.

And so, throughout the weeks when we met five nights out of seven,
from seven o'clock until before the crack of dawn, we did not break
al-Mutanabbi's trust, and never postponed today's poem to the morrow.
Yes, it would happen that you grew tired and sometimes irritated by the
idiosyncrasies of your poet, but you never made your exasperation public.
I will never forget that evening when we were reading his eulogy of Abu
Ali Haroun bin Abdul Aziz al-Awraji, the secretary,* and your tongue
stumbled and you started to make grammatical mistakes, but you struggled
on as well as you could. I was uncertain how, without offending your pride,
I could gently persuade you to abandon a reading that was close to torture,
and the only way out you saw was to suggest, in the name of pressing
hunger, that we put off the day's work till the day after.

---

* "The watchmen feel secure against your visiting me in the darkness, since wherever
you are in the shadows there is radiance." (al-Mutanabbi)

It was a suggestion in the manner of 'so be it,' which is your manner when something is bothering you. You did not let me agree or disagree, but just stood up and went to the kitchen, from where noises started to reach me. I could distinguish sounds that were familiar to me, such as water running and the clatter of glass and metal vessels, but the noises that were unfamiliar aroused my curiosity, such as that whistling, intermittent and then continuous, and that faint ticking, similar to the ticking of time bombs portrayed in films.

On that night of the Awraji poem, the limits of 'your place' still ended at the door of this study, where you had received me the first time. Naturally, after repeated visits, I knew it well. I knew all the details of the room and had some knowledge of the sections of the bookcase. I felt so comfortable moving around the room that sometimes I was tempted, enraptured by what you were reading to us, to leave this chair, which had become my chair, and walk several times the nine paces that are the width of the room. That is how matters still were between us at that stage, and so I resisted my curiosity to follow you, but confined myself to guessing what you might be preparing for us. But enough restraint: I was in love with you! My admiration for what drew you to al-Mutanabbi, and for the way you had vowed to study all the minutiae of Arabic, was matched only by my infatuation with your person and your appearance. Were these qualities not enough, that you should add to them skill at cooking? Or did you intend to embarrass me?

"Come," you said. "My banquet is modest, but it does not fear being put to the test. Would it upset you to share my habits with me, and have dinner with me in the kitchen, as I usually do?" You stepped in front of me apologetically to show me the way. We walked only a few steps, but to me it seemed a whole journey. By allowing me to penetrate your world, in spite of the short distance between here and there, were you not giving me a sign that I was worthy and eligible, and that you thought well of me?

The small square table was set as in photographs, or as one might imagine a table set by the genies of a magic lamp. The soup was perfect, as was the grilled fish garnished with vegetables on a soft bed of basmati rice. The crowning touch was the dessert, the name of which I did not know. I could make out among the ingredients the tastes of sugar, almonds, walnuts, rosewater, and saffron. I asked about it and you laughed, and instead of answering you topped up my plate and advised me to ask again later. I said: "I will, provided you promise to write down the answer." You agreed flirtatiously, and as far as I remember that was the only promise I was ever brave enough to ask of you.

You invited me to go back to the study while you made us some coffee. I asked if I could stay where I was, and volunteered to wash the dishes. "If you'd like to stay, I've no objection. As for washing the dishes, there's no need. This automatic slave (you pointed to a solid white cube next to the oven) spares us the trouble of doing that." There was a short silence, and it seemed to me that both of us were gathering our thoughts to pick up the thread of our conversation. In the manner that is conventional in such circumstances, before I had a chance to mention your promise, you set about apologizing for starting to make that rosewater hot drink without first asking me if I would really prefer it to tea. And as is also conventional, each of us gave the other a smile, and left the other to read into it what they wanted, and surmise as they pleased.

What happened between us in the kitchen was nothing remarkable if you compare it with the poems we spent many hours reading, but between me and you it was a part of the whole, so to speak.

The fragrance of the rosewater as it slipped down my throat was exquisite. It filled the air around us for some minutes, or so I imagined, and made us want to drink it straight, without questions or answers or any kind of conversation. You took your place on a low and narrow sofa, which ran against the bookcase at the far end of the room. I had thought that the three cushions lying on the sofa were only for decoration. I was wrong. You quickly picked one up and placed it behind your back against the bookcase. Perhaps you expected me to follow your example and maybe you were surprised that I did not do so. Instead, I stayed riveted to my place, but ready to take the chair just behind me and sit on it.

You watched me for some minutes as I stood nailed to the spot and then spoke to me in a soft voice, out of deference to our silence. "Take a seat," you urged, adding to your invitation by picking up a cushion from your right side and throwing it to the left.

I suggested we follow the news on television. The remote control saved you the trouble of standing up. At that time of day, two channels competed to present separate news bulletins. You had no preference for either, but switched between the two, sparing us the long commercial breaks. The day's harvest of news was meager—so-and-so met so-and-so and such-and-such had a meeting with such-and-such. The only thing that aroused my interest was a statement from the headquarters of your country's border guards, to the effect that some of their patrols, in cooperation with their counterparts on the other side, had pursued a group of 'evildoers' who were trying to infiltrate the borders in possession of weapons and other prohibited articles, and had wiped them out. I was not inclined to comment if you had not pushed me. "How long will they insist on treating people as idiots?" you asked. "Evildoers! For months we've been led to believe that what's happening on the border is a war on smuggling and smugglers. Then suddenly it emerges that these so-called smugglers are something else and that besides weapons they are smuggling in books, audio tapes, and ideas, used as a basis for describing them as 'evildoers.' I would like to have a chance to meet the genius who chose this term and ask him what he expects people to understand by it. Don't you agree that this little daily war is becoming more and more abstract the longer it continues?"

The pictures on the screen continued to flicker, silently in the moments since you put the television on mute. In silence, too, I listened to your little speech. My modesty deterred me from looking at you while I listened, but when a blonde presenter, lavishly made up and displaying all her charms, filled the screen, my modesty did not deter me from casting a lascivious glance at her, like thousands of other viewers. Your impassioned comment on the statement from the border guards almost overcame my wary reluctance to bring up the affairs and concerns of my practical life—I was reluctant to do so because I wanted you to forget who I was when I was not your guest, where I came from whenever I came to 'your place,' and where I was going when I left. My answer was simply to bemoan what was happening, the people killed, and the damage done to the country, your country and my country, from the incessant violence. Anxious to keep us off the subject and to maintain the reticence to which I had committed myself, I dwelt at length on your last comment on how "this little daily war" was becoming more and more abstract, adding that this abstractness was a victory for the outlaws, and that it expanded the scope of the war and widened the circle of those affected, because if the outlaws were merely smugglers it did not require justifications to fight them. But they had now succeeded in shaking off the label 'smugglers,' and their opponents had been forced to take a step back and describe them as 'evildoers.' So fighting them now required 'a philosophy' more powerful than the text of the laws, which impose penalties for crossing the border by stealth, possessing arms, and so on, because the laws do not impose penalties on anyone for being an evildoer, unless his evil is accompanied by illegal words or deeds.

Of course it did not occur to me when I was speaking that things were about to escalate through a chain of events (I am uncertain today what I should attribute that chain of events to—logic or chance and accident?), or that I was about to find myself in the thick of it as an advocate of peace and one of the theorists of the 'necessary violence' with which the authorities confronted the 'evildoers' and their evil doings. Did you fall for my trick, or did you see through my purpose in steering clear of the details, and then went along with me in that?

I am also uncertain about that. All I remember is that you rose from your seat and turned toward a particular shelf, took out a book in a foreign language, browsed through the back pages, which I suspected was an index of the contents, then opened it at a particular page and started to read aloud. I did not dare to interrupt and tell you that all I understood of what you were reading was a few scattered words that did not convey the meaning of the text, except that it was about religion and war. But as soon as you raised your head from the book and looked at me, you realized this spontaneously and you stumbled over your words when you tried to apologize. I stumbled too as I muttered, to spare you embarrassment, that you could carry on because I understood the general drift. Intuition came to your rescue and you gave no heed to my white lie but put the book on the table, leaned over to the bottom shelf to reach a magazine of strange format, and started to turn the pages carefully. Then you launched off again: "Forgive me for the . . . (you didn't say what). Now I recall that this text has been published in a translation that's not bad, in the third issue of this controversial magazine, which was destined to live only the shortest of lives."

You went back to your place and started to read, asking me to set you right if you made any grammatical mistakes. The substance of the text, which was dripping with sarcasm, was that when a group of people differ on theological matters, and start to massacre each other in the name of their dispute, then this indicates the highest level of development. At least for me, the subject called for thought rather than comment, but I could not possibly think about it at the time. I picked up the magazine from where it lay between us, and pretended to look through the pages for the text in question, and when I came across it I pretended to be reading it again. Meanwhile, you busied yourself switching between channels and, when the sight of a heated discussion made you stop at one of them, you turned up the volume a little and I was relieved that the discussion was in a language of which I understand nothing. I went back to the magazine, one eye reading and the other on you.

It is nothing remarkable that a man and a woman should talk openly within four walls, and nothing exceptional that they should sit on the same sofa and that one of them should watch television while the other is busy reading. But I am a man who made his living by saying that a man and a woman who are not related should never be alone together, as an article of faith inaccessible to doubt, and if I were to argue any other case, I would be vulnerable to accusations of madness or hypocrisy. It was not for that reason that I was anxious. In fact, I was about to say that if that was the reason it would have been of little importance and I would have found a way to rebut this or that accusation, and it was not my knowledge that unrelated men and women should not be alone together that spoiled our few hours together that night. The real reason was my confusion, compounded by your charm and the simple way you talked to me and dealt with me. What should have brought us together kept us apart, but I was looking at you with the eyes of a greedy man who ends up blinded by his greed.

When you yawned timidly, I did not feel I needed to take my leave, so I ignored it and continued to read the same magazine. Don't ask me from where I acquired this surprising impertinence of mine. In spite of my embarrassment, or rather my constant anxiety that my embarrassment might show, I was happy to be near you and I saw no good reason to spoil my happiness. In fact, for a moment (I don't remember how long it lasted) I forgot where I was, who I was, and who was at my side, and I went on reading as though I were at my place rather than yours.

When I tried to adjust the position of the cushion between my back and the bookcase, I noticed that the angels of slumber had encircled you and carried you off on the breeze to another world where I would have liked to find a place for myself under the sun. It was midnight. There was plenty of time till dawn, so why the hurry? Besides, supposing I had wanted to wake you up, do you think I would have dared to reach my hand out to your shoulder and tap it, or lean over toward you and whisper: "Good night, I'm going"? But since I knew nothing of your sleeping habits, I could not assume that you would be uncomfortable dozing in this position and that it would not last long. If worst came to worst, if it did last and I felt a pressing need to leave, I could move or clear my throat loudly to bring you out of your nap. In the meantime, you were mine to enjoy as I wished.

You are not at all like the blonde presenter I had stolen a glance at. Your hair is not blonde, your eyes are not blue, and your lips are not an open invitation to dig one's teeth into them. You do not have breasts so large they would almost fill a television screen. You have little in common with her and her conventional beauty, but you are beautiful in yourself, not by my inexperienced standards and my modest observations of women.

Beautiful in yourself because your beauty was not obvious to anyone looking at you for the first time. Perhaps for that reason—and although you overwhelmed me from the first meeting, if not exactly at first sight—I was uncertain about you for a long time and sometimes had doubts that you were beautiful. In fact, you had to let me into your bedroom and I had to read the signed dedications on two photographs of you by a prominent photographer before I could solve this riddle of yours. The dedications included references to how your magic casts such a spell that one cannot classify or appraise you. I do not think that the man who took your photograph fell under the spell of your magic anything like I did. So why was it so easy for him to speak about you with such certainty, yet impossible for me? Why did I concur with what he said, and still concur to this day, when I am fully confident that I know you better than he did? If the answer eludes you, it does not elude me: our whole relationship prevents me from describing you and attesting to your beauty. Can I explain water with water? But it is the truth, and sometimes the truth is disappointing because it is insubstantial, not only because it is bitter. I am under your spell, but I am a man whose business is passing on the authoritative words of others, not making them up myself.

I did not budge from my place to your left or decide to wake you up with an artificial gesture or by clearing my throat loudly. No, you took that upon yourself when you tried to turn over to the left and collided with the foreign body that was me. I do not know what surprised you most at that moment: opening your eyes to see me by your side, or the bright light.

You asked what time it was. I muttered a jumble of words—what time it was, that I was taking my leave of you, that I had not wanted to wake you up, all as you pulled yourself together and showed me to the door.

Perhaps after bolting the door behind me you went straight to your bedroom and threw yourself down on the bed as you were, but this image, although more probable than others, would not satisfy me. On my way back home I could not stop my imagination wandering: I saw you slipping out of your clothes and settling into an ample bed, rolling around in it like a child in mud that he has just discovered. I felt more and more restless and discontented the closer I got to my mosque—the mosque where I increasingly felt I was the subordinate, not the man in charge or the imam.

10

I do not remember how long we had been acquainted before news about the mosque and my two communities—the greater Muslim one and the small one at the mosque—became part of our usual conversations. Its initial absence did not surprise me at first, since I assumed you were not interested in my profession or in news about the people whose religious and secular affairs it was my duty to attend to as far as I could and intervene when necessary. That was at the beginning, but as our relationship stabilized and as I gradually came to know that your curiosity extended to a variety of subjects, some of which were not remote from my own concerns, I had to think again and guess that the reason why you avoided this subject in particular was that you were wary I might interpret your interest as intrusive. The truth is that this courtesy of yours toward me never offended me, because, whether we wanted to or not, if we came to talk about my mosque and my little community, the conversation would in some way inevitably lead to me, and this was a subject I could not talk about clearly and intelligibly. So I did my best not to let slip any word or reference that could take us down that road or would force me to let you in on my thoughts. It is for you to judge whether I really succeeded during those weeks in hiding the worries that the mosque brought on my head or whether my efforts in this direction were also fruitless, and whether the conspiracy of silence, which I thought we were in on together, was in reality a conspiracy you alone had hatched out of kindness toward me, and that when you sensed I had developed a thick skin, you abandoned the conspiracy.

It was as though you wanted to test how sensitive I was, to what extent I could tolerate simultaneously your presence, silent but moving, the specter of al-Mutanabbi (your Ahmad), and your candor. You achieved your objective and timed it well. You suggested we read the long poem *The Litany of Complaints*, which starts with the line: "He who finds fault with you is beyond reproach," and in which he describes a fever and pillories the Egyptian ruler Kafour. But as soon as we finished dissecting it, you suggested that on this occasion we drop our usual practice of choosing illustrative verses from every poem we read and that we start to prepare for another short poem of his also satirizing Kafour, the one that begins: "From which road, pray, does nobility approach you?" Under the strict regime you had devised, we were meant to compile from the poem in question a list of words suitable for use as headwords if the *Guide to al-Mutanabbi* was ever destined to see the light of day.

On the third line of the poem ("Is there anything more disgusting than a stallion with a penis, following the lead of a slave girl without a womb"), your voice lost impetus, apparently taken by surprise by the way al-Mutanabbi could utter such language, and too embarrassed to fill your mouth with the words of this line or pronounce them properly. All I could do was look away from you and stare into space until your voice recovered its vigor.

Like someone groping in the dark, warily you read the next line. You had just reached the end of the line safely and passed on to the next one— "Is it the purpose of religion that you should trim your mustache? / What a nation, at whose ignorance other nations laugh!"—when you let out a deep sigh, the essence of exasperation, and launched into a rant which you began by looking at me and saying: "Mawlana, he's speaking for us, his complaint is our complaint, his criticism is our criticism and his diagnosis is our diagnosis . . . ." Then, drawing strength from the verse and perhaps recalling that by virtue of my profession I might be one of those most vulnerable to al-Mutanabbi's sarcasm, you quickly excluded me from the group on whose behalf al-Mutanabbi was speaking and assigned me to the other party: "How long, mawlana, will you go on claiming that trimming one's mustache and growing a beard is the answer and the alternative? How long will you go on ignoring the world and wasting your time on theological minutiae of no benefit and from which no good can be expected? Doesn't it embarrass you, the state we are in—inadequate, backward, addicted to telling each other lies and taking pleasure in killing? Forgive me if I confess that cleanliness in my view is water, soap, and a toothbrush, not one of the keys to faith . . . ."*

I was disconcerted by your sudden outburst on this subject, which we had not discussed since we met, not because I objected to what you said but because you forced me to comment immediately, or else you would have seen my silence, if I remained silent, as a sign that I did not take what you said seriously, or that there was some rift between us. But my resolve did not make matters any easier for me, because your uncertainty as to which of the two camps I was in gave me warning that I should choose a place in one camp or the other and then build on the premise of that choice. Then I would either go even further than you did (and I have plenty more to say on the same subject), or take the position of someone who rejects what you said as a whole and in detail, confining my response to: "God guides whomsoever He wishes to whatsoever He wishes. Perhaps He will guide you to that which pleases Him in this world and the next. He is omnipotent, etc. . . ."

But what if, my lady, I was in both camps, not by choice but by force of circumstance? How could I tell you that that line of al-Mutanabbi not only spoke in my name, not only was it the voice of my conscience, but it also helped settle the score for me in an old feud, a feud renewed every day, not with people for whom the purpose of Islam is to preach trimming

---

* In fact, no religion in the world has shown as much interest in cleanliness as Islam, and no nation has been as concerned with cleanliness as Muslims. Islam takes such interest in it that the first thing a Muslim child studies in religious law is something called the Book of Purity, meaning cleanliness, because purity is the key to prayer, as the Prophet said: "The key to heaven is prayer, and the key to prayer is purity." Purity means cleanliness, and one of the conditions for prayer to be valid is physical purity (the body of the person praying must be clear of dirt), purity of clothes, and purity of place. Anyone about to pray must be clean and pure of body, his clothes must be clean and the place where he is praying must be clean. One of the first instructions in the Quran is: *And purify your garments.*(Quran 74:4)

mustaches, growing beards, and giving faith priority over cleanliness with water, soap, and toothbrushes, but with people of name and rank whom I meet, with whom I discuss the affairs of the community, and who, at the end of the meeting, always leave me upset, bitter, and angry that I was too cowardly to argue against them or, you could say, to argue against them along similar lines, if altogether less poetically than your al-Mutanabbi expressed it. Or should I horrify you by describing the spiritual baggage the men and women of my community come up with in my mosque? Or should I start by taking a shortcut and confide in you that, for example, Friday prayers had turned into something close to a weekly nightmare for me because of the fights, obviously staged, that punctuated the event? On one occasion the reason was that people were handing out a leaflet that on the face of it called for the promotion of virtue and the prevention of vice but was in fact a thinly veiled defense of the violent crimes the groups of 'evildoers' were engaged in; or another time, that young men insisted on standing in the way of the people leaving to collect donations for mujahidin in remote countries; or a third time, that someone made an allusion to someone among the congregation and accused him of frequenting the mosque as a spy, not to worship God.

In my turn I was uncertain what to do: should I tell you some of these details, to set your mind at ease about me and reassure you about which camp I was in? I was reluctant to do so, in case you thought I was trying to curry favor by making common cause with you. I was also reluctant because of my irritation at pretentious discussions about Islam and Muslims, which I know from experience do not tackle what is pressing and most important.

When I leave the lower city, my neighborhood, and venture into the other city, of which the neighborhood where you live is the centerpiece, I sometimes have a notion to accost some of the women and men I meet and whose appearance irritates me and ask them: "Do you know what awaits you? Do you think that these vast and towering fortresses in which you live are impregnable? And these armed young men with cruel peasant features who are posted around them, do you think that simply calling them security men will turn them into men, ensure that they follow the flag unto death for the sake of their country, and deter them from being seduced by other banners? The reports you hear about security violations here and there and on the border, do they not arouse your curiosity, if not your fears? Or am I the only frightened man in this city?"

81

Living off government money as the imam, preacher, and teacher at the Mosque of the Two Omars had not brought me, in the time since I took on the position, any obligation to wield the government's sword or invoke its authority. This was not out of presumption or boastful arrogance, but rather a policy agreed with the increasingly influential sheikh who was my mentor, and with his companions and followers. The basic principle was to keep the mosque out of the open conflict between the government and its opponents, to try to prevent a repetition of what he had seen in the past. So, taking a lesson from the experiences my predecessors had before the era of 'reform,' I distanced myself from excessive displays of loyalty to the government and those who held power, or from open hostility to its opponents, emphasizing instead the 'true faith' as a set of ideals on which there is consensus. Perhaps it was my adherence to this policy, in spite of the many sensitive situations I faced and managed to escape without resorting at the time to any public avowal of my friendships and enmities, that tempted certain people to start by negotiating with me to surrender my mosque to them amicably, or rather, you might say, to sell it to them openly. One of the last offers they made me, and the most impudent of them, included a guarantee to move me out of the country and do whatever was needed to settle me in a third country that was hospitable by virtue of its history and culture, along with—in the name of providing me a decent livelihood—a financial clause that involved a bank account in hard currency! Of course I turned them down and sent them away disappointed. Why do I say "of course"? Set aside what you now know about me, better than anyone else; set aside all my suppressed anger and exasperation, both in the past and more recently, and set aside the fact that I often skip prayers. All that is one thing, but resigning under intimidation or in response to inducements is something else altogether.

Although I was clearly a believer, my refusal, by the customs and in the judgment of the group, removed me from the neutral camp and enrolled me among the enemy. I say "me," but I mean "me and my mosque." It surprised me that some of my colleagues, even those in whose intelligence I trusted, insisted on believing that those young men had no ulterior motives but were merely acting out of enthusiasm and a desire to imitate, and so there was nothing to fear then or in the coming days. As for me, although I am no cat, which senses an earthquake before it happens, nor a Zurqaa' al-Yamama, the ancient Arabian seer with amazing visual powers, I was certain that the Friday squabbles were the prelude to something worse and that this group had resolved to 'conquer' my mosque and add it, by force if necessary, to the list of mosques that had been 'liberated.'

When I first came here, the practice of the police was to assign two policemen every Friday to regulate the traffic in front of the mosque and in the surrounding streets. Naturally, and out of respect for Friday, the two policemen did not have the authority to stop car owners from parking in no-parking zones, but only to organize the cars when they encroached on the pavements and parked in restricted areas. As the days passed, after a long series of incidents, the number of policemen assigned on Fridays began to grow, and their appearance, uniforms, and equipment began to change. Where once they had been two in number, one of them armed only with a token truncheon, which hung at his side and which he used, when he used it, so that the drivers could see him in the crowd, now the area woke up every Friday morning to a convoy of four military vehicles, two of which took up positions in the square opposite the entrance to the mosque, while the other two stopped cars entering the two roads leading to the mosque. The men who came in these forbidding and identical vehicles for weeks on end, needless to say, were quite unlike the two humble policemen in their fifties. These were young men wearing helmets, some of them holding automatic weapons, others giant shields and sophisticated truncheons that had evolved from sticks in ways one could trace only with difficulty. On top of all that, the two old policemen were familiar to the people of the area, young and old, and even the policemen at the local station had mellowed through living among the people of the area for years without replacement, until it became the rule rather than the exception to call them by their informal names, not by their ranks or other marks of respect. These new young men, however, had cruel looks, and the way they treated the people around them—including the children, who were fascinated by these vehicles, the rifles, and the shields—was extremely cautious, almost gruff, besides the fact that not one of them was ever seen in the area twice.

It did not surprise me, nor anyone else in the area, that Friday became a weekly occasion for this deployment. After statements about the clashes between the security forces and the 'evildoers' in remote areas started to appear daily in the news reports, it became normal procedure to encircle the mosque, especially on Fridays, and no one questioned the need for it, as though everyone was implicitly aware what made it necessary. Not all mosques were encircled in the same way, because those in the wealthy districts, and those which some officials thought it their duty to frequent in the company of television cameras, were protected by vehicles whose civilian appearance deceived no one. The vehicles carried people whose identity no one could mistake and parked at the nearby intersections, while in and around the mosques stood young men dressed in civilian clothes and wearing dark glasses. But at the mosques in other areas, where there were no television cameras to bear witness, the government had no interest in hiding or camouflaging its security measures—at my mosque, for example.

⁊

I said that Friday had turned into something very like a nightmare. I should add: like a nightmare I anticipated and had trouble preparing to face. Perhaps to steel myself for the occasion, perhaps because I was in a good mood that day, but unusually in any case, on the morning of the Friday before that evening of ours, I started to tease my staff. Half seriously, half in play, I began asking them to guess, one after the other: "What do you think, so-and-so? What do they have up their sleeves this week?" Someone answered: "Can they do anything more than defame and insult people?" I replied with another question: "Who do you expect they will pick on this week?" The answer was: "No, they're going to collect donations." He had a sweet tooth, so I promised him a plate of Turkish delight if he was right in predicting who they would collect for, for the mujahidin of which jungle or which remote island. And if one of them came back to me and asked: "Mawlana, which of the two do you think most likely?" I would answer: "Your two colleagues (meaning the two men who had fallen for my joke and had made predictions) are making fatwas on this matter without any knowledge, while I tend to dissociate myself from making fatwas on it, on the grounds that 'God knows best.'" It was an apposite response.

As usual, they were the first to reach the mosque. Their beards and jallabiyas gave them away, and you could tell those of them who did not wear jallabiyas if you listened to the greetings they exchanged. If someone said "Peace be upon you," and received the response: "And the mercy and

84

blessings of God," then he was one of 'the elect.' If the answer was a simple: "Peace," he was not. Rarely would they come in groups, but as soon as their leader arrived they would start trooping in one after another with amazing discipline, like a military formation. As soon as each one performed the two prostrations of salutation to the mosque and other voluntary prostrations that they and a minority of the other congregants observed, then he would join his friends. On that day they headed to a remote area close to the door. In fact, someone I trust told me that some of them spread out mats in the open area right at the mosque door, and formed lines in front of the door, although the mosque was big enough for them and for others—but he did not pay any further attention to what he saw.

In fact, it would have made no difference if he had been suspicious and had warned me what was happening, or if he had not seen anything in the first place, or if he had seen it but thought nothing of it, because the plan was masterly: minutes after the start of the call to the noon prayer, when the second call to prayer was called (this call, which comes right before the first sermon, is meant to warn the congregation that the preacher is about to start), I mounted the pulpit and sat waiting, without noticing anything to indicate that the group had planned anything outrageous. Everything was as normal and they, as I expected, were the most disciplined people there. But as soon as the call to prayer was done and I stood up to start my sermon, a voice boomed out from somewhere, jumping in ahead of me with his own "In the name of God, the Merciful, the Compassionate," and then with the prayer for the Prophet and his companions. He went on: "Praise be to God. We praise Him, seek His help, ask His forgiveness, and invoke His name against the evils inside us and against our evil deeds. He whom God guides cannot go astray, and he whom God leads astray shall have no guide. I bear witness that there is no god but God, and I bear witness that Muhammad is His servant and His prophet," exactly like someone starting a sermon. I doubt any preacher in any mosque has ever had such an experience. Yes, it has happened that imams are forced down from their pulpits, insulted, and abused. But for an imam to come forward to give his sermon and find someone he cannot see trying to elbow in on his sermon, that I have never heard of in my life, nor has anyone else heard of it before. I cannot claim that my instincts came to my rescue as quickly as I would have hoped. In fact, I could almost say that they were slow, even if the time between the beginning of the ambush and when I started to regain the initiative was no more than a minute, or maybe less. It was a long, long minute, and the least to be said of it is that during that time I experienced feelings of anger and humiliation that I would not wish anyone to experience, even an enemy. The mysterious preacher continued his sermon, while the congregation stood still as statues and I, like someone in a trance, tried to grasp what was happening around me and to stop my arms and legs from shaking. I was thinking about what was happening, though it would have been wiser to listen, because it was my ears rather than my brain that saved me. As soon as I worked out whose voice was coming out of the recording device the group had sneaked in as part of their plan (it was Sheikh So-and-so, who for some days past had been reported as either in prison or under house arrest), and as soon as I put together the pieces of what was happening, I began to shout the bismillah at the top of my voice, in the manner of a preacher who wants to calm down an indignant mob and make them listen to his voice. One of my colleagues sprang to help me and passed me the microphone connected to the main loudspeaker, after first blowing into it to check it was responding. It made a sound like a trumpet blast,* which reverberated throughout the mosque. Holding the microphone gave me a little strength, and with that I said a bismillah, prayed for "Beloved Muhammad," saluted Him with a calm resolve unrelated to my mental state, and launched into a sermon. After what had happened, I had no choice in the subject of the sermon, nor in the severe and confident, or rather violent and vituperative tone I had to adopt. Like someone reading from an open book, I improvised a speech about those who trade in God, His name, His law, and His word without respecting the sanctity of His mosques, and so on— whatever I felt inspired to say. I do not remember whether, when I took the microphone and starting speaking, I had even thought about how to bring my speech to any particular conclusion. I ignored everything around me and concentrated on the rival who had ambushed me with his magical and melodious voice, which rose from the recording device like a giant from a bottle. All I remember is that the bravest members of my congregation deliberately began to support me by shouting out, "'No god but God, and Muhammad is the Prophet of God," whenever I stopped

---

* A reference to the Quranic verse: *The day the trumpet is blown.* (78:18)

for breath, so that my rival had no chance to monopolize the scene. They coupled their cries with hostile glances at the recording device and at the young men around it. It did not escape me that the people shouting—my supporters to be frank—were a minority, and that it was fear, since there was no other reason, that deterred the others from shouting the same words out loud in public.

This farce had to end with one of the preachers overwhelming the other, so I took the opportunity of a "No god but God" that someone shouted out, and I began to berate the people who disdained to join in, using the most caustic expressions of vituperation which came to mind. I repeatedly denounced them with a fervor that fumed with rage, amplified several times over by the loudspeaker: "Praise the Lord! How can they be Muslims when they dare not proclaim His oneness?" Many of the silent ones now joined in, the place filled with cries of 'God is most great' and 'No god but God', and the voice of my rival was drowned out in the din. The ambushers realized that I had seized the initiative from them and, through all the heads in the crowd, I saw them exchanging looks and signals to withdraw, which they then did, taking with them their noisy, though meager, equipment.

I do not know if this turn of events was what they expected, but by fading into the crowd they put me in a predicament I admit I had not foreseen, since I had now aroused the fervor of the congregation. I had intended to end my first sermon at this point and a few moments later follow it up with a second one, confined to a short prayer inspired by the occasion, but I had not considered what might happen when the prayers ended and the congregants dispersed, with the 'ambushers' among them.

Their sudden disappearance made me change my mind about the length of the second sermon. Instead of keeping it short, I took it upon myself to spin it out and expand it, giving them time to withdraw and move away. That way I could avert the possibility that one of my followers would meet one of them, and that one of the two might let slip a word that, overheard by someone thirsting for revenge, would lead to an exchange of insults, and the insults to a scuffle, and the scuffle could lead to something with undesirable consequences. Perhaps my fears were exaggerated but, as subsequent testimony confirmed, they were legitimate, especially as the security men deployed around the mosque had in the meantime, under orders, gone on a higher state of alert and prepared themselves for something unexpected.

I had many visitors that Friday, unusually, and their comments were varied. The absolute strangest was what a man in his seventies, who lived near the mosque and regularly performed his prayers there, dreamed up: "Forget my partial deafness, mawlana, but by insisting on not using the microphone it was you who tempted them to play this malicious trick on you. If you were in the habit of using the loudspeaker (like the imams of other mosques, he almost said), it would never have entered their heads in the first place to raise their voice." He was referring, of course, to the sound of the elaborate amplifier they used to broadcast the sermon of their sheikh.

The others who sought me out, though supportive and full of congratulations for what they called my courage, probably left the meeting disappointed, because, instead of going along with them in portraying the outcome as a victory for us over them, as some of them were arrogant enough to describe it, I softly and gently countered their shortsightedness and their naive optimism. On my guard as much as possible not to undermine their morale, and inspired by the military metaphors they were using, I tried to explain to them that what had happened was not a war but a declaration of war, and that we would do best, as prudent men, to be fearful of what was yet to come, and not lose our cool as football fans do when their team scores a goal in the first minutes of the first half and they overconfidently assume that victory is theirs. The football season was at its height.

10

I did not mention any of this that night, but I did reprove you gently and affectionately, saying that what you had said was inaccurate in that it held Islam responsible for the sins of Muslims and held all Muslims responsible for the sins of particular groups. As you know, *No soul burdened bears the burden of another* (Quran 6:164). And as you also know, Muslims most unfortunately, like other groups of people, are not, with respect to high morals, good behavior, and broadmindedness, as identical as the teeth of a comb. As for the place of Islam and its attitude toward the world and the age, you know how thorny a question that is and how much wrangling it causes throughout the Islamic world and beyond.

I had no doubt that my opaque and feeble comments would far from satisfy you, not least because in your little speech you meant particular Muslims, the Muslims of this city, citizens and immigrants, old and new, whereas what I said was general, applicable on this occasion and on others. Although my answer did not go beyond what had already been said and did not tell you much about me, at least it showed you that there were no taboo subjects between us, and it took us back to a middle ground where you could, without contrivance, suggest that we continue our conversation in the kitchen while you finished preparing our dinner.

In the kitchen, following your example and out of solidarity, I did not want to sit down, but you insisted and, depriving me of any excuse, took a book from a distant shelf and put it in my hands. In a commanding tone, you said: "Read . . . ," leaving me to anticipate the end of the sentence: "while I finish preparing the food and setting the table." Your command took me by surprise, because the book's position on that shelf left me in no doubt that it was no coincidence that it was in the kitchen and that it was in fact a cookbook. "No, it's not to amuse you that I put this book in your hands, but to fulfill the promise you made me promise . . . to fill you in on the secret of the dessert I made last time." I turned the first pages of the book, which was neatly bound and could be kept clean, as you explained to me, by wiping it after use with a damp cloth. And there it was, in my hands, the cookbook by Ibn Sayyar al-Warraq, in a critical edition signed by an Orientalist from some country where it snows. As with many 'heritage' books, my knowledge of this book ended with the title and the name of the author, and probably it would never have fallen into my hands if I had not entered your house and you had trusted me and then invited me into the kitchen. You left me to my amazement and went off to prepare our dinner.

The small letters of the text and the dimness of the light prevented me from enjoying the substance of the book, so I made do with reading the headings. In fact, there was another reason why I refrained from trying to read, or pretending to try—a reason unrelated to the size of the letters or the dim light, although these reasons were real. As I sat comfortably on my chair, from where the whole rectangular kitchen was laid out before my eyes, you had your back toward me, and it was the first time I had had a chance to view your figure in full and see you moving about, as required by the process of preparing the various dishes—taking a few steps back and bending down to take a plate from the cupboard beneath the counter of marble with dark green veins, your operating theater; then stepping forward until the sharp edge of the counter touched you, somewhere, I suppose, below the navel; then standing on tiptoe to reach a container from a rather high cupboard; or moving to the right to inspect a frying pan, the contents of which you were cooking on a flame you had set so low that it seemed to be struggling with all its might to stay alight; or stepping to the left to concoct a mixture of salt, oil, vinegar, and aromatics of various colors; or reaching far to the left, where there was a metal sink divided into two compartments, to clean a knife you urgently needed.

At first I would throw a rapid glance at the page I was turning, then look up toward you, letting my thumb and index finger take their time looking for the bottom left corner of the page to fold it over. Little by little, when I was sure you were engrossed in what you were doing, and that I was out of your range of vision whether you turned right or left, I no longer bothered to lower my eyes at all, but instead my eyes looked straight at you, interested only in counting the breaths you took, while my thumb and index finger continued automatically to turn the pages. Luckily it was a book of several hundred pages and the meal you had chosen for our dinner that evening was too complicated for you to cook with a wave of a magic wand.

That night, resting—in the full sense of the word—in my bed, I had no feeling of remorse or guilt for my furtive glances at you, or rather for not having looked away. In fact, more than that: my conscience was not only confident that it had not committed anything that required me to chastise it or be angry with it, but it was also indifferent. From I know not where, a bedouin saying floated to the surface of my memory: when some bedouin was asked what looked most beautiful and most enjoyable, he answered: "A furtive look." I do not readily recall how long ago I had read that saying or in which book, and I do not think it struck a chord in me at the time, and I am certain I did not notice it enough to record it in the pages of that notebook, now tattered, in which I used to deposit selections from my readings, and I am sure I consigned the saying to utter oblivion as soon as I read it. Many might say there is nothing surprising about that, and I have no doubt that the most basic amateur psychiatrist could interpret the fact that I remembered that saying on that night in a way that would undermine the beauty of what I felt. Would not the analyst, whether thoroughly versed in his science or an amateur, go at least so far as to say that by trying to use a quote to put a favorable gloss on my furtive glances, I wanted to exonerate myself and deny that the way I looked at you went beyond 'pleasures of the eye?' I cannot fully confirm this interpretation, and I do not wholly reject it. In fact, I went beyond the stage of 'pleasures of the eye' before the saying came to me. I went as far as 'lust in the soul' throughout the two hours we spent over a dinner that was perhaps the longest in my life, and throughout two further hours we spent drinking refills of your rosewater drink and discussing a lecture I had been invited to give, on whatever subject I chose. In your mischievous and amusing way, you distracted me from expressing my admiration, on Ibn Sayyar al-Warraq's behalf, for your revival of his recipes (if it was a revival, then the only way to repay him was to eat them all up with relish), and instead induced me to admire the Orientalist who had spent years editing the book.

You talked about the Orientalist, about what an expert he was on the poetry of some obscure Abbasids, and about his feat in editing the cookery book, and this paved the way for us to go back to our earlier conversation about Islam and Muslims. "Forgive me my outburst and the harshness of my hasty words," you said. "Needless to say, I did not mean your person when I said: 'You.' If that was the case we wouldn't be here now, face to face. . . . Frankly, I feel naked in front of you, since you know much about me just by coming into my kitchen, and even if you know very little about my life and my past, I hardly know anything about you at all. No, I don't mean for you to tell me about your career, or how you came to be a man of religion, or how you came to our city, and other such details of your life, but I have a curiosity, if not more, to find out about you. How do you manage to reconcile your position among people, as imam of that mosque, with . . ." You hesitated for some seconds before resuming: "our friendship, let us say. Sometimes, when I'm alone of course, I try pretending that I'm calling you by your name, as friends should call one another, but 'mawlana' always stands between me and your name. When I first met you, such things didn't occur to me. I must admit that your 'civilian' disguise made it easier for me to overlook the 'profession,' if that's the right expression, that you practice, and not to treat you with formality. I must also admit that before I visited you on the first occasion I was uncertain for a long time whether I should cover my hair or not, then I thought: "As long as he's agreed to accept my invitation, then he's agreed to expose himself to the city, including the unveiled women, of whom I am but one." So I made do with a token headscarf. Little by little, I started to be troubled by thoughts and I didn't know if they were pertinent or just illusions in the form of thoughts or, more precisely, I started to ask myself, and I still do: 'Does this relationship make sense?'"

You were always braver and more eloquent than me. Do you really think I could keep pace with you and tell you openly what was seething inside me, in my mind and my heart? Luckily you did not insist, and so I took us back to the beginning of our conversation, and expressed my understanding of your outburst, assuring you that I in no way interpreted it as a personal insult: "For the reason you mentioned: that we are here now, in your kitchen, at ten o'clock in the evening, and above all that we are talking face to face, and for another reason: that the profession I practice is ambiguous by nature and can be interpreted in two ways, or the two together: there's the element of religion in its transcendent sacred sense, whereby I might be deemed to be not of this world, and the worldly element in the sense of political partisanship and endorsing one group rather than another, whereby I might be deemed to have nothing to do with religion. But the truth is that my 'profession' has a share in both elements, and on top of those a fair amount of 'social work.' Don't forget that, although my mosque is a house of God and those who come in are not asked if they are Arab or non-Arab, local or foreign, we cannot ignore the fact that it lies on the edge of the poorest neighborhood in your city, and in this neighborhood, as you know, most of the inhabitants are newcomers seeking work and a livelihood. But this, my lady, and all the details I could add about my profession, my mosque, and my people, does not take us any further. It does not eliminate the ambiguity of my position as far as you and I are concerned, and does not explain how I combine my 'profession,' as you imagine it and as it really is, with 'our friendship.' May I ask you, in order to simplify matters for you and for myself, to be more flexible and broaden the definition of 'profession' so that it is not too narrow, to include my activities and what takes up most of my time and effort?" This is roughly what I succeeded in expressing, sometimes inarticulately and at other times fluently. I suspect it did not appease you or satisfy your curiosity.

You were demanding to know how I, as someone entrusted by virtue of my profession to preserve the bounds Islam has set between what is lawful and what is unlawful (and the most immediately obvious unlawful thing is for a man to be alone with an unrelated woman), how I could allow myself to visit you, sit with you, read with you, eat with you, drink with you, and share with you many of your evening hours, and perhaps, to put it more frankly and more bluntly, you wanted to know if I was lying and who to? To myself? To you? To the others? You're right. Logically, it would not stand to reason for me to claim complete honesty. Honesty—complete honesty—would force me to admit that I am partly lying. Fine talk, but on one condition—that one demonstrate that logic is the right authority for examining matters related to human behavior, which is not something I am sure of or comfortable with.

You were not alone in having doubts about me and my honesty because, as the struggle for the mosque heated up, and with it the campaigns to discredit my humble person, it was not long before one of the leaflets described me as one of those who *in their hearts is a sickness, and God has increased their sickness, and there awaits them a painful chastisement for the lies they have uttered.*[*] On the morning of that day, when the janitor came to me gloomily with copies of this leaflet, shuffling as he came and explaining that he had found it in the courtyard and guessed that one of them had thrown it over the wall and so on, that morning I accepted the insults and the ridicule with a calm indifference that looked out of place to the anxious servant, who was worried the streets might be full of copies of the statement. When he asked me if I would like him to go around the neighborhood to investigate, I told him I would rather he made me a cup of tea. "Are we not, haji, among those *who, when the vicious address them, their only word is 'Peace'?*"[†] I am certain that the janitor, like the officer I met in my mentor's office, interpreted my apparent calm and indifference as tenacity and self-control, and even if I had sworn the most sacred of oaths, he would not have believed that I really was calmly indifferent. In fact, my inner thoughts were even more derisive than the leaflet. "Do they really need to quote the Quran to prove that I am sick—sick in spirit, in mind and in body, not just at heart?" I asked.

In short my behavior—withdrawn and contradictory, for example— was so mysterious and ambiguous that I laid myself open to accusations of hypocrisy. This was true of you and of others who had nothing in common with you. The least of my concerns was that these others should come to know 'the truth' about me and see how these contradictions were combined in my person. Besides, the contradictions were more their problem than mine, and certainly not the result of any flaw in my "psychological make-up," as one of our pedantic sheikhs went so far as to say, but it was a permanent struggle to make sure their combination in me did not make me despicable in your eyes.

As with many others, the miracle-based faith of the countryside, the faith of my childhood and early adolescence until I moved to the city, did not survive long, even after growing up in that fortress of a village,

---

* Quran 2:63
† Quran 25:63

94

isolated from the world and its temptations, a place where everyone and everything breathed 'the faith.' Don't imagine I am including myself among many in order to lose myself among them. On the contrary, I am lamenting that the profession that circumstances decreed I should study in depth and then practice deprived me of this chance to lose myself. The switch from a miracle faith to a "newfangled faith" (as someone scoffingly called it) was not difficult for those who, like me, joined the army or some government department or worked in a manual trade. Newfangled faith means you sometimes attend Friday prayers in the mosque, you fast in Ramadan or pretend to, you celebrate the two main feasts, and other than that you tuck Islam and its rules behind your ear unless disaster strikes and you turn to God in prayer, or some dispute arises between you and your brother or your neighbor, and the family or neighbors resort to some notable or sheikh to arbitrate between you. In my case, switching publicly from one faith to the other was not easy. It meant I had to restart my life from the beginning, which I did not attempt to do until after I took up employment, but before my appointment as imam of the Mosque of the Expatriates came and changed the course of my life. What made things more complicated was that I was the model of a promising and diligent student, and for reasons unrelated to the deterrent effect of religion I was also—on the surface, of course—the model of a chaste and virtuous young man. On top of that, I do not recall that the extra studying I did, above and beyond what was necessary, ever caused me any hardship. If I had been given a choice between studying and the various amusements that distracted my colleagues, I doubt I would have abandoned my studies. For all these reasons I found myself hostage to the fact that I outshone my colleagues and that a number of my sheikhs had confidence in me.

In a world such as the one where I spent my youth acquiring knowledge of religious law, it is neither possible nor proper to have an inner life where you can talk to yourself. Why would you have an inner life, so long as you are performing your duties to God as a matter of urgent priority, and your duties to mankind only insofar as the regulations and the laws require?

So much for the big headline. Now for the subtitles: people are diverse, however much it might be said that they are alike, so if there arises among them a demand for learning intended to guide mankind to some one and only acceptable right path, then most of us are bound to need our own spiritual advisers, as well as people to supervise the learning we are taught, and these advisers–supervisors are in most cases men with beards, attached to religious fraternities or schools of law. But the parts of our inner lives to which one supposes this adviser would have access rarely include the secrets of the heart and those thoughts that people are too embarrassed to put into words. Perhaps this is what distinguished me from them, or most of them, for whereas the inner lives of my colleagues were so much dross under which they seemed close to collapse, my inner life lived up to its name. Those of them who were following a Sufi path talked nonsense about their Sufism, and those who yearned for eras when Islam was making conquests and performing miracles, albeit in other countries, talked nonsense about that. But no Sufi orders tempted me and I did not find what I was looking for in activist Islam, of which I had had, by chance, a very brief experience as a member of an Islamist group. The result was that I quickly perceived what path had been set for me. I mean I quickly perceived that my Islam, in spite of all the Islamic learning I had studied and all the sayings of the Prophet, chains of transmission, and legal principles that clogged my memory, was a yearning for a childhood that was gone, never to return, and that Islam, the religion of this country and the great majority of its people, was my world and my way of life and that it was a mistake and futile to ask more of it for myself, not even some happiness or peace of mind. But my world, there and later here, did not stretch far, and my way of life, despite the controversy over it, was straitened, and still is. That is why I resort, without hesitation and on every possible occasion, to my inner life; the cave where I live out everything I do not live out among people and where I raise my voice to say all those things I do not proclaim in public. This cave of mine was a safe place, but safety is not necessarily an occasion for joy and celebration, and safety does not relieve one from the needs and demands of life in this world.

Would marriage, for example (half of religion, as they say)—marrying one of those girls my mother suggested one after another whenever I visited the village—have protected me and turned me, as far as my natural manhood is concerned, into a proper man (woe betide my simple girl if she turned out to have many children and to love being a mother!)? I cannot say with certainty. Anyway, these hypothetical questions mean nothing to me now: I did not submit to my mother's insistence and I did not follow the Prophet's advice to young men;* in fact, I went my own way, preferring a celibate life in my cave to the trouble of marrying a simple girl whom I would seek out only to satisfy my carnal desire for women,† cheating on her every now and then in remote brothels without any significant pleasure in return.

Your house is the absolute antithesis of that cave, and the clearest and most eloquent sign of that is that you opened wide its doors for me and invited me to come in, as God invites his righteous followers to enter Heaven.** You can be excused for that, because how would people who live in houses know what cave people are about, or how easily they can transform houses into caves after their own image?

To extend the analogy, my repeated visits led me to believe I could have a place in your house and find safety within it, but for my wish to come true I had to be stripped— stripped of my silence. It was a wish that was no less hard to fulfill than stripping a thorn bush or the like.

---

* "Young men, those of you who have the means should marry because it keeps your eyes from straying and preserves your chastity. Those who do not have the means should fast because it represses desire."

† "If one of you likes a woman and falls in love with her, then he should head to his wife and sleep with her, because that will satisfy his lust." (Hadith)

** *Enter therein, in peace and security!* (Quran 15:46)

10

In resigned contentment, we lived our relationship under a seal of secrecy. We did not speak about it or conspire in it by taking oaths and covenants with each other. I do not know if you divulged anything about us to your close friends or, if so, whether that helped you to accept and understand our relationship when we were living it and it was proceeding irreversibly. I did not do so, if only for two reasons—my lack of a trustworthy confidant and my crippling shyness. And now, after our relationship has gone through so many meetings, conversations, and hours of togetherness, here I am fighting the same old battle, trying to give it its due. My first duty toward it is to bring it into the open, within myself, and admit the part played by an unseen hand in pushing me in the direction that finally brought me to where I am now.

What might you perhaps say of me if I confided in you my inner self? If I declared to you that—in spite of everything, as they say—I do not at all regret that I lacked a trustworthy friend and was crippled by shyness. Otherwise I would have ruined our relationship by sharing it with someone else in the form of an incomplete version. On the contrary, I was almost happy that I preserved it for myself alone, even if that was not a matter of choice, and happy too that hoarding it to myself saved it from fragmentation through casual recollection, but preserved it for me to revive again in the way I am doing now. In this way, too, I am giving you your due: in that, for hours of clarity and peace of mind, I have been busy mulling the whys and wherefores of our relationship, and trying to work out which particular overwhelming concerns and worries of mine I regarded as the outcome of these mysterious elements. Does it strengthen my argument if I add that, because of my unfamiliarity with life in general, I must first go over my experience of life under your protection, like a diligent student revising, until I can claim that I know it by heart?

When we returned from the kitchen to the study, supplied with a jug of that rosewater drink, we turned to choosing the subject of the lecture a student group had invited me to give in one of the universities in the capital. For the first time that night, I felt that the nameless thing that was bringing us together entitled me to pose a question by way of consultation, thus overcoming our inhibitions about discussing my professional concerns and rapidly reinforcing the sense of partnership between us. You were quick to seize upon the question and, as is your wont, take me by surprise. I expected you to enumerate a few topics I could add to the list I had composed in my head, but instead you asked me, even before I told you who had invited me: "How can you ask me to suggest topics when I don't know what kind of audience is expected to consume your speech?" I was stunned by the way you phrased the question. It's not that I was indifferent to the type of audience but my instinct inclined me to look at the matter on the basis that a speech should be tailored to the occasion. Perhaps if I had consulted someone else and he had meant what you meant, he would have said something to the effect that I had to choose the subject taking into consideration the audience. I did not want to comment on your description of the audience as "consuming" the lecture. In fact, I was unable to comment on the spur of the moment because your remark had a disturbing effect on me, both emotionally and mentally, and stirred up thoughts that I wanted to store up and mull over later.

"The invitation is from some students at one of the universities in the capital, so the audience would be young and educated," I said. "I was very hesitant to accept their invitation, in case it might be said I was going beyond my mandate . . . I'm sure you know what I mean. But the personal intervention of the rector of the university, who is an influential man, and his status as a scholar, convinced me that I need not worry, because the group that invited me, he assured me, is not linked to any political organization, secret or open, and in critical times like these, as he put it, it is what each of us can do that determines his job description, not the other way round."

"Don't you think," you asked me, "that this rector you describe as influential, by his personal intervention in favor of this group, and by describing the times as critical, is hinting at what he would like to hear you tell the students in your lecture?"

"That's why I'm uncertain what to do, as you can see. Besides, I'm basically obliged to comply when he intervenes. You may have sensed that your phrase 'the audience expected to consume,' did not escape me. I was going to let it pass, in case by commenting straight away I gave you the impression that it offended me or that I was standing up for my notional audience. But now that I've explained everything to you openly you can see why it gave me pause to hear you reducing my ideas to a 'consumer product' for an audience to approve or reject." I said what I had to say, composing coherent sentences with broken words, cautiously and hesitantly, not expecting you to answer or comment, for it had become well-established between us that our conversations should be punctuated by moments of silence, indeed gaps, and that we should not try to fill these gaps with any talk or whatever else might come.

✍

Just as one person can acquire a certain habit, so can two. One of the habits we acquired was to sit down after dinner, in our usual places, on that couch facing the television. That is what happened that night, except that we both nodded off and slumped on the cushions. But we were equally anxious not to let our fatigue show, and we dozed off for just a moment before the siren of a passing police car or ambulance awoke us.

I asked leave to go, and on the spur of the moment, perhaps with a trace of disapproval, I added that "the night has tricked us." I meant it only as an observation, but my tone of voice in criticizing the hour for being so late gave you the idea that something about it embarrassed me,

100

and you quickly reassured me that the trip to the mosque at this hour, when the streets would be empty of traffic, would not take more than a quarter of an hour. The only argument I could find to prevent you accompanying me was that I could find a taxi to take me there, but my argument did not stand up to your resolve. Instead, you disappeared somewhere for some seconds, then came back with two glasses of water on a plate in your right hand and a woolen shawl on your left arm. "Drink up," you commanded. "Now that the cold season has come, you have to take precautions against the temperature difference between inside and outside." I complied with your friendly order while you skillfully wrapped yourself in the shawl. You closed the door gently behind us and we skipped down the spiral staircase. The last person to use the iron gate had not closed it, so you needed only to give it a little push. I knew that etiquette required me to make way for you to go through first, but that night, at the gate of the building where you had an apartment, the first time we ever left 'your place' together and faced the challenge of a public space, I did not know whether I should follow the dictates of etiquette or defer to your whispered invitation that I "go ahead." I did not know where we stood: for you, was being there at that hour in the company of a man something inconsequential that did not merit any precautions in the way of secrecy or haste, or, on the other hand, were you putting yourself to unnecessary inconvenience for my sake? There was a third possibility that never occurred to me at all: that we judged matters by completely different standards.

∽

There was no trace of the moon in the city sky. Did you really want me to withdraw to my mosque, my misery, and my ignorance? Suppose I were one of your books. Would you not feel a desire to browse through me and fill in the vowel signs missing from the text? For the second time in the space of a couple of minutes you whispered, "Go ahead." You not only opened the car door for me, but also waited for me to take my seat before closing it. You walked around the car without me seeing you, opened the door on the left side, and took your seat. You fastened your seat belt and asked me to do likewise. I felt for the metal buckle and pulled it toward me, but in the darkness I could not make out where I was supposed to insert the buckle between the seats. You were about to swing left to take the car out of the line of parked cars but you noticed my predicament and postponed the turn. You moved the gear lever, which was still in your right hand and, leaning slightly toward me, took the buckle from my fumbling fingers to insert it where it was meant to be. The gesture took only a fraction of a second and, when our hands touched, you said a casual "Sorry." Then you went back to maneuvering the car out from between the cars behind and in front. Although you must have performed the same maneuver maybe several times a day, I thought I should hold my breath during those moments, which I deemed critical. I held it till we left the pitch-dark side street and came out into the lights of the main road.

For years your city has seen a relentless race between, on the one hand, the poor neighborhoods, which have inevitably been built on the outskirts and which have continued to grow and expand, and, on the other hand, plans for highways the authorities advocate building. The authorities have advanced a thousand and one arguments for building the highways, even if it means the government has to go into debt or sometimes beg for funds. But what is never mentioned in the heated debate over whether these plans are a priority or economically feasible is that if the highways were built they would enclose these poor neighborhoods within concrete walls so high that someone driving through at speed would hardly detect a trace of life behind them, unless some of the young men in those neighborhoods had a mind to write their names on them, or the names of their girlfriends, or paint on them the badge of the football team they support, like prisoners on the walls of their cells. These highways, as they are called, or 'encirclement' roads, as they are not called, are the routes taken by the truck-like buses that link the two cities, including my bus, the one that bears the number 6.

The highway, the shortest way to our destination, did not tempt you, or perhaps you wanted to prolong our journey. On previous occasions when I left your place late I had chanced to travel between the two cities by taxi, passing through all the streets and intersections along the way, but our journey together from your place to my mosque was different because of the self-confidence I felt, the confidence of someone who roams around a house or strolls in a garden in the company of the owners, not as an intruder or a trespasser. I had never felt this way in a taxi, even if the driver was a neighbor or someone from my country. For this reason, I found myself discovering the city with the eyes of a man who has traveled little and is entering it for the first time.

102

Was I struck by what I saw of the city at night? Not at all. What struck me was how I had not seen it before, and, I would almost say, how I had not seen it through the eyes of envy. To tell the truth, even if that is a big word, those feelings flared up in me when we drove through a square that had a number of pavement cafés around the edges. You slowed down noticeably when we passed one of them, as though you wanted to examine the customers or see whether someone particular was there.

In general and in particular, I could not believe anything I saw that night, neither the fact that you, my lady—al-Mutanabbi's confidante, who shivered with delight when he spoke about his horses, the night, and the desert—were also a skillful driver who delighted in the sensation of speed, nor the fact that we lived in the same city. While you are like a fish in the sea, I feel that I am more than a tourist but less than a stranger, and while I am not supposed to feel lonely I feel as much a stranger here as Salih in Thamud.*

The road took us uphill and we went through a smart residential area that took its name from a place much higher above sea level than the area really is. As soon as we started going downhill again, the signs of misery and shabbiness appeared on the facades of the buildings and the faces of the few passersby. I do not think I was mistaken when it seemed to me that the level of shabbiness increased with growing rapidity as we descended, reaching its nadir when we came to a poorly lit square, one of the ones we had gone through before we went uphill. It was littered with refuse from a vegetable market. I did not want you to go any deeper into these areas, but neither did I want you to interpret that as discouraging you from entering back streets, which you knew were my world.

Inadvertently, or in despair at my inability to express myself clearly, my hand reached into the bottom of my scruffy bag, looking secretly for my keys. "And now?" you said. Had my hand given me away, or were you really unsure of the way, as you hurriedly explained? I replied that it would take me only a few minutes to finish the journey on foot. I do not doubt your good intentions when you asked me if it would embarrass me if you spared me the trouble of walking the remaining few hundred yards. I also have no doubt that you did not mean to challenge me, but your proposal

---

* "I am among a people—may God save them in His mercy—a stranger, like Salih among Thamud." (from a poem composed in al-Mutanabbi's youth)

to drive me all the way home raised two complications, one of which was the risk of being seen in the company of a woman at such an hour. I had no choice but to go with the other one: "All that worries me is that you might lose your way in the maze of these . . ." I was about to add a suitable epithet to describe the nearby streets but I lost my nerve. A junction loomed in front of us and you jumped in with a "Don't worry about me," followed by an impatient, "And now?" I faced a choice between advising you to keep driving straight on, along the somewhat wide and well-lit street, which continued in our original direction and which would soon take us on our right to the main entrance to the mosque, and on the other hand advising you to turn right into a dark and narrow lane that would soon skirt the back wall of the mosque, where I could leave you in the darkness on the pretext that by going in through the side door I would be closer to my destination (which would have been the case if this door had not in fact been closed for so many years that it had merged with the wall).

Cowardice got the better of me. I waved my hand to the right, and as soon as the small door came into view I asked you to stop. Mumbling my reason for getting out there, I thanked you for taking the trouble to drive me home and prematurely wished you a good morning. Hurriedly, I dismounted and walked around toward the door, where I repeated my farewell with a quick wave of my hand, and you waved back. I stood where I was, waiting for you to drive off so that I could retrace my steps and go into the mosque compound through the only real door it had.

❧

To ensure this therapy of yours was effective, I had to describe our night journey in full in the last passage. One of the things that never fails to surprise me about that night, even now, is how my instinct for survival (survivals of various levels and degrees) remained so acute.

That night, the ultimate survival challenge was responding to your suggestion that you drive me back home and making sure you did so in secrecy, under cover of darkness. I would not be exaggerating if I claimed that my survival depended partly on achieving both objectives. Even so, I did not forgive myself that night or after for handing over the keys to my survival, or rather my survivals, to that instinct. It also surprises me how each of us can combine emotions that we think dominate our behavior

104

and choices with calculations and rationalizations that we are hardly aware of. Would you believe, for example, that in the split second when I advised you to turn right into the dark narrow street, my only concern was that it might be so narrow that you would have to slow down and someone might see you, even someone who did not know you and did not know about our relationship? And would you believe that in those moments it completely escaped me that you were about to go back alone on the same route we had come along together and that I should have been anxious, even for the sake of courtesy? But when I checked the map of the place in my head, I remembered that the only way out of the dark narrow street was to the well-lit street, and that this was a one-way street, and all you had to do was follow it to find your bearings again, after two or three traffic lights, far away from here, yet close by, on the outskirts of your own world.

13

Behind the table, which I had restored and repainted myself, and behind glasses, which I have recently been obliged to wear when reading, I attended to the affairs of my small community as well as I could, in my opinion, and I tried hard to alleviate their concerns. The affairs and concerns of my community were not all as memorable as those I mentioned earlier; in fact, most of them arose at predictable times and were predictable in substance.

What added to the monotony, if I may use the word, is that after the sermon incident the situation on the mosque front calmed down somewhat (although the incident, as you can appreciate, did not end there, but had ramifications and gave rise to rumors, discussions, and mediation efforts that I have refrained from relating but that I might return to).

In short, that incident, which took place "in a context of escalation," as they say, coincided with the return of each party to its base to prepare for the next contest, not just in my neighborhood but in the two countries generally.

As far as I was concerned, I interpreted this short-lived truce as a marked change in their policy and plans, a change that implied they had turned from targeting the mosque to targeting the neighborhood in general.

The first onslaught came in the form of professionally printed posters bluntly inducing people to perform their prayers. "Pray before others pray over your dead body," they said, literally. It was illustrated with a crude drawing of a shrouded corpse laid out on a coffin and was signed rather threateningly: "Those Who Keep God's Bounds."*

The local people who woke up to find the posters on the walls of their houses and on shop doors (and on the front gate of the mosque) had a range of comments. Some saw the posters as a childish prank not worth discussing, while some others ridiculed such a method of admonition, failing to understand that the corpse looked like an Egyptian mummy only because it was deliberately drawn in outline to avoid any portrayal of the human form. A third group thought it had nothing to do with them. As for me, I refrained from commenting, but merely noted to myself the common orthographic error in their slogan, which, as they had written it, was addressed only to females.

As the days passed, the activities of 'Those Who Keep God's Bounds' began to expand beyond merely putting up posters, which sometimes called on people to perform their prayers, and sometimes advocated modest attire or "shunning abominations." The group began to send out personal letters, giving advice to those men and women they regarded as likely to comply and roundly rebuking others. A Muslim seen holding a golden keyring received a courteous letter reminding him, with citations from Islamic law, that it is forbidden for men to use gold for decorative purposes. Someone who was famous for his conservatism but who had lapsed on the occasion of his daughter's wedding by celebrating it with singing and dancing received a letter of reproach, accompanied by a prayer that the bride and bridegroom would live in harmony and have children. A grain merchant who sometimes charged interest found a stern letter under the door of his shop, warning him of serious consequences. My lot was to receive a similar letter written in terms that were close to insulting, faulting me, as a model to the common people, for taking a glass of water offered to me at the funeral of someone or other with my left hand rather than my right.

---

* *Those who repent, those who serve, those who pray, those who journey, those who bow, those who prostrate themselves, those who bid to honor and forbid dishonor, those who keep God's bounds—give good tidings to the believers.* (Quran 9:112)

107

For weeks these posters and letters were the only events the neighborhood witnessed. I myself did not properly "appreciate the situation," neither to myself nor in answer to a question about "my opinion on the matter," posed by a security man who came to visit me for the first time in the company of the press attaché at our embassy in the wake of the sermon incident, and who then become a regular visitor. I remember I told him sarcastically that day that "Those Who Keep God's Bounds" brought nothing new and did not show much imagination in their letter-writing campaign, because decades before them, in another Arab country, a young man who later become important had the idea of setting up an association devoted to "preventing forbidden practices." The man put his idea into practice, and writing letters was one of his methods. I said that such ideas were readily available, they were not protected by any copyright, and there was no obligation to mention their source when they were copied. "Whether it's important or not, sir, is something you should know better than me, because you are better placed to establish the facts," I added.

I thought he would interpret my response as sarcastic and evasive, but, on the contrary, he showed yet more interest and asked me questions about the source or sources to which he could refer to confirm this precedent. I provided him with what I had at hand (untroubled by any sense that I was 'collaborating'!). I was uncertain about what was happening: was it a fire that had died down but was likely to flare up again, or a fire breathing its last? The evidence pointed equally in both directions.

Because the evidence was inconclusive, I went about my business and awaited what would happen, sometimes in great anxiety. My most pressing business was to find sufficient time to get my work done without being distracted by disputes between one man and his neighbors, or between another man and his wife, or by the various letters of admonition people had received.

⁓

When I first took charge of the mosque and came to know the neighborhood and its people, I tried to insist that people who wanted to see me obtain appointments in advance, and when I failed in this attempt at 'reform' I did not give up. But I regretted imposing such a restriction all at once, and instead set aside three whole days in the week when I would receive anyone who wanted to see me, without an appointment, but this method of giving them more access did not bring about the desired result, and my office was still prey to their long and obtrusive visits. Because of my diffidence, or rather in confirmation of it, I reluctantly turned a blind eye to this for a good long time, and merely used the janitor as an intermediary between me and the visitors, in the hope that by constantly reminding them of the system he might have an effect. Their behavior irritated me as a matter of principle rather than because it wasted my time, which was in practice as good as wasted anyway. But as our relationship developed and took its place among my daily concerns, and as I went my own way with things that mattered only to me (you excepted), I could no longer endure in silence their repeated encroachments on the sanctity of my office and my time. I grew fangs from I know not where and my shyness changed into a kind of rudeness. After long thought, it seemed a good idea to involve the janitor in some of my business and make use of his help against them. He had served the mosque since it was founded, and he knew the area and the various people living around it because he had worked alongside my two predecessors. He came into my office one morning for some reason, as I was engrossed in picking apart the vocabulary, morphology, and syntax of an al-Mutanabbi poem we had agreed to read, and I thought it was a good opportunity to discuss the matter. I asked him to stay and told him how greatly annoyed I was that people were disregarding the visiting times I had set for them, especially as my workload had grown, not neglecting to add "as you can see," and pointing to the vast tome which lay in front of me and the other books that cluttered the table, as well as the slips of paper covered in annotations.

He was delighted to be involved, and reassured me that my grievance had sunk in. I thought it wise to take a step backward to strengthen his resolve before taking more steps forward and attaining my purpose: "They're our people, and we owe it to them to look after their interests," I said, "and I have no doubt that they do not intend to disturb me. But you can see the situation and we have to find a compromise that doesn't hurt their feelings but which leaves me some time for these other tasks which, God willing, will be of benefit to everyone."

At that point, the pious janitor looked disheartened, and he had no choice but to throw the ball back in my court. "Then what's to be done?" he asked, with a seriousness that showed he appreciated the importance of his mission and of what the Muslim world as a whole was missing because the local people were intruding on my office and prolonging their visits for no good reason.

"We have to get tough. My office is open to all comers on the three days we previously named, and unless there's something unexpected that requires my urgent intervention I want you to keep visitors away, as tactfully and politely as you can and with a clear conscience, and put them off until the next visiting day."

Of course I did not dare explain my request in clear terms that called things by their names, instead of restricting myself to metaphor, but the janitor surprised me by taking up the theme in a way I had not expected. "Don't worry," he said, and then proceeded to expound his own theory that it would be no sin to invent excuses that saved my time, provided I spent the time serving the community and the common good.

I thanked him for his understanding and then thanked him in advance for his trouble, but he took me by surprise a second time within a few minutes by urging me to go easy with my thanks. "Rest assured and trust me. Give me just a week with them and you'll see how I completely transform their behavior and get them used to the idea that the door to your office has hours when it opens to receive them, just as there are set times for prayer. "

Satisfied with what I had gained, I thought that the janitor, whom I had just appointed as my chamberlain, was merely trying to ingratiate himself with me, but the military discipline my visitors displayed in the days that followed our conversation and the way they went back to the appointments system that most of them had abandoned led me to conclude that perhaps I had been too hasty in attributing to sycophancy his exaggerated enthusiasm and the fact that he took my side of the argument. When one of the local dignitaries gently complained to me about the "rude" way the janitor played his role as chamberlain, I realized his commitment was genuine and I had to take him aside again to persuade him to temper his enthusiasm for his task.

I no longer remember the sequence of these events and whether you drove me to the mosque before I gave the janitor his new task or during the two weeks in which he ruled the local people who came to visit me, in my name but at his whim, or even later. In any case, there is no lesson to be drawn from putting these minor events in chronological order. What matters is that they took place within a short period and that, were it not for you, they and other more important events would not have happened at all.

By saying "were it not for you," I am imposing a responsibility on you without any reliable witnesses or any corroborative evidence, which puts my claim in the category of a 'weak report,'* and how could it be otherwise, when I was the only source? When I insist that my report is correct and that "were it not for you these events would not have happened," I do not mean to slander you or to wash my hands of what I did, or sully your hands by treating you as an accomplice by incitement. I mean it as recognition that it was thanks to you that I did what I did serenely and in full awareness, and not just thanks to you but also thanks to them, the people I have been accused of collaborating with, the people of whom they say that I "distorted Islam" to please them and serve their policies.

On the day before I was brought here, one member of the group, the most obnoxious of them, gave me to understand that they had registered my repeated visits to your place in their records, to the hour and the minute. If he had been less stupid or more agreeable, I would have told him in turn that what they knew of our relationship was no more than what they could imagine might happen between a man and a woman, and that fortunately their imagination was limited and therefore they knew very little. Perhaps I should have said more to him. I would have said, if only to be provocative, that it was you who persuaded me to launch a war of words on the 'evildoers' and encouraged me to take part in this petty intermittent strife. That would have confused him.

I have no regrets that I chose to be alone in this little house in this place, which is isolated in the first place. But there is no comparison between this solitude and the loneliness a man can feel in the midst of people. Among other people, time is constantly present. If you try to ignore it, you are reminded of it when someone knocks on the door or a telephone rings or, in the mosque, the muezzin gives the call to prayer. Here time is sickly, impotent, crippled, paralyzed, and you have to pick it up in your hands

---

* In the science of traditions about the Prophet Muhammad, a report from only one source, which may be sound or weak.

and carry it around the center of an imaginary circle for it to pass. I am not inventing the wheel, and other people, many or few, may have gone through what I am going through now, and perhaps others who have had this experience have described it better than I could possibly do, but that, and the fact that I have felt this way for months, does not lessen the impact. I say "impact" and I mean something else, but my tongue runs away with me: it does not diminish the sense one has that things are constantly on the verge of unraveling and spinning out of control.

Do not suppose that I am speaking at random on a subject I know nothing about or that I am dreaming up situations that have no basis in reality. It's not at all like that, and of course I do not want you to try to believe. But what is it that drives a man to make a stintless effort to keep time on course and to keep himself on some time track? I have no answer backed by evidence, no answer other than to recognize that the instinct to stay alive is the mother of invention and inspires us with the strength to endure.

Ignore my situation for the moment: have you not often heard talk of how this or that person lost his way in some empty quarter of the earth, and how nature conspired to test his ability to withstand heat and cold? He fought against all the odds and came back exhausted when no one expected him, and when he was asked incredulously how he managed it, the most he could answer was that he stiffened his resolve because he owed a woman he once loved an apology for a small betrayal or because it greatly worried him that a flower on the balcony of his apartment would have no one to water it. So much for the one who came home. As for the one who failed to return—trust me, nature is not to blame. His fault was that he had no woman he cared for and no flowerpot on his balcony. The instinct to survive, my lady, is something of this kind, not life itself.

When I first came here, I still felt full of what I, and we together, had been through. The way I retained that feeling was to take more interest in what was happening 'outside' than I had ever taken before. So I did not leave untouched any of the newspapers that arrived and I did not miss any of the news broadcasts on radio or television. Everything was fine: I was up to date. Then one day, my minder, the 'political security' officer assigned to me, dropped in on the pretext of visiting me and making sure that I, and "everything" (*everything?*) was as it should be. We discussed the situation in all its aspects and debated the possibilities. He examined my needs and

I asked him insincerely to send my warm regards to some of his superiors. He let his colleagues know that he was about to leave, and then shuddered theatrically as he remembered that he had something to pass on to me. Out of his briefcase he pulled a sealed brown envelope addressed to me. He took his leave once more and went on his way, with a promise that he would not be away for long, and emphasizing that I should not hesitate to contact him "for any purpose necessary."

Although I had not received any mail since I arrived here, I was in no hurry to open the envelope and find out the contents. As usual at that time of day, I caught up on the national news on television, made myself a cup of tea, and sat at the desk to leaf through some of the magazines my minder had brought me. The envelope, the last thing he had taken out of his briefcase, was resting on top of them. I picked it up and opened it carelessly to find inside it another envelope, small and also addressed to me. As soon as I saw the handwriting, my mood changed completely, from indifference to something more like a frenzy than anything else. I need not describe how gently, cautiously, slowly, and tensely I treated the rectangular white envelope, which I knew contained one of those same cards printed with your name, or how deeply I was breathing before I plucked up the courage to read the few words written on it.

As usual it was a brief message written in the third person: "Stupidity left her no choice but to take matters in hand and pack her bags. She has done so. You should do the same. Until we meet."

I do not know which of the two emotions came first: relief that you were now somewhere safe from the daily risks of death that show how precarious this country is for its people, or disappointment. But I must record that the second emotion dominated my thinking and over-whelmed me. Whereas my feeling of relief was a foregone conclusion, my feeling of disappointment was unjustified in the first place, especially as, with you where you were and I where I was, neither of us could reach out a hand to the other, let alone help each other. At the time, such sound logic was as remote from my thinking as east from west, so do not be surprised that I exaggerate and describe that feeling for a moment as "disappointment," because, in spite of being a man of religion, surely I am first and last nothing but a man in love with a woman, a man who suffers when she leaves him, even under compulsion, for another life and perhaps another man.

If I was a womanizer and you were part of my harem I would have made do with regret and brushed it off with a fond farewell, but don't forget that you are my only woman and the center of all the hopes to which I have never dared assign names. As I followed the daily news reports, which included from time to time denials from here and there of the numbers of people reported to be leaving the country, how could it not occur to me that you might be among them? In fact, how could it not occur to me that the accidents of life might have paved the way for you to meet another man, a man you liked and who liked you?

Without warning signs, or at least without me noticing them, these thoughts and questions assailed me, not in orderly sequence as I have presented them, but like a vision that terrifies and appalls. After I received the letter in which you told me you had moved, until the day I resolved to write down these notes, nothing took place, and everything took place. Nothing happened, in the sense that, as well as being cut off from the rest of the world, I was cut off from the news, which I used to follow by reading the newspapers and listening to the news broadcasts. I thought that by avoiding these I could concentrate on my worries, but I did not know that I had also lost track of time and I did not appreciate how dangerously isolated I was until I tried to reconnect with time. Everything happened in the sense that, over these weeks, most of which I spent doing nothing obvious, and sometimes pretending to be ill—my favorite trick to deter the curiosity of those around me—I turned full circle several times and went over my life from start to finish several times, forward and backward, lengthways and crossways, as a whole and in detail. Whatever direction I approached it from and however I interpreted it, my life looked to me like a big mistake. Whether it was an irrevocable mistake or a mistake that could be set right was a question I did not manage to determine, hence my constant wavering between hope and despair, between resolve and defeatism.

Sometimes I would rise from the dead, have some of the food and drink available in this place, prepare myself a cup of tea, read the newspapers, and listen to the news broadcasts, trying to catch up on 'developments' and 'events' I had missed, such as how many car bombs had exploded and where, and how many people had been killed, how many bombs had been defused before they went off, and other such mundane matters. Sometimes I would collapse and find myself in bed, taking refuge in that line of al-Mutanabbi: "With what should I console myself, being without my people and home, having neither companion, nor cup, nor any to comfort me," telling myself it was hopeless, that my endeavors were in vain, and that it was impossible that one bright morning a miracle would take me out of here, given that in the best of circumstances my life, apart from the fact that you had left it, was just a carbon copy of things I had already gone through. I know the effect your letter had on me might appear excessive to anyone, including you, or as a kind of intrusion of the unknown into human affairs. But there is no unknown, no intrusion, or anything at all. I go back to the instinct story. Isn't blindness one of instinct's characteristics? Only on that day did I see why, because I realized that blindness is instinct's greatest virtue and that when it comes into play, it takes one's hand, slows one down, and diverts one from one's plan. And when it comes into play, it ponders, adds, subtracts, makes calculations, sets its mind to work, and presents its considered advice to one's braver self. Such advice, as you know, will rarely bring the lost traveler back to water the flowers on the balcony! As soon as your brief message awakened my survival instinct, I realized that this relationship of ours, even if documented by the day and hour in the records of those idiots, will be lost to the world unless there is something to testify to it, on my part or on yours. All we can evoke to bear witness to it, all you or I can carry around with us in our separate comings and goings, is memories destined for oblivion unless they are written down.

If the walls of your house could speak and tell stories about us, they would say they heard us reading and discussing poems, and debating the affairs of the country and mankind, and sometimes the affairs of my mosque. But about us, about what we shared, I swear that the walls, even your bedroom walls, would have nothing to tell. We were talkative, but our story was silent. I do not rule out, I think, the possibility that we confided in each other and flirted, but I do not believe, or hardly, that, when every-thing was coming to a head, either of us would have warned the other that the morrow might bring something unexpected. And if I can excuse you that on the grounds that your knowledge of what was happening did not go beyond what was available in the newspapers and other media, how can I excuse myself when I could see the danger with my own eyes, closing in on me little by little, surrounding me and cutting off my options one after another? How can I forgive myself for failing to tell you, even by hints, that the morrow might be, or probably would be, another day? What harm would it have done if I had shared my fears with you and told you that I faced only two options: to press on in the certain knowledge that the death sentence against me, which was soon confirmed by a legal fatwa, was irreversible, or to entrust my safety to people I was not confident were eager to protect me, in the knowledge that by doing so I would wipe from my record all the 'courageous positions' I had taken over the last months of my 'professional life' and that later, in the eyes of friends and enemies equally, I would be held to account for choosing my safety and being happy to escape with my life!

What harm would it have done if I had shared all that with you and told you that, for the sake of our relationship and in the hope that we might resume it (I did not know how, where, or when), I was inclined toward the second option, not just in order to stay alive at whatever cost, and that I wanted you to be my partner in it and to wait for me. But could I have done that? Did I not always seek in you what I did not seek in myself, and always find it? So why should it come as a surprise that, instead of accusing myself of negligence, I accuse you of letting me down, or rather, of letting yourself down?

I do not know how this devilish idea occurred to me while I was in this abyss; the idea of taking revenge on your behalf on myself, on my inability to express myself, through writing these diaries as a testimony and perhaps as a bequest. That was how it started, no more and no less, without a clearly defined plan but just haphazardly. But it gradually dawned on me that 'writing,' even if it was just keeping a diary, did not mean imposing myself as an intermediary between, on the one hand, things I knew and events I had witnessed, and, on the other hand, the 'written text,' but rather to push this dumb animal that I am, by force and despite myself, up the rungs of articulate expression. There's no need to mention or point out that this animal was rebellious and headstrong and that taming and training it was a form of masochism, or that, whether I like it or not, for me, speaking was an acquired habit rather than part of my basic nature, and so words sometimes let me down, just as a stammer plagues a stammerer, sometimes for a reason and some-times for no obvious reason at all. Have I really trained my animal to be articulate, or have I trained him only in one form of expression: that is, 'writing'? That too is something I cannot say with certainty. In fact, I doubt I dare listen to myself saying aloud, even in a whisper, the words my pen writes in ink on paper.

There's something else I have not been sure about since recording these diaries and notes became my main preoccupation: is it the story of my life that makes writing enjoyable? Or is it the writing itself, and the authority it gives me over my life and the story of it, that seduces me and makes me want to keep writing?

On top of that, in my experience, to write is to live at a certain pace, however slow that may be or appear to be, compared with the time that flows there—beyond the walls of this resort. In fact, it is probably slow compared to any time by which it is measured. But leave aside this comparison, which does not take us anywhere, and start instead to think about the horror that gripped me before I discovered 'writing.' Day after day I saw myself wasting away. Is it not wasting away when the days form an uninterrupted sequence with the nights and you spend them, sometimes awake and sometimes asleep on your narrow bed, holding your breath, wary of making any movement, like someone besieged by pursuers, when your only hope of escaping from their clutches is to pretend you do not exist? I was seeking resurrection from this death. But whenever I came back from the dead, the most I could achieve was to beat my next death to evidence that proved that my life was not in fact total death.

When I first started writing these diaries I did not want to record the events of the day on which I was writing. On days when I was too weak to pull myself together and write, I contrived a device that I thought might deter me from succumbing to death: I started to write down the name of the day and the date, and even on days when I did not write anything else, I wrote down those two entries and left a certain number of blank lines beneath them.

At first, when these empty spaces still took up only a few pages of my thick notebook, it irritated me to see them, but not so much as to make me angry with myself. Fortunately, my irritation—suppressed, of course— did not lead me to abandon this practice I had adopted. Perhaps to the contrary: the little that I did write and the large amount I wanted to write deterred me from cheating and from trying to deceive myself. If I had been angry about my complete inability to express myself in writing, I would have had no desire to tackle these blank spaces. But in fact, not writing gradually provided a useful pang of conscience and reproach.

This 'death disease,' however, even when writing cured me of it, as I claim, did leave traces to remind me of it and by which I could chronicle it. Patience, my lady, take it easy, and give me some credence, too. Let me take advantage of the remaining trace of that disease to admit to myself and to you that, however much I have praised 'writing' and however much I yearn to write, it often happens that I do not 'write,' but rather I write for you. What a difference there is between the two forms of writing! Writing for you is to find myself far from you, even as a refugee who is anxious and in danger. Is all this distance necessary for a piece of writing to take shape? It seems so. Or it seems that what I have to tell you becomes clearer the less we are close enough to speak face to face. I wish you knew how many times, when we were together with your al-Mutanabbi or when we were alone in each other's embraces, I was alarmed when it occurred to me that you were able to reveal your inner self to me, and I contrived to obstruct the kind of communication essential for any true communion. I say "I," but "I" is not me, the shy man, confused by nature and by nurture, the man you once upon a time chose in preference to your other male acquaintances, to whom you gave refuge and took as a friend and confidant, with whom you were unstintingly patient, not the man you encouraged, by choosing him, to leave the void in which he lived and head for the wide-open spaces. And, my lady, those vestiges of what I was before I met you, and sometimes before I was born, those vestiges that kept aloof from us and stood between us as we grew closer, even now, after and in spite of everything that has happened, awake from their slumber and stand in my way. Would you like me to speak yet more harshly of myself, and say, for example, that the animal that speaks is your part of me, and the dumb animal is my part? Do you now know what I meant when I spoke earlier about the pace at which I want to live, however slow that is here compared to the pace of life there and in other situations—those I have known from personal experience and those I have discovered by guesswork? I hope so, so forgive me for refraining from trying to write to you at conversational speed and let me write to you at the speed of writing: that is, slowly.

Whatever grand contribution I can make is for your sake. Every word, every sentence I manage to wrench from inside me and deposit on these pages is a part of that contribution, not least because, for me, writing to you is something irreversible. I cannot go back from where it leads me, and because of that I have a right, my only remaining right, to be uneasy and hesitant about moving forward.

It should not surprise you that I attach so much importance to writing to you, as much importance as to life itself. Don't let it alarm you. Just remember what we shared, how our relationship evolved, and how it took root, and you will see, clear as daylight, what convergence and harmony there was between writing and life. It did not matter that it was my personality—a confused sheikh in premature old age—that made it hard to communicate. Besides, what happened between us was inevitable and irreversible, and today I can write that.

I list my memories: from the time I entered your house for the first time, a visitor on his guard against every eventuality, anxious not to misbehave, until the time when your cozy bed became our bed and we each had our own sides and our own bedside tables on which to put our books and other things. I will never forget that night when I opened the door of your house with the key you had given me and, anxious not to awake you, quietly closed the door, took off my shoes, and tiptoed to our bedroom. When I took my place on my side of our bed, you stirred and asked: "Have you been back long?"

I list my memories: from the time I entered your house for the first time as a visitor to when I left it for the last time, the eve of my transfer to this cell on death row, by which time your house had become a place to go back to, rather than a place to visit. When I look back, I see the phases of our life together mirrored precisely in the process of writing now. Remember our first trip in your car from your place to the mosque: not that day itself, but my account of the events of that night. After I wrote, I was dead for I know not how long, then I came back to life and took responsibility for myself again. I admitted frankly that I was telling the story to myself but writing for you, and I wrote all the other things I hope my incoherence will not deter you from reading. All of that is in the past, and I am still there, next to the iron door with the rusty lock, waiting for you to drive off and take me back under cover of darkness to the other door, the only one that leads to my place, that house of cobwebs nestled in the house of God.

14

I divide in two my meager salary, which hardly covers the costs of living in my country, let alone in yours, and which reaches me for some reason in the middle of each month (not the Islamic month, of course) through an account in a non-Islamic bank. I subsist on one half and transfer the other half to my home village to help pay for medical treatment for my father, who suffers from a chronic disease.

Some months ago, my brother wrote me a brief letter saying that the transfer had arrived safely, and that my father's health was constantly deteriorating.

My brother never elaborated on this deterioration or on what efforts the doctors were making to prevent it, but from the recurrence of the same phrase, in letter after letter, I could only conclude that the worst was about to happen and that the mailman would soon enough bring me a telegram, drafted after consultation with experts on the etiquette of death, saying something like: "Father's condition very troubling. Please come as quickly as possible."

Sure enough, before long, on a morning indistinguishable from any other, the mailman came to bring me the bad news.

As I had expected, the telegram did not say explicitly that my father had died and the end was over, but the phrase "as quickly as possible" was enough for me to be sure of it.

At first the news seemed more sudden than saddening, and "as quickly as possible" was not so easy to achieve, especially for someone like me who prefers to stay in one place and has never traveled except from necessity. I had to buy a plane ticket, arrange to postpone the lecture I was planning to give, contact you and tell you I would be away for about a week, have a meeting with my colleagues in the mosque, and so on. Generally, as they had on previous occasions, matters went smoothly and with a simplicity out of all proportion to my initial panic. On the very same evening, I found myself boarding the plane and heading back, for the first time in two years, to a village I had left by chance, just as I was born there by chance.

Throughout the day, my father's death was a piece of news on which I had to act, and I almost completely overlooked the solemnity of the occasion. At least one reason for the solemnity, given that my father was too modest a man to be remembered with either honor or contempt, was that death is a singular event, which strikes a man only once.

As the plane flew through the darkness, the first time I had been alone since the morning, I started to sense the smell of death that emanated from the phrase "father's death"—a phrase I had conjugated in various forms dozens of times that day. After a while, the plane landed and my relatives took me off. As soon as I arrived, they started competing to narrate the events of the last hours in tedious detail, down to every minute and second. That was inevitable, but it did not occur to any of them that for me my father had died right then, not when he breathed his last breath, nor when I received the telegram. Already, in that tube flying at an altitude of several thousand feet, I realized by myself that, once again, without great effort but as if for the first time, that death, every death, is a kind of murder,* and I recall those two verses of al-Maarri,† the bravest verses with which mankind ever addressed God on the question of death, so brave that they called him "an imbecile lunatic." The only revenge and consolation I can

---

* "If you contemplated time and its passing, you would be certain that death is a kind of murder." (al-Mutanabbi)
† "You have forbidden deliberate murder and You have sent two angels to do just that. / You have claimed that we have a second coming, but a human could well do without two lives."

find is to go even further and see death not just as any kind of murder at the hands of two angels sent by God, but as quite the most atrocious form of murder. Is there anything more atrocious than a murder where the victim is tortured beforehand and paraded in public after the event? Or else how can I explain my complete inability to summon up a comprehensive image of my father? And how can I explain the fact that when I rummage in the various regions of my memory, all I come back with is some fragments—fragments of a man who was my father?

I do not know where people in situations such as death draw the necessary physical strength, tenacity, and patience to endure. But luckily they do, and when the need calls, the body is good at managing its own affairs without demanding any attention. The need called that night!

Forget, my lady, the sad occasion for which I had come; forget that it was a dark night and that we—my three brothers, two other relatives, and I—could hardly fit in the small car that took us to the village and that panted with difficulty along roads that became rougher and rougher as we approached our destination. Forget too that, bad-tempered but anxious not to commit some gaffe, I was trying to concentrate and form an approximate idea of the scene that awaited me, a scene in which I was meant to play a prime part, despite having been away for years. Forget all that and just remember that it was the first time I had ever traveled so far so fast at one time, even if it was a journey back to a place for which the powers that be wanted me to harbor feelings of nostalgia. Would you believe that moving to your country was easier for me than this journey home? Moving to your country took place in stages, geographically and chronologically. The journey from my village to the suburbs of your city took about thirty-five years, and I had stopped along the way in several towns and villages, whereas the least that can be said of my return, though short and temporary, is that it did not observe the most basic safety regulations. Who brings a diver out of deep water to the surface all at once? My only consolation from this ordeal was that, as I promised myself, it was the last time I would ever go back. After my mother, who had died shortly before my first departure, my father had now passed away, and with his passing the last bond that tied me to this world was severed.

In our first meeting after I came back, in the course of your inquiries about the details of my trip home (and it was the first time we had touched on family matters), you were surprised to realize how weak the bonds of kinship were between me and my brothers and sisters, that we wrote to each other only on special occasions and that I had to guess how many children each of them had and so on. Of course I could have retained closer links with my family; I could have lived close to the village, if not right in it; and I could have remained attached to them even from a distance. But the last possibility was no less probable. Perhaps one of the keys to my life is that, from the first—that is, ever since I left the village, moved to the city, and went to college—I preferred to keep my distance and part ways amicably. I felt that my minimal obligation was to wish only the best for them. But to do so from afar was one thing, and sitting with them, for example, listening to what they had to say, and sharing their interests was something else I never succeeded in forcing myself to do, despite my repeated attempts. In the end (or rather, at the start!), was that because I was the weakest of them physically and so I always seemed like an intruder when they and their peers were playing rough games? For the same reason I was exempted from farm work, which was our livelihood, and so I was chosen to follow what was perhaps the only career suitable for someone to whom 'normal paths in life' were closed. Maybe, out of all my brothers, I was the one best placed to pray to God to shower mercies on my father, because he had bequeathed to them land which required great toil and trouble to extract a living from, whereas he had entrusted me, either intuitively or for lack of an alternative, to the care of God and the guardians of Islam. In fact, if you asked me today whether I was content with what my father chose for me or whether I would have preferred him to leave me dependent on my brothers, I would not hesitate to reply that I was content and more. Otherwise, how would I have met you?

As we slowly approached our destination, after talking about other things along the way, the conversation went back to the occasion that had brought us together. My elder brother told me that in the afternoon, the body had been moved from the mortuary at the provincial hospital to the house, where it had been washed and shrouded, and that the burial would take place on the next day after noon prayers, as well as other details about the burial site and how far it was from the graves of our mother and uncle.

Though death is the ultimate standstill, its rituals can be said to have gone smoothly or otherwise, as the case may be. Unfortunately for my father, the rituals of his burial did not go smoothly—far from it. In fact, what happened took everyone unawares: the burial became a family squabble in which appeals were made to Islamic law. The burial tradition in our village, and maybe elsewhere, is that after the body has been lowered into the grave and covered with a shroud, some soil is taken from under the head and kneaded with water until it turns into mud, and then put back where it came from: under the head of the dead person.

One does not require much learning to see that in this custom the living humans are imitating, in the presence of the dead, the first act of creation as represented in legends, and one may reasonably doubt that it has anything to do with the laws of Islam, as is the case with many other customs and traditions.

After we had said prayers for the dead and finished laying him in his grave—a task performed by one of my brothers—my father's only surviving brother, our uncle, insisted on the mud ritual, as custom required. But my brother, who was still in the grave, vehemently opposed the idea, advancing the irrefutable and sometimes deadly argument that this depraved custom was "an innovation," and that every innovation was heresy and that every heresy led to Hell, and so on. I knew that this brother of mine was inclined to be devout, but it was only on the edge of my father's grave, which remained open as it awaited a resolution of the argument, that I discovered that with the passage of time his naive piety had turned into "a commitment." I thought I could more easily win over my brother than I could my uncle, so I turned to him and tried to whisper to him something to the effect that all his shouting, which had prompted the uncle to respond in kind, was not appropriate to the occasion. He took no notice of what I tried to tell him, but took advantage of the fact that I was within reach of his muscular arms and pulled me forcefully toward him. If he had not caught me with equal strength, I would have lost my balance and fallen onto the body. Now there were three of us in the grave: my father, my brother, and me, each for his own reason, or someone else's reason. My concern was to ensure that my brother and my uncle made peace, the grave was filled in, and the funeral broke up peacefully, even if, after hearing the arguments they were shouting, I was certain that the peace would only last an hour or less. All that was missing for the trap to close on me was for my brother to take the initiative of consulting me, as I was sure he was about to do, on what Islamic law has to say on the question of the mud. It would be an embarrassing question, because Islamic law, of which I was the spokesman among the graves, supports my brother's view that the mud was an innovation. But for me—as the son of the dead man at the center of the dispute, the brother of one man and the nephew of the other man who would not believe that his brother's soul would rest in peace unless his head could rest on that damned lump of mud—for me mud or no mud was all the same. Despairing of convincing my brother, I tried to wriggle out of his arm in order to climb out of the grave and negotiate with the uncle, in the hope that I might succeed in convincing him, not that the mud was indeed an innovation, but that the squabble between him and my brother was disgraceful. Unfortunately someone, most probably with the best of intentions, preempted me by posing the very question I had anticipated from my brother's trembling lips.

It seemed to me that, with the exception of my brother, some of his 'committed' and pedantic colleagues, and my uncle and his few supporters, the assembly of mourners looking on was impatient to hear me arbitrate this religious family dispute, and the hardest aspect of arbitrating between the two sides was that the mourners were not of the kind that sermons would serve to placate. On the contrary, it was an unruly assembly impatient for a resolution. In fact, they were right to expect it, as was my father, who I imagine was in a hurry to have soil piled on top of him and be left alone to recover from the ordeal of his slow death.

As far as I was concerned, at least, the scandal had already taken place and there was no longer any hope of containing it, so I beckoned to my other two brothers and my uncle to approach me. When my uncle did not respond to my invitation, I made do with those who came, and spoke firmly to my brothers in this vein: "I am your brother and the son of this man here, our father, and I have a right to my opinion, just as you have a right to yours, but I refuse to take part in this farce, either in word or in deed." I jumped out of the grave with a single bound and left, to the astonishment of the mourners looking on.

That evening, I sat on the porch with its three steps leading down to the small garden in front of the house, steps which once marked the progress of my infant brothers and sisters, and then me, from the crawling stage to the walking stage. My least concern was the scraps of commentary that reached me from inside the house, where my brothers were chatting with the last of the funeral guests. I had no doubt that, the next day or the day after, I would be leaving this village, my birthplace, for the last time, and that I would never return, neither willingly on my own two feet nor carried in a hearse. And, like anyone leaving a place to which he harbors no hope of returning, even a place where he was brought by chance, I was busy enjoying it with all my five senses—or that's what I thought I was doing. While my five senses, or rather the three in operation at the time, tried to register all the sights, sounds, and smells they could pick up, my mind was drawing up plans for the coming hours and days, reflecting from time to time on what had happened in the last few hours, incredulous that "their version of Islam" had managed to penetrate as far as here and that making a distinction between tradition and innovations had become part of the puritanism of my brother, who could hardly read.

The next day, after the dawn prayer, which I would perform in the village mosque and at which I would be obliged to act as imam, I would visit my father's grave, indifferent to the objections of my brother, and then I would arrange for a car to take me in the afternoon to the main town, where there were buses heading for the capital. I would spend the spare hours in the company of the family, although I would prefer to spend them alone revisiting my childhood haunts, which I felt I had a greater obligation to say farewell to than to my family and relatives.

My determination to leave did not fail to surprise those who were expecting me to stay for at least a week, some of whom had embarked on an attempt to reconcile 'us' with the uncle, who, after what happened at the funeral, had withdrawn from 'our' assembly and was receiving condolences from the same mourners in his own house, which was only a few dozen yards from the family home. I know that my behavior violated the simplest rules of propriety and was insulting to my father rather than to the living, but neither this nor the knowledge that news of my hasty departure would ignite gossip about the family restrained me or made me hesitate. Perhaps it is true, as the proverb goes, that someone who intends to move away often commits outrages.

⟋

Homesick for you and for my life in your country, I hurried to the capital to meet the sheikh to whom I was indebted for recommending me for the post of imam at the mosque of the Two Omars; in other words, to whom I was indebted in a sense for my meeting you. When I asked to meet him it was not just to say hello, ask how he was, and chat casually about a situation of which he no doubt had more detailed and intimate knowledge than I did. I wanted to consult him as a father figure and as my benefactor about a proposal, which a reliable messenger had conveyed to me a few days earlier—an invitation to present a religious program on a television channel that was being set up.

～

When he chose to let down his mask of dignity, this sheikh in his sixties was the most cunning and skillful person I have ever known at mixing the serious with the frivolous. True to form, he turned up in a way I had not expected, in every sense of the word. After about a quarter of an hour waiting in a small hallway next to his office for someone to show up and take me in to see him, I was surprised to find a side door opening and the sheikh coming through, accompanied by someone I later discovered was his office manager.

I doubt he knew that my father's death was my motive for visiting the country and for then visiting him, and even when, while apologizing for insisting on asking for an early appointment, I told him that it was the death that had brought me back to the country, he merely said a quick prayer for my father's soul and took command of the conversation, as though it was not really around two years or more since we last met. He was going deep into details when he realized he had not introduced me to his colleague, who was sitting on his left. He broke off the conversation for this purpose and to apologize for receiving me in this hallway rather than in his office, where he said a meeting was under way. I understood from his hand gesture and the way he shook his head that it was a tedious and pointless meeting. Then, as if nothing had happened and as though he had listened to me at length, he went back to the previous subject in a confident tone: "This war knows no borders. Wherever both we and they are present, it's a battleground. Where we are present and they are not, they're likely to bring the war there. Where they are present and we are not, we must hurry to take the war there to disperse their forces, if not to win the territory back. Even if you know no more of the details than I do, you no doubt live the conflict as a daily experience. Do you think they have given up hope of taking over your mosque? Beware of delusions . . . . In any case, this is not the most important thing. The war over mosques is a

127

spurious distraction. Tell me, have the people at the new television station contacted you to discuss the possibility of you taking part in producing a program or anything else?" He gave me no chance to answer, but continued with his stream of words. "I recommended you to them, and as soon as you get back I want you to give this your full attention. The airwaves are just as important to defend as keeping our mosques safe from their nefarious propaganda and cracking down hard on anyone who wreaks havoc with slogans that have as little to do with the authentic Islam of Muhammad as west with east."

At this point, he noticed for the second time that since the start of the meeting he had not let me slip in a single word. Stealing a glance at his watch and sending his colleague off to the meeting in his office to ask them to wait a few more minutes, he asked how I was, in the manner of someone who expected only a brief answer. I adjusted my posture in readiness to stand up and then told him that in his lengthy speech he had covered all the ground, because my purpose in meeting him, apart from courtesy, was to ask him about the question of appearing on the television station, especially (and I repeated the word 'especially' twice), especially as I was a civil servant and as this channel, which was private in principle, would broadcast from another country. I did not expect him to answer at length, but my comments wound him up again and he launched into a second speech no different from the first, except that now he emphasized that our mandate as men of religion gave no weight to geographical borders.

A light tapping on the side door and the appearance of the face of the young office manager brought an end to the sheikh's monologue. He hurriedly stood up, picked up the large turban he had taken off, and put it back on his bald pate. I did not waste his valuable time, but took my leave. As usual he urged me to "stay in touch" and to inform him of any change in my circumstances. He apologized for not having been in touch recently and justified that on the grounds that he could be sure the grapevine would do its job. He led me to the door despite my insistence that he do not do so, and on the way, half serious and half joking, he gave me an eloquent farewell. "This, my friend, is a nation that God's bounds have failed to tame, so think nothing of crossing the bounds if that's what it takes to set the nation right," he whispered.

15

By now I recognized myself as one of 'the sultan's clerics,' either in the full sense of the word or in the merely pejorative sense. Those who find fault with a man on the grounds that he is one of the sultan's clerics see the sultan only as a person, or at most an office, with formidable powers that can either harm or help them. It is for exactly that reason that I have never been offended or humiliated to be classified as such. It is not that I was confident my hands were clean, instead it was because the sultan in whose service I voluntarily applied my religious and legal learning was not a person or an office, but rather the institution that I thought best able to bring about development and serve the interests of the people. I was aware that this institution was not infallible, that corruption was rife in many of its nooks and crannies, and that many of those who held high office in it were murderous thieves, but when it came to choosing between this imperfect form of government, with all its flaws and defects, and the Islamic state that they hope to set up, with their promises to fill the world with justice and equity, my choice was firm and unwavering. In fact, it was not a choice, but rather recognition of a logical necessity amply illustrated by the evidence of history. To put it simply, there is no way to combine the state and Islam without compromising one of them or giving one precedence over the other. On the one hand, Islamization is portrayed as the revival of a golden age whenever the authorities urgently need the strength of Islam to save their political legitimacy from collapse, while on the other hand, whenever Islamic principles are compromised, a consensus to remain silent and secretive prevails, even when the process takes the form of a legal stratagem. If it comes to choosing between undermining the state and undermining Islam, my preference would be to undermine Islam, gently and slowly!

Was I an oddity among my colleagues? Of course not . . . but a sheikh who works for a 'modern state' that is Islamic only to the extent that Islam is the religion of its citizens and in some sense their culture (unalterable by parliamentary legislation or presidential decree), does have an obligation toward his paymaster, that is, the state: an obligation not to publicize the fact that he is loyal to it because it is 'modern' . . . .

In order to play the roles required of him, a sheikh who works for the government has to walk one step behind the modernizing state, even when he defends that state. This was much easier for me than for some of my colleagues, who sometimes went through loyalty crises similar to the crises of adolescence. They found that the only way out for them was through legal opinions that justify serving an unrighteous ruler as the lesser of two evils, or through historic precedents and the like. I say it was easier for me because, and I take no credit for this, I do not remember ever having had a loyalty crisis caused by the learning I have acquired. How? Why? I will spare you the theory I have mastered for public consumption on how to reconcile pleasing God and serving the sultan. It is a theory for which I have mustered a whole range of arguments and evidence, but I would not like to sell you goods that are counterfeit or, if not counterfeit, then at least second-hand. It may not seem convincing to anyone but me, but this stems from my tendency toward esotericism, which has become only more refined and polished as I advance in age and learning, and which I have become increasingly skillful at deploying as it suits me to interpret the world—my small world and its small people.

I am quite sure, my lady, that all of us are hostages to our birth. If one is born on a sound footing, even in misery and poverty, then one's life holds its own and runs its course, interspersed only by the same joys, sorrows, and long periods of boredom as any other life. But if one's life does not start on a sound footing, then there's no hope of setting it right, however much one might want to and however hard one tries.

I, for example, should have been born physically strong and even-tempered, and gone casually through basic schooling, like most of my peers. The school would then have handed me over to life, and when I was hardly eighteen years old, the mothers would have chosen the right wife for me and that would be the signal for the fathers to admit me to their club, and so on.

As you know from what I have written, it did not go that way for me. Instead of tilling the fields in the open air, I found myself moving from one damp and fetid hall to another, plowing through books with footnotes. I was not physically strong enough to keep up with my brothers in their rough games, but my physical weakness did not stand between me and nature as a whole and in its diverse components. It did not stop me seeing God in nature—more by naively overhearing what the adults were saying than by looking or thinking. It was a God who, when He damaged our crops or our livestock, never did anything more drastic than warn or chide us. While we managed to stay on good terms with God, even in the most straitened and critical of times, one had to recognize that at other times He was, as my father put it, more bounteous toward us than we merited or deserved.

Of course I understood none of the principles of this commerce between man and God, nor of the accounting rules it followed, and I was no less ignorant of other adult matters in which we children were not allowed to intervene. When my father started to take me along to the mosque with him and teach me how to perform my ablutions and my prayers, things began to change somewhat for me, and God changed too. In fact, much changed. For a start, I could not understand why God would adopt as His house this small and dilapidated building (my father, his uncles, and others had lengthy discussions about repairing it), when the whole world in all its vastness belonged to Him. I could see no reason for all the precautions required for prayer, I confused ritual obligations and customary practices, and I did not know who this Abraham was, for whom and for whose family we asked God to pray whenever we performed our prayers. Perhaps, I would tell myself, he's a friend of the Prophet Muhammad, or perhaps he and his family had some part in the Prophet Muhammad's victory over his enemies. One word comes to me now to describe my inability to combine in a single deity the god of rain, birds, and colored pebbles on one hand and the god of the small dilapidated building on the other. It is a very big word and I scarcely dare to trace the letters of it, but I must . . .

Before the word 'kufr'* came into my vocabulary—though I already knew the word by heart from memorizing most verses of the Quran as the only way to please my father, and by extension my mother, I found myself uncertain, not about myself, but about God, who seemed to be deliberately picking on me and putting me down, as my brothers and their friends did whenever my mother persuaded them to let me join their games.

With my brothers and their friends, my mother was the definitive arbiter. When they excluded me I would complain to her, and I would have recourse to her when, in revenge for having to submit to her ruling that they should let me play, they were crueler toward me than toward each other. But with God I had no arbiter to turn to and complain. I was happy and felt superior to my brothers when my father took me to the mosque and boasted how many verses of the Quran I had memorized, but the price was to stand before a god who frowned, glowered, and was cantankerous, and to offer Him gestures and phrases that, needless to say, someone who has practiced for twenty or thirty years can perform more proficiently than someone who has only spent morning, noon, and afternoon in the faith. Luckily, my vocabulary was limited at that time and my confusion between the environmental activist god who was the lord of the heavens and of earth, and the god who lived in the mosque that could only be repaired by agreement between my father, my uncles, and other regulars, was an impotent confusion for which I did not have a name.

But all this was not worth mentioning compared with the ordeal in my first year at college. In this year, which counts as preparatory, the student is introduced to all the subjects he will study more fully year after year, including the study of monotheism, where the student's long voyage starts with the imam Bajouri's commentary on the *Precious Jewel of Divine Oneness*, and I doubt you can imagine what it means for a young man who still has pimples and hardly has a mustache to pore over Bajouri's work and try to understand and memorize it.

---

* Translator's note: kufr—the condition of being a kafir, an unbeliever or infidel; ingratitude for or denial of God's manifest blessings, and by extension heresy.

At college, I was given notice that the intuitive faith of my childhood, which I learned in the book of nature with its four seasons rather than in library books, lay somewhere between pantheism and monism, both of which were forms of heresy. At college, I realized that the god to whom I complained about my brothers, the god I begged to stop my nosebleed so that my peers would not take pleasure in my discomfort, the god I implored not to snatch away my mother as He had done to my best friend's mother, and the god whose gardens I had profaned without hearing a word of rebuke from him, this naive god of my childhood and my adolescence, had nothing to do with the severe and impenetrable God Bajouri describes. I also found out that God was not synonymous with the religion of which I was training to be a guardian and custodian, because "the true faith, which no one may contradict, is to follow the Book of God Almighty, the practice of His Prophet, May God Pray for Him and Grant Him Peace, and the consensus of the nation of Islam. These alone are the three sources of infallible faith, and they admit no imperfection."

At college, it became clear to me that belief in God in itself was not enough to make one a Muslim. As the imam Ibn Hazm said: "If we were to be left alone with the Quran, it would just be a collection of sentences and we would not know how to act on it," and, if only for this reason, having the illusion of acting on the Quran and its precepts was in its turn hardly enough to make one a Muslim. Given all this, it cost me much effort to get used to the idea propounded on the radio that "the practice of the Prophet was infallible in that God had made the Prophet himself infallible, because the Prophet, May God Pray for Him and Grant Him Peace, elucidated and illustrated the Quran with His words, His deeds and His judgment" and that "the Noble Prophet received the Quran and other revelations which make up his practice, which, just like the Quran, contains rulings on what is right and wrong, what is obligatory, what is to be encouraged and what is forbidden."

An inadequate summary would be to say that when I went to college I found that I was making progress, not as a student of religious law, but in embracing a religion I had imagined to be innate and learning a language I had thought was already part of me. It goes without saying, and there is no point in dwelling on the details, that this process was not a calm progression, but rather a series of leaps into the void. More importantly, this did not prevent or discourage me from acquiring learning. In fact, I can almost say that it strengthened my resolve and gave me reasons to persevere that had never occurred to me, especially as God, my God, had endowed me, as my teachers attested, with a quick mind, sound sense, a strong memory, and a diligent approach to studying and intellectual activity. I do not think that staying up late at night was an extension of these intellectual gifts, but was more probably a sign of morbid insomnia, except that I made good use of it to make rapid progress along the path that had been set for me and that I was destined to follow. So I followed it and, unlike most of my colleagues, whose handicap was clear and plain (one of our teachers summed it up as "too little understanding and too much religion"), my handicap was so secret that I could not reveal it to anyone, however much we might be friends or however much I knew they could keep a secret.

At first I did not care, or you could say that my inner life—the fact that I excelled in learning and performed the various religious rites, but remained detached from the implications of both—was a form of revenge for a childhood to which I had not given its due. "Isn't everyone with a handicap a giant?" I would tell myself, citing the proverb. If that is true, and since the proverb applies to all, then I, as someone with a handicap, had to demonstrate my strength. At the time—and I realized this only later—I was still a child at play, at play in serious matters, and at play when playing.

As you have come to know, I did not emerge after graduation as a cleric of the sultan but as a civil servant with a regular salary and a rank in a hierarchy that made no distinction between a civil servant in the Ministry of Public Works and one in the Ministry of Religious Endowments and Religious Affairs. My graduation, even magna cum laude, heralded the end of playtime, not to be succeeded by a time of pure and undiluted seriousness, but the start of a long journey that usually ended only when one reached retirement age, at which point village people like me would go back to their villages, leaving the overcrowded cities to their children.

Even my inner life, which had given me space to breathe in my college days, became more restricted for at least two reasons: firstly, the lack of competition, which had previously driven me to excel over my peers, who would hide their scanty understanding with an exaggerated display of piety, and secondly, because hypocrisy was the only type of behavior likely to overcome obstacles, obtain extended holidays, and speed up promotion.

It goes without saying that my doctrinal hypocrisy, the type to which the religious books give precedence (it had its roots in my melancholy and my uncertainty, which education only made deeper), had nothing in common with the miserly sycophancy of my colleagues. But graduating and starting a job did have at least one good aspect, in that for the first time in my life it opened a prospect, if only by a fraction, for me to move my life off the path that had been set for it for close to a quarter of a century. I did not have many options to confuse me, but just two choices—to make do with my lot or to seek a career that would take me out of the Ministry of Religious Endowments while keeping me in employment. Here again, I did not have a wide range of options, because teaching was the profession best suited to my qualifications. So I decided to obtain a degree in the Arabic language and Arabic literature. In the meantime, fate decreed that in the corridors of the ministry I should meet my sheikh himself, the professor of the principles of Islamic jurisprudence in my college days, whose name was often mentioned in connection with the 'reform' the country was going through and who had since been influential in our ministry without holding any formal position. In his blunt, jocular, and simultaneously self-important manner, he said, "Where have you been, my man? I've been looking high and low for you in this bordello," and without asking me where I was heading or taking any interest in my official duties, he took me by the arm and led me almost like my escort toward the only elevator, which led to the fifth floor, a place out of bounds to all but the lucky few because it contained the offices of the minister, the permanent secretary, and other senior officials and advisers.

When in a position of strength, the sheikh was not good at compliments and did not mince his words: "Do you think I'm joking when I say I looked for you high and low in this bordello . . . (no one else I know would dare to use such a word to describe the ministry) . . . I want to have you at my disposal . . . I have no official status here and no job title. You can stay where you are, but as an attaché in my office . . . I mean my personal attaché."

I have no idea what else he might have said, but he was cut off by the call to the noon prayer. On the lower floors of the ministry, the call to prayer was broadcast through central loudspeakers, but on the fifth floor, every office had its own sound system with a volume control that could be set on silent. Before the anonymous muezzin had finished his first "Allahu akbar," my sheikh had shut him off, casually muttering the creed and leaning his vast frame slightly forward over the desk he was sitting at. These two movements he did without standing up fully in honor of the mention of God. The short hiatus imposed by the call to prayer inspired him to try to decide my fate without consulting me. In a tone more of courtesy than of genuine curiosity, he asked me what plans and projects I was undertaking, confident perhaps that someone who had just started a new job would answer such a question only by saying he was preparing to get married or to buy an apartment with a mortgage. When I told him I was planning to study Arabic literature, he quickly reacted to the small surprise by praising me, asserting that what I was planning did not surprise him and that with his knowledge of me and my ambitions he understood my feeling of frustration and my desire to study. "Although," he said, "I don't see the teaching profession as a remedy for the discontent you're complaining of right now." He said no more, and shifting from one subject to another as was his style, a style no one I know could match, he suddenly looked up and started to rummage through the papers and files that cluttered his desk, until he stumbled upon what he was looking for, offered me an elegant brochure, then slumped back in his chair. "This conference on human rights in the Quran is taking place in about a month . . . In a month, isn't it? . . . As you can appreciate, I don't have the time to prepare the paper that we're supposed to present . . . You know best what needs to be said, all the important things and all the details . . . Wasn't it you who once prepared a paper on the subject?" It definitely was not me who prepared a paper on the subject, which had never interested me in the least, but I did not think it wise to disappoint the sheikh, so I made no comment. Instead, I left him to continue his monologue, which was more like obscure verses of poetry than meaningful sentences. He then pulled out from one of the dark recesses of his gown a scrap of paper that was dog-eared from the number of times he had folded it up and then opened it out again. He offered it to me, saying that on it he had jotted down some ideas that I could draw upon and expand.

From that day on, I became one of the ghost writers whose pens stood ready to serve the sheikh, who loved to have a platform or, failing that, any patch of rough ground which would substitute for a platform. From my new assignment I derived no material benefit to mention, or not to mention, and contrary to what one might rush to assume, it did not make me into an agent, secret or public, for one of those 'agencies' thought to have a finger in every pie. Except for the growing and renewed sense of competition between me and the other ghost writers, whose names and faces I did not know, nothing at all had changed in my life as a civil servant. Since this assignment of mine did not require me to take any positions in public (on the contrary it required complete discretion), and since, in the eyes of my colleagues, I was the archetypical naive dreamer who had gained nothing from his superior understanding and learning, since I still had the same rank, the same salary, and the same status as them, they saw nothing remarkable in the fact that I sometimes made my way to the fifth floor, other than that one of the people ensconced upstairs had discovered my talents and, encouraged by my reputation for naivety, was exploiting both me and my talents.

Fortunately, their speculation about the reason why I frequented the fifth floor was mistaken on only one point: I was being exploited with my own consent and choice, voluntarily. I was building up credit for a future day, such as when I decided to embark on a teaching career, through the small services I performed for the sheikh, and I thought I should count myself lucky that I was the one competent to perform them. Of course, the sheikh was not unaware of this and he was not naive: he did once, and only once, offer me financial compensation for my efforts, while on other occasions he merely said he would be willing to help me out financially if necessary, and I am quite confident that he was sincere in that. I do not think it would be arrogant of me to assert that he was not unaware either that I was a cut above my peers and that I was striving to excel in performing all the tasks he assigned me. As for the trust that arose between us, or rather between him and me, since it was he who took the initiative in conferring his trust on me, this was a riddle that to this day I have never succeeded in solving. Perhaps there was nothing puzzling about it at all, and I might just be exaggerating when I insist on describing his ready recourse to me as 'trust.' Perhaps, but until proven otherwise, I like to imagine the following: the sheikh, talkative to the point of being garrulous, and of awesome aspect in his stylish white turban, had come to this profession by accident, like me, and, having excelled academically and being ambitious for high office, he had no scruples about trying to scale the heights in his gown and turban, just as others descended on them through their high birth or by parachute. Perhaps the sheikh saw his inner self in me and read my silence, my shyness, my evasiveness, and the way I pretended to renounce the pleasures of this world as the desire of a handicapped child to act the wild giant.

I shall never forget one morning when the sheikh summoned me early, a few weeks after he seconded me to his service and commissioned me to prepare his lecture on human rights in the Quran. It would be an understatement to say I found him in a fury, storming and raving. Suffice it to say that he was biting his lip, and anyone who knows the sheikh does not need great understanding to realize what a state he was in if he was biting his lip. I was not offended that he did not return my greeting, for that was the least to be expected of him when he was in such a state. He passed me a newspaper opened on a particular page, and merely said: "I want you to prepare a response for publication tomorrow. These insults are not directed at me personally, but at those I represent and what I represent . . . Did they invite us to their conference only to insult us as soon as we turned our backs?" The article in question, published in the most important newspaper in the neighboring country where he had been invited to give the lecture, was a sarcastic comparison between the contents of the lecture and the 'reality' of human rights in our country. Miraculously, or perhaps inspired by the desire to show off what I was capable of, by the time the sunset prayer was called I had finished writing my response, which someone took from me page by page to type out a clean copy. The sheikh did not calm down until he had finished reading my devastating response, which took for its title the saying attributed to the caliph Othman, to the effect that "God deters wrongdoing through the sultan when he has not done it through the Quran." He regained his smile, recovered his sense of humor and fun. "I knew you were smart, but now I realize you have two hearts as well,"* he told me, and roared with laughter.

I cannot help wondering whether, like me, the sheikh was destined one day to meet a woman who would take him out of the darkness into the light, and whenever this idea occurs to me I cannot help envying him because I have no doubt he would be more eloquent than me and more open to talking about the things that men and women naturally do together. So is life merely a collection of encounters? I am almost certain

---

* *Never has God endowed any man with two hearts in one body.* (Quran 33:4). The ancient Arabs claimed that a clever man had two hearts inside him.

138

that it is, and that no life is exempt from the encounters that intersperse it. I hope that what I have said makes it clear that I was not indebted to anyone but myself when I was chosen to move to your country and take charge at the Mosque of the Expatriates. If I do owe a debt, it would be to the concatenation of chances and accidents, not to a particular person, even if these chances and accidents were the work of someone. It is the same when I talk about meeting you, even if that requires me to make some crazy assumptions—for example that Ahmad al-Mutanabbi was born, died, and was reborn through his poetry only to bring us together! Is there not a school of thought that claims that God set up the world inadvertently, and another that He created heaven and earth in play, and humankind as a whim? He is above what they say of Him, but when human beings have such beliefs about creation, do you think it implausible that we met, or that things conspired to have us meet?

16

On the evening of the sixth day after my father's death, I flew back from my trip home. I took my small bag aboard as hand baggage so that I would not need to wait with the others for it to arrive on the conveyor belt. At the sight of my special passport, the immigration officer with the rubber stamps, the gatekeeper of the paradise that is you, who was yawning and stretching, was forced to put on a show of dignity and composure, which I doubt he maintained when the waves of passengers started to crowd around his glass box. In the taxi from the airport to the mosque, after hours almost comatose on the plane and before that in the rush to board it, I realized that my break from my life in this time zone and its worries was over. Like someone who remembers an appointment at the last minute, I tried to sort out my schedule for the next day, but the task soon appeared more arduous than I had expected, and I reluctantly gave up, acknowledging that the only medicine that could reinvigorate me was a long, deep sleep. To cut short the rest of the journey to the mosque, I closed my eyes on nothingness and did not open them again until the repeated screeching of brakes warned me that we had started our descent into the heart of the city.

Faster than I expected, I resumed the rhythm of my life here. Perhaps it was because I was like anyone coming home, even from a short trip, insistently asking many questions as soon as he arrives about what has happened in his absence, but soon coming to his senses and admitting bitterly that there is rarely anything new under the sun. I made a bet with myself that I could put off contacting you for two days while I finished dealing with pending mosque matters. I held out for two hours, then hesitated for another hour, after which I could no longer restrain myself from making an appointment with you for seven o'clock. As the time approached, the first signs of apprehension began to recur, as if I were preparing to visit you for the first time. Although it is a glib expression, the type of expression that from random overuse has changed from reality to metaphor, when I say, "as if . . . for the first time," that is exactly what I mean, and the phrase 'as if' expresses with great accuracy my uncertainty about what the agenda for our meeting might include.

I was not surprised that you did not try to offer me your condolences in the conventional manner, or that you excused yourself on the grounds that you found death embarrassing as much as sad and difficult to speak about, or that you switched to asking about details of my trip and what I had seen there—the place from which danger threatened your country. I do not remember how I answered at the start of our meeting, but my answers were probably generalities that did not satisfy your curiosity. Fortunately, you had come to know what I was like, and knew that I needed time before I was ready to speak; besides, you were patient. Meanwhile, I was examining the changes you had made to the contents of the bookshelf closest to the table at which we used to sit. From the same low sofa, I noticed that something had changed in that corner, but I realized what it was only when you stood up and went into the kitchen. I stood up after you and went up to the table where we would sit when we started our sessions. There were two shelves, the upper one of which had held a collection of files (whenever I came you would dump on it all the papers and so on which had nothing to do with our session), while the lower one had housed the best-known dictionaries for the three languages you had mastered, as well as grammar books, the telephone directory, and some office supplies. In a single glance, I saw that for some reason you had devoted them to al-Mutanabbi; I mean, you had put together on them the various editions of the complete works of al-Mutanabbi, the many commentaries that had been dispersed around your library, as well as about twenty other books, which all had the name of your poet in their titles. Between two rows of books there was a pile of papers and I could see from the way they were piled up in the top right-hand corner that they were organized into groups and that each group was held together by a metal staple or something similar. I did not need to perform a divination to conclude that these papers must be articles about al-Mutanabbi, photo-copied from magazines, and when I moved closer I read at the top of the first piece of paper: "Mountains, places, and bodies of water in the poetry of al-Mutanabbi," followed by the name and title of the author and then the words: "Abul Tayyib Ahmad ibn al-Hussein al-Juafi al-Mutanabbi, who was born in Kufa in the year 303, was right when he asserted that: 'Destiny is but one of the many who recite my poems. If I speak a line of verse, destiny starts reciting it' . . . for his poetry continues to fascinate researchers today, more than ten centuries after his death, as much as it fascinated them during his life, and it will probably remain that way until God inherits the earth and everyone upon it . . . ."

From the start I thought the prominence you had given al-Mutanabbi on your bookshelves meant a new lease of life for the project that led you to seek me out and that brought us together so quickly. I deliberately stayed where I was, waiting for you to come back from the kitchen to notice by yourself that the changes you had made had caught my attention. We then moved on from talking about my trip, not because I did not want to go into details or go over what had happened, but because I did not want to do so just then. I had expected you to come back with two cups of tea, but instead there you were with two cups of some dark red juice. "Tomato juice is a better appetizer than tea, and I'm sure you haven't been watching what you eat for the last few days. No reading this evening, just a long din-ner," you said, and you were right on both counts.

For a week, the week after I received the telegram from my family, I had not enjoyed a single meal I had eaten, even by a broad interpretation of the word 'meal.' And reading, even as a way to brush the dust off the habits we had worked so hard to acquire, would not have been the best way to mark our reunion. Neither of us said openly that what we really wanted was to sit down together and listen to each other as though we were close friends. But what we wanted had the last word. Of course, I did not hesitate to ask you why you had put together within easy reach all these books related to al-Mutanabbi. You answered in stages: at first, as though you were reading my thoughts, you merely said your motive for doing so had nothing to do with 'the project.' Since I felt you were in the mood to share your thoughts, I left you to complain about how you found your work disheartening and tedious. You then recounted some of the incidents of the past week, which were indeed disheartening and tedious, and which, as you said, "make one wonder what is the point of staying in this miserly country, which is so ungenerous and unimaginative."

In fact, I paid no attention to this remark of yours at the time, and I do not think it even gave me pause, because complaining in this country, and about this country, is like the weather in other countries—a subject that serves to fill gaps in the conversation, as a substitute for dialogue or for any other purpose. Besides, it did not give me pause for another, more important reason—that it did not strike me as relevant to me in any way. If I had been an engineer, a doctor, a merchant, or even an artisan it would have struck me as plausible. But since I was a cleric whose only stock in trade was that he had mastered to some extent an ancient language, had memorized the Quran and dozens of sayings of the Prophet, and knew how to argue points of Islamic law, how could you imagine that it would occur to me to emigrate to one of those countries so attractive to others, young and old, some of whom are even prepared to run grave risks in order to reach the safety of those shores? It would be more natural for me to worry about tempting fate: by the standards of my brothers and colleagues, I was surely the model of the lucky emigrant. What better luck could one have than this—to move to your country and have a job waiting, without any competitors, and on top of that to be paid for moving, rather than to toil away for months to cover the cost? The same idea added to my sense of bereavement the day my minder brought me the letter in which you said you had moved, though when I read it I was not reminded of that casual reference to migration in your conversation that night, and it did not occur to me to call it migration.

❧

We had a long chat about the affairs and people of the country, and you helpfully pointed out things worth reading in last week's newspapers. I then unwittingly went back to asking why you had mustered that whole collection of files on al-Mutanabbi—his poetry, biography, and commentary—in a single place, giving the impression of repeated use.

"As I told you, 'the project's donkey is acting stubborn,'" you said with a laugh. "An expression I recently learned from al-Wahidi.* So I didn't put together these articles and books for any professional reason. Don't imagine I was lazy last week and didn't read. In fact, maybe I've read as much as I have since I was a student. I forgot to tell you I'm on holiday for two weeks. But I haven't read any al-Mutanabbi. I didn't . . ." (What if you were about to say, for example: "I didn't think it right to read al-Mutanabbi without you"?) ". . . But I finished reading two books about him," you added. You were speaking with a caution I had come across only when you were worried about making a slip of the tongue or inadvertently saying something that might embarrass the person you were speaking to. I left you to struggle for words, not because I enjoyed seeing and hearing you struggle, but because I was sure you would soon say what was on your mind, all at once and without regard for the consequences. That's what happened. "I'm dreaming of a private 'project' in which al-Mutanabbi would play some role, directly or indirectly. Directly in the form of a biography that would challenge the contested historical facts, or, let's say, an imaginary biography which makes free use of all the versions of his life and adds to them. Indirectly in the form of a historical novel about the times he lived in. A nebulous 'project' and I can't be sure that my enthusiasm for it will last."

Contrary to what I might have suggested, you did not monopolize the conversation or ignore me. Many times you tried to bring me into the conversation, but I deliberately brought it back to you, sometimes on some facetious pretext such as, "I'm not good at eating and talking at the same time," and sometimes on the grounds that I was seriously interested, especially when you expounded on the events I had missed over the past week, and in that I was telling the truth.

⊘

---

* "Ibn al-Jinni was one of the masters of inflection and morphology and was excellent at categorizing them, but when he spoke about semantics, his donkey was stubborn and he made mistakes."

144

I had much to say, and I had an overwhelming desire to share it with you, but where should I begin? Apart from the jumbled words I had to say about myself (and I was dying a slow death from holding them back), I knew that, since you were my closest friend, de facto and by my own choice, I had a duty to tell you about the new turn that my 'professional life' might take, and that, on top of the title by which you knew me, I was about to add another title, and did not know how I would handle it when it became public knowledge. Would I not soon appear on the new television channel, which had put enormous advance publicity posters on most of the billboards around the city? But how? How could I start to tell you that? I had gone home to attend my father's burial, so how could I explain that I had come back as the producer and presenter of a television program? How could I explain, when I had not yet been here two days, that I had had enough time to make a deal of that kind? I was hoping you might mention something that would give me an opportunity to bring it up, but I never expected you to do so by mentioning the new channel directly. So I was speechless when, in complete innocence, you asked me if the advertisements, which were the talk of the town and the topic of much gossip, had caught my eye on my way to your place. I sat up straight, like someone who is suddenly the center of attention at a crowded gathering. It was just the two of us, but perhaps I imagined myself among my colleagues at the mosque, to whom I would sooner or later have to provide a convincing story about how I had come to join the team at the new channel. Needless to say, I was much more worried about you than about my colleagues and the explanation I would have to prepare for them. My colleagues were of two kinds: on one hand, there were those who were sure that my introverted asceticism was all camouflage and that I was really a well-informed and widely connected man with a status higher than I made public; and on the other hand, there were those who accepted that I was who I was, no more and no less. Each group firmly believed what they believed, disregarding anything that might serve to undermine or weaken their belief. But you, at least as regards our relationship, had nothing in common with either group. Besides, your substantial knowledge of and familiarity with the media in your country made you quite unlike my colleagues in the way they were awestruck whenever the name of someone they knew appeared in the newspapers or his face flashed across a television screen. Even if you gave me an opportunity to break my news, I assumed

I should be cautious about taking it up. I say "assumed," because, as I realized only much later, my caution in your presence that night, as in other situations, stemmed from what one might call "guilty conscience syndrome," as in the proverb "a guilty conscience needs no accuser," which refers to how a criminal worries he might be found out and imagines that signs of his guilt are visible to others. "How could I not see the posters? They hit you in the face wherever you look," I said. "But didn't I tell you that the people in charge of that channel were interested in me, even before they covered the city and the suburbs with their posters?"

Of course I had not told you anything, not even a hint of the offer I had received. You may well wonder, just as I wonder now, whether I might have come up with a lie more plausible than this, especially as I share little with you about my personal affairs and it is completely inconceivable that I would have talked to you about a proposal of this kind and then forgotten I had done so. But that is what happened that day, and I must confess something that became clear to me with the passing of the days—that the inner life I had long preserved would not help me with the daily deceptions that are indispensable for managing and facilitating the affairs of the world.

You answered merely, "No," with a trace of contempt for my clumsy question, rather than indifference. To atone for my blatant lie, I immediately switched to a more plausible line of argument, saying that maybe I had overlooked telling you because I had shelved the offer and forgotten about it until it was put to the 'appropriate authorities' in my country and approved. Hoping to gain your sympathy, I added: "But now they've agreed, and I'm nervous almost to distraction." Then, to further lure you into supporting me, I found myself continuing: "It's only a few years ago that television broadcasts started to reach our village so you can say, by way of analogy, that I had an incomplete childhood. . . . Do you know how I try to minimize the impact of entering this battleground? I tell myself I have a good example in previous pioneers of television, those who started when television, producers, and presenters did not exist."

I expected you would ask me what kind of program it would be, when I would start my new work, and how I would reconcile it with my commitments at the mosque, but at first you made do with a malicious remark, or so it seemed to me: "So you're going to join the stars club soon and have fans—men and women." I had the impression that with your malicious remark and its scoffing tone you had obtained your revenge, and after this tacit tussle we could amicably resume the conversation. You were too shy to ask me bluntly how the people at the television channel discovered me and why their choice fell on me rather than anyone else. But these questions were implicit in the many other questions you asked about the channel and all the furor over its launch, especially as it was the first private television channel, or about my concept for the program and who would help me produce it. I did not lie to you in anything I told you, but I did not fill in the background. For example, I failed to tell you that the messenger who brought me the offer first visited me in the company of a senior official from our embassy in the aftermath of the sermon incident in the mosque. I omitted to mention the identity of the senior official from whom I obtained approval, the nature of the connection between me and him, and whether there was any link, causal or accidental or what you will, between my relationship with this official and my moving to your city and then meeting you and so on.

I also failed to disclose that the next morning I had an appointment to meet one of the people in charge of the channel—an appointment I had not asked for and had not sought, but that came about as if by magic when I received a phone call that morning. I was also delighted that your talent for generating ideas suddenly came to life and you started throwing them at me, probably unaware that I desperately needed to arm myself with such ideas in readiness for my appointment the next day.

Unusually, we did not leave the kitchen after finishing dinner to drink your rosewater drink in the usual place on that sofa in the study. Instead, we lingered at the kitchen table and you merely cleared away some of the plates. For no obvious reason, I interpreted your irritation, which you made no attempt to conceal, and the fact that we stayed in the kitchen, as another step toward a less formal relationship. I did not know that it would not stop there. When I was ready to leave, at about half past eleven, I pressed you not to drive me home because the weather was bad, and you finally gave in. As I was about to throw my coat on, you said: "Wait." From a room I had not yet entered, your bedroom, you came back with a large paper bag and took out a dark blue coat. "Try it on to see if it fits and doesn't need adjusting," you said. Without hesitation, I followed your orders and tried it on. It fit me as if it were tailor-made. You walked around me, then disappeared for a moment, and I took the opportunity to steal a glance in the mirror that covers the wall facing the door. You then came back with a pair of scissors and cut off the labels hanging from the sleeves of the coat. At first I was tongue-tied. When I managed to speak, it was a confused jumble of thanks, remonstration, and praise for your good taste. My speech became increasingly disjointed as I felt the blushes on my cheeks spread to the rest of my body and my temperature rise. Your only recourse was to urge me to take advantage of the brief lull in the weather—the rain had stopped beating against the window panes—and look for a taxi to take me back to my mosque. You grabbed the door handle to open it and wished me a warm night. I mumbled something incomprehensible and slipped through the narrow gap you had opened.

Perhaps for the first time, I had no desire that night to take advantage of your hospitality and the shelter you offered, and I did not ask myself that naive question of mine: "When any man and any woman seek shelter with each other, is there any more to it than what we share?" The question was naive because the complete opposite is true; because, if that was all there was to it, no man would take shelter with any woman, and no woman would take shelter with any man, and the world would not complain of overpopulation and no laws would be passed and no penalties instituted to limit it.

It was cold, but I was happy with my new coat, and on top of that I was proud that you had not forgotten me when I was away. The only thing to spoil my joy was the large paper bag in which you deposited my old coat. I did not dare to get rid of it or its contents for fear of losing the things I might have stuffed into the multiple pockets of the coat, but this meant I could not keep both hands warm at the same time. While I had no desire to stay as your guest, I equally did not see the cold as a good reason to retreat rapidly to my room.

I took no notice of the taxi that slowed down as it approached me. From time to time, I would plan to go as far as a junction or a crossroads and then stop to wait for a taxi to take me to my destination, but as soon as I reached the place I had fixed on, I would find myself walking on, sometimes deliberately to go around a building in front of which I could pass, or simply out of inertia. I thought I was walking on, but in fact I was wandering aimlessly, thinking of you. Two young security men standing on the pavement opposite looked more alert than all the other security men I had passed so far, as if they had just started their shift. For this reason, or simply because they were doing their duty, or in case a senior officer passed by, or because they were suspicious of me and what I was carrying, they stopped me and asked to inspect the bag. Did they stop and search me? It would be unfair on them if I were to call what they did by any other name, but such a word would be well short of what I felt. As part of the process, I was lifted up, put down, made to stand, and made to sit. I had my pockets thoroughly emptied. Although security men like them deployed around the mosque every Friday, I had never happened to come as close to them as to those two that night. In fact, I do not remember that I had ever had opportunity or occasion to speak to any of them.

In the pale light of street lamps attached to tall poles, I took my old coat out of the bag and opened it out for them to see, like a peddler hawking his wares in a street market. One of them frisked the coat: no solid bodies or anything suspicious. Inevitably, I touched the coat in turn, and it felt nothing like my new coat. Luckily, the light was so faint I did not notice its shabbiness, which surprised me later in the light of my room, when I was inspecting the pockets. The large paper bag that lay calmly on the wet pavement after I emptied it out was also inspected to see what was inside it when I picked it up to arrange the coat inside it again. "If you please," one of them said, "Off you go." The cold, which a while back I had not seen as a good reason to retreat to my room, was suddenly evident. My teeth were the first to respond, and only with the greatest difficulty could I stop them chattering. I did not "go off," as the security man had suggested, but merely moved aside from where they were standing and adopted the posture of someone waiting for a taxi.

In my nose, or in the sky, or in the city, I smelled the smell of gunpowder. Do thunder and lightning leave a smell of gunpowder? Or was it the questioning, and having my old coat searched for anything that might threaten security, that filled my nostrils? Or was it fear, which is one's only companion on dark cold nights, if one is to believe all the poetry I have memorized?

Because of how cold it was that night, and how cold I was, and how I suddenly started to have shivering fits, I could no longer tell the effects of cold from the effects of fear. Luckily, I did not have to wait long for a taxi, and it was not long before we reached our destination.

Some types of cold are impossible to keep at bay, such as the cold in my room despite the efforts of the electric heater, which I had asked the janitor to put on before he went to bed. And the coat, the robe of honor you gave me, does it not keep out the cold? Your coat, at least that night, made me feel reassured rather than warm; reassured like someone who cries out to be wrapped up and whose cry is answered.*

---

* A Quranic reference to the Prophet Muhammad, who wrapped himself in a cloak when revelations came to him.

17

My new coat, the robe of honor you gave me, puts all my other clothes to shame, not just my old coat. I discovered this on the morning of the next day, when I was dressing, trying to look as smart as possible for the sake of an appointment unprecedented in my former life. My room has no full-length mirror, just a rectangular one with black stains above the washbasin, and I use it to adjust my hair and my beard, which I always keep carefully trimmed as short as possible (compared to an average beard it hardly counts at all). So I have no way of seeing myself in full and checking my overall appearance. The most I could do was hope for the best and trust that my new coat would cover up any flaws that marred my elegance. For that reason, I resolved not to take the coat off.

At exactly nine o'clock, the janitor came in and informed me anxiously that there was someone at the door to pick me up and that a limousine was standing at the mosque gate. I automatically picked up my briefcase, which held only a volume of al-Mutanabbi's poetry and some blank paper, as if to leave without it would detract from the gravitas of the appointment. But the briefcase did not match my new coat. For a few seconds, I had doubts about whether it was worth taking and apprehensions about the impact it might have on those I would meet, but I quickly took a deep breath and imagined scenes from real life and from television in which well-dressed men appear carrying briefcases with traces of wear. Isn't wear a sign of repeated and prolonged use? The black limousine with tinted windows that had so impressed the janitor was not only standing at the mosque gate but was completely blocking the street outside. My escort walked a few paces ahead and opened the back door of the car for me. Thinking he was the driver, I was about to tell him that I would prefer to sit in the front seat next to him, but when he opened the door I realized that the driver was still in his seat.

Silence was part of the training of the two men. Throughout the drive, they did not say a word. The driver's skill and the sturdiness of the car eliminated any sense of movement, and were it not for the passing scenes you could see through the darkened windows if you wanted (they did not intrude on the eye), you would think you were in a plane with silent engines. I thought we were heading for the northern suburbs of the city, but we went through them and took a road with unfinished buildings on either side, then turned left and took a slightly narrower road going uphill, recently paved and with nothing beside it, which gave the impression it was a private road. I was not mistaken, and some minutes later the road brought us to an entrance with no gate to keep out unauthorized visitors but with a system of barriers that looked like a modern art installation. My escort had a brief walkie-talkie conversation, of which I understood nothing, with a colleague whom I could not see, but judged to be in the space-age silver box to the right of the entrance. The barriers then opened just enough to let our car through. I assumed we had arrived, and began to prepare for the meeting like a schoolboy for an exam. I was mistaken. Instead of driving toward the cluster of buildings, the driver headed in the opposite direction, toward an open area where buses and vehicles of every size and of diverse functions were gathered. When we reached the open space, he drove toward an awning under which a line of identical cars was parked. As the car braked, and before it had come to a complete halt, my escort slipped out. As soon as the car stopped, he opened the back door for me and said: "If you please."

On the previous day, when the security man said "If you please" to me, he meant I could continue on my way. But this time, where did he want me to go? Before I could follow his friendly instruction, he opened the back door of another car nearby and repeated the same words. (Later, with my successive visits to the place, I found out that cars coming from outside, almost without exception, were not allowed to drive around the compound. Everyone, staff and visitors, had to leave their cars in the parking lot and then take transport to where they wanted to go in the four buildings.) The same thing happened again a short while later when we reached our destination, with the difference that this time I got out of the car not to take another car but to take an elevator from the ground floor to a floor up high, operated by a young man just as smartly dressed as the colleagues of his I had met. Just like them, all he said was: "If you please."

In the lobby where the lift opened, I did not have to wait. A hostess grabbed me and took me to an office where she handed me over to a more senior colleague, and she in turn took me to another office, where another woman invited me with great courtesy to sit down and then whispered words I could not catch into the telephone. A moment later, with another "If you please," she invited me to stand up. She led the way and made a token knock on the door, which quickly opened, and from the other side of the room I was welcomed by the man for whose sake I had embarked on all these adventures. I had the impression that I rather let down his expectations, for what he saw in front of him was not a man with a turban on his head or a beard like a nosebag hanging down in front, but just a man of medium height in a blue coat, carrying in his right hand a briefcase battered by time. The man before me was in his fifties, youthful-looking despite his graying hair—the ruler of this kingdom, shielded behind this army of chamberlains and the doors and gates they watched over. He had no time to waste on pointless inquiries or inopportune courtesies, but what could he do faced with a hireling whose honorary boss happened to be the Lord of Heaven and Earth? I would have liked to give him a helping hand, or rather a helping tongue, and tell him: "Never mind that I'm a cleric and an employee of the Lord of the Worlds . . . This is my profession, even if it has nothing in common with yours." Your coat was very effective, as was the heating, in spite of the size of the place, which was big enough for an imposing desk and all its accessories, and a circular conference table around which I counted twelve chairs.

After a moment's greeting, in what came across as an invitation that we roll up our sleeves, he suggested that I take off my coat. I welcomed his proposal and hurried to do so, ignoring my morning's resolution to keep my coat on, firstly so as not to disappoint my host, and secondly and more importantly, to stem the flow of sweat under my armpits. As I had expected and hoped, he took control of the conversation and quoted his friend, as he described him, as saying he had recommended me, not only for my learning and for knowing when to act tough and when to play soft, but also, as he put it, because in whatever task I was entrusted everyone had confidence in me, here and in my own country! He continued: "I'll allow myself to call a spade a spade without beating about the bush. All the production units are fully staffed and organized except for the religious programs unit, and you know best why that is (did I really know best?). If we had intended to broadcast any old religious programs, it wouldn't have been a problem. We could have resorted to those that state television broadcasts and cut programs from the same cloth, or imported them from one of the Arab countries that follow an unobjectionable form of Islam. That's not what we want. Of course our religious programs will be formally under the supervision of the Ministry of Religious Endowments and its fatwa department, and on Fridays and feast days we'll carry sermons by the usual official suspects, but on top of 'canned' programs, we aspire to produce something closer to reality . . . more . . . more . . . (he muttered a word in a language I did not understand) . . . let's say less cautious, let's say more daring."

I interrupted him to give him a rest, thinking it would be impolite not to comment on what he had said with a candor to match his own: "Although I know nothing about audiovisual programs," I said, "I think I understand what you mean by programs that are less cautious and more daring, and I doubt I'd be telling you anything new if I said that the talk is far from cautious or timid in the village and slum mosques where there are daily battles to defend them and repel intruders who want to conquer them and annex them to their empire. . . . Should this war, ostensibly legalistic yet political both on and below the surface, be brought into the open on the airwaves?" My candor reassured him, judging by the way he nodded as he prepared to answer. "Politically, no problem. Legally, the channel is a project that is privately financed and with an independent status. If anyone sees any reason to object, then they can sue us in the courts," he said.

My host did not ask me if I preferred coffee or tea, and without him needing to use the telephone or any other means of communication there was a knock on the door and a professional waiter appeared, holding a silver tray with two cups of tea and two cups of coffee. When the waiter came in, my host took the opportunity to move from behind his desk to the chair facing me. As soon as the waiter had left and we were alone again, he said, "Very well, let me tell you the truth. I neither like nor dislike men of religion, but I prefer to keep my distance. My friend, your sheikh, is an exception that proves the rule, and in spite of his admiration for you and confidence in you, I was apprehensive about this meeting . . . . I confess I understand nothing of religions and doctrines, but in all modesty I can claim to know the difference between a good television program and a bad one, whether religious or not. I want a religious program of one-and-a-half hours' air time that meets two conditions: quality, and a courageous and unambiguous position on a form of Islam that I think we concur on rejecting. Do you agree to take on the challenge?" Without waiting for an answer, he added: "You'll have at your disposal a team of technicians and specialists, and you can call in whomever you see fit."

Can you imagine what I was thinking about in those moments? It might surprise you, and you might not believe me. I was thinking about how I could prove that I had outstanding talent and that I deserved you. Somehow or other, I felt my character changing, as if I had been reincarnated with the persona most likely to bring me closer to my goal: the persona of the wily student who sees that the only way to escape the fate imposed on him by birth, upbringing, religion, and education is to eclipse his peers and go his separate way. I do not know whether I told myself anything to the effect of: "Don't be fooled. This concatenation of coincidences is not a reward for your hard work, inscribed against your name on some eternal tablet, so make sure you don't let the opportunity escape you." But I did act on that basis, and I did my best to make my host feel that I was at one with him. I abandoned the logic of the dialogue and told him what I imagined he would like to hear from me. "I'm at your service," I said, "not just to prove the sheikh right in his good opinion of me and to repay your trust, but out of conviction that what you are trying to do must be done."

In a place where everyone and everything looked like a television set, it was naive of me to be surprised that the telephone did not ring for all this time. I should have known that the secretary who acted as gatekeeper could handle matters by herself, without explicit instructions. My host, my

155

new boss, went back to the chair behind his desk and summoned the secretary through some device. As she stood to his right and received his instructions about me—whom he wanted me to meet and in which order— I noticed that she slipped a piece of paper in front of him, no doubt a list of the names of people who had phoned him. He picked up a pen and made some marks on the paper.

My host did nothing to indicate he wanted to end the meeting. In fact, he started to go over in detail some of what we had agreed. "So, tomorrow morning at exactly nine o'clock you'll find the car waiting for you, and from ten o'clock you'll start your meetings with some of the members of the team . . ." he said, for example, in a clear attempt to while away the time.

The people, or whatever we were waiting for, could come in on us in only two ways: through the door or by telephone, and it was the telephone that rang. My host did not need to lift the receiver: he just pressed one or two of his buttons and the room filled with the voice of my sheikh, who addressed the manager as "mawlana" and exchanged with him greetings that were a mixture of pleasantries and private jokes. After this preamble, which I had the impression was the way they usually started serious discussions, my host told the sheikh that I was listening in. He thanked the sheikh for recommending me and informed him that from tomorrow, I would start my meetings with those I needed to see. Then, with a promise to brief him on any new developments, he signaled to me with a broad smile to come closer, take the receiver, and say hello to the sheikh.

From that day on, I had the strange feeling that I was an accomplice in a conspiracy, that countless things were likely to change if the program was destined to succeed, and that I had finally found a place that fit me perfectly—all of me: my public self and my inner self, including you! Like anyone else, I tended to exaggerate to myself the importance of what I had been invited to take part in. Only weeks after plunging into the work did I have the simple and obvious idea that 'my' program, for example, was only one of dozens of programs the channel broadcast weekly, and that the viewers had a choice between following 'my' channel's programs and those of six other channels that were easy to pick up.

The next morning, I left the mosque in the limousine in the same way, and since it was one of the days I had set aside for consultations with visitors at the mosque, I took it as an occasion to stage what amounted to a handing-over ceremony, delegating some of my duties to two colleagues who acted as my deputies. I told them that I had received 'official' instructions, emphasizing the 'official,' to help produce a series of religious programs, and for this reason I would be obliged to spend long periods away from the mosque. I added that I had full confidence in them and their wisdom. I made no reference at all to the fact that I might also be presenting the program, as I had done when I spoke to you. Before my meeting the day before, I had thought the job would be easy and the program would be no more than a lecture, but on camera. But later, when the manager had explained that what was wanted was something completely different, I regretted being so hasty in claiming I would be both producer and presenter, and I was careful not to repeat the same mistake, especially as my two colleagues and the mosque janitor were big gossips.

I went through the same "if you please" routine that morning as on the previous day, and finally found myself one of four sitting at a round table. One of them was a young woman who had been advised, apparently out of respect for me, to dress more modestly than usual for the occasion. She had wrapped her hair in a headscarf, which kept slipping and playing up on her. Of course I was reminded of our first meeting in the mosque and I almost asked her to take it off (which is what I actually did a few days later). The young woman was incontestably attractive but, although the others were about the same age as me, their behavior—extremely wary and cautious toward me, or rather toward the sheikh they initially thought I was—made me feel old in a way that I was not and that I did not know how to disprove. I was surprised how quickly I found myself engrossed in the subject. After brief introductions, the most senior of them, the producer of the program, passed me a neat folder and said it contained a preliminary proposal for what the segments of the program might be about. Everything was calculated with great precision: the length of the segments, their structure, and the breaks for advertising. As it should be, the proposal specified that every episode start with verses from the Quran and end with a prayer. Between the two there was a succession of headlines open to elaboration: "Sharia in Daily Life," "Visiting the Mosque," "Consultations on Points of Sharia," and so on, followed by a series of notes and questions, such as "selecting the Quran for the first six programs" (meaning, of course, the verses of the Quran), "obtaining a census of mosques with their addresses," "preparing a list of legal questions for the first six programs," "candidates to take part in production?

guests?" and then a number of headings I did not dwell on because I did not think they concerned me, such as "indoor/outdoor shooting," "equipment," etc. (At the end of the meeting the producers admitted to me that their 'Islamic' information came from watching the religious programs neighboring stations were broadcasting. They also had some ideas of their own, but did not know whether these would be "acceptable Islamically.") After reviewing the proposal and listening to them explain in detail what they meant by this headline or by this note or that question, the producer and chairman of the session moved on to what he called the most difficult question: "We'd like the presenter of the program to be a sheikh quite unlike the sheikhs that audiences usually see. Who do you suggest?"

I could not think of a clever answer, but he spared me the trouble. "By the way," he continued, addressing his assistants in a low voice, "if the choice was left to me I would choose mawlana. He has an excellent broadcast voice and a television face, and in any case a test would be the best proof . . . . What do you think, mawlana?" I was at a loss, and may have blushed in embarrassment at his praise for my voice and my face. I felt like someone who receives good news and tries to conceal his delight. All I could say was: "No doubt you're exaggerating," and all he could do was challenge me to try, on the grounds that, again, a test would be the best proof.

"Do you have time for us to do a test today?" he asked. Did I have something more important? "I have time, my friend, I have time," I replied. Don't ask me where that "my friend" came from but that is what I said. "My friend" issued instructions to his assistants, in a language different from the one we had been negotiating in, and at his suggestion we took a short break while they prepared the recording studio in which, as I saw it in those moments, 'my fate' would be decided. I cannot keep a secret from you. In those moments a wicked idea also occurred to me: isn't it possible I might have unconsciously allured you with my "broadcasting voice" and my "photogenic face"? I almost gave way to ideas more crazy than this, such as "What if I were a really attractive man?" but "my friend" saved me with an "if you please," and took me to a small compartment crammed with equipment I could not identify, except for the camera. The room was divided in two by a screen made of glass or some similar material. In the section stuffed with equipment, there were three of us: me, the young woman, and a third person. In the other section, the producer and his assistants sat at a table that looked liked an enormous console. The woman seated me properly and put in the buttonhole of my jacket a miniature device connected to a wire. She was trying to tuck the wire out of sight and, whenever she had to come very close, she would repeat several times the equivalent of the word 'sorry' in some foreign language, and she could hardly suppress her giggles when the third man, hiding behind the camera, made gestures making fun of her hijab. She pretended not to notice him or his gestures, and after all that, she gave a thumbs-up sign to tell the director that everything was as it should be. The director's voice suddenly assumed a commanding tone and filled the small room. "Assume that I am the audience . . . Turn toward me and ignore the camera and everything around you . . . To make it easier for you, I'll ask you some questions, which you can answer any old way. Try to speak as long as possible," he said. So I did and, on top of that, it seems I answered his questions, not only "any old way," but also with some eloquence. Without premeditation, under all those lights and in front of all those people, in that small, hot place crammed with wires and equipment, I found myself switching from colloquial to literary Arabic and opening my remarks with a bismillah and a prayer, just as I do whenever I mount the pulpit or speak at a funeral ceremony (it is odd that on happy occasions I do not switch to literary Arabic, as if happiness is nothing solemn!).

The test lasted around twenty minutes, interrupted by short breaks, sometimes to fix the miniature device attached to my buttonhole and some-times to adjust the lighting. I did not have to wait long to hear the result of the test, because I could read it straight away in the broad smile on the face of my friend the director, who was evidently proud of his sound judgment. In a compartment nearby, we sat in the dark and watched the tape we had just finished filming. The director made comments from time to time, some about my performance, and some about particulars his assistants should avoid on future occasions. Of course I was not concentrating on his comments, but was off in another world. I wondered whether, when I joined you that night, it would show that something completely unexpected had intruded on my life and that, without any effort on my part, I had been selected for a task I could not be certain I was cut out for or that I was the best person to perform. This unexpected sequence of events had ended up turning my life upside-down. Between that day, when it was established that I had all the makings of a star, as you put it, and the day when I was confirmed as one of the enemies of God (no less!), many things happened—trivial, ephemeral, and insignificant in the eyes of others, but weighty by my standards, imprinted in my memory and of incomparable significance. First and foremost among these things was a freedom to manage my own time in a way I had not been accustomed to since I moved to your city.

18

I cannot claim I was born with a natural inclination toward freedom in general, or that I grew up with the freedom to do what I wanted when I wanted. In fact, I cannot claim that I felt deprived of my freedom until I met you. Before that, freedom was no more than something one plotted by night from time to time and carried out under cover of darkness. In this sense acting freely or renouncing freedom of action was an incidental matter that would arise occasionally, like a pain that afflicts a bodily organ at certain times or under certain conditions. It would be foolish to couple what I have just said with a phrase such as "Whereas with you . . . ," or else this "whereas," which in this context would reflect the contrast between what preceded and what followed, would have to be written in giant letters out of all proportion with the other words around it, in order to prevent it from being likened to any other "whereas," either from the past or yet to come.

It is no coincidence that, as my relationship with you progressed, freedom in general became closely associated with my own lack of freedom to manage my time, because with you I discovered that my time was my life and that everything (and everyone) that restricted, wasted, or encroached on my time also restricted, wasted, or encroached on my life.

Before you came into my life I had indiscriminate desires for women, and therefore satisfying those desires whenever they arose was equally indiscriminate. My desires had a cycle, like the menstrual cycle of women, set by nature for reasons of its own and to perpetuate the species, not for its own survival, and hence without discrimination. To continue with this analogy, with you my cycles were disrupted, sometimes shortened and sometimes prolonged, and I suffered the same anxieties and so on that women suffer. To put my cycles back on a reasonable track, I needed a somewhat extended period of time to discover that I had lost the freedom to dispose of my time and to try to recover it. This endeavor continued intermittently throughout the period leading up to the time when television gave me the upper hand over those around me—my mosque, my colleagues, and my small community. As soon as I was certain I was about to appear on their screens, or rather burst on to their screens uninvited every Thursday evening, I abandoned many of the conventions that had previously governed my relationship with them, starting with the way I had divided my time evenly between my business and their business, given that much of their business was more in the nature of protocol, whether in the mosque or outside, than management or planning. I did not shun them and I was not unfriendly toward them, but I did begin to socialize with them more sparingly, not in order to gain more time to spend close to you but rather to learn about matters I had thought were beyond my area of competence. For more than two years, the community I had been sent to look after had stopped at the confines of the neighborhood where the mosque was established, whereas now my audience extended to wherever there was television reception. I cannot deny, however, that the expansion of my audience, and hence of my concerns, did enable me to visit you at times other than our usual appointments. Similarly, during the first frantic weeks of preparing 'my program,' when I was away from the mosque four days out of seven, it did often happen that on the way back from the far north of the city to the far south, I would ask the driver of the limousine to drop me off close to a small garden, which I would cross to find myself a few steps away from your building.

My selfishness and my complete preoccupation with my newly acquired 'profession' did distract me from my previous practice of reading al-Mutanabbi's poetry diligently every day in readiness for our meetings. From time to time, I would suggest we read a poem or part of a poem and you would go along with me without great enthusiasm, just as you would go along whenever I brought up my apprehensions about the television program, taking advantage of your previous experience in that field (you never wanted to elaborate on how you had acquired that experience) and profiting from your amazing ability to generate ideas. Usually, I would latch on to details of your ideas even when I thought it unlikely they would be accepted. I must have missed many opportunities to win grudging praise from my colleagues because I was too hasty in judging your ideas as brilliant but difficult to use because of their 'experimental' nature (a word that I learned from you, and that I started to throw back at you once I felt more confident). I discovered this at one of those long meetings from which the program emerged. We were discussing the "Visiting the Mosque" episode, and one of the team thought it should take the form of visits to old mosques accompanied by a historian or archeologist; another thought it should take the form of a tour of the mosques in a particular district; and a third suggested something in between. But we quickly set those ideas aside as too trite, and incompatible with the tone of the program. We were about to drop the episode and start discussing something to take its place, but at the last minute I was emboldened to propose an idea I had borrowed from you, though I was careful to present it as no more than an idle fancy. "What if we treated mosques like other so-called service facilities such as hotels, restaurants, swimming pools, and so on, so the visit would be like a report on a certain mosque—its architecture, the religious aspects, and other services, and we would end up awarding the mosque in question a number of stars," I said. When you suggested this, I had no doubt it was an amusing idea, but I had not expected to hear it called "a stroke of genius," as my friend the director put it and as the others then concurred.

Of course I did not tell any of those present, however much they praised me, that you had a copyright on the idea, nor that this was not the only idea I had plagiarized from your fertile imagination; but such an idea, an idea "so daring," as one of them described it, would need approval from above if it were to proceed, and for this it would have to be submitted in writing. "And no one but you, mawlana, can do that, because you know more than us about the services mosques provide to their congregations."

I gave a firm promise that I would come to our meeting the next day with a written proposal in my briefcase, and then hurried to your place. Our appointment that day was for five o'clock, but I arrived two hours early. I won't disguise the fact that I felt frustrated when I did not find you, or rather when I did not find you waiting for me. At first, when I retreated to the garden nearby, I did not notice or care that I had arrived two hours early. In fact, I cannot rule out the possibility that for some moments I took my failure to find you at home as a humiliation. You should not be surprised that the man who entered your home so timidly, his head and spirit bowed, should have acted so arrogantly that day, almost resentful that you were late for an appointment that did not exist in the first place! You should not be surprised, because that man, new to self-confidence and manliness, was prone to every kind of mistake, including the mistake of falling into the trap of manliness—a trap you had set with your own hands.

Before I realized what nonsense I was thinking, before I came to my senses and calmed down, I had to set out the facts of the case to myself, like a child making out the letters of a word one by one before putting them together: firstly, your appointment (I told myself) was for five o'clock; secondly, you are two hours early; and thirdly, in any case, you have no authority over her, so on what grounds are you so agitated? In what way has your dignity been offended? But I was no better off after explaining to myself that my anger was out of place and unjustified. That was because my indignation at you changed into indignation at myself, an indignation accompanied by extreme embarrassment, unmitigated by the fact that none of the few people walking in the garden in that cold weather knew who I was.

At first, I decided to spend the two hours until our appointment in the garden, but the relentless drizzle, which suggested that a rainstorm was imminent, made me abandon that plan. I did not have time to go back to the mosque, and so I was left with only two options, both unprecedented for me: to take refuge either in one of the cafés not far from here or in the nearby shopping mall. I did not hesitate to choose the latter. I would have a good excuse if I met one of my enemies in the mall, which sells everything, whereas in a café I would have no excuse to offer. Besides, a few days earlier my friend the director had taken me to the accounts department, where I had signed receipts for a certain number of coupons, valid for shopping in the clothing section of several stores and shopping malls. He had advised me that to save myself time I should start my search in this mall, where he had no doubt I would find what I was looking for. Comfortable with this 'professional' pretext, I headed to my chosen refuge from the rain, where I could go shopping if I needed an excuse for wandering around this monument to consumerism.

The building was guarded, as was necessary or as was thought to be necessary: at least two rings of security men, one in full uniform around the building and the other dispersed throughout the complex, starting with the door and all the way to the clothing section, including in the elevators and at the escalators. They were distinguishable by their standard attire, the monotony of which was broken only by their neckties, which each man was apparently free to choose. On top of this army of men, the visitor could be sure that the six-story building was also equipped with all the monitoring devices necessary, in case no one was looking, and to cover the parts of the building where human eyes could not reach. But someone visiting this monument, intent on goods and commodities, would not notice any of that, except perhaps the metal detector, which everyone coming in the door had to pass through.

As soon as they went through the door, the three women who went in before me quickly opened their elegant little handbags to satisfy the curiosity of one of the civilian security men. So as not to seem unfamiliar with the customs of the place, I followed their example and passed through safely. Having read the board showing what one could find on each floor, I followed the signs leading to the elevators and the escalators. I preferred the former, after an experience I would rather forget with an escalator when I first came to your city. Unfortunately, it was still no later than half past three, so I would have to spend at least an hour here. There was only a handful of shoppers at that time of day, and at first glance I did not detect a single man among them other than myself. The sales staff smiled at those coming in without leaving their places. As soon as I left the lift on the second floor, which was devoted to men's clothing and accessories, I faced a wing for jackets and headed toward it with resolve, like someone who knows what he wants. I pretended to be examining the merchandise, feeling the cloth and inspecting the prices. Because I was lingering in the jacket department, the saleswoman had the impression I was serious about buying. She came up very politely and offered to help me choose. I expounded at length on my professional motive for inspecting these jackets, implicitly apologizing for taking my time to choose. That made her only more eager to help me, and for that purpose she summoned one of her colleagues, who had me try on whatever jackets took his fancy and then moved me on to the shirt section, and then to the tie and handkerchief section. It was annoying to be alone with the salesman, but his presence was also reassuring, because in his company I had no fear of being accosted anew by one of his colleagues, and I would not again have to explain the 'professional motive' for my visit, which was in fact to explore rather than to buy.

As five o'clock approached, it was still raining and my tour in the company of the salesman had brought us to the section devoted to accessories such as umbrellas, bags, pipes, and other things the purpose of which I could neither make out nor understand why they were specifically classified as men's accessories. Meekly I told my companion that I wanted to buy an umbrella and that I needed his help. Perhaps he did not understand why I had suddenly succumbed, after buying nothing for more than an hour as he guided me around the various departments and acted as an intermediary between me and the other sales staff. Perhaps he was not sure I was telling the truth about wanting to buy, so he merely asked one of his colleagues to show me what she had in the way of umbrellas. She showed them to me, opening some drawers and closing others, and giving long explanations, which I thought excessive for buying an umbrella. In the end, she gave me a slip of paper, which I took like an idiot to the nearest cash desk to pay for my umbrella. I stole a glance at the paper, but there was no clear price written there, just a group of numbers and vertical lines. Obediently, I gave the cashier most of the money I had in my pocket in payment for the umbrella, but I did not understand why it was so expensive until, under its protection, I reached your place and you greeted me with a mischievous "Congratulations." I responded by telling you at length about my adventures in the shopping mall, not forgetting at the end to teasingly hold your absence from home responsible for my buying this umbrella, which, as I discovered from you, carried the label of a famous designer, obviously out of harmony with the rest of my outfit. "Better suited to those seriously committed to conspicuous consumption than to men of learning such as mawlana," as you put it.

That was the first time our meeting had begun with a joke, and with it I discovered the virtues of joking. "This umbrella is not the only sin I committed today in your name. Do you remember your crazy idea about assessing mosques by the services they provide to the congregation? I pilfered it during today's meeting and won unexpected acclaim, but the idea is so daring it has to be submitted to those in charge for their approval. For that, I have to prepare a written proposal . . . by tomorrow . . . Could we . . . work together on that?" Half joking and half serious, you answered: "So you want me to put my talents at the disposal of a dubious media project?" You took your leave, came back a few minutes later in a long black gown decorated with fine embroidery, and took your seat in front of the computer, a recent addition to the furniture of this multipurpose room. You asked if there was a particular format in which I thought the proposal should be drafted. I said no, adding only that I was unfamiliar with this form of correspondence. You did not insist, but busied yourself instead with tapping your delicate fingertips on the keyboard in front of you. From time to time, you had recourse to a device on your right, connected with a wire, which you wiped over a plastic sheet illustrated with a classic seascape scene. At your invitation, I moved closer and looked at what you had come up with while I was sitting at our table leafing through a book on al-Mutanabbi I found there. The layout of the page and the brief preamble looked to me like the work of an expert. As for your choice of "Classes of Mosques" as the title, frankly it dumbfounded me. The frivolous way you had treated the subject left me with nothing to say. "And now . . . ?" I muttered. You ignored my question, because you suddenly remembered that the water you had put on the stove must have started to boil away and you rushed to the kitchen.

When we were back on the same sofa with hot drinks in our hands, you picked up the conversation. "Now it's your turn," you said. "You take two mosques you know well and compare them. Let's say your mosque and another mosque." In the blink of an eye, the tables were turned, as they say. You were the teacher and I the pupil. Your trick worked, and without great effort the "objective criteria" (another expression to which you hold copyright) started to take shape. For fear they might evaporate, especially as, unlike the water in our tea, they could not be replaced if they escaped, you took a pen and paper and started to write down our inspirations. Shortly before ten o'clock, I sat down at the table and looked at the two pieces of paper the printer had just churned out. I was amazed at what they contained, as if I had not witnessed their birth. Leaving aside the cleanliness of the washroom for ablutions, the punctuality of the prayer times, and whether the mosque had racks at the door for the congregation's shoes, where did you get the idea of asking whether there were parking spaces close to the mosque, whether the Quran recitations were live or broadcast from a recording, and other things which had never occurred to me—the master, organizer, and resident of the Mosque of the Two Omars—or to any of its regular visitors?

You had endless surprises for me that night. As soon as we had finished printing what we thought was the final version, you remembered "something important" and asked me to tear up the pieces of paper I was holding. "We've forgotten to write 'In the Name of God, etc.' at the top of the page . . . I'll add it," you said. Crouched over your amazing device, and enjoying every moment of it, you then asked me: "Which font would you prefer?" But all this was nothing compared with what happened on the threshold of your door when I was preparing to leave and go back to my mosque. At that point, too, you remembered "something important," which it took you a moment to find when you went to look for it. "This is the key to the building and this is the key to the house. Next time you won't need to go on adventures here and there . . . You can just wait for me, here."

19

I did not need your keys the next day, because I arrived after seven o'clock. We sat down, impatiently marking time until half past seven, the time of the earliest news bulletin, when we hoped to pick up any possible information about a loud but still mysterious explosion that had echoed across the city.

When the presenter wished his audience a good evening, his tone of voice did not bode well. Even his diction, usually impeccable and tirelessly fluent, faltered at the horror of the explosion, which had happened some hours earlier in a crowded shopping street, leaving people dead and injured, starting fires and causing unaccustomed panic. No wonder. By coming into the heart of the city in a car loaded with explosives, death threatened to bring out in the open what no one yet dared to call war, and to transform it from a private to a public matter.

Eager to torment yourself, and me, with pictures, without which the 'event' would be incomplete, you rushed toward the television, which responded immediately to your commands and started to play solemn music of the kind our media broadcast on the most momentous occasions, against a background of natural scenery. We waited in silence, because speaking, saying anything, would have seemed inappropriate.

Wary of exhausting the patience of viewers, including us, or perhaps for some other reason, the natural scenery suddenly disappeared, giving way to a picture of a ornate clock with the minute hand about to reach the bottom to mark half past seven. The seconds passed and the second hand moved on past the twelve mark, heedless of the expectations we had pinned on it. I'm sure it was not the first time a news bulletin had started late, but that night the delay seemed laden with perils that neither of us dared share with the other. At last the presenter looked out grimly from the screen, wished the spectators good evening, and proceeded to read the statement in front of him. There was no news in the bulletin, just a long and tedious recitation of police communiqués and other official and unofficial statements that had come out since the explosion. The statements, almost incomprehensible in structure and vocabulary, were interspersed from time to time with indistinct pictures of a building reduced to rubble, surrounded by policemen, soldiers, and paramedics in various uniforms. It was up to the viewer to guess what had really happened.

Innocently, you broke the silence we had maintained while riveted to the screen, and asked: "Where are the dead and injured in all this? Why are they withholding their pictures from us? Do they think they have the situation under control, as they keep saying in their statements, as long as they don't show us any of the dead?" I did not comment, and nothing you did urged me to do so.

You switched between several television stations: nothing new, no details, and no exact figure for the toll of dead and injured. While the television stations friendly toward the government were content to repeat the official statement, which blamed the explosion on "a hired gang of evildoers," one of the hostile stations stood out by putting the explosion in the context of "sporadic incidents" our countries had seen in recent months and noting the surprising coincidence between our explosion and unconfirmed reports of a bomb attack on a police station in my country— a report carried only on this hostile station.

***

Was I in a cold sweat that evening, as I am now? I wish it were so, given that all I'm doing now is recalling the details of what happened. Death reduces us to silence, terrifies us, pins us to the spot, and forces us to be unusually sparing in what we say. I hesitated: should I take my leave and go back home, I wondered, or should I go along with what you wanted? You seemed to want us to stick together, wrapped in the silence that concealed our thoughts. I hesitate, so as not to write of myself that I did not hesitate and that I preferred your company to rejoining my little community, who, I have no doubt, were all ears, individually and collectively, for the news bulletins, and even more attentive to the rumors, which, again without doubt, had started to multiply like a cancer as soon as news of the explosion spread, as if they had taken form inside the bomb and then flown in all directions with all the torn flesh and splinters of glass when it exploded.

With your magical device, you can tell the television to shut up and go dark and it obeys at once. The television was like a third person, and as long as it was with us it forced you to sit up straight and prevented you from relaxing. Now that it was gone and we were alone again, there was nothing to stop you stretching out and making yourself comfortable in what I now know to be your favorite position—lying right down on the carpet with your head resting on the edge of the sofa.

I do not remember, and I do not want to remember, how long I remained in the position you left me in when you lay down on the carpet, too frightened to move, say a word, or even look at you. Your regular breathing was the only proof that you were awake rather than dreaming. I had no idea where you were or what thoughts had carried you off to sea. And if that simile is apt and you were indeed sailing, then I was wallowing in my thoughts: here we were, a man and a woman alone, with no fear of being disturbed by anyone, so where was the devil? Were you so trusting of me that you could behave in my presence as if I did not exist? Or were you gambling on my lack of self-confidence? Are not the two things one and the same? Is it not true that I did not even dare to look at you?

From the beginning to the end of our relationship, you always held the initiative. It was the same that night. Totally ignorant of your past and of much of your present life, I can be forgiven for knowing absolutely nothing of your sleeping habits; for example, what side you prefer to turn on when you grow tired of lying flat on your back. I was to your right and there was nothing to your left, and then I felt you changing position and took it as an opportunity to look at you. There you were, nodding off, turning on to your right side. Your head rolled slowly and came to rest just above my knee, on the lower part of my left thigh. Your right arm slipped down into the gap between us while your left arm reached out and rested on my right thigh.

Does it surprise you that I should spend so much time describing the details? I do so for the simplest of reasons: unless I dwell on the details I would not be me, and perhaps I would not be here now. I forgive you if you cannot understand why I was so hesitant. I forgive you, because my motive for being so careful is beyond belief: never before had I been alone with a woman in such peace and serenity as I found with you. In fact, I had never been alone with any woman other than with those women who meet the needs of men for a fee, and worse than that was the way the devil refused on those occasions to join us as my accomplice!

So there I was, forced to choose between two options: to pretend to be chaste and leave your house never to return, or surrender to you and to your judgment, answering a mysterious call and uncertain what I should attribute it to—to life or to nature, or a mixture of the two?

I felt somewhat reassured when you did not wake up at the glances I could not help but throw at you, I mean at us. Perhaps, deep in your slumber, deliberately careless, you wanted to give me enough time to grow accustomed to us being so near to each other and to discover for myself that for a man and a woman to be close should be like a shining city on a hill, not something done furtively. Forget all this nonsense . . . All that happened is that, by staying asleep, despite moving me and touching me, you gave me time to recover and catch my breath.

It wasn't lust that made me reach out and run my fingers through your hair, wrap my hands around your hand and squeeze it, or adjust the way you were lying. It was not lust . . . or else it was pure lust, and lust for everything about you.

I imagine I can hear you whispering to me in jest: "Go easy on yourself, man, it doesn't matter if you desired me, because in the end, despite everything you have told me about yourself and despite your lack of experience in dealing with women, are you not a man to whom the laws of nature apply, no more and no less? Suppose you were someone else, someone who does not share your affliction, would not the muezzin of nature inside you have summoned you, would not the same feelings and sensations have stirred and teemed inside you?"

❦

You are not here in my safe resort to whisper any such thing to me, but that is only a part of what is so terrible about my present situation, as on previous occasions when I have been unable to proceed with my account because of objections I imagined you raising against me. I took my imaginings seriously and worked hard to counter your cogent objections.

Today I will not do so; or rather, I will not do so in this particular case. Even if you are right in saying that, whether I like it or not, I am a man just like other men, I insist that my lust for you that night was quite the opposite of a 'sudden impulse.' If you want me to be more masochistic, I would remind you that whenever I tried to satisfy my 'sudden impulses' I always came back empty-handed or worse, and I took my wretched experiences, some of which I have recounted, as proof of what I say. But this objection, if we are still talking about objections, does not satisfy me, especially as I have an objection that is yet more devastating and powerful. I hold that my lust for you conjured up hope for me and made me feel happy: why not, when, spontaneously and out of nowhere, what you did ended up making me count in your life?

❦

I did not need to move close to you. I put my right hand on the left side of your brow and my trembling fingertips started to comb the tresses of your hair in the same direction, touching your left ear. You did not say or do anything to object—not in the least. On the contrary, a few moments later I found you adjusting the way you were lying, turning very slowly and gently so that all your head rested on my thigh. My right hand covered as much of your forehead as it could and my fingertips explored your hair without fear of straying from time to time to the right or the left toward one of your ears and fondling them.

❦

Writing in the morning is different from writing at night, at least with this kind of writing. Yesterday, when I went to bed a little after midnight, I did not do so because I was too tired or irritated to continue with my account of our relationship. I did so because I wanted to save the next part for myself, if only overnight. Besides, in recording it, I found myself sifting through the details in a way that might suggest I was looking for the clauses of the pact we made that night, the pact that took us across the last expanse of unexplored territory that lay between us. I felt that laying out all the details would help cure the two of us from what happened between us.

Now, in the morning, the matter is quite changed. Yesterday I had no doubt that the morning would bring change, but it reassures me to discover that my suspicion was well-placed and that, having reached the point when our intimacy started, I cannot now retreat.

⁂

Did my tender caresses bring you out of your sleep? Were you pretending to be asleep? Yes, you were. You were kind to me, and with the tips of your toes you flicked the light switch, plunging us into darkness. In the darkness we embraced and kissed, and lay together on the floor, resting our heads on the sofa. You unbuttoned my shirt and I unbuttoned your blouse, and with your hands and lips you explored my chest and I did likewise. Then, I do not remember how, we ended up completely naked. We tossed and turned, until finally I was done and collapsed on top of you to recover my breath. Yes, that's what happened.

But however fine and lengthy my description of what happened, I cannot do it justice, not because it wasn't a big deal— it certainly was— but because I am afraid it might come across that way and that what I say about it may seem too little. Who would now believe me if I were to say that, as soon as I plucked up courage and put my hand on your brow, a magic wand waved away all the barriers that had stood between us since we first met, and that what followed fanned the flames, rather than lit the fire?

⁂

Al-Mutanabbi's collected works lay on the table where we left it when we sat up to watch the news. I looked at it and it looked at me. It reminded me that I was not the only man under that roof and between those walls. For some minutes, I had been awaiting your return and I was impatient. I was hesitant: it had never been your practice to drop hints when plain words will suffice, or would your usual candor (if, for example, you wanted to tell me I should leave) have been out of place that night? I discovered I was naked, and I hurriedly gathered up my clothes and put them on, unable to resist stealing some glances at your clothes, scattered for some reason across a wider circle than my own. The least I could do, for politeness' sake, was wish you a good morning, even if it was before the break of dawn. I tiptoed toward the pale light emanating from a room at the end of the corridor, down which I had never ventured. In cowardice, I hoped to find you dozing so that I could retrace my steps and make do with a hurried "good morning" scribbled on a slip of paper on top of al-Mutanabbi's works. Through the crack of the door, I saw your shadow motionless on the wall opposite. In case you took offense if I was wrong in thinking you were deep in slumber, I pushed the door gently. Your hand slipped out from under the cover and reached toward me.

All the heartbeats my heart had missed for the past hour now beat. Almost in a trance, I continued to advance and knelt by your bed. You reached for the light switch and fiddled with it, until the light, already soft, dimmed to a faint glow that was more yellow than white. Then your hand came down on my head and played in my short hair. Having dared come into your room, I gave no sign I wanted to move any closer. I left you in full control, but . . . but like a child with a secret plan I took advantage of the darkness and my kneeling position to furtively remove my shoes. I was not in a hurry to move closer. On the contrary, I was in a hurry to find out what you would decide for me—your verdict on what had started between us. That is how we were placed: you in your bed and me kneeling beside it. I was just a premise on which you could build what you wanted: you could decide that we should stay like this for the whole two hours before the time came for me to leave. You might courteously suggest driving me home, and I would understand that you wanted to be alone; or you might pull me toward you, or hint that you would do so, and I would understand that your desire for me, like my desire for you, had not yet abated.

I do not know how long we spent like that before it occurred to me that maybe you too were leaving the decision to me, and waiting just as I was waiting, and that I was fooling myself when I told myself it was up to you alone. But then, was it not you who took the initiative and put out your hand to invite me closer? "How come you dare not return the greeting in kind?" I thought to myself. "Why not respond? Say something, spin a web of words to wrap the two of us together, something to the effect of 'You seem to be tired and on the verge of deep sleep, so I ask leave of you to depart.' Young man of the pulpits, where is that eloquence of yours, attested to by friends and enemies alike? Indeed, what kind of eloquence is this, so ready to be forceful and assertive when it comes to talking about religion, the world, and life and death, but that fails you when you are called upon to speak gently, in a soft voice, not thunder like a preacher?"

I did not have the courage to speak, only to act. As I learned with you, deeds are very often less of a burden than words. Your right hand was still on my head playing in my hair. You lifted my left hand and held it, and when I was sure that our fingers were entwined I squeezed it slowly, and the squeeze spoke for me, and spoke for my inability to look up into your eyes and whisper my thoughts to you.

Had it not been for the darkness and the sheet that covered you, or part of you, I would have been abashed by your nakedness. Fearfully, hesitantly, in a daze, I slowly reached for you, caressed your soft body from end to end as far as my arms could reach, as far as your knees. I relished the smell of you and had an urge to hold you tight with all my strength, but I restrained myself. It was not hard for me to do so, because the physical arousal did not make me forget that I was a novice who had never shared such pleasures with a woman in her bed. For fear of doing something to betray my inexperience, I took my time. Maybe you thought I was teasing, and you reached out to embrace me. All I could do was follow your example and let my instincts override my fears, with some help from genuine desire and my trust in your experience of worldly things. Even now I cannot explain that smile on your lips: was it an ironic comment as you read my thoughts, or a sign of satisfaction and approval? You clung to me and I interpreted that as meaning that you were putting me in charge. I obeyed, or rather you obeyed. I unwrapped your arms from around my neck, and when they were free I wrapped my arms around you under your armpits. You turned from your side on to your back and I found myself on top of you. I bent my head down, kissed and licked your breasts, while your tongue and lips played on my neck. You shuddered beneath me and wrapped your legs over mine, while I lay straight between your thighs. Our bodies converged and I sought a way to penetrate you. You enjoyed my explorations and wanted more. I gave you more and pulled myself up, holding back because I sensed that I could not wait much longer for your rapture. I pulled my right arm from under your back and reached down toward your vagina to rub my fingers in your wetness. You were gentle with me. You pushed my hand aside and with a quick shudder you set me straight and guided me right into the very depths of you.

❦

It was as hard for us to leave your bed as it had been to reach it in the first place. You took the initiative of course, but not only that. When you told me you were ready to drive me back to my mosque, and I was still in your bed, wrapped in your sheet, you had the good sense to withdraw somewhere where I could not hear a sound from you, sparing me the embarrassment of my nakedness. I do not know how I could have stood naked in your presence.

I know that both of us had a yearning to be alone, and on the way I did not utter a word, and neither did you. When we reached the mosque, we gave each other a perfunctory farewell, which did not embarrass either of us, even if it was not worthy of what had happened between us.

I wavered a while between waiting for dawn in my room and waiting in the mosque, and for no good reason I chose the second option. Here too, under the pulpit, whether I wanted it or not, and however strange it may seem, I was at home in God's house, my home and my place of work, a place with which I was as familiar as someone else would be in his apartment or his house, or in his office in a government department, or at his place behind a machine in a factory. And just like someone else in his office or factory, it happens that I am energetic one day and less so on another day, and on a third day in a bad mood and impatient for my shift to end. Here or in my room, I could see only your face and felt a strange tension, something between peace of mind and anxiety.

I passed close to an hour waiting for dawn to break, going over everything that had happened since seven o'clock the day before and trying to put it all together in an intelligible sequence. The strangest thing about it was that in this attempt of mine it was not thoughts about you that preoccupied me, but thoughts about myself.

177

Whether I liked it or not, my body and some of my muscles, which I had the impression I had never used before, gave a thousand good reasons for this egotism. I did not realize that I was praying in a state of ritual impurity until I had finished praying.

20

For the last few days, I have deliberately avoided writing for you. Ever since I started recording my account of events, I have often felt embarrassed to the point of cowardice when writing, but I have rarely been so hesitant to reconstruct our conversations, so unable to decide which was most important. That is why I made a commitment not to write, and turned instead to reading various passages in the few books I have accumulated here. Now I am abandoning this commitment, not because I know which of the matters pressing upon me makes it worth my while to pick up my pen, but under the impact of a sudden feeling that my situation here is starting to look unsettled and that the time I am destined to spend in this isolation is beginning to run out. At first, that time seemed to stretch to eternity, like an ocean with no shores and no floor, and I imagined there was no escape from its bland monotony and pallid colors. But now I feel that the time I have left is short, that I have been given a deadline to finish a task I took upon myself in a rare moment of thoughtless vanity—the task of writing down parts of my life and of our story in a genuine record, a trace of which might just survive if I am struck irreversibly dead. More than that: my delight at this deadline is matched only by the pleasure and enjoyment that writing for you brings me. The last thing I want to do is boast or succumb to superlatives, but what I have already said is, for me, the most serious confession I have made so far. That does not mean that only now have I been overcome by this double feeling of pleasure and enjoyment. Of course not. Ever since I started inking these pages, writing (for you)—a path I had never taken in the past—has acquired the status of an imperative and irresistible passion. Otherwise I would have given up at the first test I faced in that task—when I tried to make these pages bear witness for me in a way that left no place for secrets.* I would have given in to defeat and taken refuge in silence; I mean, in the safety and cover of silence. But I did not, and only today, in fact right now, do I dare to name those two feelings by their proper names. When I see those names in writing or hear them in speech, they never fail to arouse ideas and fancies that are hard to reconcile with the signs of modesty and circumspection that you associate with me and by which I have long defined myself.

As for you, my lady, rest assured that my disappointment will be immense if I am removed from this place to anywhere else, even to where you are now, before I finish these chapters of the story of my life, which appears to be about to make progress. I am driven to this apprehension by thoughts provoked on the occasion of my minder's visit a week ago and his promise to visit me again in the coming days to find out what I think of the proposal he conveyed to me.

My minder did not know that the only news I cared to hear from him was that he did not bring any 'happy news' to suggest that my isolation might be interrupted and my writing task disrupted, because neither he nor anyone else appreciates how engrossed I have become in my story in recent days and how this obsession has changed my situation. Spontaneously, or with deliberate intent to draw me out, my minder did not conceal his surprise at how "serene" my state of mind was, as he put it. In fact, he expressed his surprise with an affection and kindliness I had not previously seen from him. I was somewhat embarrassed that my demeanor and my words should so easily betray my newfound tranquility.

He asked me if I had been following the news and I answered casually: "I prefer not to hear it." He did not press the question, but instead asked another question, about what I was reading. I had the impression he was

---

* "Secrecy has a place in me inaccessible to any confidant, impregnable even when I'm drinking." (al-Mutanabbi)

180

using his question as an excuse to throw an inquisitive glance over the contents of the table, in case, I imagined, they might produce a convincing explanation for the change he had detected in my mood. He did not need to examine the contents, for they were the same as they had been since I had first arrived: my bare-bones library—an anthology of authenticated traditions of the Prophet, Ragheb al-Isfahani's glossary of rare words in the Quran, as well as an edition of the complete works of al-Mutanabbi, without any commentary. "Don't you get bored reading these dictionaries?" he asked, probably ready to praise my diligence after the 'No' he expected. I disappointed him when I answered with a decisive "Of course." I was not being deliberately provocative but it was what I felt, and maybe he gave my "of course" a wider interpretation and assumed it was in answer to a more general question such as: "Don't you feel bored?" I felt sorry for him, though grateful that I was not in his position. I was also worried about leaving him to speculate, even if my worries were misplaced, and in my desire to compensate I saw no alternative but to act helpless, so I told him I wanted to get hold of certain books and the only way for me to do so was to entrust him with this chore. My expectation was not mistaken: he latched on to my request and proceeded to respond in various ways, the gist of which was that it would be no trouble at all and all I had to do was provide him with the titles of the books I wanted to obtain. In that way, I was again the petitioner and he was again the person in charge. In order to entrench him in this role, I picked up a slip of paper and wrote the titles of three books on it. I passed him the piece of paper, which he examined carefully. He then gave it back to me, insisting I add other books that I wanted. He was more persuasive than me, and came close to coercing me, but at just the right moment I instinctively came up with an argument to which there could be no response: "I swear by God these are the only books I would like."

"With your oath, mawlana, you disarm me completely and leave no room for negotiation." That is how he answered me, careful not to reveal all the cunning that lay beneath what he said, but not so much that I missed the subtext, which was that an oath is the argument of the weak. I ignored what he said, turned a deaf ear to the subtext, and left him to manage the rest of our meeting as he wished.

I have no idea how matters went between him and the other residents of this refuge entrusted to his care, but my relationship with him, at least from my point of view, was always ambiguous, in that we would each compete to implicitly relinquish the status of host and willingly assume the role of guest—the unwelcome guest, no less—and I have no doubt that the ambiguity in our relationship was much more irksome to him than to me. Whereas his visits to me, when he visited, came to an end—as far as I was concerned—as soon as he left and I was alone again, I do not think they came to an end so easily for him, because I have no master to whom I have to explain myself, other than the master I have chosen (you, that is), whereas his masters were no doubt less gentle and indulgent than you, and more ruthlessly analytical and coldhearted, with nothing beautiful or elegant to say. Maybe he pays them his dues loyally, bowing to the demands and formal obligations of this world, or maybe, if he has a choice in the matter, with a view to sorting out his affairs, packing his bags and seeking for himself and his family a place to live under a sky that rains water rather than blood. Who knows, maybe he is one of those who have already moved their families to safe countries and who, when they protect the security of this country, act like mercenaries in the best of times, but like guard dogs in the worst of times.

I wonder what my minder writes in the reports he submits after every visit. Does he observe the fluctuations in my moods? Does he notice there is no sign that the newspapers piled up near the door have been read? Will he attach to his report on this visit a copy of the slip of paper on which I wrote the titles of the books?

Because I controlled, or thought I controlled, the meeting between me and my minder, I was confident enough to accept without hesitation his invitation that we take the opportunity of the mild weather to take a walk outside and continue our conversation. My minder did not seem to know what he was inviting me to do and, when I readily agreed, he did not see how my state of mind had changed. I tried to remember whether he had made such a suggestion before, but all I could recall from our previous meetings was the gloom and despondency that I brought to them and that he would accept with good grace—the good grace of a doctor paid to be patient, not of a generous friend. This would inflame rather than placate my suppressed anger, and would push me, in order to test his endurance, to even more introversion, gloom, and despondency. Not only that; in fact, what really irritated me was not his good cheer but that beyond or under it, or wherever you like, I detected an erroneous interpretation of my state of mind. Many a time, especially in our first meetings, I almost lost my self-control and confronted him with the truth: the truth that his interpretation of what was up with me, which was most probably based on analogy with the concerns and worries of the other residents of the refuge, was completely mistaken, and that my sorrows, if only he knew it or believed it, were intimate, private sorrows untinged by nostalgia for any passing glory, and it did not matter to my sorrows whether that glory was restored or whether it was past and never to return . . . and that my sorrows, even if they sometimes looked like the sorrows of mourning, their mourning was not in anticipation of losing a life I feared I might be deprived of but for a piece of my life, which from my point of view was life itself, a piece of life that stood apart from my life before and after. But, as you would expect, since horses know their riders best, I would hold my tongue, suppress my anger, and conceal my real state of mind. Between those days and today my minder gained no new knowledge of my inner thoughts and I did not bother to enlighten him, and perhaps because of this and not for any other reason, he was not surprised that I accepted his invitation to explore an outside world that, as soon as I crossed the threshold of this death row, I had always considered forbidden territory where I could not tread, except in cases of absolute necessity—for example, for my monthly medical check-up in the central building; or for the regular maintenance tests on the security systems, which also necessitated moving me to the same building; or, last but not least, for the insecticide-spraying campaign that last month forced me to vacate my wing for forty-eight hours. If I am correct in assuming that the human beings and mechanical devices that guard the place track my every movement, then it is not impossible that my minder saw my acceptance of his invitation as confirmation of his own inter- pretation of my depression—that is, that it was a 'natural' and ephemeral condition, which might reasonably afflict anyone so secluded from others, whose only remaining place in the world was under a sun that rose over high walls equipped with electric barbed wire and protected by sentries with their hands on their hearts and their fingers on the triggers of their rifles—a condition that would no doubt pass as soon as the inmate resigned himself to his lot or acknowledged, however reluctantly, that living under this sun was only a chapter in the story of his destiny.

Had it not been for my growing self-assurance, and my confidence in this explanation for his lack of surprise, I doubt I would have accepted his invitation or willingly submitted myself to an ordeal I never imagined life was cunning enough to contrive.

We walked for longer than I had expected, under the gaze of my minder's companions in their smart civilian clothes, with their dark glasses and concealed weapons, unlike the usual guards, who were masked, wore tight camouflage fatigues—rather like sports clothes in the way they accentuated the shape of their bodies and muscles—and were mostly armed with rifles with telescopic sights.

As a prelude, and without warning, my minder launched into a political analysis that portrayed the interests of major powers and small states as intertwined, and said that because of a conjuncture of interests certain circumstances had arisen, or at any rate were about to arise, and that other circumstances would no longer apply. It was not long before, in this interplay of interests, I detected the smell of oil, mining interests, and dubious political deals. Out of politeness, from time to time I would make mumbling noises to indicate that I was all ears for what he was saying, and in fact, although I was also preoccupied with enjoying the lushness of nature around us, I was listening to him to some extent. As he gradually went into the details and started to call things by their proper names and identify the people concerned, I began to pay more attention, and longed to know what his purpose might be in his elaborate presentation.

Did he deliberately make sure that we did not turn back until he had finished his analysis and was ready to draw his conclusion? That is what happened: "Unfortunately, one can't say everything one knows . . . and if one did, it wouldn't be understood or taken seriously," he said. "The hardest aspect of this war of interests (I was surprised that he used the expression without reservation) is that it's waged against us in the name of God, His book and His law . . . and the ways and the words of God are so diverse and tortuous that one can hardly tell which of them might lead to illegal activity! As you well know . . . someone who passes on heresy is not necessarily a heretic, is he? But he might sometimes hesitate to pass it on. That's where I stand, and that's also what led me to speak at such length and put off the task of passing on the message I have been asked to give you. To put it simply, and how simple it is, I have been commissioned to sound you out on how willing you might be to appear on television again and present a weekly religious lesson or something of that kind. On my way here I went over for the thousandth time all the possibilities and ideas and doubts that might occur to you as a result of this proposal. I have no doubt that you are now whispering to yourself something along the lines of: 'Aren't they satisfied that I have already put my own life in danger once, from a fatwa that will not lapse with the passage of time and that can be carried out wherever I am found?' or 'I have already drowned, so why should they worry about me getting wet?' You have the right to mistrust us and to think such thoughts, and even worse thoughts, but don't forget that the success you achieved through producing and presenting that program, even if there were only fifteen episodes, was unprecedented in the annals of religious television. I don't need to say I'm not exaggerating, because it's self-evident. Isn't it because of that success that you have been here for months?"

I was not misrepresenting my true feelings when I told him he had taken me by surprise, that this proposal was the last thing I expected to hear, and that I would need some time to reflect on the matter. What I did not tell him, and what I also felt, was that I had a strong and urgent desire to go back to my room, to be alone and consider my situation. It did occur to me to ask my minder if there was any way I could contact my sheikh, the one who had recommended me in the first place, but I abandoned the idea when I realized that in fact I had nothing to say to him and nothing to consult him on, but amazingly, just at that moment, my minder happened to think along exactly the same lines. After months without bringing me regards from the sheikh, he suddenly remembered that the sheikh had asked him to convey his greetings and his hope that we could soon meet.

The message from the sheikh only made me more tense and more anxious that my minder leave me alone. He did not seem to be in a hurry. I trusted that when we reached my room our meeting would come to an end, but he gave no sign that would happen, and asked if he could come inside with me. Without thinking, I said: "Make yourself at home, come on in." Did I really say it in a sarcastic tone? Or was it he who heard it as sarcastic and then thought it his duty to explain anew that the proposal implied no obligation and I was free to choose whether to refuse or accept it? My sarcastic remark, which had prompted this lengthy clarification, apparently deterred him from saying what he had intended to add when he followed me inside, and instead he merely asked me to think about the matter and promised me another visit . . . and the books.

In front of me on the table lies the draft of a letter to my sheikh, intended as my response to the proposal my minder had conveyed. My only concern is to win more time, and this letter, which opens with thanks for his regards and goes on to assert that I never take any decision without referring to him and that I await his guidance, is the only way I can win time, whether or not the letter reaches him; or at least that is what I am betting on. I do not know how my minder and his masters will read the letter, and I do not even know what kind of connection there is between my sheikh and these people, who in my memory have no faces and no names, and I do not care to know or bother about this matter. I have a legitimate right to be frightened, and my chief fear is that I will lose this right. The most obvious assumption is that I am afraid of death; not any death, but death by murder; and not any murder, but murder after torture at the hands of people who are confident they are carrying out a divine decree and that God is holding their hand. I may be afraid of death, but that is not the primary fear from my point of view; not because I am brave, but because I have a greater fear: a fear that something might prevent my martyrdom from running its course to the very end.

It was the custom of the ancients, whenever they digressed from the subject, to say something such as "Let's go back to where we were," and then resume the conversation where it had broken off. I wish I could go back to where I was with such ease and pick up my story. But far from it! From now on I will live and write what is left of my book in the knowledge that it may be a race against time . . . I mean, that the time may not be enough for me, and for my only life which indisputably deserves the name of life.

21

I t is no time for modesty, which sometimes means calling things by
other names—euphemistically, metaphorically, or, more simply, just
by allusion. It is no time for modesty, and so it is also no time for
making excuses for things that might seem gross or crude, or that must be
treated with discretion in polite society.

One rainy day you entrusted me with the keys to your house, and for
a woman to trust a man with the keys to her house means she trusts him
with herself. Trust in this case does not mean custody alone, but custody
and the right of use. I do not know whether you expected me to exercise
those rights of use without an explicit invitation from you. Maybe you had
to wait that week to be sure that I would act on that basis and then found
you had no choice but to accept it. And then what happened happened,
as I remember very well!

After that day, the day when the final barrier came down between us
as man and woman, I loosened up in innumerable ways, often without any
visible evidence or overt signs. From that day on, too, I felt free to enter
all the rooms in your house, and I started to drop in without advance
appointment. Little by little, my visits began to merge into permanent
residence. You now call the computer table my table, and you have brought

for the computer another smaller table with wheels and put it next to your table, the one where we grew to know each other. For my papers and stationery you have set aside one of the shelves of the bookcase, and for my clothes, which have started to multiply and become smarter, part of your giant wardrobe. The pace of my life has picked up, and I have kept up with it, breathlessly at times, seeking your help whenever possible and tapping my own inner strength when necessary. But it is not only my life that has picked up speed, but also the cycle of life and death in your country and mine. It is true that death in my country was always cheaper than death is here, and the war there was more overt than it is here, but the difference between the two places and whether I was in one rather than the other did not prevent the two wars from affecting me. Even before I had personal experience of it, as imam, preacher, and teacher, I realized by tangible daily evidence that managing and guiding people's faith is a most difficult task. I often wondered, especially when I was working in the Ministry of Religious Endowments, in the department in charge of running and supervising mosques, how it was that many mosques were left to themselves, or rather to the local clerics, for them to talk about God in any way they liked. I was not reassured by the bureaucratic inquiries our department would receive from time to time from the religious activities branch in some security agency, asking about some mosque. After examining our records, we would soon ascertain that the mosque in question had been built on land bought by some charity as a religious endowment, and that we did not know who the imam was, or we would find that the imam registered with us had died years earlier. That might seem surprising when the country was under such tight control, but surely what happens here and there is ample proof that such surprise is misplaced. The iron fist that strikes terror in people's hearts and, when terror alone is not enough, throws people in jail or opens fire at them, hesitates when it comes to breaking down the door of a house of God, to say nothing of the fact that it has no authority over what lurks in people's hearts.

"We're trying to catch up with people who have already had their say,"* said one of the participants in that 'closed' meeting between officials from the ministries of religious endowments in the two countries and

---

* A reference to Quran 20:129: *Were it not for a prior Word from your Lord, judgment would have been passed and a set term appointed.*

188

others from the religious activities branches of the security agencies. "Unless we acknowledge that they have beaten us to it, and unless we try, among our measures, to catch up and keep an eye on the religious lessons given in mosques, then our efforts will be in vain . . . I'm not saying that he who makes the first move must necessarily win; I'm just observing that we're like people who have been caught napping."

It was a sign of the times that the meeting took place on the initiative of the security people, not of the mosque people, and that the proposal I supported—namely, that religious lessons in mosques should be monitored and that we should counterattack with our own lessons—also came from the security people. After all, like hundreds of others, in principle and according to my job description, I was paid to perform three functions— to lead prayers, to give the sermon on Friday and at the two main feasts, and to teach.

While the first two needed no explanation and could be controlled, there was no agreed and comprehensive formula for the teaching function. The subject of the lessons might be Arabic grammar and morphology, just as the lessons might be on Quranic exegesis, or the sayings and practices of the Prophet, and as long as that was the case, who could give assurances to anyone on how one sheikh or another might interpret the verses of the Quran that deal, for example, with the promotion of virtue and the prevention of vice? And who could guarantee that some cleric or enthusiast or anyone else was not the kind of person it would take the greatest faith to trust, especially when the "greatest faith" in this context could imply vigilante justice?* And who could guarantee what someone or other might say to explain what the Prophet meant when he said: "I have been commanded to fight people until they say 'There is no god but God,' and those who say 'There is no god but God' shall be secure in their property and their lives," or when he said: "The Israelites have split into seventy-two factions, and you will split up likewise, and all but one of those factions will go to Hell." Besides, as I once heard a preacher on the radio say, teaching

---

* A saying of the Prophet Muhammad reads: "If any of you see an abomination and you can intervene physically to prevent it, then do so. If you cannot intervene physically, then use your tongue. If that is not possible, then condemn it in your heart, but that is the weakest form of faith." (Author's note) Many Islamist activists have cited the saying to justify their own unofficial policing activities. (Translator's note)

in mosques counts as proselytizing, and "all religious scholars versed in the Quran and the Sunna everywhere have a duty to proselytize, teach, promote virtue and prevent vice . . . they should pass on God's message wherever they are—in the mosque, at home, in the street, in cars, planes, and trains." And who can give assurances that someone or other is really learned? Add to this the fact that the management and supervision of mosques, even if they are the houses of God, are not assigned to archangels, but rather to human beings whose clerical status does not save them from being civil servants, lazy ones most of the time.

Take, for example, an upright government-appointed sheikh who does his duty in full and gives a lesson once or twice a week. If his lessons are boring and he tells boring stories in a boring way, don't you think that his disciples will abandon his lessons and his mosque, to join the circle of a sheikh who is eloquent, intelligent, and interesting? Assume the best of him, of his honesty and his logic. How could he stop anyone from coming to his mosque, praying there, mixing with the congregation, and spreading his religious message in their ranks? I'm not saying I am exempt from all the vices I have enumerated. When I arrived in your city, armed with my three titles (imam, preacher, and teacher), I found that my predecessor had made do with giving a few lessons, more like ethical homilies, on special occasions and during the month of Ramadan. For form's sake and to liven up the mosque, I tried to organize a weekly public lesson on the model of my predecessor's lessons—that is, more like a sermon, between sunset and the evening prayer every Thursday. In the first weeks, the size of the audience was significant, but most of them came either with intent to get to know me, to please the new sheikh, or to request a favor, and most of them were men of middle age or older. As the weeks passed the audience shrank, or rather the only people there were those who prayed regularly in the mosque, and the lesson evolved into a discussion that sometimes went on beyond the time for evening prayers. For sure, colleagues of mine had tried as I tried and had failed as I failed, but my failure was mitigated by the knowledge that the local people came to my mosque for mundane rather than spiritual purposes, and this enabled me to confine my contacts to those of them who were devout. Before the start of the attempts to take over the mosque, some of which I have already mentioned, all this helped me accept the events that befell the mosque, the neighborhood, and the country as inevitable events for which the warning signs were clear. And do not forget that God in His creation works in mysterious ways, and that every human is fated to experience both things he wants and things he does not want, things that are worth taking risks for and things that are not worth taking risks for. This applies to those who bear the title of sheikh as much as it applies to others. For example, when my name comes up as the imam of a mosque, my admirers say I defended my mosque to my last breath (no doubt they are exaggerating a little, since I have now been breathing this last breath for months!). Did I defend my mosque? Yes, I did, or rather I pretended I was determined to defend it, and perhaps my pretense of resolve protected it more than my defense of it. But can I say that I succeeded in turning my mosque into a model house of God? I cannot claim that. In fact, I would almost go so far as to say that the fate of my mosque made it the worst possible example, an example of the evil that none of us, whether killers or victims, can wash our hands of.

～

When I first started appearing on television, Fridays at the mosque took on a new lease of life. I did not in fact expect my status as a fledgling star to have such a rapid impact or that the mosque would benefit from it to such an extent, but that is what happened.

On the Friday after my third television appearance, I knew beyond any doubt that the number of faces unfamiliar to me was constantly growing. This impression was corroborated by the large number of people who gathered around me after the end of prayers, some merely to say hello, some to say hello and to congratulate me on some remark I had made, some to say hello, praise the program in general, and state some objection to the remark which someone else had been praising, and others to say hello and request an appointment for a personal consultation.

Saying hello was the essential element and what came with it, if anything, was just a means to that end. We often talked about this, and when I expressed surprise at my rapid transformation into a star behind whom people sought to pray and to whom people wanted to say hello, your answer was: "Stop pretending to be modest. You well know that modesty is a form of arrogance." But in fact my surprise was very far from being contrived, firstly by analogy with myself: I do not remember making the slightest effort to say hello to any television celebrity, neither at university,

191

while I was working in the ministry, nor after; and secondly and more importantly because preparing the episodes of the program and playing the role of presenter was a constant worry throughout the week: no sooner had I finished recording the program on Wednesday afternoon than I fell back into the snare of the program on Saturday morning, at the weekly meeting, which brought together all the members of the team and which made plans for the next episode. Needless to say, this meeting itself required preparation.

All of this, I have no doubt, was completely unknown to the mass of Muslims who saw of me only what appeared on screen. One of your favorite aphorisms was that "stardom is a profession" and you sometimes dropped all pretense of reserve and told me frankly, sometimes bluntly, but without reproof or contempt, that "in the end" (that is, from the point of view of television, that giant udder which feeds mankind indiscriminately with pictures, ideas, and fantasies), though the audiences may differ, there was no difference with respect to "social function" (another phrase I have borrowed from you) between me and a rising young singer idolized by a segment of adolescents, or that young and pretty colleague of mine who presents the game show, or other stars whom fans rush to greet. Nevertheless, I did not really understand your remarks, and the reality of my new personality did not strike home until one day I found an analogy drawn from my own upbringing. That was the day when I asked myself, tentatively, and with a certain naivety: "When they insist on saying hello to me and others like me, isn't that a form of seeking baraka, spiritual power?" I could not help but conclude that it was.

For you, the subject was a matter of indifference, and you saw it with experienced and irreverent eyes, judiciously and decisively, so my repeated talk about the spell I sometimes found myself inadvertently casting on people far and near inspired in you an idea that was no less sharp than your proposal to sort mosques into classes. (That proposal was adopted and, when it was shot and broadcast, it gave rise to so many passions that we came close to deciding not to continue with the idea, but the man with the final decision insisted and threatened to suspend the whole program if we dropped it.) In this case, you said, "In most religious programs open to audience participation, all the audience can do is ask questions and seek rulings on points of Islamic law. Why don't we turn that upside down and ask the audience what they think about practical matters relevant to themselves and religion?" I did not comment on your proposal, but as usual I stored it away in my memory just in case. Some days later, before I had had a chance to retrieve it from memory, you surprised me with a detailed proposal, laid out so persuasively that all I had to do was submit it. You and the program team, including me and those whose judgment I trusted, agreed that the weakest segments in the program were those related to news about Muslims in the world, but we, the team, lacked any substitute for them, or perhaps were too lazy to come up with better alternatives. When you gave me your proposal, I was at a loss what to do. I could have put it aside and claimed that I had submitted it and it had been rejected, but that idea never occurred to me. In fact, I did submit it, and within a few days a committee, including the team and an influential official at the station, was set up to look into the details. At the time, the city was preoccupied with a series of murders targeting a number of prostitutes, responsibility for which was claimed by a group called "the Defense of Virtue."* Inspired by you, I suggested that this topic of the moment should be the subject of the short segment, which we divided into two parts: a first part, taking up two-thirds of the allotted time, in which an invited audience from the general public would discuss the chosen topic, and a second part, taking up the remaining third of the time, in which I would explain the view of Islamic law. After some hesitation my proposal was adopted, although I myself was about to back out of it after some of my colleagues took fright and urged us to choose a subject less provocative toward "religious feelings." I do not need to tell you what impact the affair had. The four guests were unanimous in condemning vice and prostitution, while maintaining that the murder of these prostitutes was a crime, even if the perpetrators had clean hands and pure intentions. Islamic law, as expressed by me, took the side of the audience, on the grounds that, although Islamic law strongly condemns vice, preventing vice is not a right that anyone can exercise at random. It was quite unprecedented to say that on a television channel respected by the majority of spectators, according to opinion polls, and as part of a religious program entitled "Peace Be

---

* Of course, before long it emerged that this group never existed and that the perpetrators of these crimes were people hired to carry out these killings by a rogue security agency.

Upon You" (the first part of the traditional Islamic greeting*). It aroused the rancor and resentment of some, but it only added to the fame of the program and to the star status of yours truly, your distinguished pupil.

Like all stars, your distinguished disciple became the center of attention and an object of envy; in fact, the more envied he was, the more he became the center of attention. Naturally, the most prominent of the malcontents were colleagues of mine from your country, who saw me as 'the foreigner' of dubious learning (on the grounds that the educational disparity between our two countries also applied to institutes of Islamic jurisprudence) and begrudged me the success that I rather than they had reaped. I may have been a foreigner but the world of Islam, whether they like it or not, is one country, if not a single town,† and I could cite thousands upon thousands of good precedents for Muslim clerics roaming the world to seek and propagate learning far from their places of birth. As for my learning, it was no less than that of the most learned of them, and when I made a mistake, I resorted to my eloquence to silence them when I could not defeat them by argument. Although the two arguments—my foreign status and my celebrity—failed to discredit me in public, the envious, even those of them who preached in favor of an Islam based on the Quran and the Balance rather than an Islam of Iron,** did not lack for a third argument, more

---

* "It is related that when a Bedouin Arab met someone from his own clan and family, he would greet him by wishing him peace—that is, a comfortable and pleasant life, free from pillage, raids, captivity, and coercion, and would also wish death upon his enemies: that is, anyone who was not from his tribe. The Arab greeting, the second part of which early Islam omitted (i.e., the part wishing death) . . . combined peace for the family, the tribe, and relatives by marriage with death for the foreign outsider." Wadah Sharara, *Death to Your Enemy* (Beirut: Dar al-Jadid, 1991), 97–98.

† "If the enemies of Islam enter the land of Islam, then there is no doubt that they must be driven out, initially by those closest to the point of entry." Ibn Taymiyyah, *Majmu al-Fatawa*, vol. 28.

** Through his Prophet, God revealed the Quran, the Balance and Iron. *We sent our messengers with evident wonders, and sent down with them the Book and the Balance that mankind may act with fairness. And We sent down iron, in which there is great strength and benefits to mankind, so that God may know who will come forward to support Him and His Messengers, in the Unseen. God is All-Powerful, Almighty.* (Quran 57:25). His book guides to the truth and the iron sets aright those who stray from the truth. This is the only way to make people righteous. When one of the two—the Quran or iron—is ineffective, iniquity and ruin result. The Prophet said, "I have sent the sword ahead of the Hour so that God alone is worshiped." (Hadith)

eloquent than the first two and more likely to convince both common people and the elite, I mean the elite of the common people, namely, that in everything I did and said I was the plaything of a hidden hand, the very same that had brought me to the Mosque of the Expatriates some years ago, that had made me a star and protected me.

Oddly, those colleagues of mine who envied my sudden stardom were not the only ones who propagated this rumor. It was also propagated, very widely and more vigorously and by every means, not just by word of mouth, by the group of adversaries that had reached the fringes of the mosque and that preached the Islam of Iron and of painful punishment. In fact what annoyed me about the rumor was not that it was propagated but that it was so stupid, because the fact that some hand or hands had taken me by the hand, brought me to your city as imam of the Mosque of the Expatriates, and then recommended me as producer and presenter of the program was not something I denied. On the contrary, since I started work in television, it often happened that I deliberately admitted the patronage of the influential sheikh. But I thought it sheer stupidity to describe this influence as secret. How could it be secret when no one other than him, either in this country or my country, had such power to make or break? Although this fact was as clear as the sun in July, the idea that it was mysterious was deeply rooted and impossible to dislodge. On top of that, the rumor irritated me because the one and only hand that guided me and deserved to be described as mysterious was your hand, but I could not give it credit in public.

In the meantime, our life together took its course within the walls of your house, with nothing to disturb its serenity.

Since I started writing down these notes, whenever I tried to tell the story of our relationship, I could not help stopping from time to time in wonder at what happened. I was still amazed that the sheikh of the Mosque of the Expatriates, in other words me, should have had the good fortune to come into contact with a woman in the prime of life who was so fascinating in every way. Today, although that sense of surprise still recurs from time to time, we do still have a right to be surprised that we understood each other so well, with such a minimum of discussion; that

195

is, with hardly any discussion at all. In fact, as our relationship evolved, as I progressed from being a chance encounter in your life to being a close companion and lover, and you progressed from being a woman wrapped in mystery to being a lover and confidante, how could I not be surprised that, for all that to happen and to endure, we needed only to begin? Once we started, it became a way of life.

It also happened that, without any overt agreement, neither of us ever brought up the subject of 'the future' to which this intimacy might lead. The truth is that when 'the future' is off the agenda of a man and a woman bound together as strongly and intimately as we were, it is a rare and wonderful opportunity. Without talking and without overt agreement, we also made good use of that opportunity day after day. If that had been known to others, it would definitely have made them envious of us!

If I must add something, I would add this: that everything I have said so far about our relationship would be incomplete if I did not give full credit to the learning we exchanged. There's no comparison between what I learned from you and what you learned from me. All you gained from me was a few rules of grammar or morphology, and it would make no difference whether you knew them or not and, besides, anyone with a grasp of grammar and morphology could have explained them to you as well as or better than I did. But as for what I gained from you, the least one could say is that it is immeasurable. I am not one of those who claim that life is a science one can master. Before I was born again through you, life was nothing worth mentioning. Afterward, life was breathed into every-thing and all things, even the most trivial and insignificant. From then on, life was no longer inconsequential and immaterial. I am not exaggerating, believe me. Monotheistic theology robbed me of the God I had seen in the wonder of His creation and Whom I loved without anyone's help. My life before you made life repugnant to me and robbed me of my desire to live . . . I met no one who restored God to me or me to God. Deep inside, I shied away from sharing my God with anyone I met. But I did meet someone who reconciled me to life and brought me back to life, and that was you. A second birth or a first resurrection are nothing but pale metaphors that have a dubious resonance but fall short of describing my gradual transformation as our relationship grew stronger. I know that however much I enumerate the aspects and details of life that I discovered thanks to you, someone will come out and ask contemptuously: "Is that life?" But for me, life embraces everything, and I do not care that others despise or pretend to despise some aspects of life, probably because they are unaware of them or have never experienced them. Leave aside how I learned again at your hands how to read al-Mutanabbi's works; leave aside our discussions and how they helped me to discover, if not always new ideas, then at least new expressions or new usages of well-known terms; leave aside how my vision, dulled by education, explored new and unknown horizons. Leave aside all that, because it is not what matters, because you could not have conveyed all that to me unless you had cured me of what, somewhere in these notes, I called my "premature senescence." Yes, it does sometimes happen that the symptoms of this senescence recur, not to mention that some devil sometimes whispers temptations in my ear. But it is one thing to experience such furtive thoughts and temptations, and then to stand up to them and fight them off, armed with what I have gained from you, and quite another thing to stand aside and let them destroy me. All the good luck I may have had—the luck that brought me from poverty and obscurity to renown as sheikh of the Mosque of the Expatriates—is not worth, in my view, the happiness your company has trained me to enjoy and without which I would not have walked with sure steps, or hardly, to where I am now. I owe it to you that I changed my appearance, and no one knows better than you that it is no small thing for a man to be persuaded, at a time when he has no need for clothes at all, that there is no shame in dressing well or as lightly as is comfortable. I also owe it to you that I learned that when a man and a woman are alone behind closed doors, the devil is not necessarily a third presence, and that I discovered for certain that the books of Islamic law of the four schools, or five or six, or as many as you want, despite their prolixity and their obscure jargon, are not big enough to mention what a man and a woman may feel in a moment of epiphany (no, I am not speaking in the language of the Sufis, and I do not mean it in the Sufi sense!).

I do not remember which night it was that you asked me a question to the effect of "Aren't you envious of him? I mean Ahmad al-Mutanabbi. Aren't you curious to inquire how I spend these long hours among his works, these papers and files?" I answered that of course I was envious of him, but I was leaving you to grow tired of him, and then I would not need to make the slightest effort to win you back. And when you failed to respond in a way that stood up to my argument, you justified your pride with a certain flirtatiousness and asked me a question I had to reply to: "Don't you think he disapproves of us? Doesn't he deserve that we give him his share of our time?" I stipulated that I should choose the poem, and you agreed. I warned you that the poem was something he wrote in his early youth. You asked me what I meant by my warning. I busied myself looking for it in the index, and it took me a while, although poems ending in the letter 'qaf' are rare. You asked again, and I merely said it was something the man said in his youth. Perhaps you understood what I meant, or perhaps the joke you made up—"The kind of thing an old man pretending to be young might write?"—dumbfounded me. I opened the book at the page where the poem starts—his eulogy of Abul Muntasir Shujaa bin Muhammad bin Aws bin Maan bin al-Rida al-Azadi—and put it in front of you and left you to read it, with something in mind other than to draw your attention to the fact that the predicate of "the ordeal of longing" in the second line is the clause "that it be" and when he writes "what" in "what goes out" in the fourth line it creates a verbal noun and that this line contains a grammatical joke, which refers to a certain dispute between the grammarians of Basra and those of Kufa and may contain an additional piece of evidence that al-Mutanabbi, either instinctively or deliberately, wrote some of his poetry in the language of the Quran or something similar, not just in Arabic.

I left you to read, with a mind to confess to you that the first six lines of this poem helped to console me in my love for you, and although I recognize my debt to your Ahmad, I have now grown out of his thrall and no longer need to criticize or forgive those in love, because I have become one of them. I had a mind to match my words with deeds by interrupting your reading and pulling you toward me . . . and before you reached the sixth line, that's what I did.

Without warning, I rose from my chair, stood behind you, and put my hands on your bare shoulders. Your voice trembled. I took no notice and did not explain what I was doing by inviting you to follow me or anything like that. Before your voice faded completely, I slipped my hands down close to your armpits and in the flash of an eye put them under your arms and lifted you up. In fact, I did not need to, because you stood up willingly, and willingly we walked to your bedroom, pressed together, with me behind you. I moved you close to the wall and turned you till you were facing me. I put one hand behind your head to cushion it from the wall, while my other hand started to caress your buttocks. While I was busy with your lips and neck, I felt your hand undoing my trousers, which fell to the ground. I was barefoot, so it took little effort to slip out of them. I tried to push you to the bed, but you knelt down and took my penis in your hands like someone picking up a burden which was large rather than heavy. You brought it toward your lips and it slowly began to disappear into your mouth. For a while you closed your lips over it and then, just as slowly, you began to rock your head back and forth. No sooner did part of it appear than it would all disappear again, as it filled with blood and as I filled with pleasure. During those moments, which lasted I know not how long, I must confess that I neglected you, attending only to my pleasure.

When I felt I could wait no longer, I realized that you were waiting for me. Knowing me intimately, you did not abandon me. My body was reeling and you were worried I might be feeling guilty.* Instead, you took me gently and walked us in an embrace to your comfortable bed. Then you stood up and went to your spacious bathroom, which I had never entered when you were in it or even thought of entering. But my desire for you was stronger than my inhibitions. The gurgle of water, which indicated you had finished doing your intimate business, encouraged me to join you. In the mirror, you saw me approaching naked. You carried on brushing your teeth and then flossing with the tip of the toothbrush. I was drawn to

---

* I was right about your apprehensions, because at that very moment I suddenly remembered the details of an incident that had an effect on me and from which I learned much. I used to attend the public lectures that one of my teachers gave after evening prayers every Thursday in a mosque near my college. After the lecture, he would open the floor to questions and requests for legal rulings. One evening, the sheikh lingered unusually long in reading out to the audience in his loud voice one of the written questions he had received, and when he took matters in hand and started to read out his answer, his loud voice had a resolve and a strain that were impossible to miss. The question from the pious student did indeed deserve careful treatment: "Is it lawful for a wife to take her husband's penis in her hands and her mouth like a sandwich?" I don't know how the rest of the audience reacted to the question because I did not turn to see them. I was focused on my sheikh, not wanting to miss anything of how he would handle it, certain that he would do it well. I imagined myself sweating profusely in the same situation. He cleared his throat and swallowed several times before replying: "The questioner's question is gross, but the answer is that it is lawful." He then quickly moved on to the next question. It was a lesson like no other!
The answer is correct: see Sheikh Muhammad Ahmad Kanaan, *The Rules of Married Life* (Beirut: Dar al-Basha'ir al-Islamiya, 1993), 99.

you irresistibly, until I found myself pressing against you, my arms wrapped around you and my hands caressing your breasts while my penis tried hard to nestle between your buttocks. When my efforts failed, I saw no alternative but to seek the help of my hand, which began to play in the sensitive spots hidden in the triangle of hair below your stomach. You did not hold out long against my playing fingertips. Unbeknownst to you, or so it seemed to me, you sprouted wings and began to writhe, and when the writhing exhausted you or was unable to contain your pleasure, you spontaneously stretched out, resting on the edge of the washing machine and spreading your legs. Just as a bird does not need to be taught how to fly, I did not need to have experienced this style of intercourse before to know what to do next, once you had paved the way for me, nor how I should lead our lustful dance. Once you had orgasmed, followed shortly by me, we did not want to go back to your bed separately. Locked together, we tried to walk slowly. We failed and reluctantly separated. But before long, we nimbly renewed our amorous adventures aboard your bed.

That night I found out for sure that the sum total of pleasure is not two naked bodies in one bed; I mean, it is not just two naked bodies in one bed!

22

My minder's long absence troubles me more than it reassures me. He has never made me promises, other than those I extracted from him at the time of his last visit, but he has never failed to turn up for an appointment. I want him to stay away, and stay away for a long time, as long as I know what prevents him from visiting, so that I know whether to write in brief or at length. He said he would come back to visit me within a week, and since that week elapsed I have wavered between writing slowly and hurrying up. Have they given up the idea of bringing me out of hiding? If so, why do they need to keep protecting me and watching over me? Is it not possible that someone will come, today or tomorrow, to tell me that the reasons that required them to bring me here have lapsed, or, worse yet, that the authorities who have me in their power want me to go back where I came from? These questions haunt me like a mild but constant headache, and I cannot dispel or quell them. Now that, in the story of my life, I am coming to the death threats and my move here, the uncertainties have an even more powerful grip on me. I do not want this strange coincidence between my anxiety these days and my lightheart-edness in those days to affect me or throw its shadow over me. But my will alone, however strong it may be, is not enough to prevent that. Perhaps I should just pretend that there is nothing new under the sun. Why am I so reluctant to take this way out when I have taken it so often in the past?

When I look at what happened and how it happened, especially in the days just before I came here, I can hardly believe how recklessly and naively I was living, or how I overlooked what the consequences might be. Of course I realized what I was dealing with and which side I was on, and I was fully at ease with the opinions I expressed in public, but very often my excitement with myself, with you and with our relationship, would sweep all that aside or consign it to some abyss of oblivion. The best evidence for that is the way I was deaf to the many alarm bells that rang time and again and that a sensible, responsible man should have heeded. Anyway, I do not discount the possibility that I deliberately turned a deaf ear to them. I also do not discount the possibility that it was the renown I had acquired that baffled my opponents and made them hesitant to mobilize and finish me off quickly.

I am quite sure they could easily have killed me, because they had already shown enviable skill in circumventing security measures and infiltrating protected enclaves, and similar ingenuity in carrying out their killings. Besides, killing me would not have required any great effort or any considerable subtlety on their part, because, despite much advice, I had not changed any of my routines. In fact, I refused to travel around by private car or have people assigned to protect me, and I went on in that manner until a few days before I was moved here, when I was informed that from then on I would have no choice in my movements and my security.

It is strange for a man to explain the reasons why people refrained from killing him, almost as if he were apologizing for remaining alive, apologizing both to the dead, whose number he was fated not to join, and to the living, among whom he is an intruder. When I first appeared on television, the statements put out by my opponents described me as "the clown," in a manner that was derogatory rather than polemical. But as Friday prayers in my mosque began to flourish, it seems they had second thoughts about the 'clown' epithet and about the wisdom of attacking me in person. They then expanded their target and spoke of "the Secessionist

202

Mosque* and its heretical buffoon imam." This only made me more euphoric, and blinder, because, unlike the other mosques in the city and its environs, mine was the only mosque visited by television cameras, not to test the quality of the services it provided to its congregation, but to ask the congregants why they were not afraid to come and pray behind its imam.

My 'friends' in security have their own explanation, backed with dates and details, for why they spared my life—they say that their restraint was attributable to the success of security operations in dismantling the networks of 'evildoers.' Perhaps their explanation is closest to the truth, but even today it is not enough to convince me. I still maintain that it was their role in describing me as "the clown" that saved my skin throughout those months, because my only response was one of disdain. Sometimes I quoted the Quranic verse *We have our deeds and you have your deeds. Peace be upon you! We have no truck with the vicious,*† and at other times I cited one of two sayings by your poet—either "If someone deficient slanders me to you, to me that is evidence that I am perfect," which I supplemented with a disclaimer of pride or any claim to perfection; or else "Who bites the dog if the dog bites him,"**— and sometimes with both. If others did not dwell on the way I combined in a single context a quotation from the Quran and quotations from al-Mutanabbi, you were aware that I was not doing so by chance but deliberately and intentionally, because in those days you had brought me in on the secret of your personal interest in al-Mutanabbi, separately from the 'project' that helped bring us together, and on the fact that you had collected various passages, some connected with his character and his era, and some related to more general subjects, such as the history of prophecy in Islam and studies on the language of the Muwallad poets,†† on Ibn Jinni, al-Farabi, and so on.

---

* A reference to Quran 9:107–8: *And for those who built a mosque, out of malice and blasphemy and to sow discord among the believers, and as a spying post for one who had previously fought against God and His Messenger—they will no doubt swear: "We only intended a good deed." Yet God testifies that they are liars. You are never to pray in it. A mosque founded on piety from the very first day is more worthy for you to pray in.*

† Quran 28:55

** The full line reads: "In my contempt for him, I did not speak to him. Who bites the dog if the dog bites him?"

†† Poets of mixed descent writing in Arabic. (Translator's note)

"I do not claim that my modest learning qualifies me to enter the field of scholarly research," you said, "but I do claim that my amateur familiarity with the work of al-Mutanabbi qualifies me to record, impressionistically so to speak, some of my thoughts on the subject. I do not yet dare say that my endeavors in this field might one day take the form of a book, or, if they were to do so, that the book would find any readers. If it does end in a book, when the time comes that I decide to stop work on it, then I see it divided into chapters, perhaps thirteen, one of them, of course, on al-Mutanabbi's 'abnormal' birth (in the view of some*) and his confusing genealogy, and another on the coincidence, of unlimited significance when one thinks about it, that he was a contemporary of Farabi and that both were proteges at the court of Sayfaddawla.† I am not concerned whether or not they met, whether one of them did or did not hear the other speak, or whether Sayfaddawla's audience chamber was big enough for the two of them. What strikes me is how reading the works of the two of them suggests that in that remote age, the Arabic language had already diverged into completely disparate forms. What is left of a tongue that writes poetry in one language and philosophizes, or tries to philosophize, in another language? It sometimes seems to me that al-Mutanabbi (who wrote his poems twice, firstly when he wrote each one and secondly when he chose what deserved to be retained and threw away the rest) was writing against Farabi . . . Tell me, do you believe that al-Mutanabbi claimed to be a prophet?"

I had no idea why you suddenly switched to this question from your previous remarks, but I had my reply ready, because the subject had long intrigued me, this subject of prophethood, and I was even more intrigued after reading him at your suggestion. "I don't know how you will take this,"

---

* "All this suffices to convince me that al-Mutanabbi's birth was abnormal and that al-Mutanabbi was aware that it was abnormal and that he was affected by this throughout his life." Taha Hussein, *With al-Mutanabbi* (Cairo: Dar al-Maarif, 1986), 25.

† Despite the age difference between al-Mutanabbi and Farabi (the first was born in 915 CE and the second in 870 CE), al-Mutanabbi and Sayfaddawla met in 948, whereas Farabi visited the court of Sayfaddawla between AH 334 (about 945 CE) and AH 336 (about 947 CE), moved to Egypt in AH 337 (948 CE), and then returned to Damascus in AH 338. See the dates for Farabi's travels in Abdel Rahman Badawi, "al-Farabi," in *Encyclopedia of Philosophy*, vol. 2. (Beirut: Arab Foundation for Studies and Publishing, 1984), 93 ff.

I said, "but, frankly, I do not rule out the possibility that he had a notion to claim the status of prophet as the shortest way to obtain what he wanted, what he considered too sublime to be named.* In fact, it surprises me that some people voluntarily try to prove him not guilty of this charge. In a world where the culture had always had a fascination with prophets, quasi-prophets, and those who play that role, or fill that gap, in this 'prophetosphere,' if I may use the expression (morphologically the word is sound), the least one would expect from an ambitious young man of good family, a man who might rise God knows how high, is that he should seek his fortune by means of prophethood, but this in my opinion is not the most important thing. The most important thing is that he quickly realized that his claim was vulgar and retracted it, not out of a sense of guilt, but in order to turn to poetry, and that was his masterstroke, if not to say his genius.†

---

* "They say to me: What are you in every country and what do you seek? What I seek is too sublime to be named." (al-Mutanabbi)
† The standard version of his life runs as follows: Abul Tayyib al-Mutanabbi, whose full name was Ahmad ibn al-Hussein ibn al-Hassan ibn Abdel Samad al-Juafi al-Kindi the Kufan, was born in the year AH 303 in a place called Kinda, near Kufa in modern Iraq, from where he takes his last two names. He was not from the tribe of Kinda, but from the Juaf tribe.

He grew up in Kufa. It is said that his father was a water carrier there and then moved with his son to Syria, and he grew up there, too. One poet refers to this in a poem satirizing al-Mutanabbi: "What's the virtue of a poet who seeks favors from people morning and evening / A poet who lived for a time selling water in Kufa, and for a time selling his self-respect?"

But Mahmoud Muhammad Shakir does not object to favoring the view that al-Mutanabbi was an Alawi, a descendant of Ali, which would explain all the mystery about the life of the man and about the fabricated versions of his lineage. According to this author, the facts of the case are as follows:

"A man descended from Ali, an important one, of course, married the daughter of al-Mutanabbi's grandmother. She got pregnant and gave birth to Ahmad ibn al-Hussein, and for some reason the Alawi was induced to divorce his wife and leave her. The Alawis persuaded him to do that, and so he left her and divorced her and she went back to her mother, either pregnant or with her baby, stricken with a sadness that killed her. The child remained and his grandmother took custody of him and looked after him until he was a young man. She told him the truth about himself and his real lineage. Prudently, she warned the young man of the consequences of speaking out about his lineage and made him give promises and oaths, by her love for him and his love for her. She told him that speaking out would spell ruination for her and for him. He was disgruntled about this until an incident in which he claimed descent from Ali

"Perhaps your Ahmad, in his pillory of willow-wood,* at an age between adolescence and manhood, did not know what fate had in store for him (unless it is true that he had prophetic powers): for example, that Ibn Jinni would quote his poetry, defying the strict grammarians who had refused to quote anyone later than the poet Ibrahim ibn Harama, who died more than a hundred years before al-Mutanabbi was born,† and that Gamal al-Din bin Rashiq would quote a line of his poetry** in a fatwa prescribing murder in defense of the Prophet Muhammad's honor. Even if he did not know all this, I am certain that from that day on he had more trust in poetry than in prophethood.

---

in Syria and was arrested and forced to desist from such claims. He was careful to obey his grandmother's order after understanding her prudence and good judgment and how she had given him honest advice.

"This version of the question of al-Mutanabbi is what explains al-Mutanabbi's long silence about his lineage and why he concealed it as much as he could from gossipers. It also explains the origin of the story of his father the water carrier, and why they were so keen to make it up and present it with such embellishment. This version provides solid evidence on how al-Mutanabbi went to the Quran school of the Alawi nobility in Kufa and studied Alawi doctrines. It also explains why al-Mutanabbi refrained from eulogizing the Alawis, including those of them who had prestige and authority, when he was in Kufa; and why he refused to eulogize Abul Qasim, the Alawi and the companion of Prince ibn Tughj, when he was in Ramla, and what happened earlier when the Alawis had their slaves lie in wait for him at Kafr Aqib." (Mahmoud Muhammad Shakir, *al-Mutanabbi*, Book One, 2nd edition (Cairo: Madani Press, 1977), 45–46.)

* The Fatimids, the Alawis, and the state then ruling in Syria all kept their eyes on al-Mutanabbi, and when he appeared among the Bani Uday they sent a contingent to arrest him and chased him from place to place. He was in hiding from them until he finally fell into the hands of Ibn Alim, who was a Hashemite and an Alawi, in a village called Kutkin. He was arrested, and the carpenter was ordered to attach two blocks of willow wood to his legs and his neck, to which al-Mutanabbi responded: 'The man resident in Kutkin claimed to be from the house of Hashim bin Abd Manaf' / To which I replied: 'Since you became one of them, their shackles have been made of willow.'"

Al-Mutanabbi stayed in prison from late AH 321 or early 322 until 323, when he was released. (Mahmoud Muhammad Shakir, *al-Mutanabbi*, Book One, 103–104.)
† Mahmoud al-Tannahi, *The Future of Arab Culture*, al-Hilal 581 (1999): 220
** "Similarly, Gamal al-Din bin Rashiq quoted a line of al-Mutanabbi in the case of a Christian who slandered the Prophet Muhammad when al-Malik al-Salih first came to power in Egypt. The line of al-Mutanabbi was: 'And high honor is not safe from injury, until blood has been spilled on its flanks,' and bin Rashiq acted in accordance with it." Ibn Khallikan, *Wafayat al-uyun*, vol. 1 (Beirut: Dar Sadir, 1994), 22–23.

"By the way, I have for you a saying of the Prophet worth quoting when you talk about the conflicting accounts of how he acquired the nickname al-Mutanabbi. The gist of the saying, if my memory does not mislead me, is 'Don't pray for the nabi,' and the amusing aspect of the saying is that the word 'nabi,' which of course usually means prophet, has been glossed by the commentators in the sense of a high place or a path.

"You agree with me that al-Mutanabbi was the opposite of Farabi and that a young man who had already achieved renown in the prime of youth was the opposite of an old man who was 'the most ascetic of people in the world' and who, according to Ibn Khallikan, lived on four dirhams a day. He was the opposite of a 'philosopher' who did not dare to deny prophethood and of whose philosophy nothing would remain unless he recognized it wholeheartedly, so he saw no alternative but to dedicate a chapter to it in his most famous work, *The Virtuous City*, immediately after the chapter on the causes of dreams. As for the quality of his writing when he writes about 'revelation and the vision of the archangel' and other such matters, much could be said. There are some people it is better to hear about than to see, and it is better to hear about Farabi than to suffer his Arabic."

You also spoke to me about other chapters, for some of which you were still collecting the material, and a third that was under revision and that you wanted me to make observations on and correct any mistakes in syntax or morphology. The subjects of these chapters were all surprising, but, to go back to what I was saying, before I digressed, about the "two miracles"—the Quran and al-Mutanabbi's poetry—and my deliberate citing of the two together, I have to give you your due, because you were planning to devote one of the chapters of your book to al-Mutanabbi's two disciples—Abu Othman ibn Jinni and Aboul Alaa al-Maarri, who revered al-Mutanabbi's works and put them on the highest pedestal.

Ibn Jinni, who is known for choosing fine names for his books,* saw no fitter name for his large commentary on the works of 'the Poet'* than

---

* "He left behind fine books, which indicate his ample virtue and his abundant learning, and he also chose fine names for them, so much so that it is said that Sheikh Abu Ishaq al-Shirazi, who died in AH 476 and was a professor at the Nizamiya School, named some of his books after books by Ibn Jinni." A study by Muhammad Ali al-Najjar (Beirut: Dar al-Huda for Printing and Publishing, 2nd edition, undated, page 60 of the researcher's introduction).

The Explanation. Aboul Alaa al-Maarri, who, like his 'Poet,' had no scruples about seeking to emulate the eloquence of the Quran† (if it is indeed true that al-Mutanabbi attempted to do so), and whose collection of poems entitled *Unnecessary Necessity* contained—as has escaped the attention of no one—113 chapters, the same number as the Quran,** was quite explicit about his views on the matter when he gave his selection of al-Mutanabbi's verse the title *Ahmad's Miracle.*

The subject of that chapter is a foregone conclusion—the rivalry between the Quran and poetry.

On the grounds that it was an extension of your own idea, you asked me for permission to "steal" the idea I referred to earlier—my firm belief that, when al-Mutanabbi stepped back from his claim to prophethood, it was in order to turn to poetry, not because he was giving up an unrealistic ambition. I did not respond to your request; instead, when you went to your table to write down what I assumed were thoughts that had crossed your mind, I asked you for permission to go into the kitchen and prepare our supper.

---

* "I have been informed that Aboul Alaa al-Maarri used to call al-Mutanabbi 'the Poet,' while he called other poets by their names, and that he used to say: 'In his poetry there is no expression that can be replaced by some other expression with the same meaning.'" Ibn al-Adim, "Tarjamat al-Mutanabbi min baghiyat al-talab" in Mahmoud Muhammad Shaker, *al-Mutanabbi,* Book Two, 283.

† "In his book on the sarfa theory, the poet Abdullah ibn Muhammad ibn Said ibn Sinan al-Khafaji claimed that the Quran was not so unusually eloquent that it can be considered a miracle performed by the Prophet Muhammad, and that anyone with a good command of Arabic would be able to produce something similar, but they have refrained from doing so in order to ensure the Quran in itself appears to be a miracle of eloquence. This is the school of thought of a group of theologians and Shi'i." Yaqut, *Encyclopedia of Literary Men,* vol. 3, 139–40.

** "The ancients had doubts about his prose works and accused him of emulating the Quran in his book *al-Fusul wa-l-ghayat,* and I also note that his book of poems, Luzum Ma La Yalzam, is made up of 113 chapters, while the number of chapters in the Quran is also 113. Was that deliberate, I wonder?" (Maroun Abboud, *Abul Alaa al-Maarri, Zawbaat al-Duhour,* 4th edition (Beirut: Dar al-Thaqafa/Dar Maroun Abboud, 1980), 25–26.

It is commonly said that there are 114 chapters in the Quran, but this footnote is not the place to take up the dispute over this; for more details, see for example the chapter entitled "On the Number of Chapters, Verses, Words, and Letters in the Quran" in Imam Suyuti, *al-Itqan fi ulum al-Quran.*

Everything that has happened, everything I have seen and taken part in, has only made me more confident of the conclusion I came to that evening: that prophethood in its diverse forms is the religion of the common people.

When I say this, I am not excluding myself. In my work on television or from the pulpit of the mosque, was I not something like a prophet? Were my opponents—the amirs who received pledges of obedience and death, as well as the lesser ones who spoke in favor of an Islam of Iron—anything but quasi-prophets? Was our daily squabbling over verses of the Quran, sayings of the Prophet, traditions of his companions, and other arguments anything but a war between two religions, each with its own prophets and evangelists, though the two religions happened to bear the same name, cited the same saying of the Prophet,* and each claimed to have won the love of Layla, and more?

I know that behind the war between the two religions and their prophets lay things that had nothing to do with the Lord of Heaven, but rather with the lords of the earth and lesser mortals, strong and weak alike, and that some people read this war in a language full of numbers and statistical diagrams completely incomprehensible to me and to people more knowledgeable than me about religion; people more committed to emulate the Prophet's conduct and with a better memory for his sayings. But all this does not change the case in any way, and neither do the plans to "raise the level of services" in the overpopulated villages and in country areas isolated because of poor transport, not because of distance, or the "attempts to provide incentives for investment" as a way to "create" I do not know how many jobs. In the meantime, and until the world is filled with equity, justice, and job opportunities, the keys to Heaven, stamped with the name of God, His Prophet, and the only acceptable religion, are being copied by the hundreds and given out to young men in a hurry to leave this world, within the narrow confines of which they have spent very little time, for a next world that is more enticing and more in tune with their boundless dreams. They would kill and be killed, and death would

---

* "The end of the world will come only when two groups with a single creed come to blows." (a saying of the Prophet)

win round after round without asking who was the killer and who the slain, because, whether we liked it or not, we were all on the same side—the side of death.

It was a solid chain of coincidences, similar to inexorable fate, that brought me to where I now am and gave me chance after chance to express my innermost feelings. That too changes nothing of the case, because in this internecine war, in which death has been and remains the undisputed victor, no one has had occasion to follow the advice of the Prophet when he said that he who sits is better than he who stands, and he who stands is better than he who walks.* After everything that has happened and in light of all the consequences of this war, if I was asked today whether I regretted taking part and inciting others to take part in it, and with my words maybe killing, or abetting murder, or making light of murder, then I would say, "no," not out of arrogance or obstinacy, but because I see nothing to regret. Do you think I should regret that in the end (what end?) all I did was take sides with the cause of life and oppose to the death the cause of death?

They called themselves "the Victorious Group," and my favorite nickname for them was "the Group Victorious in Death"—the death of reason, of emotion, and of the body. I do not think I was exaggerating, because they elevated to the status of a ritual their quest for a death that was nothing but torpor, or at most a painless sacrifice: hence its corrosive force, its over-whelming potency, and simultaneously its magic. Faced with this death, I have to admit that the life whose side I claimed to have taken was puny, stunted, and unfair. When it was not like that—puny, stunted, and unfair—I could not take its side openly. I must also admit that the Islam for which I campaigned vociferously does not guarantee entrance to paradise, and even when I took the side of life, don't forget that I did so in the name of God, His Prophet, and True Religion!

---

* "Abu Huraira reported the Messenger of God as saying: 'There will soon be a period of turmoil in which the one who sits will be better than one who stands and the one who stands will be better than one who walks and the one who walks will be better than one who runs. He who would watch them will be drawn by them. So he who finds a refuge or shelter against it should make it as his resort.'"

210

23

In the three weeks before I was brought here, it was like waiting for the Hour of Judgment, the time of which no one knows. After we postponed my lecture at that university three times—firstly from my side, because of my father's death; secondly on the part of the rector, "because of circumstances"; and a third time by me on the grounds of my new commitments, we finally agreed on a fourth date, with an amendment to the format to reflect my newly acquired status. Instead of a lecture on "Islam and Modern Political Systems," people were invited to a "Dialogue with an Islamic Media Personality on His Experience in the Television Sector." The title made us laugh to tears, and you affectionately made fun to your heart's content of the term "media personality." You chose the clothes for me to wear that day and pressed me not to let my shyness get the better of me and not to neglect to notify my colleagues at the television station of the lecture and of when I would give it. You took it upon yourself to invite my 'colleagues' from other media organizations. In that way, everything was as it should be, or so it seemed to me.

As in all universities, the Islamist students at this university had a considerable and forbidding presence, and included a good number with long police records. So I did not rule out the possibility that they might intend to stir up trouble during the lecture. I brought up my concerns with the rector, and his answer was that trouble on campus was better than trouble outside. I took this answer as a license to speak my mind freely. But what the rector and I overlooked was the nature of the trouble they intended to make, or perhaps we implicitly assumed that it would be no more than the kind of trouble they usually resorted to on such occasions. In fact, when I, on your advice, told my colleagues about the lecture and when it would take place, and when their boss immediately assigned a camera crew to "cover the event," my shyness got the better of me and I did not tell the rector that 'the event' might receive 'media coverage' and that this 'coverage' might encourage our friends to cause trouble to suit the occasion. But even if I had told him, would that have made any difference?

We reached the platform from a side door and I took my seat between the rector of the university and the dean of the faculty that had invited me: the faculty of mass communications and public relations. I immediately realized that the Islamists made up the great majority of the audience. Except for a few front rows where men and women sat together without displaying any symbols of Islam, those sitting on the other benches wore beards and hijabs, not to mention the fact that this part of the audience was divided in two, with young men on the right and young women on the left, and that most of the women wearing hijabs were covering their faces, except their eyes, with notebooks, paper handkerchiefs, or the like. Some months earlier, for security reasons, the niqab or full face-veil had been banned in universities, and observant women students had been obliged to interpret more liberally—if the term is appropriate—the Quranic verses on which the Islamic rules on women's dress are based.*

---

* "To describe the niqab as an imported innovation which has nothing to do with religion or Islam, but which was introduced to Muslims during periods of extreme decadence, is in fact neither scientific or objective. It is a simplification that distorts the facts of the case and evades a realistic examination of the subject. No one familiar with the learned sources and with the views of scholars can dispute that the question is contested, by which I mean the question of whether women can show their faces or should cover them up, along with their hands. Scholars—religious lawyers, interpreters of the Quran, and specialists in the traditions of the Prophet—disagreed on this point in ancient times, and continue to disagree today.

"The disagreement stems from their position on the texts relevant to the subject and on the extent to which they understand them, since there is no text that is both of uncontested authority and of absolute clarity. If there was, the matter would have been

212

Accordingly, it seemed superfluous when the dean of the faculty leaned toward me and whispered: "They've deliberately taken over the hall to prevent . . . ." When I nodded to him to say there was no need for him to explain further, he took no notice and started a new sentence: "It looks like they've filled the corridor leading to the hall to stop anyone coming in."

Anxious not to get flustered, an anxiety that never left me despite the 'experience' attributed to me, I took off my glasses, and I think that was a good move. As soon as I finished my lecture, which, based on your advice, was written in the first person and focused on real and sometimes funny incidents and details drawn from my short experience, the host opened the floor to questions and hands went up. Even without my glasses, my eyes could not fail to identify the rows where most of the hands were raised. I was worried that the two university officials might be overawed or that one of them might take fright and pass over the few hands raised in the front

---

settled. They disagree on how to interpret the Quranic injunction: *to display of their adornment only that which is apparent*. (Quran 24:31)

"They have cited Ibn Masoud as saying that *only that which is apparent* refers to women's clothes; that is, the outer clothes which cannot be hidden. They have cited Ibn Abbas as interpreting *only that which is apparent* as reference to kohl on their eyes and any rings they are wearing. Anas ibn Malik is quoted to have said the same, and Aisha to have said something very similar. Sometimes, to kohl and rings, Ibn Abbas adds hennaed hands, bracelets, earrings, and necklaces, and says that references to such decorative accessories may in fact refer to the part of the body where they are found. Ibn Abbas says it refers to the face and the palm of the hand. The same is also attributed to Said ibn Jubayr and Ataa' and others. Some of them include parts of the arm as covered by *only that which is apparent* and Ibn Atiya interpreted it as meaning parts that become visible by force of circumstance, as when the wind uncovers them, or the like.

"They also disagree over how to interpret the Quranic verse, *O Prophet, tell your wives and your daughters and the women of the believers to wrap their outer garments closely around them, for this makes it more likely that they will be recognized and will not be harassed. God is All-Forgiving, Compassionate to each.* (Quran 33:59). What is meant here by *wrap their outer garments closely around them*?

"One of the second generation of Muslims, Ubayda al-Salmani, is quoted as interpreting the phrase as meaning in practice covering the face and head and most of the left eye. Muhammad ibn Kaab al-Qarazi says much the same. Akrama, a dependent of Ibn Abbas, disagreed with them and said that it meant covering her cleavage with her gown.

"Said ibn Jubayr said: 'A Muslim woman should not be seen by a strange man unless she has a mask on top of her headscarf with which she has covered her head and the upper part of her chest.'" Yusuf al-Qaradawi, *The Niqab for Women* (Beirut: The Islamic Bookshop, 1993), 10–12.

rows and select their colleagues in the other rows, so I quickly picked on the only raised hand among the few unveiled women and invited her to ask her question. She did so, and it was such an incisive and bold question that I almost thought that you were behind it. "Do you think your program, which is evangelical whether you like it or not, has been as successful in winning converts as it has been as a television program?" In answering, I went as far as I could, saying that there was nothing pejorative about it being evangelical, and that its success as a program was a boast I would not make. As for its success in the competition between rival religious ideologies, I could not resist answering in jest: "The best evidence for that, as you can see, young lady, and as I can see, is the audience that has honored me by attending this meeting."

My joke made everyone laugh, including the Islamists, whose mood I had gauged, even if the back rows did stop laughing sooner than those at the front.

For the sake of fairness, if only a fairness distorted in advance by the weight of numbers, I called on a group of people who had raised their hands, without singling one out. After exchanging hardly a glance between themselves, one of the leaders stood up and asked a long question, starting with "In the name of God the Merciful . . ." and including all the citations he could remember that supported the view that the Quranic phrase *only that which is apparent* and the reference to *bringing down the outer garments* in the two contentious verses* prescribed the niqab rather than any other form of modesty in dress. He ended by asking about the legitimacy of the decision by the university authorities to ban the niqab and prevent any woman wearing the niqab from coming on campus.

The dean of the faculty quickly objected to the question on the grounds that it was "out of order" and "a flagrant attempt to take advantage of this public meeting to bring up internal university matters." The rector followed him up with the same argument. In my view, the man who asked the question and those who were with him expected nothing less and only intended to assert their presence and show others they were capable of stealing the limelight. That was exactly what happened, in that the hall began to ring with successive cries of disapproval along the lines of "The niqab for women is a university matter? Since when has obeying

---

* This refers to the two Quranic versions discussed at length in previous footnote.

the injunctions and prohibitions of Islamic law been a university matter?" Some of them even shouted out things such as: "And the depravity of half-dressed women,* why isn't that a university matter?"

For some seconds, or maybe more, I was uncertain what to do: should I say my piece on the subject or should I dissemble and consider that what was happening around me on camera was indeed a university matter on which I could not intrude? The cowardice of the dean and the rector, or what looked to me like cowardice, and the fact that the group of Islamists was starting to withdraw from the hall in an orderly and theatrical manner to chants of "There is no god but God, Muhammad is the prophet of God," by which they declared the meeting over, left me with no choice. I stood up, took the microphone, and shouted at their spokesman, who was standing in the aisle with his back to the platform, like a commander watching his troops withdraw from the battlefield. "You asked a question and I have the answer for you." He took no notice of what I said and I ignored his evasion. "You say that the niqab is not only a university matter and I agree with you on that. To go back to your question, I would go further than that, to what you did not say, out of respect for the sanctity of the campus. The decision to ban female students from wearing the niqab is not the responsibility of the university authorities but of the government. But I tell you, and anyone who wants to listen—and I am willing to take responsibility for what I say—that under Islamic law the ruler, and in our age the ruler means the state, including the executive, which is the government, has the right to suspend temporarily whatever provisions of Islamic law it sees fit if suspending some provision or other at any given time achieves some public interest or, at the least, prevents some wrong. So, even assuming that wearing the niqab is an established and definitive requirement under Islamic law, which is very far from being the case anyway, then there can be nothing wrong in suspending it, as long as the aim is to prevent it being used to sow strife and cause harm. Today the niqab, in universities and other institutions, is a pretext that leads to 'overriding harm,' and in this case the consensus of those learned in Islam is that recourse to such pretexts

---

* Abu Huraira quoted the Prophet as saying that women "who are dressed but appear to be naked, who are inclined towards evil and make their husbands incline toward evil" will not enter heaven.

must be prevented, so it is pointless to invoke the sharia in the matter of the ban on the niqab in universities and so on."* Only at this point, as the last platoon of the student leader's troops was heading for the door, did he turn toward me and shout out at the top of his voice: "Anyone who suspends one rule suspends them all. Enough nonsense, you sheikh of suspension." He turned on his heels and, bringing up the rear, followed in the footsteps of his colleagues.

I was about to continue the meeting with those who remained, but the two university officials decided against it. Politely, I accepted their invitation to have coffee in the office of one of them. Although they lauded my courage, they were clearly shaken. I sipped my coffee as fast as I could without being rude, and left them grappling with the concerns of that day and the next. I hurried to your place, to find you had beaten me there. I did not stay there long, either. The incident, and the skill with which it was contrived, had also struck you. I listened as you passed on some of the comments you had heard from your neighbors sitting in the front rows. But I was distracted from all that by an insight inspired by the details of the brief exchange between me and that young man, and by a speculative question, which on the surface looked very simple: "Is there any way to reconcile Islam with the requirements of living in this world other than suspending most of the rules of Islam, or at least declaring that those rules that apply only to individuals are optional, however difficult it might be to distinguish obligations that apply solely to individuals from those that apply to the community as a whole? In all aspects of public and private life, by various means, sometimes by various subterfuges and sometimes by deliberately turning a blind eye, except where we are bound by a definitive religious text, are we not always trying to prove that the objectives of Islam are consistent with the dominant ideals of the age, regardless of why those ideals predominate?"

---

* "A pretext that leads to harm is a course of action that was originally intended to attain a legitimate purpose, and was not intended to achieve harm, but which generally does lead to harm, such that the result is more likely to be harmful than beneficial. An example would be insulting the gods of the polytheists in their presence, because it is a means to a legitimate purpose and is not intended to lead to harm, but it might lead to harm in the sense that the infidels might insult God Almighty in response to the insults to their gods, hence most people learned in Islamic law believe that such a course of action is to be avoided." Qutb Mustafa Sinno, *Dictionary of Islamic Legal Terms* (Damascus: Dar al-Fikr al-Muasir, 2000), 213.

For a long time, I had not dabbled in such general speculations, which some people might consider 'profound,' while in my case they were with me whether I was thinking or speaking, as close to me as my jugular vein. For that reason, I preferred that day to follow my impulse to be alone and go back to my mosque, rather than accept your invitation that I stay in your company.

There was no news at the mosque, except for a passing reference from the janitor to the fact that a certain sheikh, "who hasn't been to see us in a long time," had come by with a man and two girls, had waited for me an hour, and would drop in again to see me early the next morning. I did not bother to seek any further information. No doubt, judging by the man and the two girls, he had come to ask a favor.

Hoping that it would be a simple request, and not one that involved saving someone from execution, I closed the door of my room on myself and my demons.

24

The man and his retinue turned up earlier than I had expected. Luckily, I was in my office and his early arrival did not disturb me or require him to apologize. We exchanged greetings, said how much we had missed each other, asked after each other's health, and gently reproached each other for not visiting for so long. Then we called on the janitor to expedite two cups of tea, all before it occurred to me to ask him about his companions who, as I had been told, had come the previous day and had waited for me with him. He waved his hand to suggest it was nothing urgent. Then, a moment later, he explained his gesture: "Were it not for them, despite my desire to visit you, I would not have undergone the rigors of this journey which, as you know well, is most agreeable to me. Let's leave them aside for now . . . . They're outside . . . . We'll go back and talk about them later . . . . Of course, as much as your time allows."

His tone of voice was meek in a way I had not known of him before, but not in the manner of a supplicant. Before I became a star, he had often come to me seeking favors on behalf of someone or other from the village where for many years he had served as imam of the mosque and where he had acquired property, married, and settled down. On those occasions, his charm and his memory for poetry meant he could ask for what he wanted as though he was not asking, without long preambles and without being undignified or obsequious. But now it was the meekness of defeat. This was apparent within a few minutes of his coming in, when the conversation faltered several times and he launched into the kind of compliments we used to exchange only in jest. I was troubled and could not help pressing him with questions about his health and the health of his family, as if illness were the least of evils. "For my age I'm in excellent health, thank God," he said, "and my family and kids are well, but . . . haven't you heard what happened to me?" In fact, I had not heard talk of what had happened to him, and unless I heard it directly from him I doubt the news would have reached me by any other channel. I did not want to make him more disheartened by saying, for example, that his doings did not make it to the newspaper headlines, a retort I would not have hesitated to make in former times. I apologized for my ignorance by saying that my duties had forced me to neglect keeping track of my friends. He ignored my apology and repeated the question: "Do you really not know what happened? I would have thought you would be the first to hear and follow the details." He was like a man at his wits' end, when he finds himself forced to acknowledge that he has suffered a double misfortune: not only the original calamity, but on top of it the fact that news of it has not spread in the way he had expected and in a way that might have given him some consolation. I tried to alleviate the air of gloom that weighed on us with a little banter, imitating the way he, one of the best mimics I have ever known, whenever he came and found me depressed, would tell me: "What's the trouble, man?" His only response was to sigh and mutter: "Those were the days!" I then took his sadness seriously and left him to emerge from his silence at his own pace. If he had not wanted to share his thoughts with me, I told myself, he would not have wanted to be alone with me nor put off discussing the purpose of his visit. I did not have to wait long, and I was not mistaken. "Since you don't know what happened to me, then for sure you also don't know that I no longer wear this gown or this turban, except on special occasions, and were it not for the fact that your friends at the mosque would have asked what had befallen me, I wouldn't have come to you wearing what I have come to see as equivalent to fancy dress."

I understood nothing of what he said and I made no secret of it.

"Some months ago, my friend," he continued, "they took control of my mosque and drove me out. Now my only wards are plants and animals: the trees and vegetables in my little orchard, some sheep and some chickens, led by a white rooster who sets an example for how to treat them all equally!"

There was a rancor and bitterness in what he said, but I was somewhat reassured, if that is the right word, when I noticed that his sense of humor had survived despite the bitterness. That encouraged me to ask more questions about what had happened. "I don't think that what my mosque saw was very different from what happened in other mosques, especially in outlying areas. At first it was an unprecedented wave of religious enthusiasm among the ranks of the young, coupled with a boom in mosque attendance. I saw the congregation of my mosque increase in size and change in nature. My mosque had been like a private club frequented by men of old or middle age, but now it suddenly opened up to new faces, a new language, and activities it had never known before. It was only at prayer time that the two groups mixed, and even the word 'mixed' is rather an exaggeration, since in the front row you would rarely see people from both groups together. Before and after prayers, each group had its own corner—on one side the old-timers chatting as they might chat anywhere else, and on the other, whispering and confiding in each other, the faithful of the last rain, the age of whose faith could be measured in each case by the length of the man's beard. In the first weeks, the only distinguishing features of their presence were their strict adherence to certain traditional practices and their public display of this adherence, and sometimes their 'brotherly' criticism of someone or other for the way he did his ablutions or performed his prayers and so on. This criticism, although brotherly, was not well received, or taken as advice. Although the disputes caused by this criticism did not lead to anything more than an unequal exchange of arguments—the claims of seniority and precedence on one side versus meticulous performance of the rituals, even to excess, on the other—the breakdown in dialogue and tolerance added to the antipathy between the two groups and made them more wary, or rather made the old-timers wary of the others, if only because the new group showed such confidence in itself, after God of course, and such a firm belief that they were right in everything they did and said, that the others, including me, could not go along with them.

"From time to time I wonder whether I did everything I could to defend my mosque, and hence myself and my position, and I never reach a satisfactory answer. Sometimes I think I could not have done more, while at other times I accuse myself of cowardice, because one day, for example, I might have looked down to avoid their hostile stares, while on another day I hesitated and did not have the courage to stand up to their prattling fraud of a sage, with his own perverse interpretations of God's law. Tell me, and I pray you tell me the truth: Do you think I fell short? But just a moment. Let me tell you what happened and then I'll let you speak. The first incident worthy of the name between me and them happened when they came and asked that the mosque doors should stay open day and night. As you well know, this was a legitimate request with malicious intent. Even if no one can stop believers from visiting houses of God,* I was not about to present the mosque to them on a silver platter. After assuring them that houses of God should indeed be the last places to have their doors closed, I said I was responsible to the Ministry of Religious Endowments for running the mosque and that the delay in assigning someone as caretaker forced me to close the doors outside prayer times. Of course my argument was feeble and could be challenged on several grounds. At first they suggested taking turns in acting as caretakers, and when I said that I didn't have the authority to agree to that, they took the dispute to a higher level. 'Since when have mosques opened and closed their doors on the basis of decrees that may or may not be issued by government departments that at the very least must be deemed corrupt?' they said. I refused to go along with them and dug in my heels. Maybe I was wrong, telling them I refused to be dragged into matters that had nothing to do with me. They exchanged glances and made do with something like a mysterious 'Very well, then,' and a tepid farewell. That same night, under cover of darkness, they took the mosque door off its hinges, and from then on they took turns stationed there day and night like soldiers protecting a front-line position. To be honest, I should add that at dawn the next day their leader met me with great courtesy at the mosque door and explained that what they had

---

* *Who could be more wicked than those who prevent the mention of God's name from His houses of worship and strive for their ruin.* (Quran, 2:114)

done was not meant as defiance of me or to disparage my status but 'As you know, "no obedience is due to any mortal when it comes to disobeying the Creator."'* He finally suggested that, to meet my obligation toward the Ministry of Religious Endowments, I submit a report to the police station explaining what had happened! Just as I was reluctant to report the matter to the ministry, the local police chief hesitated a good while before he reported it to his superiors, for them to report it in turn higher and higher. In the meantime, with our hesitation and the indifference of officialdom, the appearance of the mosque changed in every sense of the word. Defying the ministry and the laws, they set to work renovating the mosque, appropriating square meters wholesale from the approach road, which of course they did not delay in paving. They renovated the washroom for ablutions and atop the minaret they installed four loudspeakers to broadcast their thunderous pieties to the four quarters. Their civility, which smacked of military discipline, and the conscientious way they handled the mosque and most of the people of the village was like a silent but violent earthquake that shook our little world. One of the most prominent outcomes of it was the gradual growth of overt sympathy for them, coupled with a tendency to treat their dogmas, which at first looked like a ridiculous fad, as an example worthy of emulation, and to treat their rhetoric as inspired revelation. In explaining their repeated conquests, both of territory and of hearts and minds, they avoided any arrogance that might have unsettled or perturbed the villagers. I saw them adopt a policy that included 'good works,' cooperating with the local council in its modest projects, helping shepherds find treatment for their sick livestock, organizing free supplementary lessons for school children, and so on. The way they treated me was above reproach, and they continued to let me lead them in prayer, though they sabotaged my Friday services. Every Friday morning, they and their new followers, joined by some of the old-timers, would head to a nearby village where the preacher was one of their leading sheikhs. The congregation at my mosque fell short of the quorum needed to hold proper Friday prayers, so we could merely hold noon prayers, as on other days. Grudgingly, out of necessity, I held my tongue when I heard how some of these enraptured disciples compared my boring, repetitive, and

---

* Hadith

timorous sermons with the stimulating, fiery, and courageous sermons of my colleague. Sometimes I suspected, and I don't think I was mistaken, that the formal civility and obsequious humility I mentioned were, at least as far as I was concerned, a kind of daily torture designed to unnerve me and eventually to push me over the edge in such a way that it would seem I had done so spontaneously, for some purpose known only to me. That is in fact what happened. One Saturday afternoon, the loudspeakers conveyed to the people of the village the news of the arrest of my colleague and deadly rival, the sheikh for the pleasure of whose fiery sermons they took the trouble to repair to the mosque in the next village every Friday. After the news, the loudspeakers began to broadcast the text of a political statement accusing 'the evil, despotic, and violent regime' of downright oppression and tyranny, and so on, till the end of the refrain, and threatening the regime and its fellow travelers with serious consequences and an unpleasant fate.

"Whether the regime was righteous or iniquitous, whether the sheikh with the golden tongue had been wronged, whether people wanted to extinguish the light of God*—none of these considerations interested me or gave me pause the moment the loudspeakers installed on the minaret of my mosque started to spew their lava. Enraged and aggrieved, I hurried to my mosque, not to find out what was happening nor to register my objections but, naively, to win back the mosque, deluding myself into thinking that this ploy of theirs revealed their true nature, that by their own words and deeds they were now incriminating themselves, and that none of the villagers, including their disciples, would approve of turning the mosque, the house of God, into a platform for broadcasting political propaganda that I thought we should have nothing to do with. If the rest of the story was merely what you would expect, I would spare you the details, but it was more horrendous and humiliating. Of course they sent me packing and no one raised his voice in my support. If that had been the end of it, it wouldn't have mattered much, but having succeeded in embarrassing me and driving me out they took the opportunity to settle all their scores once and for all and, because I had urged them not to mix religion and politics and not to confuse their enemies with the enemies of God, they

---

* *They seek to quench the light of God with their mouths, but God insists on blazoning forth his light.* (Quran 9:32)

accused me of diverting people from God's path and of 'collaboration with the security services.' 'Take care of your soul, mawlana,' said their spiritual guide, speaking offhand in his cold, poisonous tone of voice, 'and hurry to seek forgiveness of God before it's too late.' They did not give me time to consider my position or decide whether I had in fact offended God or some human. At exactly midnight the same day, several young men broke into my house, tied my hands together, and took me away to a camp of theirs somewhere in the hills, about an hour and a half's drive away.

"From the moment I was seized, I had visions of a horrible death, and my only prayer to God was that they do it quickly and that the task of killing me be assigned to some novice who would go straight to it, not to one of those monsters who left their murder victims in such a state in the wake of their disciplinary campaigns that the descriptions alone were enough to make anyone pray to God as I prayed. It might occur to you to commit the stupidity of congratulating me on my survival, just as some of the villagers did the day after my release. Please don't do that. The worse thing that can happen to someone who faces being killed, in any manner whatsoever, and who survives is to have someone doubt his word when he says that death now runs in his veins like blood. In the case of someone with leukemia, for example, we are willing to say that death is the twin sister of the person's soul (and body), so why do we have no faith in the close kinship between the survivor and death after he has escaped it? Escaping death, my friend, is not always to have death pass you by, or to pass by death yourself, but sometimes—in fact, most of the time—it's to have death pierce you like a quivering arrow. For two days I was interrogated, and to most of their questions I had no answers, convincing or otherwise. I think they knew what I would and wouldn't know, so they refrained from using violence when they questioned me, unlike others whose anonymous cries and desperate entreaties I could hear.

"Before the break of dawn on the third day they brought me a document which they asked me to copy out and sign. It was a confession that I had 'cooperated with the security services under duress and provided them with information which could cause harm to their Holy Movement,' as well as a promise to turn faithfully to God and to dissociate myself from the regime and from regime personnel. Frankly, I didn't hesitate to obey their orders to copy it out and sign it, although I knew that complying with their orders was no guarantee of survival, should their leader decree otherwise. They took me out of the hut where I had been detained and one of them, as curtly as possible, ordered me to wait while he and his companions went off to where their friends had gathered to perform their dawn prayers. From the way they left me unguarded, I had forebodings of mischief and I did not budge from the spot.

"The way they prayed was quite extraordinary. I had to watch what was happening in front of my eyes for quite a while before I realized they were performing the dawn prayer according to the rules for a 'fear prayer,'* something I had read about in books but had never seen performed

---

* "God has been lenient to His people and has not imposed any religious observance that is irksome. When He ordered them to pray, He allowed some flexibility in the performance, so that someone who is traveling, is afraid or is facing an enemy, or is sick or has some other excuse, need only perform as much of the prayer as is possible. That is the origin of the 'fear prayer,' which has been endorsed for use by warriors, especially when they face their enemy and fear they might be ambushed while they are at prayer. In such cases they do not all assemble for communal prayers in the usual way, but instead they perform the 'fear prayer.' Authority for the 'fear prayer' comes from the Quran: *When you set out on an expedition in the land, no blame attaches to you if you curtail your prayer, if you fear the unbelievers will take you by surprise; for the unbelievers are your manifest enemy. If you happen to be present among them, and stand to lead them in prayer, let a group among them stand with you, and let them take up their arms. When they prostrate themselves in prayer let them be in the rear and let another group who have not yet prayed come forward to pray with you; let them be on their guard and take up their weapons. The unbelievers long for you to be negligent with your weapons and equipment, and thus would attack you in one rush. If pelted by the rain or if you are sick, no blame attaches to you if you put your weapons aside, but be on your guard. God had readied for the unbelievers an abusing torment. Once having finished prayer, make mention of God, standing, sitting, or reclining. Once you feel secure, perform the prayer, for prayer at a set time is decreed upon the believers.* (Quran 4:101, 102, 103)
"Fear is of two kinds:
"The first kind is a fear that prevents performing the prayers in their full form, when time is critical or when war is declared. In this case, prayers are postponed until close to the last possible moment, and people then pray however they can, even walking or running, with token prostrations towards Mecca and so on, with whatever words or gestures as needed.
"The second kind of fear is that which arises when the enemy is expected to attack if all the Muslims are busy praying, in which case they are allowed to pray in disorder or in separate groups, following separate leaders. There are many manners of performing such a prayer, and in contemporary wars, with the new capabilities to bomb and destroy, warriors pray in whatever manner is practical, in separate groups, or in disorder so that they are not all in one group for the enemy to bomb or shell them." Ahmad Ali al-Imam, *Contemporary Reflections on the Law of Jihad* (Beirut: The Islamic Library, 2000), 88 ff.

until that day. After the prayer, someone came and took me to where they had gathered to pray and gave me a place in the circle around a man I concluded was their leader. From what he said, I found out that he was on a visit to the camp. He gave us a brief lecture on the virtues of military service and protecting the front lines, and answered a few questions on points of Islamic law. Then he graciously pointed toward me and added, as if he were continuing a conversation the first part of which I had missed: 'They say we spill the blood of the innocent. If that was the case, would we have left this man alive? (meaning me). We asked him to repent and he confessed his past sins, turned back to God, and renounced the iniquitous tyrants. When it was clear he did not deserve one of the punishments prescribed in God's law, we held him in captivity for a few days and he is now free to go back to his family and his children. If anyone says that we kill the innocent, tell him that we act on the basis of the Quranic verse: *And slay not the soul God has forbidden, except by right. Whoever is slain unjustly, We have granted authority to his next-of-kin: but let him not exceed in slaying; he shall be helped.** I didn't believe my ears when I heard him talking about releasing me and later, many days after my release, I began to dare to remember those moments, to think about them and appreciate the true horror of them. My release was delayed until close to midnight, when they took me back to the outskirts of the village, blindfolded in a car that appeared by magic. Until today, I hadn't told anyone in such detail what I lived through for those three days. The truth is, I couldn't and didn't have to do so, because the day after my release the rumors were already out, spread deliberately or by people who were misled. 'Our sheikh, whose piety we admired and whose wit we enjoyed,' they said, 'have you at last discovered him as he really is? Did you know who was hiding beneath that ragged gown? *The truth has come out, and falsehood has vanished away.*† Your much-revered sheikh was no more than a minor informer . . . He has admitted everything . . . And if God's law on the death penalty had been applied without regard for his status as an old sheikh, he would have met the fate he deserved.' Do you remember what I told you at the start, about how this gown and this turban have come to feel like fancy dress?'"

---

* Quran 17:33
† Quran 17:81

226

Out of kindness, and for fear he would have a seizure, I interrupted his tale, unconvinced that letting him bring the story to its close would allay my fears. I do not think I said anything significant, firstly because there was nothing to be said, and secondly because I was busy imagining what impact his story could have if it was allowed to be recorded and broadcast. It did not occur to me that what he had said was only a drop in the ocean.

He wet his throat with constant sips from his cup of tea, which had gone cold during his lengthy testimony. Then, like someone who realizes he has made a mistake for which he must apologize, he looked at me and his hands began to shake. I found myself rising from my chair, walking up to him, bending down, and kissing him on the forehead. His trembling hands held my hands and I could almost hear his teeth chatter. I stayed in place with difficulty, worried I might lose my balance and reluctant to say a word or move an inch. I do not know how long I stayed like that, but it ended when he felt strong enough to rise from his chair, squeezing my hands and simultaneously releasing them from his grip. "Forgive me," he said, "this isn't why I came to see you." I suggested he wash his face, and he had no objection. A few seconds later, he came back, ready to resume the conversation. "I have a special esteem for this man, who came with me with his two daughters, otherwise I wouldn't have come to you in the hope that God will enable you to help him. May I invite them to come in? It's an embarrassing subject, so I would prefer to let them lay it out," he said.

I called to the janitor to let them in—a man in his sixties and two girls, one in her twenties and the other rather younger. The man and the elder girl greeted me. They took their seats and said nothing. At a single glance the man realized that the floor was his: "This girl of mine, mawlana," he said, pointing to the younger one, "is not as she should be. Not that I'm objecting to the will of God Almighty, but . . . ." The older girl came to the rescue of her stammering father, whose tremulous, strangled voice showed how distressing it would be for him to continue speaking. Firmly, boldly, and in vocabulary drawn from modernity, she told the story in brief: "This sister of mine, for reasons I don't think God is responsible for, but rather my parents, suffers from severe mental retardation. She is fifteen and her physical development is complete, but according to the doctors she has a mental age of no more than eight . . . We have tried to protect her from the worst to be feared in the case of a girl with the body of a woman who can be seduced with a doll or a piece of candy but . . . it has happened, and she is probably at the end of the second month of pregnancy." As the girl, whose tenacity I admired, proceeded with her narrative, the helpless father retreated into his shell, as if trying to shrivel to the point of invisibility. He curled up as much as possible, pulling his legs together, hunching his shoulders, and bowing his head, and when he could do no more he froze, with nothing to indicate his presence among us other than the suppressed sighs that escaped him. The other girl, the younger one who was being talked about, showed no obvious sign of mental retardation, except that I noticed a certain dullness deep in her eyes when I looked at her closely while listening to the elder one's story. Until then, I had deliberately avoided looking at the girls, who seemed to be having trouble arranging the scarves that covered their hair. Perhaps I also failed to notice because of the younger girl's swollen cheeks and her blue chapped lips (I was right to take my time in judging her appearance—the elder girl told me in a telephone conversation later that when her mother discovered her daughter was pregnant, it aggravated an existing nervous disorder and routinely, every day, she would lay into the girl remorselessly, in the hope this would make her miscarry). "Of course," the girl continued, "my parents' only concern is to prevent a scandal and stop the neighbors gloating, and that's what has deterred them from pressing charges against the man who made her pregnant."

She fell silent, which was odd, because the girl had spoken the last sentence in a way that suggested she was holding back something she was about to reveal. My colleague the sheikh was quick to break the silence unceremoniously: "There's another reason, my friend, for not pressing charges, apart from averting a scandal," he said. "It turns out that the two young men who seduced her and took turns raping her, either of whom may be the father of the child, joined the Brigade of the Chosen in their mountain strongholds several weeks ago, and when the father, along with some village elders and wise men, went to complain privately to someone known for his close links with the group, the answer came back a few days later that there was no evidence that the two youths were implicated and that, even if there had been, they had clearly repented, since they were now proving their worth in the field of jihad. And when someone dared to ask the group's local representative what kind of jihad this was when waged by rapists, the agent dismissed the question with words to the effect that to advance His religion God uses the righteous and the unrighteous without discrimination."* The conversation between me and my colleague digressed somewhat before we went back to the question: how could the girl get an abortion? I reassured them, if that's the right word, that given the state of her pregnancy it would not be difficult and I promised to follow the matter up in the coming days.

I had spoken and given my promise on the spur of the moment, reckoning that I could persuade 'my friends' in television to arrange an abortion for the girl and possibly find her a place in an institution that looked after mentally retarded people. I also thought I could use the incident for access to the stricken family and thus to an exclusive media scoop. Of course, I also thought about how we would need to record the testimony of my friend the sheikh on camera, but I did not think the time was right that day to bring this up with him, and in fact, at the end of the meeting I found myself reconsidering my initial enthusiasm in the light of reason and seeing that I had been thoroughly reckless. As usual, my only recourse was to put off any decision on my various ideas until I heard your view, because self-confidence in the company of my people and those who came to me with requests was one thing, but self-confidence in your presence was something else.

They had to set off back to their village only minutes before noon prayers. I waited for the call to prayer, prayed the four prostrations with the people at the mosque, and then apologized for being unable to have lunch with them. I headed to your place, hoping to have some time to myself while I awaited your return to consult you. I had come to share with you a pressing concern, and suddenly your answers to my inquiries enabled me to see the complete picture, whereas previously, living three separate lives—one with you, one at the mosque, and the other at the television station, I was able to see only the details. The last question you asked was: "Did you assure your sheikh or the girl and her family that they wouldn't come to any harm if you turned their tragedy into documentary material?" In fact, throughout the two hours I had spent waiting for you, this question had been almost my only worry, even if I framed it in a rather

---

* "The biographies of the Prophet assert that a man called Qazman, a polytheist, fought on the Prophet's side at the battle of Uhud and killed three members of the Bani Abdel Dar tribe, who were carrying the polytheists' standard. The Prophet said on the occasion: 'God is strengthening this religion with an unrighteous man.'" Ahmad Ali al-Imam, *Contemporary Reflections on the Law of Jihad,* 71–72.

more subdued form: "How can I put his story on television without putting the people in danger?" Now that you had asked the question, it had to be answered. I had not ruled out the possibility that you might spring this question on me, but there is a difference between expecting something and being prepared for it, even fully prepared. Even if one's mind has taken precautions, one's facial expressions and body language may not be able to conceal one's nervousness. But the strangest thing about it is that throughout those two hours of conversation we did not once remark that simply by presenting this program I would be putting myself in the danger zone, so how could I convince my friend the sheikh to let us broadcast his testimony? How could I exploit the tragedy of this family in the war raging between 'good' and 'evil'? You sensed what was on my mind, and maybe you guessed at the stream of ideas and images that went through my mind during our conversation, and realized that asking too many questions would only make me more distressed, so you withdrew to the kitchen and invited me to join you in eight minutes!

That was one of the code words we had established. I will never forget the brilliant performance of that magic oven: you put frozen dishes into it, and within eight minutes the radiation made them tasty and delicious, as on that day. Instead of obeying you, I rushed after you and began to apologize for dragging you into concerns that had nothing to do with you. You fended me off and turned the conversation to completely unrelated matters, saying you were increasingly persuaded by "my theory" about al-Mutanabbi and prophethood, which, when you translated it into your own language, become roughly that his claim to prophethood was the childish phase of his constant quest for power, a morbid phase, in fact a form of infantilism, and that the evidence for that was that his quest shifted, as much of his poetry shows, to something more serious than claiming the status of prophet, which would only have made him one of many prophets or aspiring prophets: it shifted toward becoming the Seal of Poets writing in Arabic. "Leave aside the question of whether he succeeded or failed," you said. "Isn't it amazing that in this culture, in the persons of the Prophet Muhammad and its greatest poet, the ultimate trophy should be to have uttered the definitive word, after which there is nothing to be said: the word that sums everything up, and after which anything else is superfluous, banal, or tainted? Do you see, as I do, what that means? What it means for a word to dream of repeating itself for eternity? In that case, what's the difference between repetition and silence, or isn't death the ultimate silent repetition? In the realm of politics, the politics of real people, what stands between this passion for the definitive word and using it for murder? Is there anything like murder, or the threat of it, for silencing people, for gagging them, for making speech redundant? I have a mind to give what I'm writing about al-Mutanabbi and prophethood the title *Shahwat al-kalima al-fasl*, which can of course be read in two ways— as 'Passion for the Definitive Word,' or as 'Definitive Passion for the Word.'" And, because one thing leads to another, you gave us a digression on the rules in Arabic grammar, which you had recently learned, for the case-endings on detached qualifiers such as 'fasl' in your putative title. You then went back to the life of al-Mutanabbi, and complained of the trouble you were having finding the commentaries of Abu Shujaa Fatik,* that madman of whom it was said that al-Mutanabbi never spoke so truly as when he praised him and mourned him. I tried to leave my seat to help you pick up the dinner things, but you pinned me down by giving me a book you took from a shelf several inches higher than yourself with a stretch that showed me an aspect of your agility I had not seen before. "Read it . . . choose something to cook tomorrow or the day after . . . Do you want these frozen dishes to become our staple diet?" Of course I could not decipher a word of it or work out what it all meant, but out of modesty, my constant companion in your presence although we lived together and were friends, I did not want you to see the urgent desire for you that my face would have betrayed. I shielded myself with your book in the hope that, hidden from your sight, I could get my breath back. You told me to read, but as I turned the pages the only image I saw was that of your breasts as you reached up for the book, rising for a moment and then falling, and the image of your bottom, moving in rhythm with your breasts as your waist contracted. This little detail aroused me a great deal— not the first time some such detail had such an effect. But this time, I was ashamed of my timidity and of hiding from you. I decided to disobey you. I closed the book, recovered my breath, and set aside my lustful thoughts. I put the book back in its place and beat you to the cloth that hung, always

---

* One thing we missed that day, but which you soon caught, was the extraordinary coincidence of names between this Fatik and Fatik ibn Abi al-Jahl, who killed al-Mutanabbi.

231

damp, next to the sink at which you were standing, dealing with the plates before putting them into the dishwasher. I bent over the table and set to work wiping it. You left off what you were doing, turned toward me, put your hands on my shoulders, and muttered: "Back to your place. It's the thought that counts and it's enough that you had the intention." That's all you said, but the shiver that ran through me was out of all proportion with what you had done. In fact, I might almost say that it exceeded what I could imagine. Besides, I was somewhat confused about the desire for you to which I was in thrall. I desired you not just as the peerless lover (surely a woman deserves to be described as peerless when she has civilized a man, saving him from the ignorance and stupidity of his maleness), but also as a woman who was a unique blend between the humility of learning and the strength and courage of knowledge. On top of all that, I desired you for the way you drove a car with restraint or put together dishes that, even those so straightforward that you did not have to consult your recipe books, never lacked a touch that showed how refined your taste was.

Although I was so aroused that I was leaking what we clerics call preseminal fluid,* I was completely confused about my desire for you, not somewhat confused as I said earlier. I had a mind to wrap my arms around you and walk you to your bedroom, our bedroom, in order to express my desire in the form of lust. I never thought I would live to see the day when I would distinguish between my lust and my desire, but that is what happened on that day, when I enjoyed restraining myself; in fact, I took you by surprise by standing up all at once and moving in four or five quick steps from the table to the sink where you had been rinsing the dishes before putting them into the dishwasher. In front of the sink, I began with difficulty to roll up the sleeves of my jacket and the shirt beneath it. I was not trying to be funny, but what I did made you roar with laughter. "Forgive me," you said, "but you needn't go to such trouble just to rinse the plates. . . . In any case, because you so insist, I won't disappoint you." From behind the kitchen door you took a waterproof apron, embroidered with a design that I had no doubt you had chosen with great care, and offered it to me with both hands, as if to show me how to put it on, sparing me the embarrassment of looking stupid if I tried to put it on myself. I

---

* Sunni jurists unanimously agree that under Islamic law such fluid makes one 'impure' and requires ritual ablution before prayer.

bowed my head slightly to put it through the circle between the thin cord and the yoke of the apron, but you stopped me and suggested I take off my jacket, which was made of material so thick I could hardly roll up the sleeves. I could only obey you, given how quite ridiculous I looked with my jacket still on.

In that way, too, even if it was one of my last visits to that house, the bond between us grew stronger, without any grand promises or solemn oaths. When I say this, a host of similar incidents comes to mind, and I cannot help but wonder, with a naivety that in my case is quite sincere: could our relationship have blossomed without those tiny incidents, witnessed only by the books in your bookcase, the pots and pans in your kitchen, and the walls of your bedroom? And would it have been our fate to share those intimacies—the embraces, the sweet nothings, the solidarity, the bonding, and the sighs of passion—if all we had shared was reading the works of your Ahmad and discussing the affairs of a nation that persists in proving right his description of it as "the laughing-stock of nations?" My spontaneous answer is: without those tiniest of incidents, not only would our relationship never have been fated, but I myself would not be who I am today.

However arrogant I am, however humble I am, however difficult it is to believe what I say, however tempted the listener is to take this as a metaphor, I have to acknowledge that my second (and last) apprenticeship was at your hands. The last thing I want to do is suggest that ideas and other abstractions were the only things I learned from you, and from living with you. How could I disregard the fact that it was you who gave me the first pair of sunglasses I ever wore in my life, that it was you who changed the way I dress and showed me how to operate various electrical appliances?

At the end of this autobiography of mine, as I race against time to complete it, the only favor I ask of you in return is that you believe me, or rather that you abandon your own version of what happened between us and adopt my version, that you find interesting those parts that I found interesting, and overlook the parts of our story that I have overlooked. Feel free to wonder at the way I have crossed so nimbly from one bank to the other, and my stream of thoughts will, I hope, enlighten you about the turmoil I have been through. How, you might ask, can I jump from talking about the dishwasher to asking you to believe my version of our story? How from nothing do I jump to tackling the whole thing? Don't bother to explore how that could be. That is the way it is, and perhaps my ultimate aim is just to breathe some meaning into my homage to what happened between us—a meaning other than grieving at its passing.

I do not seek that as a luxury or to pass the time while I wait to see what will become of me: I seek it out of necessity. And where do I still draw the strength to seek it? From writing for you, not from any wish or hope. So, believe or don't believe, among the ruins of my life that I revisit, like a shadow moving from west to east, weeds spring up as I write and, though sparse, the weeds change the appearance of this house of ruins, this death chamber. It is writing for you, not any wish or hope, that gives me the idea that I should see my stay here, in this isolated stronghold, as a blessing, one that increases my share in the life of this world, and after living it in the blink of an eye, without having a chance to examine it closely, I will not be deprived of the chance to live it in reverse, in slow motion when I feel like it, lingering when it suits me and skipping whatever might pain me, even if, when those bitter moments call on me to give them their due in my story, I rarely succeed in blocking my ears.

⟞⟞

In the previous pages I went into more detail than I expected and tarried more than was appropriate for a man in a hurry. I should also remind you that the two incidents that dominated the previous pages—the visit of my friend the sheikh, accompanied by the unfortunate family, and my visit to you—came in the wake of the 'dialogue meeting' in the university where I publicly and irreversibly crossed swords with 'them.' Although the argument was heated, I admit that I did not consider it close to its end. In the days that followed, in spite of the misgivings that came to light through our discussion, I did not deviate from the plan I had made. I recruited my friends at the television station, after obtaining approval from my superiors, to arrange for the girl to go into hospital for an abortion and then to be given shelter in an institution for those with special needs. I deployed my newly acquired self-confidence in long telephone conversations with her sister, discovering that she was a nurse and did not spend all her time in

234

the village, but in the nearest town, and so on . . . and that she was prepared to give a detailed account of the ordeal of her village and her sister.

As a reward for all these exertions, I gave myself permission on the next Thursday to dine at your place, not just to pass by, as was our custom.

We dined together, and I went back to my mosque at about midnight and slept serenely. At dawn on Friday, I awoke serenely, and after dawn prayers I went off to prepare the sermon for the day. From eight o'clock onward, local people dropped in on me and everything proceeded as it should until exactly half past eleven, about an hour before the congregation starts to trickle in for Friday prayers. Not far from the mosque there was a loud boom, and it soon emerged that the source of it was a small home-made bomb, which had been placed in one of the rubbish bins at the entrance to the neighborhood as one comes toward the mosque (the mosque is not only a house of God, but also a local landmark). Although the bomb was small, and no one was injured and the material damage was insignificant, within minutes the whole area turned into a war zone in every sense of the word. The news spread like lightning throughout the area and beyond, judging by the phone calls I started to receive, and with equal speed dozens of policemen turned up to join their colleagues who, as on every Friday, had arrived in the early morning.

The bomb was unremarkable and was not intended to kill or cause destruction, according to an explosives expert who inspected the scene, but the fact that it did not kill anyone or destroy any buildings made no difference. The next day I read in the newspapers, "At exactly 11:30 a.m. yesterday, an explosion took place in a rubbish bin one hundred meters from the Mosque of the Two Omars. Fortunately, it did not cause any injuries or damage to property. In the wake of the explosion, security forces sealed off the area and searched for any other bombs the evildoers might have planted." They did not find any other bombs, but the explosion, however modest, did cause the cancellation of Friday prayers, which apparently was the most those behind it intended to achieve.

ـملـ

My instinctive deduction, shared by those who visited me late that night—my allies by necessity—was confirmed the following day when a twelve-page letter entitled "The Last Cry of Warning to the Iniquitous

235

Sheikh" reached the parties concerned, including me, the media and some local dignitaries.

The letter did not overtly claim responsibility for the previous day's explosion, but the coincidence in timing between the explosion and the letter left no room for doubt that those who signed the letter were the same people who omitted to leave their signature on the bomb. With some pride, I read the letter, which was addressed to "those misguided people who continue to see this man—the Balaam of his age—as a man of learning dedicated to the triumph of Islam, to those seduced by the man's logic, to those who continue to journey to listen to the man in the belief that he can teach them something of religious and secular value, to all those ignorant of the man, to those who do not know him." If my sense of pride may seem inappropriate, I suspect that the most cowardly of cowards would have felt the same way when he noticed how each and every one of his words had been held against him, how he had caught people's attention and achieved a certain fame, even if the people in question were stalking him with evil intentions. After a brief preamble about heretics and their works, how from the beginning of Islam's mission to the present day they never ceased to plot against the Muslim community ("and what is to be expected of an impostor, an intruder into sharia learning, a man who is not only a charlatan but also a lackey of the government and its agencies?"), the drafters of the letter proceeded to support their allegations with evidence. They recalled that I had been appointed imam of the Mosque of the Two Omars "under suspicious circumstances" and that ever since "this Holy Movement" began I had taken a position of "open hostility" toward it. They also recalled that in the previous Ramadan, for example, I had banned vigils and nighttime prayers in the mosque.* They laid out all their evidence to support their conclusion that I was the natural choice

---

* This was true in the sense that I was duty-bound to do what I had myself proposed, that is, to close mosques early to prevent anyone taking advantage of the holy month to occupy more of them, if only temporarily. My proposal, which was adopted, was in fact based on the practice of the Prophet, who made life easier for Muslims by abridging the special evening prayers in mosques from twenty prostrations to eight prostrations, on the understanding that Muslims would perform the other twelve prostrations at home. Their allegation that I called in the police to enforce this was a 'cheap fabrication,' as they say. All that happened is that the security forces did take certain measures around mosques during the month, including the Mosque of the Two Omars, but I had nothing to do with those measures.

"to spread poison across the airwaves from a television station that had known links with imperialist circles that are still trying to catch their breath" and so on, and that my task there was "to promote vice and prohibit virtue." "But what is not at all natural," the letter continued, "is that this howling dog should be left to bark at the caravan of the authentic Islam of the Prophet Muhammad, though the caravan itself follows relentlessly the True Path under the watchful eye of God, oblivious of this vengeful man and his likes." It went on, "If we had to stop and comment on every word the man says, it would be a long session and our answers would fill a whole book. But we do not have time for that, and besides, this vile flatterer in the embrace of idols does not deserve so much attention. Our time is more valuable than him, his masters, and his idols. Were it not for the need to warn the Muslim community of the errors and heresies of this doomed man—a man whose intrigues have spread and ensnared many Muslims—we would not have mentioned him or answered him in the first place."

After that came the passage that perhaps made me proudest—a listing, drawn from my television programs, of "what this ignorant impostor, who has set himself up as an authority on fatwas, calls opinions on points of Islamic law." After every opinion I had expressed there was an answer, intended by the authors to refute my argument and expose my ignorance. I need not explain why these pages made me prouder than the rest of the letter: they had at least watched the programs from start to finish, and on top of that they had watched them in torment!

After all this rhetorical effort, this arduous quest for Quranic verses, for traditions of the Prophet and legal arguments to challenge my opinions, one could have expected that some verdict would follow, and that is indeed how the letter ended:

> "As we stated earlier, if we wanted to dwell on every word uttered by this aforementioned man, and discuss them from the point of view of Islamic law or of reason, or examine how true or realistic they are, it would take much time and we would end up with a complete book. We have therefore confined our comments on them and on their author to the following:

"What this man has said counts as overt and total subservience to the forces of heresy and to the cult of the ruling tyrant and his regime. No two people with knowledge of the religion of God Almighty would disagree on whether he is an infidel and an ally of the forces of evil.

"An analogous case would be that of Balaam, the Israelite sage who was once the most learned man in his community but who abandoned the word of God and God's religion when he said a prayer on behalf of Israelite infidels against monotheistic members of the tribe. 'And recite to them the tale of him to whom We gave our signs, but who cast them off, and Satan followed after him, and he strayed into grievous error. And had We willed, We could have raised him up through Our revelations; but he inclined toward the things of this world and followed his lust. He was like a dog: if you attack it, it lolls its tongue out, or if you leave it, it lolls its tongue out.'"*

"Those who specialize in interpretation, and indeed distortion, however powerful they may be and however skilled, cannot explain away the blatant heresy this man has already spoken as anything less than heresy, or find any term for it that saves it from description as blatant heresy, unless in their interpretations and distortions they exceed the bounds of sharia concepts and conventional semantic usage.

"For the blatant heresy he has exhibited and continues to exhibit, the man cannot be exonerated by any of the considerations that prevent declaring people infidels, such as the excuse that he was ignorant, misunderstood, or acting under duress, or any other of the recognized impediments.

"However hard some might try to find an excuse for him, they have found overt expressions of heresy that thwart their efforts and rebut the interpretations by which they intended to exonerate the man and disregard

---

* Quran 7:175-76

238

his errors.

"Consequently, the principle that proof must be established before someone is declared infidel does not apply in this case, since this principle properly applies when the charge is made against someone who lapsed into heresy for reasons recognized under Islamic law.

"For all the reasons laid out above we have no choice but to declare this man to be a genuine heretic and apostate, subject to all the penalties and consequences of apostasy in this world and in the afterlife, until such time as he publicly dissociates himself from the False God and his legions, and from all the blatant and conclusively proven heresy he has engaged in.

"This judgment is in no way invalidated by the fact that the man is a doctor of sharia law,* or that he is a man of renown and reputation, or that he performed useful work in the initial stages of his education and as a cleric. None of that will count in his favor in the face of blatant and heinous heresy, because it is the final stage, how one finishes off a process, that matters, as the Prophet said: 'And by him who has my soul in His hand, one of you may do the deeds of the people of Paradise till there is only an arm's length between him and Paradise, but then his destiny intervenes, and he does the deeds of the people of Hell and enters it; and a man may do the deeds of the people of Hell till there is only an arm's length between him and Hell, and then his destiny intervenes and he does the deeds of the people of Paradise and enters it.'†

---

* I don't know where they found this doctorate of mine, and I have always been amused by the way some of my colleagues, including those whose only aspiration is to obtain a doctorate, insist on giving each other the title "Sheikh Doctor," even before the person in question has been awarded the doctorate. It gives the impression that the title 'sheikh' by itself does not imply learning worthy of respect.
† Various almost identical versions in Sahih al-Bukhari.
** Musnad Ahmad ibn Hanbal, hadith no. 11, 804

"The Prophet also said, 'Don't admire someone's deeds until you have seen how he finishes. A man may do good deeds for a period in his life and if he died at that stage he would enter Paradise, but then he may change and do evil deeds for a period in his life and if he died then he would enter Hell, then he may change again and do good deeds, and if God wishes him well, He will have him do good deeds before he dies, and then let him die.'** We ask God Almighty for forgiveness and for a good ending."

Contrary to what they might have expected, forcing me to choose between public repentance and the judgment of God did not strike terror in my heart. Maybe my sense of unbroken pride pushed aside and outweighed the terror, especially as the two options both amounted to death, even if the more pleasant of the two was bloodier.

So my only option was a third one: to raise the stakes in response. The quickest response required that I speed up the process of having the girl admitted to hospital so that I could tape her sister's testimony—an arrangement on which the sister and I had already agreed. The wind blew in my favor and I was surprised at the courage, composure, and sound logic of the sister. All I had to do was piece together her testimony. Because my choice was to raise the stakes, not just to reply in kind, I made an appointment to visit my friend the ousted sheikh in his village the following Sunday (without, of course, disclosing that my purpose was to persuade him to share his own testimony with me—lure him into it, if you will!). Finally, I had no doubt that the end was approaching: the end of my life.

Today, as I go over those final hours minute by minute and in boring detail, it strikes me that on that Thursday, in a way to which I was not accustomed, it did not worry me that the next day was Friday and that this Friday would be unlike all previous Fridays because of what had happened a week earlier.

With a light heart, I headed to your place about an hour before the program was due to air so that we could watch it together. We did watch it, observed by the books in your library as we sat lovingly on the sofa facing the television, and by the walls of your kitchen and the pots and pans of our last supper. A little after midnight, I left you to go back to my mosque. But that night I did not reach my destination, and I am certain I will never go to that mosque again.

Postscript

n end but not the end. This is where I conclude my digressions. If I had had some extra time, I might have whiled it away describing what happened to me in those two weeks I spent far from you and from my mosque, 'fate unknown.' During that time I was the guest of security personnel who saw fit to give 'the public' more than their fill of me as a star and who concocted for the media an ingenious story that I was abducted by a group of 'evildoers.' The second and final chapter of the story told how the forces of good, personified by the security forces, succeeded in freeing me from their clutches.

As I said, luckily I ran out of time and I have been spared the trouble of going over the events of days and nights about which I have conflicting feelings that I have not yet been able to reconcile. In a sense, I want to believe that when they ran off with me as I was on my way back to the mosque that night, in what looked like a 'kidnapping operation,' it really was "a preventive measure based on hard information" that the disciples of a certain leader were about to abduct me. On the other hand, although it was not at all a remote possibility that I might be abducted or even assassinated, to be rescued in this dubious manner, and then to hear that I had been kidnapped and that a "complex" security operation had resulted in my release, makes me feel anxious, distressed, mistrustful of those around me, and dissatisfied with myself. On top of all that, the two weeks that I spent in that military complex—it combined simultaneously the austerity of a barracks and the luxury of an officers' club—was my very first opportunity to have close and constant contact with men from what are called the security agencies, despite the fact that incessant rumors, sometimes whispered in private and sometimes aired in public, especially when I worked at the television station, alleged that I was their creation and their hireling. The truth that no one will believe—neither those who launch random accusations or others in general—is that I am not the creature of the security agencies, but rather a creature of coincidence and of having met you, at least if I must be attributed to some creator. The other truth is that, although I am aware that the opinions I advocated gave comfort to one party and antagonized another, I was speaking only for myself in all my inadequacy.

I should not, of course, overburden myself or burn all my boats. I should instead launch into 'sentimental' confessions, such as saying that only now, when I see things from a distance, do I realize that I chose one group of murderers over another. It does not matter if, from time to time, I have to hear people say that I was deluded or that I was so caught up in what I was doing that there was no way back, or other excuses that may exonerate me. Is there anything you think I should do, anything I should regret not having done? To have peace of mind? Don't worry about me, my lady; my mind will never be at peace. Or do you think I should try to save what can be saved in the hope that things will change? Even in the worst moments I spent between the four walls of that refuge, alone and dejected, I never dreamed of resuming my former life when I came out. As a child, my only recurrent dream was that a magician would whisk me away in the middle of the night, far from this country that no one would wish on his enemies, never to return. I say "a magician" because I had lost hope that this dream has even the slightest chance of coming true, but that showed a lack of confidence in you and your obstinacy, for which I can only apologize, now and forever.

***

On that day, as every day, as the sun began to sink toward the horizon, I reluctantly acknowledged that the news that my minder was meant to bring me had been delayed till the morrow, in the best of circumstances. Before dusk, I took to my bed in the hope that sleep would rapidly spare me the ordeal of seeing night fall, with the demons it brought to torment me. I believe I dozed off without too much tossing and turning, and then slept long and deep, judging by the way the telephone operator, a man I did not know personally, apologized profusely for insisting on waking me (though in fact I had heard only the last few rings of his call). He then informed me that a certain captain wanted to talk to me. The captain introduced himself briefly and politely in a way that added no new information about himself or his status, and then told me he had instructions to escort me to a meeting 'outside,' and asked me to inform him as soon as I was ready.

I had not set foot 'outside' for months, but in fact it was not the idea of facing the 'outside' again that preoccupied me, but rather what was behind it. Like anyone in such circumstances, I was in a hurry to find out what awaited me—even fearful and anxious. Luckily, there was no way to play for time or delay. I quickly smartened myself up as best I could and informed the mysterious captain I was ready. He immediately replied that I could open the door myself from the inside, which I had almost forgotten. I realized that there was nothing to be gained from asking the officer in charge where we were heading, so I merely wished him a good evening and held my tongue throughout the journey, which lasted an hour and a half and brought us to a wealthy neighborhood not far from the television station. The obsession with security, which infected me to some extent, in spite of myself, made me think we were deliberately taking a detour to disguise our true destination, the television station, from any pursuers who might be following in our tracks. But my faith in my security skills was misplaced. The car carrying me and my escort was joined by two other cars, which appeared without me noticing when and whence they came, and our motorcade soon came to a halt at the entrance to a building, where the escort in charge handed me over to what I assumed was a colleague of his. Here too my security skills let me down. I said to myself that this swanky building in this swanky neighborhood must be the front for a government department that, because of the importance of the tasks assigned to it, worked day and night under this cover of luxurious secrecy. But when the door opened to the penthouse apartment on the top and eleventh floor, I saw nothing to suggest that my guess was correct. The man who opened the door looked more like a butler than a guard, and the hall where I waited a few seconds, although sparsely furnished, evinced a discreet and stylish grandeur quite unlike the vulgar grandeur I had seen in the offices at the military complex where I had spent two weeks after my purported abduction.

Before I could conclude that I was in a house and could start thinking whose house it might be, the owner rushed to embrace me with palpable sincerity and warmth. Before I could mumble more than a few unintelligible words in response to his greetings, he took me by the arm, walked me to the reception room, and went straight to the point. "I know you didn't expect to be brought here," he said. "But this isn't the only surprise awaiting you, my friend, so keep calm." It was good of him to warn me, because the least one could say of the series of surprises I had that evening is that they fully deserved the description.

On the balcony beyond the large reception room, I caught sight of two men, neither of them dressed in a way that suggested they were either men of religion or military men, and I did not try to guess who they might be. They were seated facing the city spread out in the darkness, so near and yet so far, and as we moved closer to the balcony, they picked up the sound of our footsteps and it looked as if they were preparing to stand up. Even then I could not make out who they were. I will spare you my description of how I felt when they turned toward us and I recognized one of them as my sheikh, the patron who had changed the course of my life. But my surprise was soon overwhelmed by another feeling, which I can only describe as a feeling of relief, although it was much stronger than just a feeling and more than relief. It was the relief of a lost and desperate man who meets someone to whom he can entrust his freedom and surrender control of his life. After these two surprises, it was no surprise to discover that the other man was a certain general, a man too famous to need introduction, the tsar of the security services in our country at one time. After a friendly if not warm greeting, the three of them continued their conversation. I was pleased they did not fuss over me. That suited me well, because it gave me a chance to let my relief mellow into a sense of relaxation, which included all the muscles in my body. It also gave me a chance to find out in a general way where matters stood, why my sheikh was staying in your country, and why the three men were gathered on this balcony, over glasses of I know not what, for what was, as it emerged from their conversation, the latest of a series of meetings they had held in recent weeks.

Although they were talking about weighty matters, my initial relief persisted, and the fact that I was there with them, undoubtedly on the initiative of my sheikh, was conclusive evidence that he would not abandon me to my fate. That was the most I hoped for at the time, even if my future prospects seemed, despite their candid talk, to be wrapped in mystery.

I do not know whether my sheikh had deliberately arranged for things to happen this way, so that I would discover for myself, by listening to them, what had happened over the previous few months, or whether it was a sudden whim that gave him the idea that bringing me in on their meeting would be the quickest way to brief me on the latest events, which had turned things upside down and which were about to bring about dramatic changes in policies and personnel.

Like someone who has finished with one subject and moves on to another according to some prearranged plan, my mentor concluded his conversation with his friends by saying that, for the time being, and as long as he had not been notified that he was persona non grata here, he preferred to "stay close to the scene of events." He then turned to me, and this time addressed his words to all three of us. "But I don't want to implicate him (meaning me) in this decision of mine," he said. "As you have gathered from our conversation, my friend," he added, now addressing me, "today isn't yesterday. Your sheikh, who once had authority and an influential voice, now lives here, honored and respected, but in voluntary exile. Most of your sheikh's friends there have turned against him, accusing him of failure, along with the policy he advocated. And the same accusations against him, and against others there, are of course being leveled at those who shared his opinions and those who are with him here, including these two men (he pointed to our host and the general). I don't know whether we failed, each of us in his role and within the bounds of his mandate, or whether the cause we defended was a lost cause from the start and no policy would have worked. Anyway, let's leave them to try their kid-glove policy of dialogue and conciliation, while we mind our own business. You, what do you think?"

For a moment I assumed he was joking. "How could he ask me such a question?" I thought. "Doesn't he know where I've been for the last few months? Has he no concept of the ordeal I've been through?" Probably I was flustered and it showed. If it did not show, then probably my failure to respond prompted my mentor to keep talking as if he had not asked and did not expect me to answer in the first place. "Like any of us, you have two options," he said. "You can stay here until God decides your fate, I mean until this country, too, becomes so upset about us that we can no longer stay. If this is your choice, we can arrange a job for you and you can stay at my side for better or for worse. Or you can move somewhere else in the big wide world, and if that's your choice, the way is open for you. If I were you, I wouldn't hesitate, especially since you seem to be luckier than the rest of us."

I understood I had a choice between staying and leaving, and if he were me, he would not hesitate to choose the latter, but I had no idea what he meant when he said that "the way is open" and that I was "luckier than the rest." After a sincere attempt to thank him, which he dismissed with a wave of his hand, I had to summon up all my strength to ask him to explain what he meant. He was surprised by my question. "How so?" he said. "Don't you know that your woman friend has mobilized all her acquaintances to get you out of here and take you in where she's living now? . . . Haven't you received her letters?"

It would be pointless to elaborate on what I felt then. However hard I try, and I have tried, I doubt I could ever enumerate all the emotions that swept my mind and body in those few seconds between the moment he asked about your letters (which had never arrived) and the moment he again asked me which decision I would take. I was too speechless to answer his question, and the man could not resist a spontaneous witticism. Switching from one form of Arabic to another without his friends noticing, he remarked, "On this Day of Judgment I wish I too had a consort I could flee to. . . . Don't you hesitate." The other men laughed and agreed, even if they did not realize what was behind the reference.* As for me, I did not hesitate.

---

* And when the Blast shall sound, that will be a Day when a man flees from his brother, his mother, his father, his consort, his sons, every man that day shall have business to suffice him. (Quran, 80:33–37)

Translator's Afterword

Translation always entails compromises, and in the case of Rasha al Ameer's *Judgment Day*, more than in most contemporary Arabic novels, many of the compromises arose from an unexpected quarter—the different histories and sociolinguistic frameworks of the Arabic and English languages. Arabic is a corpus of possible utterances that spans more than 1,500 years, indigenous in a territory that stretches at least 4,500 miles from west to east, and embracing every possible social and professional milieu—from the humblest peasant to the erudite scholar steeped in a rich literary tradition. By social convention, one form of the language has had unique prestige since the early centuries of Islam, when it was codified by grammarians such as Sibawayh, who died at the end of the eighth century CE. That form of the language is no one's mother tongue, but rather the common heritage of all those diligent and studious enough to adopt it as a vehicle for their thoughts. Rasha al Ameer has chosen that path. Modern Standard Arabic, the contemporary lingua franca of official discourse and literature, is a linear descendant of this idealized language, but in the last two centuries it has evolved in subtle ways, often opaque even to Arabs other than experts, sometimes under the influence of translations from the languages of the nations that have dominated the Arab world: mainly French and English. Only a few pages into *Judgment Day*, the word 'premodern' sprung to my mind to describe the peculiar and distinctive quality of Rasha's writing. If one could really go back in time, it would be interesting to see if al-Mutanabbi himself could have read *Judgment Day* with ease—something that could not said of a twenty-first century newspaper. I see that some commentators whose first language is Arabic have described her style as 'classical,' though in English the word suggests misleading comparisons with patrician writers in Latin such as Cicero or Virgil. But *Judgment Day* is not some antiquarian folly, or a clever pastiche of the kind that James Joyce indulged in when he wrote the *Oxen of the Sun* episode of *Ulysses*. On the contrary, Rasha has written with mathematical precision and concision, choosing words with great care from the vast corpus available, and taking full advantage of the morpho-logical twists and turns that the unusual structure of the Arabic language allows. Some of the words she uses do not appear in any dictionary that I could find, yet the meaning was usually transparent. Sometimes she acknowledges that she has "made them up," as in the case of *"manba'a,"* which I ended up translating rather inadequately as "prophetosphere," a cultural environment populated by numerous prophets. If her sentences are sometimes labyrinthine (I counted one at some 150 words), it is because the ideas are complex. To break them up would have severed some of the links in the matrix of semantic units. As I wrote to Rasha when I volun-teered to take on the task of translating her book, I was reminded of Jane Austen and Marcel Proust, two writers also famous for their complexities. What they all have in common is an obsession with dissecting the workings of human motivation—not something easy to put into a linear text made up of mere words, but ultimately one of the prime objectives of any literature that goes beyond mere storytelling.

In conveying all this in English, I ran a serious risk of appearing pedantic or obscurantist, which would have done her work an injustice and frightened off readers whom I wanted to share her ideas on religion, sex, modernity, and tradition, and above all, the transformative power of love. As reviewer Mona Zaki wrote in *Banipal*, the magazine of modern Arabic literature, "The work's classical Arabic style casts a hypnotic spell that might be problematic and difficult to convey should the novel be trans-lated." Modern literary English, the only medium I could conceivably employ, is much too firmly tied to the world we live in. The English language has no equivalent of a register that comes close to transcending time and place. On the other hand, her anonymous sheikh, living in his anonymous city and falling in love with an anonymous woman, is indeed often a little pedantic, and I hope I have allowed that to come through, to about the same extent as the Arabic original implies.

Other commentators have given variously al-Mutanabbi the poet or the Arabic language, or both, the status of full-fledged characters in this novel, the counterparts of the devil who does or does not turn up when the sheikh and 'my lady' are alone together. Translating the poetry of al-Mutanabbi (so boastful, such a braggart, so bombastic) was a challenge in itself, and perhaps I should not have been surprised to find that, with the notable exception of Arberry's all too brief selection (*The Poems of al-Mutannabi*, Cambridge University Press), few scholars or translators have made a sustained effort to present 'The Poet' to an English-reading audience. In the case of two lines of al-Mutanabbi, I confess that I gave up completely and merely referred to them obliquely as "two absurdly impossible lines that consist of just a string of forty imperatives, many of them derived from the obscurest of verbs." It would be gratifying if this translation of *Judgment Day* were to help inspire some future scholar to take on the task of translating his complete works. I also omitted Rasha's lengthy footnote on what I called "the rules in Arabic grammar . . . for the case-endings on detached qualifiers," somewhat reluctantly because the information was new to me and readers with a knowledge of Arabic might have appreciated it. It would also have illustrated Rasha's meticulous approach to the intricacies of a subject that is clearly dear to her heart. For the many Quranic verses, I found none of the existing translations adequate stylistically, so I took the bold step of translating them myself, naturally with guidance from all those who have gone before me. I trust my versions do not offend any sensibilities. For the translations of hadith (accounts of the sayings and doings of the Prophet Muhammad and his companions), I am indebted to the University of Southern California, where the Center for Muslim–Jewish Engagement has done some amazingly thorough translation work and posted the results on the Internet.

But most of all I am indebted to Rasha, who gave me three days of her time to go over difficult parts of the text and answered all my written questions, even if I had already asked them in different forms once before. I hope that the result of our labors will win her book the audience it deserves and give English-language readers some insights into matters of immense topicality, not least the diversity and abundant heritage of that nation "at whose ignorance other nations laugh," as al-Mutanabbi put it in deliberate self-deprecation more than a thousand years ago. Enjoy.

Modern Arabic Literature
from the American University in Cairo Press

Bahaa Abdelmegid *Saint Theresa* and *Sleeping with Strangers*
Ibrahim Abdel Meguid *Birds of Amber* • *Distant Train*
No One Sleeps in Alexandria • *The Other Place*
Yahya Taher Abdullah *The Collar and the Bracelet* • *The Mountain of Green Tea*
Leila Abouzeid *The Last Chapter*
Hamdi Abu Golayyel *A Dog with No Tail* • *Thieves in Retirement*
Yusuf Abu Rayya *Wedding Night*
Ahmed Alaidy *Being Abbas el Abd*
Idris Ali *Dongola* • *Poor*
Rasha al Ameer *Judgment Day*
Radwa Ashour *Granada* • *Specters*
Ibrahim Aslan *The Heron* • *Nile Sparrows*
Alaa Al Aswany *Chicago* • *Friendly Fire* • *The Yacoubian Building*
Fadi Azzam *Sarmada*
Fadhil al-Azzawi *Cell Block Five* • *The Last of the Angels* • *The Traveler and the Innkeeper*
Ali Bader *Papa Sartre*
Liana Badr *The Eye of the Mirror*
Hala El Badry *A Certain Woman* • *Muntaha*
Salwa Bakr *The Golden Chariot* • *The Man from Bashmour* • *The Wiles of Men*
Halim Barakat *The Crane*
Hoda Barakat *Disciples of Passion* • *The Tiller of Waters*
Mourid Barghouti *I Saw Ramallah* • *I Was Born There, I Was Born Here*
Mohamed Berrada *Like a Summer Never to Be Repeated*
Mohamed El-Bisatie *Clamor of the Lake* • *Drumbeat* • *Hunger* • *Over the Bridge*
Mahmoud Darwish *The Butterfly's Burden*
Tarek Eltayeb *Cities without Palms* • *The Palm House*
Mansoura Ez Eldin *Maryam's Maze*
Ibrahim Farghali *The Smiles of the Saints*
Hamdy el-Gazzar *Black Magic*
Randa Ghazy *Dreaming of Palestine*
Gamal al-Ghitani *Pyramid Texts* • *The Zafarani Files* • *Zayni Barakat*
Tawfiq al-Hakim *The Essential Tawfiq al-Hakim*
Yahya Hakki *The Lamp of Umm Hashim*
Abdelilah Hamdouchi *The Final Bet*
Bensalem Himmich *The Polymath* • *The Theocrat*
Taha Hussein *The Days*
Sonallah Ibrahim *Cairo: From Edge to Edge* • *The Committee* • *Zaat*
Yusuf Idris *City of Love and Ashes* • *The Essential Yusuf Idris*
Denys Johnson-Davies *The AUC Press Book of Modern Arabic Literature* • *Homecoming*
In a Fertile Desert • *Under the Naked Sky*
Said al-Kafrawi *The Hill of Gypsies*
Mai Khaled *The Magic of Turquoise*
Sahar Khalifeh *The End of Spring*
The Image, the Icon and the Covenant • *The Inheritance*
Edwar al-Kharrat *Rama and the Dragon* • *Stones of Bobello*

Betool Khedairi *Absent*
Mohammed Khudayyir *Basrayatha*
Ibrahim al-Koni *Anubis* • *Gold Dust* • *The Puppet* • *The Seven Veils of Seth*
Naguib Mahfouz *Adrift on the Nile* • *Akhenaten: Dweller in Truth*
Arabian Nights and Days • *Autumn Quail* • *Before the Throne* • *The Beggar*
The Beginning and the End • *Cairo Modern* • *The Cairo Trilogy: Palace Walk*
Palace of Desire • *Sugar Street* • *Children of the Alley* • *The Coffeehouse*
The Day the Leader Was Killed • *The Dreams* • *Dreams of Departure*
Echoes of an Autobiography • *The Essential Naguib Mahfouz* • *The Final Hour*
The Harafish • *Heart of the Night* • *In the Time of Love*
The Journey of Ibn Fattouma • *Karnak Cafe* • *Khan al-Khalili* • *Khufu's Wisdom*
Life's Wisdom • *Love in the Rain* • *Midaq Alley* • *The Mirage* • *Miramar* • *Mirrors*
Morning and Evening Talk • *Naguib Mahfouz at Sidi Gaber* • *Respected Sir*
Rhadopis of Nubia • *The Search* • *The Seventh Heaven* • *Thebes at War*
The Thief and the Dogs • *The Time and the Place* • *Voices from the Other World*
Wedding Song • *The Wisdom of Naguib Mahfouz*
Mohamed Makhzangi *Memories of a Meltdown*
Alia Mamdouh *The Loved Ones* • *Naphtalene*
Selim Matar *The Woman of the Flask*
Ibrahim al-Mazini *Ten Again*
Yousef Al-Mohaimeed *Munira's Bottle* • *Wolves of the Crescent Moon*
Hassouna Mosbahi *A Tunisian Tale*
Ahlam Mosteghanemi *Chaos of the Senses* • *Memory in the Flesh*
Shakir Mustafa *Contemporary Iraqi Fiction: An Anthology*
Mohamed Mustagab *Tales from Dayrut*
Buthaina Al Nasiri *Final Night*
Ibrahim Nasrallah *Inside the Night* • *Time of White Horses*
Haggag Hassan Oddoul *Nights of Musk*
Mona Prince *So You May See*
Mohamed Mansi Qandil *Moon over Samarqand*
Abd al-Hakim Qasim *Rites of Assent*
Somaya Ramadan *Leaves of Narcissus*
Mekkawi Said *Cairo Swan Song*
Ghada Samman *The Night of the First Billion*
Mahdi Issa al-Saqr *East Winds, West Winds*
Rafik Schami *The Calligrapher's Secret* • *Damascus Nights*
The Dark Side of Love
Habib Selmi *The Scents of Marie-Claire*
Khairy Shalaby *The Hashish Waiter* • *The Lodging House*
The Time-Travels of the Man Who Sold Pickles and Sweets
Miral al-Tahawy *Blue Aubergine* • *Brooklyn Heights* • *Gazelle Tracks* • *The Tent*
Bahaa Taher *As Doha Said* • *Love in Exile*
Fuad al-Takarli *The Long Way Back*
Zakaria Tamer *The Hedgehog*
M. M. Tawfik *Murder in the Tower of Happiness*
Mahmoud Al-Wardani *Heads Ripe for Plucking*
Amina Zaydan *Red Wine*
Latifa al-Zayyat *The Open Door*